STEALING
HOPE

Also by David Temple

Discovering Grace

STEALING HOPE

The story of one family's relentless
battle to find hope

DAVID TEMPLE

ST SIMONS PRESS

For more information, or for special discounts for bulk purchases, please contact:
St Simons Press
1235 East Boulevard, Suite 109
Charlotte, NC 28203-5870
business@stsimonspress.com

ISBN: 978-0-9891865-1-3
Library of Congress Control Number: 2013905801

Published by St Simons Press
www.stsimonspress.com

Cover design by Andrea White
Images by iStockphoto.com
Headshot by Jim McGuire
Lyrics by Faith Fisher
Book design by David Temple & Faith Fisher

Published & manufactured in the United States of America

To the girls in my life -
Mom, Kay, Barbara Ann, Brenda
Dawn, Katie, Caroline and Lauren

And in loving memory of:
Amy Woody Melkonian

She fought the good fight and shared a life of hope.

ACKNOWLEDGEMENTS

There are so many people I want to thank for the support and encouragement given me during the journey of writing this book. Several have worked diligently behind the scenes to make this book the wondrous slice of magic it has become. And without any of them, I would not have been able to fulfill yet another dream of a story that lies inside my mind.

A dear friend recently shared a quote. She must have sensed, as she often does, how this quote would be perfect at this juncture of my life. It is by Maya Angelou and she writes, *"There is no greater agony than bearing an untold story inside you."*

Just as teachers teach and painters paint and preachers preach and policemen protect and artists create—so should writers, write. Writing is my true passion. I hope you enjoy.

To my managing editor and longtime friend, Faith Fisher. I thank you from the bottom of my heart for being there, without fail, without judgment and without complaint. Thank you for your willingness to provide a patient ear, a kind heart and a tough stance. Your hearty appetite to never let anything slip is inspiring, and your tenacious eye to detail is amazing. Your daily words of encouragement were always perfectly timed and patiently shared. After suffering all those sleepless hours, I hope you'll please work with me again. I promise to concentrate on my tenses, confirm my historical data and correct my continual lines of...ellipsis. Know this: I couldn't have completed this book without you. Most importantly, thank you for a deep friendship that has spanned decades.

To Lauren Black, my mutual dog-lover, food-fan and friend. Thank you for the nudges to keep going. I believe your unique and creative voice should be heard. Write on!

To Jennifer Coots, my wine-partner, co-daydreamer and dear friend. Thank you for never doubting for a second that I would create great things.

To Clare Sente, a soul mate who has been an integral part of my life for more than two decades. Your whispers of enlightenment have come when I needed them most, and your laughter makes my heart smile.

To Amy McIntire, my long-time gal-pal. I deeply admire you and cherish our friendship. It keeps me going, even during the cloudiest of days.

Finally, to my three favorite girls: Alice Kay and Barbara Ann, you're the best sisters a brother could ever dream for, and Mom, your unwavering encouragement and creative eye helped birth this book. Thank you all for reminding me that my voice is worth hearing.

Do not spoil what you have by desiring what you have not; but remember that what you now have was once among the things you only hoped for.   -Epicurus

PROLOGUE

CHRISTOPHER SHIELDS HIS EYES from the bright sun, squinting as he looks up into the enormous oaks. These same trees have shaded his family's property for nearly a century. The deep Carolina blue sky is a sharp contrast to the enormous white clouds hanging overhead. He thinks, *This moment couldn't be more perfect.* A dozen or more children play in the yard, their laughter bouncing through the trees and echoing throughout the neighborhood. They chase one another, designing imaginary playgrounds and enjoying the last weekend of summer before school begins.

Suddenly, a screen door slams against the house, followed by the shriek of a young girl.

"You're it, Grace!" several children shout.

The eldest of three, Christopher tries to chase his sister, while David hangs on his brother's back. Christopher's hot pursuit becomes lukewarm thanks to the extra baggage onboard.

"C'mon, Chrissy!" Grace shouts. "Put down that sack of books and show me what ya got!"

They all laugh as David jumps off Christopher's back.

"Go ahead, Chris. You're not gonna let a girl win, are you?" David chides.

Christopher looks into his little brother's eyes, enjoying the friendly taunt, high-fives David and sets out to catch his younger sister.

Their mother, Angela, lounges in a chaise, enjoying the shade. Her eyes meet Christopher's and she smiles, turning to see her baby girl run circles around the others then back toward the house.

"You show 'em who's boss, Gracie!" Angela shouts.

Their father, Jonathan, snoozes on a nearby lounge chair, unfazed by the screams of the children. Angela returns to her novel.

Like the high school running back he once dreamt of becoming, Christopher playfully pushes off the children who are piling atop him. They cheer on Grace as she plans her escape.

Now, just inside the house, Grace sticks her head out the screen door and taunts, "Do you *really* think you can catch me?"

Christopher, now fully goaded, unloads the gaggle of neighborhood children.

"Okay, L'il Professor, you heard Sis—let me show her who's king of this yard."

"We know who's faster," David says with a grin.

Christopher is gone in the blink of an eye.

As he enters the house, Grace is being shooed away by their grandmother, Daphne. He starts in one direction—around the large sofa, just as she fakes him out, heading in the opposite direction. Grace looks over her shoulder, shrieks and sprints down the long hallway, extending an arm to the old plaster wall for balance. The sound of their running feet becomes muffled as they reach the carpeted hallway.

At the end of the hall she heads to the left, hesitates, then darts right toward the guest room.

Christopher approaches the doorway to the quiet dark room, waiting for his eyes to adjust. He doesn't see Grace, as he nears the bed. He stops to catch his breath.

Suddenly, Grace pops up from behind the bed and giggles, shaking their uncle, who lies motionless on the large four-poster bed. She shouts, "Wake up, Uncle Carter!"

He doesn't move.

"Don't bother him, Gracie. He's taking a nap."

She sees a glass of water on the bedside table and picks it up.

Christopher notices a vodka bottle on the back of the nightstand and whispers loudly, "Stop, Gracie! That's a grown-up drink."

She quickly spits it out.

"Yuck!"

"I told you. C'mon, let's go back out. It's your turn to be *It*."

"Why do people drink that stuff?"

"Makes them feel good, I guess. C'mon, let's go."

Grace reaches to shake her uncle once more, but he doesn't move.

"Let's GO!" Christopher whispers even louder, before turning to leave and is back in the hall when Grace shouts.

"Look what I found!" Christopher turns to see her holding a pistol.

"Grace! Put that down!" he gasps. "It's not a toy!"

She waves it around and says, "Let's play *Cowboys and Indians* and this time, I'll be the cowboy!"

Panicked, he starts toward her.

"C'mon, Gracie! Stop, it could be loaded. Come back outside and play."

He turns to leave, hoping she'll follow, but glancing back, he sees Grace looking down the barrel of the gun.

Terrified, he shouts, "Grace! Put it down—Now!"

Startled, her hand slips. BANG!

"GRAAAAAAAAACIEEEEEEEE!"

PART ONE: Painful Memories

CHAPTER 1

AS THE GUNSHOT BLAST echoes throughout the house, Christopher sits upright in bed—his t-shirt and sheets, soaked with sweat. The blue of the full moon outside his window casts scary shadows across the bed. *That looks like a body facedown.* His eyes dart around the room, looking for her. The fan overhead spins slowly, reminding him of that awful moment. Was he still there? Were the dark shadows scattered across the wall her blood, or memories meant to torment him? His heart had been racing, his breathing quick and short, yet now, he's not breathing at all. *Am I dead?* He runs his hands across the covers, searching for a tangible clue that he is alive—in the present. Blood running cold—*Is that what I'm experiencing? Death?* He screams as loudly as he can, to either be heard or wake himself.

Suddenly, the door whips open, slamming against the wall. Angela turns on the overheard light and stands there with a look of horror on her face. As they both squint—their eyes adjusting to the light and the rude awakening, they stare at one another as if in the same horrible dream. Slowly, they both let out a long exhale. Their bodies relax, slouching inches lower.

"Are you all right?" Angela asks, slowly catching her breath.

Christopher's eyes again search the room, looking for the source of the gunshot. The long, body-shaped shadows he saw moments before are from tree limbs just outside his window—the open drapes make that evident now. He looks up. The fan above the bed was *his,* not the one above Carter—that day in the guestroom. It's coming back to him, yet he absently asks the question that's pounding inside his skull, begging for an answer.

"Did you hear…?"

Reality quickly sets in.

Angela forces a tight smile and gently sits on the side of the bed, slowly shaking her head. She quietly says, "Son, there was no gunshot."

His mind fights for the answer. *Was that just a bad dream and Grace is asleep down the hall? Or, was it true?* His thoughts slow their frantic pace, but find no easy solution.

As the tension releases its grip and his breathing slowly returns to normal, his mind gets quiet and, lowering his head, he manages a whisper, "I know."

Angela looks at him with a loving, yet pained expression and, placing a soft hand on his cheek, whispers, "I'm so sorry."

At that moment, she felt as though her heart would shear in half. She wanted to *make it all better*—as only a mother can do. But she could do nothing of the sort, except be there for him to lean upon.

His eyes, that were moments ago filled with terror, now give way to a heavy sadness. He goes to speak and hesitates then tries again, and finally ekes out words that once again tear at his mother's heart.

"One way or the other, something…has got to give, Mom."

She waits, hanging on his fragile words—feeling so helpless.

"I feel like my chest is going to explode," he says, his chin quivering with pain. "Either that, or my head."

"All I can tell you is, it's been my experience that time has a way of healing. And we just have to leave it in the hands of God. But the short answer?" she says, trying to comfort him, "Soon. I promise."

Time suddenly felt like the enemy and he wanted relief NOW. And with that realization, he finally bursts out crying, losing all control and letting months and months of squelched pain come rushing like a flood through a dam. Angela pulls him close, letting him bury his face in her chest while the tears pour out.

Lost in thought, as well as in pain, she slowly looks up to find Jonathan standing at the door—agony creasing his face. Angela finds herself unable to decide whose pain will crush her heart the most—her son's, her husband's, or her very own. And so the cycle begins, all over again.

Jonathan puts one hand on Angela's shoulder and the other on Christopher's head. In another moment or two, Christopher's sobs slowly subside.

"Son, I'm here for you. Mom's here for you. We're *all* here for you," Jonathan calmly says, allowing each sentence plenty of space to breathe and relieve.

Christopher nods, slowly pulling away from Angela and wiping his face on his shirtsleeve and whispers, "I know."

The sounds of the night seemed to have stopped—a momentary interlude, perhaps to allow a family's pain to take center stage. In reality, it was more likely their ears had become deaf to anything aside from their pain. And after another few minutes, Christopher quietly adds, "It's just…I can't seem to get those images…and those last few minutes of her life…I can't erase them from my mind. They just play over and over and over."

He looks up at his dad, and the face Jonathan sees is that of a frightened little boy, not the cocky high school graduate-to-be.

"Son, I think…your mother and I both think that it's time…that the three of us, find some relief." Jonathan looks to Angela. "Again."

Christopher's eyelids are heavy from carrying the weight of pain for entirely too long.

"I know the first time it was *my* turn. I think now it may be good for you. How does that sound son?" Angela asks, managing a sweet, if not troubled, smile.

Christopher pauses for a long moment, but then realizes there is no more resistance in him, so he nods, "I'd consider anything right about now," and lets out a long, exhausted sigh.

She pats his hand and says, "You're a brave young man, Christopher, and we're both so proud of you. Just remember, we're all in this together."

In the next room, David's sweaty palms and warm ear hug the cool plaster wall as he eavesdrops on his hurting family. He had been glued to that spot for the past 20 minutes or more, hoping for resolution, feeling his older brother's pain and daydreaming of the day when these nightly attacks will stop.

Quietly, he climbs off the bed and kneels on the floor, propping his elbows on the edge of the bed. The moonlight pours in the window, shining on the back of his head, casting an angelic glow.

"Dear God, please help Christopher. He's in a whole lot of pain and we all sure could use your help. You and I both know nothing's too big for you." He pauses. "Well, you and Gracie."

Just then, he hears a tiny tapping at the window. He turns to see a large, unusual and colorful butterfly—her wings, fluttering on the glass.

It's gone in a blink.

Grinning from ear to ear, he whispers to the night, "Looks like you're both on duty!"

CHAPTER 2

THE NEXT MORNING, THE Matheson home is filled
with bright sunshine and the smell of a home-cooked
breakfast. David sits at the kitchen table eating French toast
and surfing the web. On the screen are pictures of exotic
butterflies. One in particular, resembles the one he saw last
night at his window.

David had always been an exceptional child. To
those around him, it seemed quite likely he would be or do
whatever he wished. He had an insatiable appetite to learn.
Moreover, his parents were convinced that he had a
photographic memory, at least close to one. He could look
at an image, or read a description and recall it—in extreme
detail, weeks, if not months later. It could be a bit
intimidating, as he was only 14. He would most likely
breeze through junior high and perhaps even skip a year or
so, and sail through high school as well. It would be no
surprise at all if he were accepted into any college he
desired. As impressive as his unique abilities were, he had
never developed an inflated ego. David had a highly
sensitive nature that made him aware of a great many
things; his intuition was uncanny. Neither of his parents
paid it much attention, as he'd been that way since birth.
One thing was for sure—you'd have to go a long way to
pull something over on him.
Angela walks in from outside—a newspaper tucked
under her arm. She rubs David's head, drops the paper on
the kitchen table and goes to the cupboards, taking down a
bottle of pills.
"Studying already, L'il Professor?"
David watches from the corner of his eye, as she
swallows another pill—the second, this morning.
"Uh huh." He continues clicking from picture to
picture.

"You feeling okay, Mom?"

"Just a headache. I was up late last night. Christopher was having bad dreams."

"Again?"

"Yep. And I couldn't sleep much after that."

He unfolds the newspaper and scans the headlines, absently nodding. "Yeah, me either. Tossed and turned. Must have been that new fabric softener you bought. Smells kinda like a girl, Mom."

She turns and crosses her arms. "Yes, it does. And I like it. But if you men of the house don't, I suppose I could buy something more *manly*." She returns to breakfast preparations.

David can't quite tell if she is being serious, or playing with him. So, he makes a dramatic point of raising both hands and saying, "Whoa, I didn't mean anything by it, I was just…"

"You were just being a smarty," she replies, vigorously whipping more French toast batter.

David watches his mother for a moment—his eyebrows raised as he observes the zealousness with which she whips the batter. He was going to say something smart like, *I'm wondering if you're mad at the batter, because it looks like you're beating it to death.* Or, something along the lines of, *Swing batter, batter. Swing!* Instead, he chose to play it safe and simply reply, "I'm praying for him."

She slows the torrent of the whisk, snorts a tiny chuckle—at herself, and looking over her shoulder, says, "Thank you, Pastor."

Jonathan is heading down the steps and catches the last of their conversation. "Wait, there's only one pastor in this house, and it happens to be me." He sneaks bacon from David's plate.

"Hey, that's mine!"

Jonathan winks. David returns the familiar gesture.

"You're praying for who?"

"You mean whom," David replies.

"What?" Jonathan fusses with his tie.

"It's, praying for *whom*."

"Okay, for *whom*?" Jonathan retorts.

"For him." Angela nods upstairs, but Jonathan doesn't see her.

Starting to chuckle, Jonathan asks, "For *which* him?"

"For the only other *him* in the house!" David chuckles. "Who's on first?"

They're all laughing, as Christopher shuffles down the stairs.

"What's so funny?"

They stifle more laughter as he unintentionally continues the famous Abbott and Costello routine.

"Your brother."

"Got that right," Christopher smirks, pouring a cup of coffee.

Changing the subject and filling empty plates with stacks of French toast, Angela walks to the table, placing a heavy tower of toast at Christopher's chair. She kisses David on the top of his head and asks, "Son, how would you like to join your father, brother and me for an *outing*?"

"Isn't that the old code word for *seeing Dr. Long*?"

Christopher interjects, "But Ma…"

"I think it's a great idea. Besides, he's not just a good doctor…he's a friend, too."

"Since when did doctors become friends?" Christopher asks.

"Dr. Vaden has been our family doctor since you were in diapers."

David chimes in, "But he still wears them, Ma."

Christopher smacks the back of David's head. "Very funny, Little Man."

Jonathan says, "Dr. Long was kind enough to help this family a year ago…and we just thought that perhaps it may be a good time to tap into his expertise again. I mean, prayer certainly works, but sometimes you need a little booster."

"Yeah, like that stuff you put in the SUV, right Dad?" David asks.

"Kind of, but that stuff's more about helping gas mileage."

Christopher nudges David. "Yeah, he needs better gas mileage…with that lead foot."

"Oh, no you di'nt!" David jokes.

This sort of banter started every day at the Matheson home. The family, like the town of Mission Grove, was known for being there for one another. Thick or thin, up or down, good times and bad—this family and hundreds like them all across the county were people of simple needs. Give them honesty, days full of hard work, healthy families and hearty laugher, and they were happy. The laughs this morning, shared between this tightly knit family, were the kind that came from the bottom of your soul. And it had been a long time since they enjoyed even a glimpse of that kind of joy.

CHAPTER 3

CARTER CHOPS WOOD OUTSIDE his country home. *Sun's bearing down on me like a prison guard*, he thinks. *Reminds me of another time. War was Hell. Hot and hostile. Dangerous and dirty.* The violence and lack of humanity were the killers. After weeks and months of disassociation though, one simply forgot the rules of ordinary engagement and chose to forget *normal* by making new rules. Often, it got ugly. *Today, I'm a free man, in my own backyard, chopping my wood from my hundred-n-some acres.* And he was tending to his own private world.

He stops to take a breather and wipe the pouring sweat from his scarred brow. His tight black t-shirt reveals sinewy muscles, strengthened by hard work. He was proud of being able to stay in this good of shape at 49. He'd worked hard every day to get there. *And when I die, I'll leave having worn this body out—not trying to preserve it.* It was more than he could say about his dying father—a once strong-as-a-bull man. *Whatever. Randall made decisions that were strictly his own and nobody else's,* he thinks to himself. His father, for as long as Carter could recall, was all about what was in it for *him.* Carter had always assumed that these were just the rules by which the Matheson family lived—the rules, a silent code if you will, that said you had to do it *his* way. *Why in the world am I thinking about that SOB right now—that miserable, complicated old man?*

"Shoulda put him out of his misery when I had the chance," he mumbles to no one.

Carter stuffs his handkerchief into his back pocket, picks up the axe, checks the blade for sharpness and returns to chopping. Just as the blade meets the log, as if on cue, a phone rings in the distance. He doesn't hear it. He adjusts the log and swings again. Again, a phone rings just as the wood splits. He tosses the pieces aside and places another log on the stump.

Ring!

Carter looks around.

Just then, Samson exits the doggie door from the kitchen and comes running around the house.

"What is it, Boy?"

Ring!

"Oh yeah, the phone," he snorts, rubbing the dog's head. "Hell, that thing's only rung, what, twice in the past year? Once, from Johnny for a barbecue…"

Ring!

He sticks the axe in the trunk and leisurely walks toward the house, "And the other was…"

Ring!

Stepping inside the darkened house, he picks up the phone and barks, "Yeah?"

Long pause.

"What kind a greeting is that?" a scratchy voice crackles.

Carter is shocked. He walks over to the front window and pulls back the curtains.

"The kind that greets any and all old *coots* who call this place."

A cough rattles on the other end. "Nice."

"What's on your mind, Randall?" Carter asks, calling him by name more to make a point than anything else.

"No, hey, how are you? How ya feeling?"

Carter's trying to figure out something: *How come, in the middle of minding my own business, do I get a call, out of the blue, from Mr. Randall Matheson, just after I was thinking about him, for the first time in…who knows when? What a freakin' coincidence.*

"Hello?" Randall asks, trying once again to get a response.

"Yeah. I mean, no. No pleasantries, just what's up?"

"For a man with two boys who hate him, you'd think just once in a while, they'd give the old man a break."

"We might. *If* that old man weren't such a hateful ass...our entire lives."

A series of guttural coughs explode from the other end. *Sounds like somebody's choking him.*

"Put down the smokes," Carter says with a sinister grin.

"I did. Years ago. It's just that...(cough)...life has a way of (cough, cough)...reminding you of past damage."

Without missing a beat, Carter snorts, "Present, too."

Another long pause.

"You can be a mean young man, Son."

"And you can be a bitter old man...*Sir*."

Another series of coughs, a deep breath and then, "Okay, we could go at this for hours..."

"Not me. Got too much to do," Carter interrupts, growing impatient.

"Me too. Dying a little more every day," Randall adds.

"Aren't we all?"

"Some faster than others."

"Uh huh."

"Trust me. The reason I called..."

"I don't. And there *is* a reason?" Carter snarls.

"If you'd shut the hell up and let your old man get out a sentence between these annoying coughs...and someone's smart-assed quips...maybe you'd learn a thing or two," Randall barks.

"Some things never change," Carter mumbles.

"I'm ignoring that."

And this is how it went—for the better part of Carter and Jonathan's life. *The Bull* would state his way. Everyone else around him would try to state their interests. But, to no avail. It was his way—you guessed it, or the highway. No if's, and's or but's. You could go two days, two months or two years without talking to him and he just might pick up the phone—like he was doing right now, and call you, asking for a favor. And that favor? It always benefited him; hardly ever could Carter recall the results, good, bad or indifferent, benefitting anyone else.

"Here's the thing…(cough)…" Randall continues. "I was wondering if you'd be interested in helping me out with a small…job."

Through the years, Randall and Carter had worked many a job. Randall, being a Lieutenant Colonel in the Marine Corps had seen his fair share of jobs: good, bad and anywhere in between. Carter, despite similar training, traveled mostly in worlds *between the lines*, working in *areas of gray*—that questionable place between black and white. And it was up to you to make the call which side was right or wrong. Nonetheless, he had a particular skillset. And he was damn good at it.

"What sort of…job?" Carter asks. "I'm not in that business anymore."

"You don't even know what type of business I'm talking about."

"Well, if you're behind it, I'm sure it's nothing good."

"Well…let's just call it *my last request*," Randall responds quietly.

"As interesting as this sounds, I'm not much for helping out…" he stops for a moment to reconsider, then adds, "All right, let's hear it. Guess I could do one charity case a year."

There is another long pause—this time, not for effect, but Randall was beginning to feel as though he might be breathing his last breaths.

"I was hoping you'd help me find…your sister."

Carter nearly drops the phone.

"My WHAT?"

CHAPTER 4

DR. LONG'S OFFICE IS handsomely appointed. As a doctor of counseling, he helped patients to become mentally healthy by way of therapy. Some might expect an office that was more austere, or *removed*. However, as an avid lover of history, architecture and sports, his office was warm and comfortable and well stocked with literally hundreds of books on everything from all the world wars, Japanese culture and an expansive overview of politics. He enjoyed learning about exotic butterflies, rare coins and architectural influences from the past hundred years. He could speak eloquently on topics ranging from nanotechnology, stem cell research and the future of drones, both for use in the military, as well as for the civilian. And his love of the water and everything in it or floats above it was vast. A large salt water aquarium sat in the middle of his office and the 40-foot yacht he sailed back and forth between Charleston and any number of islands, was something he enjoyed as much as life itself.

From an early age, Long was grateful for the opportunities he had been given by his father. Their family had always enjoyed many of the finer things of life, at a time when many of his classmates struggled. The fact that his father was one of the first African-American dentists in Charleston proved surprising to some circles; however, the fact that Jefferson, like his father, was so well educated, proved quickly that the Longs would become known for impeccable credentials in their respective fields. Jefferson also realized that being a black counselor in a conservative, affluent and predominantly white community like Mission Grove would have its own set of challenges. The interesting thing is, in all the years that he has lived and worked in this suburb of Charlotte, he has yet to ever have it openly remarked about.

The study of mental health, from both a scientific and a spiritual standpoint, was something he had been intrigued with for most of his adult life. The human mind and all that assists in understanding this incredible machine was his life's passion. And his office, combining intricate detail with a harmonious vibe and tasteful décor, gained the attention of all who visited.

Dr. Jefferson Wainwright Long, handsomely dressed, sits at his large, neatly arranged desk, chatting on the phone with his much younger girlfriend, Sammy. Listening, he looks at picture frames that line the mahogany bookshelves. One in particular shows he and Sammy, arm in arm on a sailboat, docked at *The Mega Dock,* an enormous marina in downtown Charleston, South Carolina.

Speaking in hushed, romantic tones, he says, "Yes, I know Thanksgiving is only two weeks away. There's still plenty of time to plan." He smiles. "And that's one of the things you do best."

Samantha coos on the other end of the phone, "So, do you want to go away for the holidays, or what?"

"If that's what you want, Baby."

"Well, you know my family situation is nothing to write home about. Being an only child has a way of making holidays either really great, or nearly non-existent. Mom has a new boyfriend and he will no doubt have her preoccupied this holiday. Besides, I just saw her over the Labor Day weekend, so…"

"Okay, Key West it is. We both love the heat and I'd like to take the boat out for one more long trip before *old man winter* comes to visit."

Sammy is playful. "Baby, I have a feeling *Lady Giselle* will get out to sea before getting stored for the winter."

The intercom buzzes.

"Just a second, Baby."

Click. "Yes, Eloise?"

"Your nine o'clock appointment has arrived. Would you like me to send them in?"

"Give me just a moment, please, and I'll be right there. Thank you."

Dr. Long double-checks the room, being sure everything is in place and clicks back to Sammy.

"Love, I have to go. Can we finish this conversation over dinner tonight?"

"Sure, I'll look for you around 6:30? And I am so excited; this is going to be the perfect break before I start my new job."

"It'll be a good change and a huge step up. I'm so proud of you. See you tonight."

He hangs up, checks his tie in the mirror and opens the door to welcome Jonathan and Angela.

Jonathan and Jefferson exchange a handshake, as Angela forces a smile and tries to intercept Long's look of surprise by shrugging her shoulders.

"I know." She holds up her hands. "Something about his...not feeling it."

"What's that even mean?" Jonathan asks. Entering the office, he holds the back of a chair for Angela.

"Self-conscious," Dr. Long replies, as he follows them in, motioning to take a seat. "It could be something to do with David."

"How's that?" Jonathans asks.

"He wants to appear strong and in control in front of his little brother. If my instincts are right...they're probably working it through—in their own way, right now. You'll see."

Angela sits stiffly, smooths her skirt, takes a deep breath and trying to relax, says, "His nightmares have recently reached an all-time high."

"How often?"

Jonathan fidgets, looking around the office. "Three, maybe four times a week?"

"Sometimes more," Angela adds. "And for the past 6 or 7 months." She looks down at her hands. Jonathan takes one and squeezes it. She manages a tiny smile.

"It's been, what…" Dr. Long starts.

"Just over a year now," Angela interrupts. "And frankly, I'm…I mean…we…are at our wit's end."

Dr. Long removes his glasses and wipes them with a handkerchief he takes from his breast pocket. It was a move he had learned from an attorney friend of his—meant to buy time, come to a conclusion, or merely allow a conversation to evolve with little noise. A puzzled look crosses his face.

"Has it been that long already?"

Jonathan nods, "Last time you saw us…for business, was last summer. It was just a bit over a year. You were such a help."

"Yes. And we're hoping that perhaps—along with prayer…" Angela says, looking first to Jonathan then back to Long, "that perhaps you could consider being an equally powerful help to us again. Now." She is fighting to keep from crying.

"Time certainly has flown," Dr. Long says quietly. "And of course, I'm here whenever and for as long as you need my help."

"Come to think of it, the last time we saw you—for a casual reason, was the…" Jonathan stops to think, then realizes it wasn't at the concert where Christopher and his band, *Solstice*, won the competition.

"Memorial Day weekend. It was a party at your home," Long interjects. "I seem to recall an enormous barbeque. And an *animated* Carter."

Jonathan rolls his eyes. "Yeah, well, some things never change."

Angela is having trouble keeping a happy face, starts to say something then stops. Long notices.

Looking at a photo behind Long, she says, "Sammy's such a lovely person. You both look so happy."

"Yes, she is. And…we are." Long's smile puts Angela at ease.

"Is it getting serious?"

"Oh, I don't know. She's still…I mean, *it's* still young."

This catches Jonathan off-guard and he chuckles. Cupping his hands to his mouth, he says, "Attention, Dr. Freud. You have a slip at the front desk."

Jefferson and Sammy met over a year ago when she worked in the local public library. He had been doing some research, and she helped him find a good deal of material he needed for an essay. Needless to say, his long hours became their long hours, and they started meeting for coffee. They've been a couple ever since.

"Anyway, about Christopher and his struggles…" Angela says quietly, bringing the conversation back around.

Long clears his throat, adjusts the pad on his desk and says, "Yes. Can you tell me what in particular, or rather—how is he coping on a daily basis, besides the nightmares?"

"His grades have dropped and he's been getting into trouble at school," Angela replies. "And I don't recall if I mentioned this when I called to make the appointment, but he came up short a couple of classes. So, he's got to either squeeze in some extra course work, or he'll be back for an extra semester. And that, as you can imagine—what with the possibility of not being able to graduate with his peers, has been hard on him."

"That's certainly not the Christopher we all know," Long adds.

"It gets worse," Jonathan says quietly.

ðœ

In the parking lot of Dr. Long's office, David and Christopher sit in silence in the SUV. David taps away at his iPad, swiping the screen from one website to another.

Christopher listens to music on his ever-present iPod, staring out the window and biting a nail.

After a long silence, David quietly says, "That's disgusting."

"Huh?" Christopher halfway asks.

"Just didn't want you to ruin your appetite." He grins without moving his eyes from the screen.

"I didn't ask you," Christopher snorts.

"I know."

"*Know-it-all.* That's what you are."

"No, I don't," David responds.

"Just shut it, 'kay? What do you know?"

"You just said it."

"Huh?" Christopher shifts in his seat. "Oh. Right."

After another short silence, Christopher smacks his lips. "Look, D, I'm not trying to take it out on you. I, just want—" He stops, shakes his head and returns the buds to his ears and cranks the volume up.

"I know what you want," David says.

Christopher shouts, "Huh?"

"You want someone to blame!" David shouts in return.

This shocks Christopher. "What…do you mean?"

"You want someone to blame so you can push this guilt onto *them*," David replies, without looking up.

No response.

Christopher turns the volume down, but leaves the buds in his ears.

"Dad said that while Grace's death was his and Uncle Carter's fault…at the end of the day, it was an *accident*," David says, drawing out the last word for effect.

Christopher can't decide which is worse: having a younger brother who is clearly smarter, or the fact that he always has an answer for everything. And if he doesn't, then he will research for days, even weeks if necessary, to find the correct answer. Christopher ponders, *He doesn't do it for any other reason than to help others. Zero ego.*

"Should either you or Grace have wandered into the guest room that day? Who knows? Should Carter have had a gun with him—something Dad specifically had asked him NOT to do, on several occasions? No. But, good or bad, he *is* our uncle and we still love him."

"Yeah." Christopher mumbles.

"Maybe   it   was   just   a   matter   of circumstances...misaligning."

"English, please?"

David grins. "Wrong place—wrong time. And, who knows? Maybe Mom's right."

"About what?"

Hesitating a moment, David realizes what he's going to say next won't likely sit well with Christopher, for a number of reasons; however, he also knows that not saying anything—especially when it could be the truth, isn't fair to his brother.

"About it being Grace's time. Maybe her job was done."

Christopher grimaces, "Now you sound like Dad. He's always saying preachy stuff like that."

He knew it. That's exactly what he was expecting to hear from Christopher. Perhaps he'll try a tactic that he believes is closer to his own personal reality.

"Maybe it's true. I don't know. I'm probably more into the science of why things happen than anything else. But at the end of the day..." He hesitates.

"Yeah?" Christopher asks without looking up.

"Who really knows?"

Christopher knows that on some level his brother is just trying to help. But he, like everyone else, wasn't witness to the horror that Christopher saw—not that he wished that scene on anyone. Frankly, he doesn't think that either one of his parents would be sane to this day...if they saw what he had seen.

David adds, "And as much as it hurts you to relive what you saw..."

"You have NO idea WHAT I saw!" Christopher shouts.

David sits quietly, thinking about what Christopher had to have seen. He can't imagine. He doesn't want to. In fact, David was not allowed to enter that room for weeks, as it had to be cleaned thoroughly, get a fresh coat of paint, and the parents threw out anything that had any porous nature to it—that included bedspreads, blankets, carpets and the draperies that hung on either side of all the windows. David recalls that he didn't even step foot in the guest room for two months when, one day, Angela asked him to go and find an antique flower vase for some fresh flowers. He remembered walking in, looking around and having the weirdest feeling go through his body. He felt a warm rush over his body, like someone had wrapped a blanket around him. He recalled standing in the middle of the room, smiling and feeling that everything was going to be okay. Then he picked up the vase and was on his way. After that, he was no longer afraid of that room.

After a long silence that felt nearly deafening, yet somewhat cathartic, David quietly speaks.

"I know I haven't learned as much as you have, but I have a pretty good idea...what a gun at that range...would do to..." He stops.

David stares out the window and, for the first time since the funeral, allows tears to fill his eyes—in front of his brother. He wasn't going to fall apart, but talking about it aloud as they were, made him feel a pain—like the pain Christopher must be feeling, and it was a pain he worked hard to keep from surfacing.

Christopher, still looking out the window, reaches over and pats his kid brother's knee and mumbles, "You're definitely smarter than me."

David kids, "Excellent point."

Christopher picks up his backpack, coils up the earbuds, stuffs them in his pocket and grabs the door handle. Turning to David, he looks him straight in the eye.

"I just want..." He pauses. "No, I *need*...it to stop, David."

"It will. I promise."

"How can you?"

David cocks his head to the side and smirks, "Cuz, I'm the L'il Professor. I can do anything!"

Stepping out of the SUV, they laugh and head toward the doctor's office. David has a feeling of relief from sharing with his big brother how he felt—whether it was good or bad, right or wrong. The bond between brothers had to be pure and unconditional. It was one of the only safe places in this world.

Putting his arm around his kid brother, Christopher says, "You're prolly right. Now, let's get this emotional crap over with."

CHAPTER 5

JONATHAN, ANGELA AND DR. Long patiently wait for Christopher to have a seat as he hesitantly makes his way into the room. David is across the room looking at the doctor's vast collection of books.

"You have quite the library, Dr. Long. Impressive."

Long smiles and responds, "Thank you, David. That's a nice compliment coming from someone of your intellectual ilk." Long had learned from talking with Angela at length one day of David's near obsession with learning. She said that books and his brother and sister were his best friends and that he didn't find the need for a great many others.

David looks over his shoulder at his parents and beams. They smile with pride.

"Not bad for a teenager, huh?" He turns back to the books and adds, "Don't mind me, Christopher. I have plenty to keep me busy." He pulls down a book on Japanese rituals and sits on the lounge chair in the corner.

Long notices his choice and comments, "Ah, one of my favorites. You'll enjoy it. Be sure to spend time looking at the temples and gardens."

"Thank you." In seconds, David is lost in a world that is all his own.

Christopher watches his little brother and thinks to himself, *Why can't I be normal like him? And smart.* He looks to his parents and wonders, *Do they see me as abnormal? I mean, I am sitting in the office of a shrink.*

"Tell me, Christopher, how are things at school?"

It's back to reality, as Christopher slides down in his chair and proceeds to *tune out.*

But Angela won't have any part of it.

"Son, Dr. Long asked you a question. Please engage here, would you? We're here for you."

"Are you?"

"What's that supposed to mean?" Angela asks, with a look of surprise.

"Nothing," he mumbles.

Jonathan interjects, "Son, please sit up in your chair, answer your mother's question and don't waste the doctor's time."

As Christopher studies his hands, Long looks to Jonathan and nods, adding, "I have all the time in the world. Your family, Christopher, is my family. I hope we established this early on. I want to help you in any way that I can right now, just as I hope I've been able to help in the past."

Silence.

"You have," Christopher mumbles.

"What's that, Son?" Jonathan demands.

"I said, you have...helped...Dr. Long, Sir." Agitated, he shakes his head and begins to withdraw again.

Angela speaks up, "Christopher?"

He continues to stare at his hands.

"Please look at me, Son."

"Yes?" He looks at her.

"That's better. Look, if you don't want to do this, fine. We can come another day, or another month, or never, if that's what you want."

"Really?" he asks.

"However, we do need to find some sort of help for you...as it pertains to these nightmares." He gets an instant look of anxiety on his face. She continues. "And I think— as does your father, that Dr. Long is our number two choice for assistance, in matters of the heart and mind."

Long has a questioned look on his face. Jonathan points heavenward.

Long says, "Ah. Of course. Good company."

Several smiles help break the ice and Christopher begins to relax.

"You're right. Something has to give. I mean, as depressed as I feel..."

Angela raises her eyebrows as she looks to Jonathan. Christopher doesn't see them.

"…there has to be something that will help me shut them down."

Long speaks up, "There are several ways. And they range from quite easy to rather…strong."

Christopher looks up, first to Long, then to his parents.

"What's rather strong?"

"Well, that would be very strong medication and intensive therapy. But that," he adds in a comforting voice, "is certainly not something we need here, I don't believe."

Christopher sighs and his shoulders relax. "Good, then let's hear it for quite easy."

Dr. Long claps his hands together once and stands.

"Now, that's what I call a good start. Let's wrap it up for today and I'll have Eloise make an appointment for later in the week."

Long escorts them to the door and wraps one arm around Christopher's shoulder. "Perhaps your dad could bring you, and just you and I could chat, or…"

"I can bring myself. I drive, you know," Christopher interrupts.

"Done," Dr. Long says. "That'll work just fine."

Across the room, David sees the meeting has adjourned so returns to the bookcase to replace the book.

"David, please, feel free to take that with you," Long says. "You certainly seemed to be enjoying it."

"Can I really?"

"Of course," the doctor replies.

"Thanks. There are so many interesting things about the Japanese culture," he says to Jonathan, nearly skipping out of the office with delight as he shares his newfound knowledge.

"C'mon on boys. Let's head out," Jonathan says.

Angela hangs behind, as the men proceed to the waiting room. She takes the arm of Dr. Long.

"Thank you so much for all you do, Dr. Long. You're a blessing to us all."

"Angela, how many times do I have to tell you? It's Jefferson...and it's my pleasure." He smiles, patting her hand.

"Just one other thing before I go. Could I get another prescription? Christopher's not the only one that's not sleeping well these days."

"Of course, Dear." He hesitates a moment then adds, "I thought we just filled that."

"No, it's been quite a while. I'm pretty sure. Just need to get over this bump in the road—especially with Christopher suffering so much." She hesitates then adds, "You understand."

"Of course."

He writes the scrip, as the others leave the building and head to the car.

"It really helps. And Christopher will see you in the next day or so. Thanks again."

As she leaves, Long waves, turns and smiles at Eloise.

"Lovely family," Eloise kindly says.

"Indeed." He returns to his office, closing the door behind him, and walks to his desk. He pulls out a patient ledger and finds *Matheson*, then slides his finger across the page and down a long column. He stops, double-checks, then shakes his head.

Looking out the window, he frowns and mumbles, "Best not play with fire lest you get burned."

CHAPTER 6

CARTER STANDS IN HIS dining room, staring out the window. His cool blue eyes are focused on nothing in particular, but his keen mind is racing, trying desperately to capture something. *I have a sister? That is the craziest thing I've ever heard,* he thinks. He hears a tiny voice far in the distance when he realizes that he has been holding the phone away from his ear.

"You did say *sister,* right?"

"Yes," Randall confirms.

"I don't have a sister," Carter responds, confused.

"Well...it's something you didn't know about," Randall says, sheepishly. "But, yes, you do."

Carter is not happy, as he's not big on surprises. "When in the wide world of wonder were you...no...never mind. With you, I've just come to expect one cluster..."

"Point made," Randall interrupts. "I got it, okay? And as lame as this is going to sound, I've been meaning to tell you. But..."

"When?" Carter interrupts. "And why now? Most importantly, what do you mean by *find?* How does one go about *losing* a daughter?"

"By..." Randall tries to say, but Carter doesn't let him finish.

"That is *if* she's actually your daughter."

There is a long silence on the phone, then Randall finally responds.

"Again, if you'd shut up for one minute, I'll explain."

Carter pats his pocket for a cigarette—a long habit, recently removed. Instead, he walks to the fridge and pulls out a beer, pops the cap and takes a long drink.

"She's actually, well, a half-sister."

Taking a breath, Carter quietly responds, "Uh huh."

"After your mother died—God rest her soul..."

Carter interrupts, "Don't you…"

"Give it a rest, Son…(cough)…As I was saying, I was still in the service, of course, and was…(cough)…stationed overseas. We didn't know when we were going to come back, so I…selfishly…lived for the moment."

"Big surprise." Carter says through gritted teeth.

Randall ignores this and continues, "I met this woman and, well, you get the picture."

"Uh huh," Carter quips.

"So, I come back. Time goes by. I get married again. More time goes by. Then, one day, this…girl shows up. As you can imagine, I'm…taken aback."

"Sure," Carter snorts, adding, "I guess."

"Okay, long story short. With times as they were…especially given the fact that I…had come into some money…"

"What? How?" Carter blasts.

"That's a story for another time, but suffice it to say…"

"You disappeared on Jonathan and me so long ago I don't even know which president was in office! Then, a year ago, out of the blue, you call to tell me you're dying. And at that time, you don't even know that your only granddaughter is dead! Then, another year later, you call me to say, 'Hi, and oh yeah, you have a sister—thing is, I've, uh, kinda LOST her! Can you help me find her?'"

Carter is enraged.

"Just let me…" Randall gets cut off.

"Hold on!" He shouts into the phone, then slams it onto the counter and walks to the fridge. He pulls out another beer and pops the cap while walking out the back door and into the yard. He circles the spot where he had been chopping wood, taking a long drink in the process.

"Of all the nerve…" He takes another drink. "Here I am trying to do good…" He takes another drink. "What a selfish…" And he finishes the bottle. Samson sits at his feet patiently awaiting some attention. Carter takes a deep breath and rubs his dog's head.

"Sorry, Boy. It's not you. Just somebody trying to rattle me."

Walking back inside, he picks up the phone and continues.

"Okay. I'm back. Had to catch a breather."

Silence.

"You still there?" Carter asks.

More silence.

"Yeah, I'm here. Bet you went out for a drink, huh?"

Carter looks around then says, "Uh huh."

"Probably needed it. Certainly deserve it. That's my boy."

"Don't start…with the *my boy* stuff again."

A lone, gravelly cough echoes across the line, followed by, "Fair 'nuff."

Carter finishes with, "Let's just…take this one step at a time."

CHAPTER 7

THE MATHESON'S SUV IS traveling up I-77, having left Long's office in Davidson. It's a good-looking day and that certainly helps the somewhat strained mood. Jonathan and Angela drive in silence, looking to one another from time to time, as the boys in the back seat provide a play-by-play wrap-up of their meeting.

"Nice *outing*," David says sarcastically, adding, "Actually, I liked it. He's a cool guy and I got this great book for hanging out while you got your head checked."

"More like a shrink rap. Hah...get it?" Christopher says, punching David in the arm for extra effect.

"Ouch, Turd-face. That hurt," David whines.

Jonathan watches from the rearview and smiles.

"Ouch...that hurt," Christopher mockingly replies.

"Boys. Please," Angela begs. "My head hurts and frankly, I'm not in the mood."

The bickering in the back seat continues as the parenting does the same from the front.

Jonathan turns to Angela and says, "You seem to have a lot of them lately."

"I'm okay, Love. Just need more sleep." She nods toward the backseat.

"Gotchya. Just worried about my baby, that's all."

"And Baby appreciates it, too," she beams.

Jonathan pulls off at their exit, glides through a couple of traffic lights and is soon driving through the gates of their neighborhood entrance. Christopher starts to put things back into his backpack. Jonathan notices.

"Son, you can hang out. I'm giving you both a ride to school."

"Nah, that's okay, Dad. I'm gonna drive myself. Grabbing lunch with the guys, then off to soccer practice. May hang out for a while."

"Okay. Just not too late, huh? School night and all that."

They pull up to the house and Christopher jumps out. "Thanks for the ride! See ya, Professor!"

"Later, Chris!" David shouts, gathering his things.

Angela leans over for a goodbye kiss.

From the backseat, David sighs, "Really?"

In between kisses, Angela says, "Yes, really."

"I'll call ya later, Babe," Jonathan says, as she gets out.

"Looking forward to it."

David has already jumped out of the SUV and run around to the front, waiting to ride beside his dad.

"Shotgun!"

"And tell me," looking at his watch, "would a hot chocolate ruin your lunch?" Jonathan winks.

"Nah. In fact, it's been proven that chocolate actually increases your appetite as it releases all sorts of dandy chemicals into your bloodstream. You see…"

Jonathan holds up a hand, "Okay, I believe you. Starbucks, here we come!"

He and David both lower their windows and wave goodbye. Angela stands waving and smiling at her two boys.

క

Inside the house, Angela drops her things on the kitchen table, gets a pill bottle from her purse, pours a tall glass of water and takes a long drink.

Grabbing her temples, she lets out a big, "Whew!"

Just then the phone rings. Startled, she jumps.

"Hello, Matheson's residence."

"Hey Baby Girl, listen, I know you just got in—saw you pull up, but was wondering if I could swing by in a little while. I have some great news I want to share."

"Sure Mom," she says, rolling her eyes.

"Okay, give me about 20 minutes and I'll be over. I have an interview to finish up. I'll tell you all about it in a bit."

Angela hangs up and stops to look at a picture of Grace on the fridge. Touching her girl's face, she begins to cry. Leaning on the fridge, she slowly slides down to the floor, where she sits and cries.

ϟ

Jonathan and David are nearly to school as David empties the last of his hot chocolate. He cuts a look at his father who is peeking at his smartphone.

"Shouldn't text and drive, Dad," David says quietly.

Surprised, he tosses the phone up on the dash, almost too quickly—like a child caught doing something bad.

"Huh? No, no...not texting. Dangerous. Just...uh, looking at my calendar. Got a full day."

"Right."

They drive in silence as Jonathan contemplates his day. *I've got meetings to attend: two for the Center, one for a couple of new employees and something else. It'll come to me.*

David is lost in his own world. *That book is cool. I'm going to make a study on exotic butterflies. All my homework is done. I have one big test today—piece of cake. Speaking of—wonder what's for lunch.*

There are a few more minutes of silence before David speaks up.

"Dad, what do you think about the after-life?"

Lost in thought, it takes Jonathan a moment to respond.

"The after-life, huh? You mean Heaven."

"Yeah. And Hell, if there is one."

"Oh, there is one all right."

"You're sure…" David says, cutting a look in his father's direction.

"If I know you, you're getting at something specific, right? What is it?"

David opens his smartphone and pulls up a picture of a beautiful butterfly.

"Dad, you're a pretty smart guy. And you've got a lot of degrees, from some very impressive schools, so I know you know a lot of things. So, let's just consider, for the sake of argument, that someone you knew had passed away."

Jonathan looks at David and cocks his head to the side.

"You mean…someone like your little sister?"

"Okay, yes. Let's use Grace as an example. Well, I've heard tell…"

"You've…*heard tell*? Son, you sound like a Wild Western storyteller."

"You get the picture," he says, rolling his eyes. "Anyhow, I've studied stuff and…" He poses with both thumbs under each arm, affecting a country storyteller. "I've given myself to a-studying, and I say here…"

Jonathan nearly spews his coffee across the inside windshield.

"Whoa there, Pardner…ya best be…" David stops the act and shakes his head. "Okay, enough of that."

"And, we're almost at school. How about you give me the *Reader's Digest* version, please."

"Some religions, or theorists, believe that friends, family—souls in general, can often return to earth in a different form, like an insect or animal…just to let their friends or family know that everything is okay."

Jonathan listens, then slowly starts to nod his head and finally says, "Yes. I have heard of this. And what insect, or animal, or whatever…have you seen lately that has you thinking about this?"

Jonathan pulls up in front of the school and puts the car in park, but doesn't take his attention away from David for a second.

"Well, last night, when you and Mom were in Christopher's room?"

"How did you…"

"Dad," he interrupts, "do you have any idea how many times Chris wakes me up with his night terrors?"

"He's having a difficult time."

"No, I understand—maybe better today than ever before. But here's the thing…"

Jonathan leans closer, beaming with pride, hanging on his son's every word.

"Last night, when things got quiet in there, I knelt on my knees to pray to God and ask Him for help for Christopher."

"That's great, Son. You're such a good brother."

"And it was then that I heard something tapping on my window. I turned and there was a beautiful butterfly…at the very same time that I was praying for Chris."

Jonathan nods, "And you're sure it wasn't a moth?"

David shakes his head, "Dad, I know the difference between a butterfly and a moth. And this was no ordinary butterfly. It was a Blue Morpho butterfly. A *Morpho Didius*—from the *Nymphalidae* Family, to be exact."

Just then, a horn blows from behind. Jonathan looks in his rearview and waves.

"Wow, Son, a *Bluemorphonymph*…that's neat. And I genuinely appreciate your sharing, but from the looks of it…" Jonathan nods behind them, "we may have to talk about this more tonight at dinner, okay?"

David is already gathering his things and opening the door to get out.

"Sure, Dad. Have a great day."

As he closes the door, Jonathan lowers the window and shouts, "Love you, Son!"

David spins around and shouts, "Love you, too. And it's a rare *Japanese* butterfly, Dad!"

And with that, he runs up the sidewalk and into school.

ॐ

Driving to work, Jonathan is still smiling, thinking about the story David shared. He's not only amazed at his amount of knowledge on so many fronts, but also the hunger with which he attacks everything. *I always liked school, but I was never that self-motivated.* Jonathan is certain his young boy will attend any school he chooses, going at the rate he is.

He picks up his phone and hits speed-dial to call Angela. The phone rings several times before he gets a message, "Hello, this is Angela, I must be out working on the yard, or taking care of my three boys, so please leave me a message and I'll ring you back!"

BEEP.

"Hey Hon, bet you're plantin' mums with Momma. Just wanted to share a story our son shared with me on the way to school. Let's just say, I had no idea he knew so much about butterflies. Okay, see ya at dinner. Love you." He tosses the phone in the passenger seat and whistles a happy tune.

ॐ

At the other end of that phone, Angela lies on the kitchen floor, unconscious.

CHAPTER 8

THE MISSION GROVE COMMUNITY Church boardroom is filled with a number of people from both the church and the local community. Pastor Matheson sits at the head of the table—handsome, animated and both fully in control and completely admired by this room, and this community of people. On his right, sits—appropriately, his right-hand man, Joshua Ridge. Josh is the associate pastor and is a gregarious, enthusiastic and loyal second-in-command heir to the pulpit. Whenever Matheson is away, which is very seldom as Jonathan loves this church and local community as his own family, Josh handles all the pastor's duties.

To his left, sits the church secretary, Claire. She is efficient, lovely and appreciated by her peers, as she's been by the pastor's side since he arrived nearly two decades ago.

Sitting at the opposite end of the table is Mayor Forrester W. Garvin, stalwart in the community and Pastor Matheson's best golfing buddy. Garvin is a large, happy fellow who always approaches people with a hearty handshake and a booming voice—one that Jonathan has tried to recruit to the choir for years, but to no avail. Come to learn, the mayor is tone deaf. He's always been a big supporter of this church and sees it as one of the best parts of the Mission Grove community.

On the mayor's right is one of the newest additions to Mission Grove. Although not a member of the church, Stephan DeAngelo has become a big fan. DeAngelo is the new vice-president of American Bank, the number three and fastest growing bank in the Carolinas—slowly gaining on Wells Fargo and Bank of America. He recently moved to Charlotte from Paris, where he was Manager of International Business for one of the premier banks of Europe, *BNP Paribas*. He saw working in the States as an opportunity to become a much larger player. Plus, his wife was from New York, but they wanted to raise their daughter in a smaller, simpler town. So, after spending two weeks vacationing between Charlotte and Charleston, they decided that the charming Charlotte suburb of Mission Grove was the place for them.

Across the table from him and on the mayor's left, is the director of business affairs for the church, Ray Benson, not your typical quiet accountant type. He has a solid nose for business, but he's also an equally efficient basketball player. The church ladies call him *Bachelor Boy,* because he's in his late 40s but looks and acts like late 20s. He is leader of the men's basketball tournaments.

Rounding out one of the last two slots is Sheriff Danny Mahler. He and the pastor have been friends since college. Actually, they were roommates their junior and senior years. And although he was caught in a compromising position last summer, all charges were dropped and his reputation has been cleared, making him one of the most admired men in the community.

Finally, there is Stuart Owensby, Jonathan's father-in-law and the man they call the *Godfather of Mission Grove.* His family started this church in 1921, and Stuart has been on every board since he graduated college. He's the most rock-solid and consistent man at the church, and someone who everyone adores.

"Thank you again to each of you for being here today. This is an important time in the life of our church as we are facing the most exciting expansion since—what? Stuart..." Jonathan looks to Stuart for backup.

"Since my great grandfather and his friends built the original church building so many years ago...I fear to count," he says with great pride.

"And since that time, we've come to love this church and her family more by each passing year. Now, on the anniversary of my daughter's passing…" The heads of everyone slowly nod in quiet respect. "Since Grace went to be with her Heavenly Father, her earthly father has work to do. And we're just the people to do it."

"Here, here!" says Mayor Garvin.

"Absolutely," Stuart adds, pounding the table.

"You bet!" echoes Ray Benson, while clapping.

And Stephan DeAngelo chimes in with, "Bueno!"

"Thank you, Stephan. And this may be a good time to let you take the floor. After all, you're about to help us build the floor!" Everyone laughs, as he stands and moves to an easel where he begins his presentation.

Stephan is a classically handsome Italian man—well-dressed, polite, professional, but with a sex appeal that everyone, especially the ladies, admires, and the kind of person you have a hard time not liking.

"First of all, I want to say thank you so very much for your allowing me and my bank to help your church to create the first of its kind multi-purpose facility that will be able to not only house the ever-growing Mission Grove Community Church congregation…" he nods, as the group quietly golf-claps, "…but also support the arts with concerts, sporting events and much more, providing the entire metro with handsome tax incentives while utilizing the space for conventions and such."

He rolls a small cart over to the side of the conference table and lifts a veil, displaying a model of the proposed building.

"Announcing Mission Grove's *Grace Family Center*!"

Everyone claps—their mouths agape, and stands in wonder at the beautiful structure and adjoining grounds.

CHAPTER 9

CARTER CLIMBS UP INTO his old pickup truck and drives down his worn, gravel driveway. *Time for lunch. I'm starved,* he thinks. He'd worked up an appetite and knew just the place that would scratch that itch. It's late for him to be having lunch, but he had been distracted by a surprise phone call—one that had surprised him in more ways than one.

Carter reflected on how Randall hadn't spoken to him for more than a year—not long after Grace had died. And that was after having not spoken to him for years—not long after Jonathan and Angela were married. Plus, he was surprised that he was asking for help. *Is what I've been thinking all along, finally about to come to pass? Am I going to be set up by my own father in hopes of burying that safely guarded secret once and for all? Was that why Lt. Colonel Matheson called—so that he could act as judge and jury over his oldest son and put to rest the shroud that covered us both for nearly a lifetime? He didn't sound like a man full of vengeance, but then, I don't trust Randall as far as I can toss my Ford F-150.*

Carter has merged onto the four-lane, just a few minutes from his favorite lunch spot. It was a place he and Jonathan had frequented over the years and a place they loved to take Christopher, David and Grace when they were still small. He thought about David and how different he was from the other two. He'd have to take him there some day—just the two of them. *I need to be a better uncle to those kids,* he thinks.

He pulls into The Derby Diner and parks in the back corner, just like always. As he enters, the bell overhead signals to the wait staff that another customer has arrived. As had been the case for as long as he could recall, Buster, the owner, sticks his face out from around back, or through the service window, or from behind the counter with a friendly smile and a quick, "Hello and thanks for coming. Grab any seat you like and we'll be right with you."

Day or night, cold or hot, fresh or tired, just like clockwork, if Buster was working—and he worked nearly 6 days a week for the past 30-plus years, any and every customer was going to hear that greeting.

Carter flips through the menu as though it's his first visit, even though he always got the same thing, every time: double BLT with crispy bacon and extra mayo, crinkle-cut fries and coffee, black.

Teresa, his favorite waitress walks over with coffee in hand, just like always. He liked Teresa. She was pretty in a girl-next-door sort of way, but with a mischievous look in her eye. But she was true—about her age, what she liked about any number of topics, and what she had in mind about doing with Carter. Some day.

"Hey, Carter. How's it hanging?"

He smiles.

"Just about the same way it does every day, Teresa. What's new in your world?"

"Just wondering when you're going to let me make you a home-cooked meal. Something besides a BLT and fries," she says with enough sex appeal to distract him. "That's all."

"One of these days, Teresa. Soon."

She grins, nods and shifts her weight to the other hip and asks, "What's on your plate today, Carter? That is, besides your usual?"

He drifts for a second, thinking about her and replies, "Just chopping wood. And thinking."

"Yeah, well, you just keep on thinking and I'll get to chopping some of that bacon for you, okay, Sweet-pea?"

She winks and leaves.

He watches her wiggle—knowing the little something extra was for his benefit alone.

CHAPTER 10

AS CHRISTOPHER WALKS ACROSS the high school parking lot toward his truck, he is lost in thought. *Is it really that important to get good grades if all I really want to do is to sing and play in a band? I mean, who needs history or algebra to write and perform in concerts all around the world? Maybe I should just focus on writing more good songs and honing my playing skills. Everything else will take care of itself.*

Two classmates come from behind the building and startle Christopher.

"Yo, Chris. Where ya goin'?" shouts Peter Vaughan, a classmate and all around not-so-nice guy.

"Yeah, American Idol, whassup?" a guy named Jeff chimes in. Chris had seen him around school, but didn't think that either one of them were the kind of guys that would make great pals. He remembered Jeff hanging around Botany class, noting that he didn't seem like someone interested in greenhouses and plants.

"I'm starved. Gonna grab some lunch!" he shouts back, nervously hoping they'll just keep walking.

The two boys look at one another, say something that Christopher can't hear, then start running toward him. Not sure exactly what to do, Christopher tries to play it cool and nonchalantly, yet briskly, heads toward his truck. The guys are gaining on him and his palms start to sweat. He tosses his bag in the back of his pickup, just as the two boys approach the vehicle.

Peter is out of breath and manages to say between deep breaths, "Can we come?"

Jeff says nothing, but looks around the campus. They're between classes, so there isn't much traffic on the school grounds.

"Sure. Why not?"

❧

Christopher, Jeff and Peter made for an unlikely trio. Peter was the kid who got into a fight with Christopher last school year, after making a comment that Christopher will never forget. He and his girlfriend at the time, Kym, were just minding their own business when this punk approached Christopher, knocked his books out from under his arm and asked a question that made his blood boil. *Hey, Christ-opher, tell us, what's it like seeing your little sister's head blown off?* Christopher recalls that moment like it was ten minutes ago. At the time, all he could do was turn around and swing, knocking the ever-loving crap out of this character. That scuffle got them both suspended for two days. But for right now, he is choosing to just play it cool.

Jeff was Peter's pal and one of the *darker* characters at school. He was a new kid at the school and one that people tried to stay away from, as his looks were handsome, but dark. He reminded girls of that pretty boy from the *Twilight* movies. Given most guys thought he was a badass, not to mention he was built like a linebacker, they just left him alone.

They're about a mile away from school before anyone says anything.

"Thanks for driving," Jeff says. "My old man's Pontiac is a deathtrap."

"True dat," Peter laughs. "And my Jeep is really wacked. Needs a tune-up, or something like that."

"It's cool," Christopher replies. Feeling more relaxed and confident, he picks up speed and cranks the stereo, shaking his head and banging his hand on the steering wheel, keeping perfect beat to the music. The two passengers watch him shamelessly jam to the music.

"Damn, Bro, this heap can move," Jeff shouts above the blaring song.

"Thanks."

"But what's that noise, Dude?" Peter asks, nodding toward the dash.

"That's my band," he turns down the music, "well…former band, *Solstice*. Cool, huh?"

"Not my thing. But…a halfway decent beat, I guess," Jeff adds.

"Sorta crap, if you ask me. Who's the girl singing lead," Peter jokes, punching Jeff in the side.

"Watch it, Vaughan. Unless you want that elbow up your ass," Jeff barks.

Christopher watches the interchange and realizes how much different these guys are than his old band-mates. But then, those guys don't get it. Artists have to step outside their comfort zone and experience different sides of life—if they're going to be true artists.

Jeff pulls pot from a baggie and rolls a joint. The speed with which he makes it surprises Christopher. Peter watches Jeff's manual dexterity as though he were creating art.

As if he were reading their minds, Jeff says, "Yeah, ain't my first rodeo, Jeffro!"

Jeff and Peter laugh, then light up the joint and take a few hits before offering it to Christopher.

"Yeah, not right now. Driving, ya know. Maybe later."

"Whatever," the boys say in unison, as they take another hit and blow the smoke toward Christopher. He swats it away and adds, "Yeah…whatever."

CHAPTER 11

DAPHNE HAS CROSSED THE vast property that she and Stuart share with Jonathan and Angela. Often, they'll use a small four-wheel drive *Gator* to traverse the several acres. This time, however, Daphne chose to walk. Angela's car is in the driveway, so she's puzzled. Besides, she just called a half hour ago. She looks at her watch.

"I had no idea we'd take an hour and a half!" she mumbles to herself, walking around the side of the yard to see if Angela was up to her planting duties. She wasn't.

Heading back toward the kitchen door, she peeks in the window and gasps when she sees Angela lying on the floor. Panicked, she rushes to her daughter's side.

Looking around, she searches for any clues as to what happened. Nothing. Leaning over, she listens for a heartbeat. Faint. She stops and thinks: *Stuart? No, he's at a board meeting. Jonathan? With Stuart. What about Danny? He's there too. Okay, 911.* She picks up the phone and dials. In an instant, someone picks up.

"911, what's your emergency?" the calm voice says on the other end.

"It's my daughter. She's passed out. I just got here and…"

"Mom?"

Daphne turns and sees Angela propping up on one arm. She lays the phone down.

"Baby? Are you okay? What happened?"

Angela is groggy, but manages a very quiet, "I don't know. One minute I was…"

"Hello? Hello? Miss?" a tiny voice echoes in the distance.

Daphne turns and sees that she had absently laid the phone down. She picks it up and says, "Yes, uh, she appears okay." She nervously laughs. "False alarm, I guess.

I'm sorry. Thank you." She hangs up the phone and turns her full attention to her daughter in distress.

"What in Heaven's name? You had me scared out of my mind. How did you get here…I mean, when did you pass out, and where…"

Angela interrupts, as she attempts to stand, "Mom, one at a time."

"Stop, Daughter. I'll help you up. Just…here, wait…"

Daphne pulls out a chair then grabs Angela by the arm and helps her to sit.

"Okay, let's see. One: I'm sorry I scared you. Two: I don't know how I got here, but I think I fell." She smiles. "Three: I guess I passed out, well…" she looks at her watch, "must have been about a half hour, because you said you were coming over…"

"Okay, about that. I'm sorry, but you see, the person…"

Angela interrupts, "Whoa, I'm not finished. So, it's evidently been longer than that. Let's see, where was I? Four: I was coming in from outside. Jonathan dropped me off from Dr. Long's…"

Daphne takes a very big breath and sighs it out, rather dramatically.

"Okay. I see you're fine. But you scared the pickle outta me."

Angela chuckles, "Well, I'm sure that's a sight. Listen, Mother," she continues, as she starts to stand, "I have not…"

"Wait. I'll get it. What do you…"

Angela smacks her hand lightly. "Stop, I'll get it. I'm fine. As I was saying, I was just standing here, taking some medication and simply fainted."

Daphne scowls, walks to the counter, picks up the prescription bottle and, taking her glasses from her pocket, reads the fine print.

"Angela Elizabeth, what are you taking here?"

At that moment, Angela has to think: *I owe it her to be honest, but frankly, she'll just ask me a hundred questions—none of which will provide satisfactory answers. It's MY life and I have to cope with MY crap the way I have to.*

"It's just something to help me...cope. Dr. Long prescribed them a while back and..."

"Does Jonathan..."

"No, he does not know and I would appreciate it if you..." she gets up in her mother's face, "would not say anything to him." She backs away and walks to the fridge.

"Okay. Okay. I just think..."

Angela holds up her hand and takes a deep breath, running over a few things to say in her head first. *Here she goes. I don't WANT her opinion. I don't WANT anyone's opinion. EVERYONE else gets to do what THEY want, AS they want, WHEN they want.*

"I know you think everything should be discussed between partners. That's probably how you and Daddy did things, but this is different. Jonathan has enough on him right now, what with the new church expansion, his boys'...our boys' sports leagues starting up for fall. Then, there's Thanksgiving which is just a couple of weeks away..." She trails off and shakes her head.

"What?" Daphne asks.

After a big sigh, Angela continues, "Not to mention, Christopher is now seeing the family *shrink wrap* as he put it earlier. First, Jonathan, then me and now our oldest. Who's next? David?"

Angela stares out the window. *When will all this madness stop!*

Daphne leaves the silence alone so her daughter can focus.

"And here I am, after a little more than a year, just now starting to come to grips...being able to handle...but barely, Grace's passing. I mean, I have always tried...you taught me to always be strong. You and Daddy have always been so strong, and here I was trying, really trying, to be so very strong for so long." She takes several deep breaths, looks at her trembling hands, then back out the window.

"Even other women in our fellowship group—behind my back, no less, just kept commenting, 'How can she be so strong? How can she be so chipper? How could she have just lost her only daughter and be so *Super Mom Of The Month*!'" Angela grabs either side of the sink, hangs her head and starts to quietly cry. *Just leave me be, people. I'm doing the best I can!*

Daphne walks over, turns Angela around and wraps her arms around her. Angela's tears become a steady stream, accompanied by a deep moaning.

Then, as only a mother can, Daphne allows Angela a safe haven of release. She pats her daughter's head, pushing strands of hair from her face, and lets Angela empty her bucket of pain—a bucket that had passed its capacity long ago, and was now spilling over in the form of deep, soul-wrenching sobs.

CHAPTER 12

THE DERBY DINER HAS a hustle-bustle atmosphere. Not only is does it serve the best home-cooked food— bringing people from miles around to sample any number of hand-crafted dishes, but it also sits alone on this long stretch of road. The parking is always full, from just before noon to well after 1:30, for the main lunch rush. Any other part of the day, it continues to have a steady stream of hungry patrons. Part of its charm is its nod to the '50s, as the décor hasn't changed much since she opened in 1955. The over-sized windows let in plenty of sunlight along with the surrounding vista of the distant Blue Ridge Mountains. Barstools still spin red vinyl mushroom tops, while the original freckled Formica counter retains the same luster it did nearly sixty years ago. The soda fountain and ice-cream counter, with brightly polished quilt-patterned backsplash, was as fresh as the day they opened. Their neighborhood diner was a sacred place where patrons could step back in time and remember how simple life used to be.

Carter pushes his empty plate away. Nothing is left but a few crumbs. Teresa comes over with a fresh pot of coffee.

"Well, Mister Man, you certainly made haste with that," she nods toward the plate, then adds, "Don't recall the last time you ate *two* plates of the same. Must be some kinda record."

He catches a twinkle in her eye, the kind of twinkle that says, *I want you.*

"Yeah. Suppose I was hungry. Lotta wood today. Lot on my mind," he says in his best Sam Shepard voice— something playful. *Another kind of record being set*, he thinks to himself.

Teresa leans over a bit closer this time, as she pours another cup of coffee. He can smell the perfume in her hair. It was clean like rain, with a hint of vanilla, or cinnamon, or something like that. *Sexy is what she is,* he thinks. It had been a long time since he'd been with a woman. And if she kept this up, things were going to overheat pretty fast.

"You smell nice," he says shyly.

"Why, thank you, Mr. Carter. Nice of you to notice."

She starts to walk away, turns and comes back to his table.

"Almost forgot," she coos, placing the check on the table. "Doubt you'll be hungry for a while. But if you need anything, there's a number on the back. We also deliver." She winks, turns and is back to the kitchen before his smile dissolves into a frown, as he concentrates. Trying to focus on the task at hand, he ponders whether or not he'll help his father find his daughter—Carter's half-sister. *Surprise!* Randall's unclear motive makes him more than a bit hesitant.

A small commotion breaks Carter's concentration and gets his attention. As he looks up from his coffee cup, he sees Christopher and two young hooligans sliding into a booth in the corner. It isn't ten seconds before Christopher sees him, looks around nervously, says something to his crew, gets up and walks over to Carter's booth.

"Hey, Uncle Carter."

"Hey, Christopher."

"How's it going?"

"Not bad." He looks around Christopher to where the boys sit. They're cutting up and making too much noise for a family restaurant. Christopher follows Carter's gaze.

"Schoolmates," Christopher says, turning back to face Carter.

"Uh huh. From here, they look baked."

Confused, Christopher asks, "Whaddya mean?"

Carter grins, motions for Christopher to sit, then waves Teresa over, motioning for two coffees.

"Baked?"

No response.

"Toast?" Carter says.

Christopher still acts dumb.

"High?"

Christopher looks around as though he's about to get busted and, wiping sweaty palms on his jeans, leans over to whisper, "Oh. No, I wasn't—I mean, they were…"

"Hello, men," Teresa says, startling Christopher as she places two fresh cups of coffee on the table between them.

"Teresa, this is my brilliantly talented nephew, Christopher."

He nods.

"Christopher, this is my, uh…Miss Teresa, a likewise talented…waitress." He almost blushes.

Noticing Carter's embarrassment, she smiles and turns her attention to Christopher.

Reaching for her extended hand, he starts to get up, but can't as he's in a booth.

She laughs, "No need to get up, but thank you for the respectful notion." They shake hands.

"Nice to meet you. And thank you for the coffee," Christopher says quietly.

"My pleasure. You two enjoy yourself. I can see there's plenty of handsome to go around in the Matheson family." And she walks away.

They look at one another. Silence. Then a small chuckle erupts from Christopher, followed by one from Carter.

"Wow. She's hot, Uncle Carter."

"Duh!" he responds.

They laugh harder now. But not as loudly as the two punks in the corner.

Carter straightens. "Chris, it's none of my business. I mean, you're a big boy and can make your own decisions, but from where I'm sitting, I'd say you're hanging with some…bad fruit."

"Huh? Oh, yeah, they're pals from school. Well, not exactly pals, but some guys we hang around."

Carter looks at the space beside Christopher and says, "We? I don't see anyone else in that side of the booth but you."

"I mean…you know what I mean. Besides, the guys I always hang out with aren't as…cool."

"You're shi—, I mean, you're kidding me, right? Cool? Again, it's your business, but those guys? They're about as cool as a warm dump."

"That's disgusting."

"Sorry. Just trying to force a point. Look, Christopher, you're obviously smarter than them and way more talented…"

As Carter talks, Peter and Jeff walk up the aisle to where Carter sits.

"Hold on, here come Mutt and Jeff." Carter sneers.

"Sup, Old Man," Peter says through bloodshot eyes.

"Sup?" Carter coldly replies.

Jeff, also a bit behind the eight ball, stands to the side not saying anything, but looking like he could chew a spoon.

"Uncle Carter, this is Jeff…and Peter. Friends from school."

Peter holds out his hand to shake and as Carter obliges, Peter jerks his hand back. "Psyche!"

Carter isn't amused.

After a moment of shooting him eye darts, Carter says, "Son, you impress me as a big nobody…on a long road to nowhere. Now, why don't you and your girlfriend here just run along."

All three boys just stare at Carter. The two outsiders look at one another, smirking. Christopher thinks, *Did he just say what I thought he did?*

"But Dude, Christopher gave us a ride," Peter whines as Jeff flairs up just enough to get attention, but not enough to cause a scene.

Before the situation gets any more volatile, Carter sets the duo straight. "Tell ya what. I happen to know that school's not out for the day…and Christopher's gonna be headin' back alone."

He looks down at their feet, "And since you both appear to have both of your feet, I'd say you put them to work and just hike your keisters right down the street."

Glancing across the street, he checks his watch, then says, "In fact, if those heels are too painful to walk all the way back to school, why don't you catch the Number 52, right over there." He points to the bus stop across the street and adds, "It'll be here in less than five."

They both notice Carter has placed his hands on the table. They may be slower than usual, but they get the fact his muscular arms could easily damage their faces—if he had a mind to.

Jeff smacks Peter's arm and nods toward the door, saying, "Good idea. Let's hit it. There's nothing going on in this place anyhow." Peter, being the weaker of the two, follows along. "Sure."

They both nod to Christopher and start to leave, but not before Carter grabs Jeff by the arm. Jeff tries not to show it, but Carter's grip nearly takes his breath away. He plays it cool, as Carter reaches in his other pocket and pulls out a five-dollar bill.

"Now, be a good lad, and place this over there on the table where you *used* to sit. Do it on your way out so that Miss Teresa won't think you two are some kinda Neanderthals. 'Kay?"

Jeff manages a faint, "Yes, Sir."

"Thanks. Now, run along. Ladies."

They walk briskly down the aisle, and Jeff drops the five on their table, nods shyly to Teresa, looks back at Carter and they vanish out the door.

Christopher cranes his neck to watch them head down the street.

Peter turns around, shoots him *the bird*, and they blend in with the traffic.

Christopher slowly turns back around and just stares at Carter who calmly sips his coffee.

"Damn," Christopher finally says.

"Uh huh," Carter quietly says as he continues to sip his coffee.

"You are one cool cat, Uncle Carter."

After a long beat, he adds, "You too, Christopher. You are too."

CHAPTER 13

SEVERAL HOURS HAVE PASSED, as the group has discussed budgets and future projections for expansion. They also covered a variety of topics of *add-ons* that they were confident would be appreciated by the church. Being as *green* as possible was a priority they all agreed on; therefore, a roof-top garden, solar panels and recycled rain water were the top contenders.

The church board finally adjourns, and several members remain in the boardroom where Stephan DeAngelo holds court with Jonathan, Joshua and the mayor. Several employees are in the lobby area, congratulating one another, looking at the model of the proposed building and chatting it up. Stephan has made quite the impression—not only on the board members, for his adept presentation skills, professional acumen and assistance in helping the church get the small bridge loan needed to complete the Grace Family Center, but also on the women of the church office. They've gathered around Claire's desk, acting as if they're busy performing clerical duties, but instead are waiting to see the *Italian Stallion*— as he's already being called in their circles, to see if he's married.

"Girls, first of all, this is a professional organization," church secretary Claire says. "I don't think Pastor Jonathan would appreciate you all," she looks around, "okay, *us all* standing around ogling the liaison from the bank, much less, placing bets—figuratively of course, on whether or not he's married."

"True, Claire, but it doesn't hurt to dream. I mean, what's the harm in window shopping?" says Patricia Cootson, the social media consultant & web developer for MGCC.

A deliveryman, with a *Causby Caterers* logo on his cap and a name badge that reads *Wesley*, walks in and stands behind them, quietly awaiting a signature. Dee Ridge, the assistant pastor's wife, flashes her diamond adding, "Hey, I'm happily married, but there's no harm in appreciating God's handiwork."

Finally, Wesley says, "I see what you mean, girls," eyeing Stephan from a distance. "Two words: Dee-Vine!"

Dee spins around, embarrassed and says, "It's about time to head home."

Claire snickers, signing his clipboard, as everyone gets a good laugh. He takes the clipboard and sashays out of the office.

"Now, *that* was funny," adds Claire.

Just then, Jonathan and Stephan emerge from the boardroom. The girls scatter like ants under a magnifying glass.

"Claire, would you do me a favor?" Jonathan asks. "Would you see to it that Stephan here gets front row seats to this Sunday's service and luncheon after? Seems as though he and his daughter are brand new to town and I'd like to make sure they feel welcome."

Claire cuts a quick look in the direction of some of the girls down the hall, just out of sight of the two men, then responds, "Of course. Will do." She smiles at Stephan then clumsily reaches for some documents on her desk, until she realizes that Jonathan was joking about an *official* ticket.

They enjoy the gag.

"Got me, Pastor." Claire says, blushing.

"Sorry. Just having fun." He turns to Stephan and continues, "Stephan, seriously, we look forward to having you at our service on Sunday. Stay for lunch. I'd like to introduce you to my family."

"Thank you, Pastor Matheson. Janabelle and I will look forward to it. Thanks again."

He nods to everyone, gathers his briefcase and walks down the hall. Jonathan can't help but notice the effect he has on the office personnel. In fact, he walks over to the edge of the hallway, out of sight from the girls, and winks at Claire—waiting for her to give the *coast is clear* sign. Then, he steps out and catches all the girls watching Stephan walk to his car.

"Girls! Really!"

They're all embarrassed until he bends over laughing. He claps, and they all join in the laughter.

A cell phone rings in the distance. He looks around when he realizes it's his phone. He returns to the conference room and finds it next to his briefcase. Answering it, the look on his face changes instantly.

"Yes, Daphne. I'll be right there." He looks at his watch. "15 minutes. Stay with her."

He turns to Claire and says quietly, "It's Angela. Something's wrong. I have to run. Please finish this up for me, okay?"

She nods, and he's out the door.

CHAPTER 14

CARTER PULLS UP TO THE entrance of a Verizon Wireless store and gets out of the car just as Officer Reddick is leaving the store. Carter's in his own world and doesn't see him until he's nearly at the door.

"Well, look who it is, as I live and breathe," Reddick says to Carter. Surprised, Carter extends a hand and they vigorously shake.

"Man oh man, it's good to see you. How in the world are you?" Carter asks.

Nodding, Reddick says, "Good, good. Just picking up a new phone charger. My dog chewed up my old one."

"Dog? Wow. That's some commitment, huh?"

"Yeah, thought if I was going to hang out here, why not set some roots. And getting a dog seemed like a good enough place to start."

"What kind?"

"What else? Lab," Reddick nods.

"Good choice. Man's best friend. And his name—I hope it's a him," Carter jokes.

"Yeah. *His* name is Dexter."

"Like the TV detective show?"

Reddick laughs, "Nah, less serial killer, and more the name of the street I grew up on as a kid."

"Cool name. Why not bring him by the house sometime and let my Samson give him a run for his money?"

"Sounds good. We'll do that. Uh, just one thing. He's still a puppy, so, your boy may get a workout."

"Bring it on!"

Reddick's radio chirps, and he starts to leave, but first says, "Oh, another thing. Guess you heard about Danny, huh?"

"Something about making captain? Geez, they'll let anybody run the force," Carter jokes.

"Yeah, well, run the pencils across the desk is more like it. Actually, he's practically a suit."

"So, does that make you…"

He nods. "Sergeant. He figured somebody had to take his place."

"That's great news."

"Yeah, thanks. I like it. But here's the thing—my replacement?"

"Uh huh."

"A guy named Bobby Durkin. They, or we, call him Durk. Behind his back, we call him Dick—for obvious reasons."

Carter smirks.

"But here's the rub. He's new. Ex-army. Got something to prove. Not sure what. And he's got a real grind for guys who drive and…" Reddick gestures drinking from a bottle. "I mean, we were mostly busting your balls, but word is he's more likely to bust your back. Just saying."

Carter looks him dead in the eye and says, "Don't you worry about me, Buddy. If I had a dollar for every cop clown that tried to hang me out to dry, I could buy Barnum *and* Bailey."

Reddick smiles a wicked grin and tips his cap, "Understood."

"Come see me. Off the clock. We'll drop a few in the backyard. Get caught up. Been too long."

"Sounds good."

They shake hands and Reddick walks to his car. Just as Carter reaches the storefront, he stops and turns. He wants to satisfy a curiosity. "Still got that damn limp," he mumbles. *Gotta help him get rid of that one day.*

Not fifteen minutes later, Carter is leaving the store when he sees Jonathan's Escalade race by.

"What the—"

He climbs in the truck, tossing his bag on the seat, puts it in gear and tears out after Jonathan. Checking his rearview, he sees very little traffic and steps on it. The light ahead turns yellow just as Jonathan approaches then slides through. It catches Carter. He bangs the wheel in disgust. Sitting there, he strums his fingers on the steering wheel— it doesn't help, especially given that an old Vietnamese man and teenage boy slowly cross the intersection.

The old man tries to keep up with the teenager, but his cane slows him down. The boy ignores him, lost in the over-sized headphones. His head bobs in sync with invisible music.

The light changes. Carter takes off. Jonathan is well ahead, but Carter's enhanced F-150 allows him to catch up two lights later. He pulls up next to Jonathan and toots his horn. Jonathan sees him and lowers the window while saying goodbye to someone on his cell phone.

"What's the hurry, Old Man?"

The expression on Jonathan's face says he's not interested in idle chat.

"It's Angela. Daphne just called. Said she went to the house and found her unconscious on the floor."

"What?" Carter barks.

Just then, the light changes and Jonathan shouts as he pulls away, "I'm sure she's fine. I'll call you later."

Jonathan was gone before Carter could get out, "Okay."

A horn blows from behind, and Carter has to think twice before deciding not to get out and punch their face. He watches as Jonathan speeds ahead.

Jonathan slides to a stop in their gravel driveway and is out of the SUV and halfway through the kitchen door when he shouts, "Angela?"

"Sshh…." Daphne loudly shushes, as she comes down the steps. "She's lying down." She waves him over to the kitchen table and sits.

"I'm sorry if I startled you, it's just…"

"You did, Daphne," he interrupts. "I think I just set a land speed record getting from the office to here. What happened?"

She pats his hand, seeing that he is still breathing heavily.

"Deep breath. Well, I came over to share some news with her, but I was running late. You see, I was on the phone with…"

"Daphne. Please," he interrupts again.

"Sorry. Cut to the chase, of course. Anyhow, I came over and found her out like a light. I was going to call you, but—well, anyway, I got 911 on the line."

"And?"

"And, just as I was about to give them the details, which was shallow breathing and slow heart rate…"

"Yes?"

"Well, she woke up."

He finally sighs, relaxing his shoulders and quietly responds, "THANK YOU for being here and taking care of her. I don't know what I would do without…"

"She's my girl. Our girl. And she's going to be fine. Frankly, I think she's just over-exerted herself…among other things."

"You're right…and thank you again. Do you think we should see Dr. Vaden?"

"That's exactly what I suggested, but she said no. Adding that, depending upon how she felt tomorrow, she would go. You know her—she can be stubborn."

"No doubt. Well, I'm going to go check on her, then…" he looks around, "I'll finish my work here in the home office, and later…I guess start dinner."

Daphne raises her eyebrows, "Really?"

"Yes. Really. I can cook."

She smiles broadly, "Oh, I know you can cook…a hamburger or barbeque on the grill, but how about in here?" she chuckles, pointing to the expansive, button-adorned Viking stove.

He hesitates, then, "Well, you could help me," he says with a boyish grin.

She looks at him and grins, shaking her head. "Okay, you run along, I'll see what we have to work with. If I need to rob Peter to pay Paul, all it will take will be a jingle to Stuart."

Jonathan leans over and kisses her forehead, "You are a saint. Thank you."

As he walks away, she swats a hand-towel, saying, "*Charmer*. Now, git!"

&

Jonathan taps softly at the bedroom door and enters the curtain-drawn room. Angela is lying on the bed with a compress on her eyes and her shoes off. She breathes softly. Sitting on the side of the bed, he takes her hand. He sits quietly for a few moments, remembering all the reasons he loved her. The patience of a saint, the strength of ten women, her godly faith, her ability to make everything work so smoothly, and not to mention the fact that, even after all these years, she still makes his heart skip a beat from across the room. He kisses the back of her hand and she smiles, lifting the compress to peek at him. He leans over and kisses her. She moans.

"Thank you, Baby. I needed that."

"The pleasure is mine. How ya feeling?"

"Better. Much better, in fact. And Hon, I'm fine. Don't worry. I heard you flying up the driveway and sliding on the gravel." She shakes her head. "A regular Jimmy Johnson."

"Maybe older. But just as fast."

"And brave. My knight in shining armor."

She starts to get up, adding, "I better…"

He gently pushes her back down. "Nope. You just lie there. Daphne and I have it all under control. You don't have to worry about a thing. Well, perhaps until tomorrow," he chuckles, "but for now, your job is to just relax."

"Thank you."

"Is there anything I can get you? Fresh compress? Water? Aspirin? Glass of wine?"

"Hhmm…"

"Anything?"

"No, I'm fine," she points to the nightstand. "I have most of those bases covered. What's Daphne making for dinner?"

He stands and removes his tie, placing it on the back of the closet door. "Don't know, but I'm sure it will be great."

"Of course. She's a walking cookbook."

"I do have a few things I must get done before the end of the day…"

"Oh…"

"No, no, I'm doing it here, in my office. Didn't want you to think I was a *hit-n-run*." He turns to leave, then turns back, "Babe, before I go, are you sure there's nothing wrong…well, besides all the everyday stress and stuff?"

"I'm fine. Just overloaded—that's all. No breakfast, running ragged, playing *Super Mom*—it just caught up. That's it. Seriously. Go finish whatever it is you have to do and we'll catch up on the day at dinner."

"Okay. In fact, tell you what, I'm going to run you a hot bath. Your favorite. I'll toss in those—what do you call them, *yummy* soaking salts? And is that the brand name, or a descriptive?"

"Very funny. You are an angel. That sounds perfect." She sits up on the edge of the bed and kisses him.

"That's my girl," he smiles, walks to the bathroom and starts the bath. A moment later, he comes out to find her undressing. He raises his eyebrows. She smiles and bounces her eyebrows in return.

"Okay, I'll just be in the office…trying to concentrate on work…"

Angela smiles, flashing him a moment, then walks into the bathroom.

"Yup, I'll just be downstairs…concentrating hard…on getting my work done."

"Bye now. Love you," she says, pulling the bathroom door nearly closed.

Jonathan starts to leave, stands there a moment, listening for her to get in the tub. He walks to her make-up table, picks up her purse and looks inside. At the bottom of the bag he finds a prescription bottle and reads the label. Frowning, he looks toward the bathroom then quietly places the bag exactly where he got it and heads downstairs.

CHAPTER 15

BACK AT HIS HOUSE, Carter empties a variety of electronics from his recent shopping spree and spreads them out on the dining room table: the latest and greatest smartphone, a GPS, an infrared camera, a pocket HD camera—the size of a pack of cigarettes, a tiny voice-recorder—the size of a pack of gum and two pairs of handcuffs.

Then, he reaches in a nearby drawer and pulls out an extra-large pack of Nicorette gum, a pocket sewing kit and two 12-packs of BC Powders.

Satisfied, he smiles and says aloud, "Now, that should do it."

Just then, the phone on the wall rings.

"Carter."

"Randall."

Good. Straight forward. All about business, Carter thinks. *Now, we're getting somewhere.*

"Top of the morning."

"Well, don't you (cough) sound chipper, Old Boy. As I recall, you're happiest when you have a plan. A mission."

"You recall correctly. What's up?"

"I've been studying the situation, turning it over and over in my mind, and I think I've come to a slightly different conclusion than I had made before."

Randall's tendency to dangle things, people, and opportunities in front of people like they were carrots, made Carter's stomach tighten. *Been here. Done this.*

"What is it now?" Carter grunts.

"Before you go getting your boots in a twist, just hear me out. It doesn't change your mission...as much as it changes both the immediacy and the intensity of said mission."

"Meaning?" Carter asks.

"Meaning, I don't think your sister ran away, as much as I think she was…"

"Oh spit it out, Old Man. She what?"

Silence.

"I think she was kidnapped."

Reddick rides down I-77 lost in a daydream. He flashes back to last summer. The car wreck near Dead Man's Twist, overlooking Lake Mitchell. The speed he was going. *Silly*, he thinks to himself. *That crash nearly killed me.* And the guy who he'd been hired to scare—and nearly kill, is now a friend. He considers, *If it weren't for Carter jumping in that water and pulling me to safety then making sure I had enough blood to stay alive,* he lets out a small chuckle, *I wouldn't be here. Even with this limp, I'm damn lucky to be alive.* He drives in silence, shaking his head and grinning. He takes a long, deep breath and says aloud, "It's a funny old life."

Carter has the phone cradled on his shoulder, listening to all the details Randall is sharing. But now, he's come to the distinct conclusion that he's going to need a bit more…*power* behind his mission.

"I'm still here. Just adjusting my game plan is all."

"Got it. So, I have it on good authority—meaning a couple of my old pals in the service, that there are some people who have been watching me."

Carter walks into the hallway and taps a panel on the wall. It looks like one of those old built-in ironing boards from the '50s. In fact, that's where Carter got the idea, except that this board releases a secret panel. A passerby would never think anything of it.

"Go on. Someone's watching you."

Carter continues listening and working. He pushes a button that reveals a concealed handle. Pulling that handle down, a tray appears.

"Yeah. As you saw, I have a rather sizeable house…in a very nice neighborhood."

"Roger that," Carter confirms.

"So, a friend of mine works as a local security guard—and no, the coincidental humor of that was not lost on me, given your *incognito get-up* of last year."

"Okay, Funny Man. Keep kidding, or start spilling."

"Anyhow, he's noticed an out-of-the-ordinary traffic pattern from two cars in particular. Out-of-state plates—which isn't too unusual, given that there are so few locals, but I'll get to that later. It's also that one of those cars was spotted at a bar where your sister works."

Carter stops what he's doing and asks. "Wait. Two things. First, can we please put a name with my supposed sister? Second, she works at a bar? How old did you say she was?"

Carter continues to work, removing the short tray and a small, worn duffle bag. He empties the contents onto the table.

"You're right. First of all, her given name is Elizabeth—just like your mom's. Elizabeth Hope, actually. But she goes by the name of Shasta. Don't ask."

"Okay," Carter replies, not missing a word as he continues to organize. Joining the electronic spread are a 9MM Glock, a 9MM Sig Sauer and his favorite custom .357 revolver.

"And second," Randall continues, "she's 18, looks 25 and acts 30. Look, she wanted to get out of the house. I was tired of her just hanging out and mooching off me all the time. She was bored. You get the idea."

"Got it. So tell me, what makes you think…Shasta…was kidnapped rather than disappearing on her own accord?" Carter asks, while still emptying the bag onto the table: ammo, a retractable razor knife, mace in a fountain pen, a pack of zip ties, a roll of black Gorilla Duct Tape and a bottle of Visine eye-drops.

"Well, she lives in one of the finest 'hoods in West Palm Beach, in a $5 million dollar home, drives a nice car that her old man gave her, has hot meals served any time she's home…"

"Got it. She's pampered. So, why up and vaporize if you got all the creature comforts?" He stops and eyeballs everything on the table, pointing and counting.

"Yes. Well pampered. Decent job, even though she's way smarter than what she does," Randall adds.

Carter continues organizing everything in a neat and specific order.

"And she gets a small allowance from me…you know, just for personal stuff. Anyhow, without this turning into a damn *Oprah* show, what I'm trying to tell you is, A: She's got all this and isn't about to just give it up, B: She's been hanging out with some sketchy characters lately, and C: She's been gone for three days!"

"Okay. But three days doesn't much of a kidnap make."

"What are you, some poet?" Randall barks, adding a short round of guttural coughs.

There is a long silence between the two men.

"Sorry. Here I am asking for your help and giving you a hard time," Randall wheezes.

Carter nods his head, smirking.

"Here's the thing. I can't do this myself; I don't have the strength or the energy. You do. Have both. In spades. Besides, you've always been good at this sort of thing."

"Stop the sentimental crap. I'm in. I just need to know what I'm in *to*," Carter adds for effect.

"As I said, I'll make it worth your while. I'll give you all the resources you need to bring my baby back. And…"

Carter picks up a miniature camera and photographs the layout of tools. He then stops, waiting for Randall to continue.

"You still there, Old Boy?"

"Yeah, still here. Just not feeling good. Listen, let me go and I'll get back to you with more details…in a short time."

"Sounds good. And call me the instant you know anything more. Like, perhaps a ransom note?"

"Will do."

They hang up. Carter surveys the spread. "That should just about do it."

CHAPTER 16

DAPHNE STANDS AT THE stove chopping vegetables for a vegetarian spaghetti dish that the boys love. Jonathan quietly enters the room. "What a day!"

Startled, she jumps. "For great goodness sake, Son, you nearly dropped me in the grave."

"Sorry," he sheepishly says. "Just trying to keep the house peaceful. Doing my part, ya know, for harmony and such."

"Huh?"

"Nothing. Just something I'm reading at work. Foreign relations stuff." He sticks his face over the pot and inhales. "Smells divine."

She smiles. "Divine, indeed. Heaven inspired!"

Jonathan bends over and pulls a bottle of red wine from the under-counter wine fridge. "Care to join me?" he asks, lifting the bottle in the air. "I'm having just one glass."

"After a day like today? Absolutely!"

The phone rings. She drops the knife and gets it before the second ring, looking in the direction of upstairs.

"Hello? Yes. Bring the garlic bread. I made it earlier. It's wrapped in foil and on top of the stove. See you in 20 or so. Bye."

"Stuart. Bread duty," she says and returns to marinating veggies.

Jonathan has poured two glasses and places one on the counter beside her.

"Thank you."

He nods, toasts her glass, swirls the wine and takes a sip. Leaning against the counter, he stares into space. She stops what she's doing, takes a sip, says, "Mmmm…," and then returns to cooking.

After a longer than normal period of silence, she finally asks, "What is it?"

"What? Just enjoying being home early..." He looks at his wine, "And this. That's all."

"Uh huh. I know you better. You don't sit still this long. For anything. Or, anybody."

"Guilty as charged, Your Honor," he replies, cutting a look out of the side of his eye.

"Exactly." She takes another sip.

He sets down the glass, crosses his arms and asks, "So, tell me...just how long were you going to wait before you told me about Angela's...drug addiction?" Daphne nearly spits the wine out of her nose. He just watches.

Catching her breath, she returns to stirring, adding, "Wrong pipe."

David lies on his bed studying Dr. Long's book on Japanese culture. He has gathered several other books that include: *Botanical Wonders of the World, Reincarnation: A Study—A Solution, Quantum Physics: An Essay in Life Matter and Energy*, a modern copy of *Psalms & Proverbs* and *Exotic Butterflies from Around the World*.

He is deeply engrossed in taking notes while sketching a picture from the butterfly book. Next to him lies his laptop aglow with a picture of a space shuttle floating in orbit. When he touches the screen, a box appears asking for a sign-in security password. He taps out a series of keystrokes and the screen comes to life. On it are several photos of exotic butterflies.

"Interesting," he says to himself. "Who knew there were so many butterfly varieties in the world?"

He checks his wristwatch and picks up his phone. After scanning through his contacts, he punches a key and lets it ring.

"Hello, Dr. Long's Family Practice. This is Eloise. How may I help you?"

"Hello, Miss Eloise. This is David Matheson. Is Dr. Long still there?"

"Hi, David. Yes, but he's just getting ready to leave." She pauses. "Looks like he's in there giving his fish their final feeding of the day. Is there something I can help you with?"

"Yes, I would like to ask him just one question. Promise I won't keep him long at all. I would really appreciate it."

"Just a moment." She places him on hold and some canned music plays on the line.

"Hmm, that's easy," David says to himself. "*In The Air Tonight* by Phil Collins, from the album, *Face Value*. 1981, but originally recorded in '79 as the first single of his ca—"

"Hello, David. I'm about to run off to dinner with Sammy. Is there something I can help you with?"

"Yes. Would it be possible for me to keep this book on Japan just a few more days?"

"But of course. As long as you like."

"Thank you. And I don't want to get greedy, but there were a few others I'd like to read, if I may. Maybe Mom can drive me by?"

"Absolutely. Just have her call to make sure I'm here, and you're more than welcome to any of my books, David. I'm just thrilled you have such a thirst for knowledge."

"Thanks. I really appreciate it. I'm working on a theory, of sorts, and think you may be a key to my discovery."

"Well, excellent. I'll look forward to hearing more. You take care, give my best to your family and I'll see you very soon."

"Yes, I will. Thanks again. G'night."

David lies back, propping himself up on a mound of pillows, and basks in the excitement of new knowledge.

"Wait until they hear what I've got cooking." He sits up straight in bed, takes a big sniff and says, "Speaking of which…" He closes his laptop, jumps off the bed and is out of the room and down the hall in a blink.

ॐ

Daphne scoops dinner onto plates while Jonathan gathers glasses from the cupboards.

"I'm just saying, as close as you two are, it's hard for either one of you to keep anything—much less something this important, from one another. And to be honest, I just wish that she felt comfortable enough with me, after all these years…"

"She does, Son," Daphne interrupts. "You know that. It's just that, she doesn't want to worry you, or to…"

Just then, David jumps down the steps, two at time, landing loudly on the hardwood floor. He shouts, "Tah-dah!"

They both stop what they're doing and give him a quiet round of applause.

"What's the tah-dah for, Professor?"

"Oh, just me making a grand entrance is all, Pops," he says to Jonathan, then asks Daphne, "What's for dinner, Grandma?"

"One of your favorites, veggie spaghetti. Now wash up and…" Daphne stops and looks out the kitchen door before continuing, "…right on time. How about you take the plates and set the table for me, okay?"

"Sure thing," he says, taking the plates from Daphne and winking at his dad. Jonathan returns the gesture and offers Daphne another glass of wine. She holds up her hand, "No thanks. One is enough." She lowers her voice, "You already have me giving up too much information as it is."

Christopher comes in the door, listening to his iPod, and passes them by with nothing but a glance. Jonathan slides into his path and stops his progress.

"Hello, Dad. Nice to see you. How was your day? Mine was great. I made all straight A's," Jonathan says, jokingly.

Christopher stops, is about to act belligerent, then cracks a smile and says, pulling the buds from his ears, "Funny, Dad. Very funny."

"I thought so. Thanks. Do me a favor will you…"

"Dad, I just got here," he interrupts.

"Hold on. Before you get all up in it—or, whatever it is you all say, just do me one small favor and knock on your mother's door and tell Her Majesty that dinner is served. Can you do that? Your brother is setting the table."

David waves from inside the dining room.

"Okay," he says, walking away. "I'll dump my stuff and get her." He leaps up the steps, two at a time.

Jonathan turns to Daphne and whispers, "Boys!" Then, he cocks his head to the side and adds, "Wait a minute. Girls!" while pointing from Daphne to Angela's room and back.

"Wise guy, huh?" Daphne cracks.

CHAPTER 17

HAPPY WITH THE PREPPED display for his upcoming *mission*, Carter pours himself a short drink over ice and starts toward the front porch. Looking at his watch, he stops a moment to think and sip. He pulls the receipt from lunch out of his wallet and dials the number. After four rings, she picks up.

"Hello, this is Teresa."

"Man your voice is just as sexy on the phone—"

"As it is slopping hash at the diner," she interrupts.

"Well, not exactly what I was going to say—"

"But it'll get 'er done, right?"

"Got that right. Listen. I know it's late—"

"I am. And it isn't. What's on your mind?"

He shakes his head.

"Well, if you'd give me half a second, I'll fill you in. Wanna grab dinner and some drinks. I can—"

"Yes. I'll be ready in 20."

"Wow. Okay, I'll meet you—"

"I can text you my address. Got a smartphone?"

He looks at the table at his brand new gadget.

"In fact, I do."

"Good. Then, I'll just send it back to this number."

He looks confused.

"Uh, no. Let me give you that number…"

He fumbles for the paperwork that contains the number.

"Okay, here ya go. Ready?"

"Born."

He grins, giving her the number, adding, "Same area code, of course."

"Of course. Now, fancy or casual?"

"Huh?" He looks down. "Uh, how about casual. Kinda my style. Not much a one for—"

"Okay. Casual it is. See you in 20."

"See you in 20."

She rings off and he stands there, basking in the moment. Sampson looks up from his favorite spot on the porch. Carter smiles.

Just then his smartphone pings. He picks it up, looks at the screen and smiles. Punches one button and it displays the address, route and is calculating the time. It reads: Estimated distance in time, 18.5 minutes.

"Now *that's* a smart phone," he says, as Samson walks over to Carter, then adds, "It's a good day, Boy." He rubs Samson's head. "About time."

ॐ

Teresa has just enough time to run a cursory blade across her long well-toned legs, bounce out of the shower, remove a shower cap, pull her hair into a pony-tail and start to get dressed.

"Sassy!" she says to the mirror and thinks, *But the well-worn undies? Not working.* She makes a quick change.

Looking at the clock on her nightstand, she does a quick calculation in her head and says, "Okay, *Mr. By-The-Book*, I said 20, you'll be here in 19—so as to not keep a lady waiting. I hung up a little more than 15 minutes ago; that leaves me 3, maybe 4 minutes. Sugar-snap!"

She spins around, opens her closet, flips through a meager selection of sundresses, reaches for one and then recalls, "Oh. Casual." A big sigh leads to burrowing through a pile of clothes in the corner. "Jeans. Check."

Next, she bends over and digs around in the pile of shoes at the bottom of the closet. "Cowboy boots, or sandals?" she asks her over-sized Tabby who sits on a stack of pillows on her bed.

"Meow."

"Boots it is, Mr. Peepers!" Sitting on the side of the bed, Teresa pulls on one boot, then the other. "Excellent call—it's rugged, tough, but with a sense of sexiness." She looks at the clock. "Oh boy, this is gonna be—"

Just then, a knock at the door signals her date.

She jumps up and down in an over-dramatic pseudo temper tantrum, flips her pony tail over her shoulder, sticks her chest out—oops, the one without a top! She grabs the closest top that's hanging on the hook on the back of her door, slips it on, takes a deep breath and sashays to the front door and opens it dramatically.

Carter stands there, rugged, handsome, in complete control with just a hint of nervousness in his eyes. *Good*, she thinks.

"Hey there. Just sitting around, waiting for you to get your sorry ass up here." She winks, but it comes across more as a squint.

Cute, he thinks, as he says, "Nice to see you, too."

He smiles then looks down at her top. Frowning, he cocks his head to the side as he tries to read it.

Confused, she looks down and notices her t-shirt is wrong side out. She steps in front of a nearby mirror and the reversed image reads: The Derby Diner Softball League Champions, 2007.

"Oh brother," she says.

CHAPTER 18

"OH BROTHER, WHERE ART thou?" David shouts to Christopher who has not come to the dinner table yet. Jonathan and Angela, Stuart and Daphne and David wait patiently for their sixth and final dinner guest. Just then, he shuffles down the steps and slides into his seat next to David.

"Sorry," he mumbles. "It was Kym, and I guess I lost track of time."

Jonathan smiles at Angela, then puts on a phony stern face and says, "That's what watches are for, Son." This gets a light giggle from the table.

"Let's pray," Jonathan says as everyone takes one another's hands. "Dear God, thank you so very much for the blessings you shower us with every day. We can hardly fathom your love for us, but we thank you so very much. Thank you for watching over My Love..." he opens one eye to see Angela smile, "and for allowing the love of all of our lives, Daphne, to be present at just the right time. You are a wonderful and an awesome God. Finally, thank you for my two boys, my incredible Poppa-in-law, and for this bounty that we're about to receive. And they said..."

Everyone chimes in simultaneously, "Amen."

David instantly adds, "Dive in."

Stuart grins at David. "Never gets old, does it, Son?"

"Nope," David replies and reaches for a biscuit.

"Sooo, besides a near mishap with your mother and my wife, how was everyone's day?" Jonathan asks.

Christopher looks around and stares. "What?"

"It's called a conversation starter, Son," Jonathan says.

"It's nothing, Son. And despite what that appeared like, your father is actually concerned and just trying to lighten the mood on what he thinks could have been tragic," Angela quietly says.

"Angela, it could have been much worse than it was," Daphne chimes in, adding, "but for the grace of God…"

"Absolutely," Stuart adds. "I'm just thankful that my girl was nearby. See? This is why it's so important to always have family around. Right, boys?"

They both nod, but Christopher further inquires, "What happened, Mom? Seriously. And without all the holy-moly, good-golly stuff."

"Well, not so sure what that's all about, but simply put—I got overtaxed. Between work, helping your father, taking care of you boys—which is my number one pleasure, by the way, I guess it's just been a lot."

"And the anniversary of Grace…." David trails off.

Angela smiles and looks at David, adding, "Yes. Thank you for honoring her memory."

Jonathan places his hand on hers. Christopher rolls his eyes. Jonathan catches his expression and starts to react, but Angela intercepts by squeezing his hand tightly, then turning her attention to Christopher. She asks, "How was your day?"

Christopher sits there for a moment, playing with his food then, after another moment of fidgeting—as though he were processing something very intense, he responds with, "Pretty good. Best part of the day? Watching Uncle Carter help a couple of loser friends," he adds air-quotes around the words as he continues, "*get their attitudes adjusted.*" He laughs.

Jonathan looks at Angela, and she to him, when they both say, "Huh?"

"Okay, news flash: I'm hanging out with some…different people than I was last summer. I'm sure you wouldn't approve, but then, that's not my immediate concern."

"Now, just a minute, Son." Jonathan exerts.

Angela grabs his knee under the table and says, "What your father is trying to say, is—"

"What I *am* saying is—you will show respect to this family and not mock us with your teenage angst!"

The table is quiet. Jonathan is a bit self-conscious, but stands his ground.

"I'm sorry, Son, but I'm serious. You're skating on thin ice. Your grades are—"

"Okay, just great. Here we go. Let's start with the grades—as though they're the most important thing."

"SON. I think it may be a good idea for you go to your room until you can re-think your attitude, then maybe you'd like to return to this dinner table…with your *own* attitude adjustment."

Christopher stands. His nostrils flare. Everyone is waiting for the next emotional explosion, but there isn't one. He calmly drops his napkin on his plate, slides his chair back and quietly walks up the stairs to his room. The last sound they hear is the slamming of his bedroom door.

Jonathan sits down.

David says, "Well, that daily recap went well."

Everyone tries their best not to laugh.

After an uncomfortable silence, Jonathan finally says, "The new family center is approved. Met with the new banking liaison and we're good to go. Should break ground sometime between Thanksgiving and Christmas. Appropriate, huh?"

Everyone nods.

"That's exciting, Son. What a blessing to the community and an honor to this family," Daphne says.

Angela, after a moment of silence, turns to Daphne and asks, "Well, Mom, what is your good news?"

Daphne stands and heads toward the kitchen when she stops and says, "Oh, it's nothing…" She adds some warm biscuits to a serving basket and returns to the dining room with a very loud, "Except that I've been asked by the publishers of *Good Housekeeping* to submit my favorite recipes for a new cookbook!"

She shakes her fists in the air, not able to contain her enthusiasm.

Jonathan and Daphne look at one another, mouths agape, and high-five one another shouting, "WOW!"

Jonathan adds, "That's great! Now, all of America can experience what the Matheson family experiences every week!"

Angela wraps her arms around Daphne's neck. "That's fantastic, Momma! That's what you were coming over to tell me today. And here I was so self-absorbed. I'm SO proud of you."

By now, Stuart and Jonathan and David are all standing, high-fiving one another.

Stuart, beaming with excitement, says, "FINALLY! People, besides our family, will be able to experience the magic of my girl's homemade biscuits!"

They cheer in unison—including Christopher, who has come downstairs and stands on the bottom step, watching from a distance. When the cheering stops, they all look at Christopher who says, "I'm sorry, y'all."

They smile. He nods then says, "Way to rock, Gramma!"

The dishes are clean and put away. The house is quiet. Jonathan and Angela sit at the kitchen table sipping a cup of tea and sharing a quiet moment before calling it a day.

"I'm so proud of Mom. It's time something like this happened for her," Angela quietly says.

"Yep. She does so much for us—without ever asking for a thing in return. She's amazing." He touches her hand. "Just like her daughter."

Angela smiles, looking at him with the same romance and passion as they've always shared. "YOU are amazing, Mr. Matheson," she coos. "Working hard to provide for your family. Rushing home to once again be my hero. And still managing to be a full-time dad, molding your boys into the men God wants them to be."

He basks in the moment, knowing his wife meant those words with all her heart.

"Thank you. As for Christopher...well, he's going to take a little extra molding," Jonathan jokes.

"I know. It's just that he...is trying so very hard to become a man. And he has these forces all around him, both good and evil, trying to grab his attention. But if he doesn't focus for the rest of these two final semesters, I'm afraid he won't ever see graduation." Angela wrings her hands and sighs deeply.

"Now, Babe, before you take on any more stress, especially at this time of night, please know that we have, and are doing, the best that we can. The rest is up to him. You can lead a horse to water—"

"But you can't make him think," she winks.

"Something like that."

"That's something Momma used to say when we were in school. *Momma's Wisdom.*" She pauses to think. "Hey, maybe she could add that to her cookbook. As a heading, or...as one of the necessary ingredients to life!"

Angela is rather proud of herself for such a neat idea. She reaches over to fist-bump Jonathan, but doesn't get the position quite right. "Now, how do you guys do this?"

Jonathan takes her fist and repositions it to the right place. "There you go."

"Thank you," she grins, picking up their cups and taking them to the sink. "You want to check on your boys while I put these in the dishwasher?"

He joins her, kissing her forehead, both cheeks and then on the lips. "Thank you, Love. Good idea. Been a long day."

"No kidding. I'll be up in a blink."

Before he reaches the top of the stairs, he says, "Your blink better be a blink, 'cause my eyes are about to sink. Lights out and toes up in five!"

"Okay, okay," she quips. Placing the cups in the dishwasher, she stops for a second and looks at the floor where, just this morning, she'd taken an hour nap. Shaking her head, she bites the inside of her lip—deep in thought, then walks over to a side cabinet where she keeps vitamins and such. Taking down a large box of alcohol swabs, she reaches for a prescription bottle behind it, removes a pill and returns both. Standing at the sink, she looks out at the moon, takes a deep breath and whispers, "I've got to get some sleep."

With that, she washes down the pill and turns out the light.

CHAPTER 19

INSIDE THE HANDLE BAR, Teresa and Carter are having a good time. They high-five one another as their shot glasses come slamming to the table. Those glasses join four empty beer bottles and two well-devoured racks of ribs.

Teresa licks her fingers, saying, "Who knew this joint had such good ribs?" To which, Carter replies, "And who knew you could eat so much?"

She punches him and he continues with, "I mean, for such a petite, young lady."

"Not much petite about me," she says, wiping her mouth with the back of her hand, posing like a big fat guy.

Carter looks her over from head to toe and says, "I beg to differ, Ma'am."

"Well, that's because you're what some would call a gentleman."

He shakes his head, then with an over-blown country hick accent says, "Now, don't you go getting your mind wrapped up in the fact that I'm some kinda good person…cuz, I'm not."

She laughs. "Who said anything about being good. I'd settle for normal. Heck, even a dose of old-fashioned would be a nice change of pace."

Carter quietly snorts, "Seems I wrote the book on messed up. Even have it in hardback."

As soon as he said that, he frowns with a look of where'd that come from?

"Oh, I don't know. I've written a good many chapter of a book called, *My Life As Crap*."

Carter slaps both of his knees and says, "Okay, this is getting too sad-sack for me." He waves the waitress over, motioning for *two more* then says, "Nothing like a shot of the Devil to better appreciate Heaven!"

Teresa laughs, "Never heard that before, but I like it. And you know what, Mr. Carter Man...I like you, too!"

They look at one another—eyes wide open.

"Okay, I said it. Big deal." She adds, "And supremely obvious too, don't you think?"

"Then why do we both look like...someone just farted in church?"

They burst out laughing.

The parking lot of The Handle Bar is nearly empty—just three vehicles are left. Carter and Teresa are leaning against Carter's truck, staring at the ink-black sky full of bright stars and a full moon.

"One of my favorite things about living in the country," Carter quietly says.

"Being able to enjoy living room furniture on your front porch?" she chuckles.

"Yeah, well, there's that," he smiles, "and the fact you can park your truck anywhere in the yard."

"Or on that same front porch, if you like," she adds quietly.

He chuckles.

"The stars? I'm with you," she says, turning to him. Gently touching either side of his face, she looks into his eyes and says, "Just in case you were wondering..." She kisses him.

After several moments of great kissing, he says, "I wasn't. And me, too."

࿇

Carter puts the truck in Park, turns it off and sits there a moment before saying, "That was one of the best nights I've had in...a very long time. Thank you."

"What? Thank *you*. This big city girl likes your small town ways. It has a nice...fit."

He looks at his hands, nodding. After another moment, he says, "Just so you know—and not to get all heavy right out of the gate, because we aren't kids anymore…"

"Got that right. And speaking of which, I have one." She stares straight ahead.

Carter tries not to look caught off-guard.

"Aaaaaaand *Scene*," she chuckles.

"What?" he asks, wrinkling his brow.

"An old theatre term. College. Sorry. Doesn't…really fit…does it?" she trails off.

He puts his hand on hers. "Teresa, that's not—"

"What you're signing up for," she interrupts. "I get it, I should have…"

"No. Stop. What I was going to say was that's not an issue. As long as we have something like this," he motions between the two of them, "it's all good in my book."

She looks into his eyes and says, "Wow, wasn't expecting that."

He looks away to be sure he's ready to complete this conversation.

"And as much as it is the first date, you and I both know that chemistry like this doesn't happen every day. And once too often we've both let chances slip by that we later regretted."

Her mouth is agape.

"Tell me something, Carter. Is my jaw hanging open?—because I'm pretty blown away by a tough old loner like yourself, no offense, coming out of the gate with that much sensitivity." She suppresses a laugh, with both hands.

"Okay, if that's a laugh waiting to happen, you can just let it out, Little Lady. I'm just saying…again…I'm not perfect, got a LOT of old baggage I'm trying to take to the landfill, but…"

"But nothing. You had me at *chemistry*."

Effortlessly, they laugh again.

"Three tours of duty left me pretty wacked out. Two ex-wives left me wiped out. One son-of-a-bitch dad leaves me pretty stressed out."

"Nicely put." She adjusts her sitting position, with body language that says, okay, that's what you've got? Here's what I've got. "Me? My current tour of duty is slopping hash and trying to raise a kid—neither one of which is my strongest of suits. Just one ex. Thank goodness. And my dad? Hah! Wish I knew where he was. Haven't seen him since…" She gets lost a moment. "Well, let's just say I don't recall what president was in office the last time I saw him."

Carter slowly grins, saying, "Nice." He nods his head even more slowly and adds, "Sounds like a match made in Heaven, huh?"

"You betchya, Soldier! Now walk me to my door and give this lady a proper good night kiss. I've got double-duty tomorrow."

He salutes and says, "Yes, Sir!"

Even with a full moon, neither of them notice the car parked across the street beneath a lamppost where there once was light. The intoxication, both of love and alcohol, cloud their eyes from seeing a cigarette's burning ember glowing just outside the driver's side window.

CHAPTER 20

IT'S LATE WHEN CHRISTOPHER quietly taps on David's bedroom door. A soft, "Come in," whispers from inside. Christopher enters to find a nearly asleep young David. His bed is littered with stacks of books. Nothing unusual there. What is unusual is the overhead slide show. What was once a galaxy of stars and planets has been replaced with a tropical paradise with swarms of multi-colored butterflies.

"Wow, David. You may have outdone yourself with this one."

Waking up, David beams with pride and asks, "Really? You think?"

"Oh yeah. The animated slide show at Gracie's wake was one thing. Your interplanetary thingamajig was another, but this—this is amazing. Have Mom and Dad seen it yet?"

"Nah. I'm still working on it. Trying to add a 3D element. Gonna take some time," he yawns. "You're the first to see it."

"Cool." Christopher starts to fidget as David takes the books from his bed and stacks them on his desk.

"What's up?"

"Couldn't sleep."

David doesn't turn around—so as to not embarrass his brother, as he says, "Or afraid to, huh?"

"Yeah, kinda. But there's something else."

David has cleared his bed and now gets in and under the covers, propping himself against a stack of pillows and pats his bed, motioning Christopher to sit.

"I'm sure you've heard about…some of the guys…I've been hanging out with."

David nods nonchalantly.

"Well, I do miss some of my musician buddies—although since last year's competition, I've kinda wanted to just go out on my own, ya know?"

David nods again, trying to suppress another yawn.

"Sorry to keep you up, I—"

"Dude, seriously? No biggie."

"Well, I'll cut this short. I just wanted to say…I really want to try it on my own. I mean, the BIG *on my own*…as in go to New York and try to get a record deal." He waits for some sort of reaction.

Knowing how important this is to him, David wants to be careful not to immediately over-react and squelch his brother's dreams. He taps his chin, as though deep in thought, and says, "Well, that's probably not going to happen overnight, right?"

Christopher nods.

"And it's going to take money, right?"

Christopher nods again.

"And, in a perfect world, you would have to graduate in May…in order to be able to follow through with this, by say…next summer?"

"Yep. And before you slam my dre—"

"I'm not doing that, Bro. I know where your heart is. And what do I know? I'm a kid, but—"

"Just the smartest kid I…or anybody else…has ever known," he says, reaching over to get a fist-bump from his kid brother.

"So, I guess what I'm thinking—that is, if you're asking my opinion…"

"Which I am."

"Well, I say you go for it."

Christopher excitedly reacts.

"Course, you'll have to save some money up."

"Got that covered. Gonna talk to Dad about a little extra allowance—you know, helping around the house. May even get a part-time job somewhere."

"That's good."

Christopher's enthusiasm suddenly disappears, as he stares at the floor.

"What?" David asks.

"Well, there's another thing," he hesitates, "that I really need your help on."

"Name it."

"My grades suck, because I've been a slack-ass— and if I'm going to graduate by May, I need some help. *Your* help."

David realizes just how hard this is for Christopher to do. He imagines how embarrassing this may be for him—given that his younger brother, by three years, needs his help to graduate high school. But he also knows that they have a bond like none other. And he knows that he would do anything to help his big brother achieve his dreams. And as much as it will crush David to see him go, he knows all too well how supremely important it is for Christopher to realize those dreams; and, he would never let anything in the world step in the way of that happening. In the still on the night, under the safe haven of home and family, David knows deep within himself that this is a moment that will never come again in his lifetime. So, he takes it all in, cherishing the opportunity as he quietly responds, "Christopher, whatever I can do to help you…consider it done."

Christopher fist bumps David, trying to suppress tears.

He stands to leave, stops, then walks back over to his kid brother. Leaning over, he hugs him and whispers in his ear, "Thank you, David. I love you." David squeezes tightly and says, "Me too, Big Brother."

As Christopher pulls away, David adds, "Now, get to bed. The professor has to get his beauty sleep."

Still suppressing some tears, Christopher laughs, then says through the closing door, "Hey. Guess *Little Professor's* about to take on a whole new meaning, huh?"

David smiles from ear to ear, winks at Christopher and turns off the light as the door closes.

In the dark, his quiet voice says, "Thank you, God. And thank you, Gracie."

≈

Carter is well down the road when his new smartphone chimes. He picks it up to see that he accidently set it to ping a *top of the hour* reminder. He clicks on the date. It reads, MISSION: SHASTA. An alarm is set to 5 A.M. He glances at the dash clock. It reads 1:16 A.M.

"Damn," he mumbles, shaking his sloshing head. *Gotta get some rest if I'm going to be worth anything tomorrow,* he thinks to himself.

As he looks back up, he has to suddenly jerk the wheel to keep from veering into the median and oncoming traffic. Moments later, and from out of nowhere, a set of high beams and flashing blue lights flood his rearview mirror, nearly blinding him.

"WHAT THE—"

A blaring siren shrills an exclamation point to the rest of his caustic sentence.

He quickly glances at the speedometer, noting the speed: 59. He immediately recalls that this stretch of the highway has a speed limit of 55.

"Shit," he yells, trying to will instant sobriety. *One mile over misses it,* he thinks. He slams the steering wheel repeatedly, takes a deep breath and checks the rearview once more—squinting. He pulls over.

Within seconds, an outstretched hand pokes in his window with an accompanying husky voice, stating, "Title and Registration, please."

A super-bright Maglite pierces his retinas, rendering him temporarily blind.

The faceless voice adds, "Sir, have you been drinking?"

Carter has only a second to consider his response. The new laws pretty much screw him. *No more sobering up in the overnight tank,* he thinks to himself. Knowing such, he surrenders—but not without some attitude.

"What do you think?" he responds with sarcasm that cuts the night air like a blade.

Without missing a beat, *The Voice* blinds Carter again then barks, "Get out of the car, Sir. Right now!"

Carter obliges, but upon exit, doesn't see the officer's outstretched leg and trips and falls to the ground.

"I'd say so," he laughs. "Stand up and place your hands against the hood!" he shouts.

"No need to yell, Officer...I'm right here," he smirks, more for his own enjoyment.

"A smart-ass, I see. Spread your legs. I'm going to pat you down for any weapons."

Starting to turn, perhaps too quickly, Carter manages, "I don't have—"

SMACK!

Carter's head absorbs the Maglite and slams into the hood of the truck.

"Hey! There's NO reason to—"

"Shut it! You shouldn't have tried to swing at me."

Carter can't take it. Too much unwarranted violence in his life to stand for it. He suddenly drops to one knee, spinning around with his other leg outstretched, thus kicking the officer's legs from beneath him.

The Voice hits the ground with a thud, causing his Maglite to roll across the gravel; its light dances in the darkness.

His next move surprises Carter. The officer takes the momentum of the fall and uses it to his advantage, throwing himself into a roll, and landing on his feet. At the same time, he reaches around and pulls a Taser gun from the back of his belt.

While Carter tries to stand and wipe the pouring blood from the side of his head, the officer zaps him with everything he has.

Carter's body shakes with convulsions.

Between the blood and the buzz, Carter goes nighty-night...*By the Light of the Silvery Moon.*

CHAPTER 21

ANGELA HAS TOSSED AND turned for most of the night. She rolls over and looks at the clock. It reads: 2:05 A.M. Quietly, she slides out of bed, being sure not to disturb Jonathan, and tiptoes downstairs.

Reaching in the hall closet, she takes out a lightweight overcoat and a hat. Unlocking the kitchen door, she steps out into the cool, moonlit air and takes a deep breath. Spreading her arms out to either side, she smiles up at the moon. After standing there motionless for a few moments, she walks barefoot through the moist grass toward the garage.

When Carter awakes, he can't decide which was worse: the over-sized egg on the back of his head—where he vaguely recalls getting it cracked by some jack-hammer when he got pulled over, or the combination of beer, tequila, barbeque and jalapeno sliders that percolates in his belly like a foul soup.

Rolling over on his side, he hurls all the contents of the aforementioned soup on the floor beside him, on what looks to be a pair of standard-issue boots.

"Nice one, Asshole!" barks the same voice he *speed-dated* earlier this evening.

Through his blurry vision, he makes out the shape of a shaved head.

"Nice melon, Jerky Boy," Carter spews, wiping the vomit from his mouth.

"That's Officer Durkin to you, Numbnuts."

Carter tries to sit up, except the nurse who is attempting to sew him up still has a needle and thread attached to the side of his head.

"Whoa, Cowboy. Let me finish crocheting your handsome and ever so hard head and then you can sit up. That is, *if* you promise not to puke again on the boots of one Officer Cranky-Pants."

Carter obliges, not that he has much of a choice.

"I may be cranky, Nurse Ratched, but it's because I'm an officer of the law just trying to do my duty. Protect and serve, Ma'am. Nothing more...nothing less," Officer Durkin proudly announces.

She looks at him, then half salutes and asks, "Can you please give me a few inches? Make that a few feet. In fact, since you smell like the inside of this man's stomach, would you care to head over to that restroom and wipe yourself?"

He looks at her name-tag, then with a bad attempt at humor, responds, "Sure, whatever Nurse Symon says." He chokes out a stupid chuckle on the way to the restroom. At the same time, a tired and weary looking janitor arrives with a mop and bucket and begins to mop up Carter's vomit.

"Sorry about that," Carter says to the janitor.

The guy looks at him with complete neutrality and mumbles, "No worry, Gramps. Nothing else to do in this graveyard...shift." He makes quick work of the cleanup and is gone.

"You seem to have such a way with people, Carter," Nurse Symon says, as she snips the last of the thread and places a large bandage on the wound.

Carter tries to slowly sit up. Symon helps him, chiding, "You may want to go slow. I had to give you something to let me stitch you up and I'd say..." she looks at the front of his shirt that is partially covered in blood and vomit, "it didn't exactly agree with you."

Without missing a beat, she adds, "That, or the one too many drinks on top of bar food."

Nodding, he says, "Then, there's that."

Carter notices that Nurse Symon is much too attractive to be working third shift. *Not as attractive as*

Teresa, of course, he thinks to himself. He cocks his head to the side and says, "Wait. Don't I know you?"

Cleaning up the tray of needles, bandages and such, she grins and says, "Yup. You helped save my boyfriends' lives…last summer."

"Boy *friends*?" Carter asks.

Starting to leave, she leans toward Carter while quietly sharing, "Well, now that's the thing of it. You gave me so much work to do—what with tending after two of them, simultaneously. I got rather attached to both of them."

She pats his hand and disappears behind a nearby curtain. Five seconds later, she shouts, "One of 'em will be here any minute now!"

Officer Durkin returns, drying his hands on a paper towel. He tosses the towel toward a nearby waste-basket. It misses.

"Nice shot, Chimp."

Durkin grins, "I think we both know who got the…nice shot."

He's just about to slap some cuffs on Carter when Office Reddick comes around the corner dressed in jeans, a sweatshirt and flip-flops. He looks like he just got out of bed.

"Well, look who's here," Carter smiles, thinking he's about to go free.

"Hold up, Reddick," Durkin barks. "I've got it all under control. Don't need your help, thank you very much." He continues to cuff Carter.

"You hold up, Durk. I can help here," Reddick chimes in.

Durkin gets up in Reddick's face—in typical schoolyard style, and says, "No. You cannot. It's my arrest. I am the one on duty…" looking Reddick up and down, "not you. So why don't you run along and do whatever Nurse Symon says."

"You've already worn that one out, *Durk*," Carter smirks.

Durkin spins around with enough fury that Carter's hair would have fluttered in the breeze if he didn't have a tight cut.

"It's OFFICER DURKIN, Punk, and why don't you keep your trap SHUT until we get you to the station. Then, when I LOCK you in the can, you can run that silly TRAP of yours the rest of the NIGHT, and likely well into TOMORROW." Durkin has gotten a little closer with each emphasis until he is literally inches from Carter's face when he gets to the word *tomorrow*.

"Nice breath, Durk. Have a turd sandwich for dinner?" Carter smirks.

Reddick steps in between them and attempts to cool things off.

"Okay, so he's...this is your...case. Got it. But I'm following you to the station. He's got his one phone call. And I'm the guy to be sure he makes it."

"Whatever, Reddick" he spits. "Just get out of my way and don't pollute my evidence." He spins Carter around and cuffs his wrists behind his back.

Reddick is completely confused and mumbles, "What?"

Carter rolls his eyes and says, "No biggie. This isn't as bad as it looks."

Without missing a beat, Durkin sneers his best Clint Eastwood *Dirty Harry* impersonation, "Really, Punk? Driving while intoxicated, resisting arrest and attacking an officer?"

"What the—" Carter shouts at first then mumbles, "You're high, Donkey Boy. We'll see who ends up on top of this one."

Carter cuts Reddick a tiny smile, as Durkin escorts him, handcuffed, from the Emergency Room. Durkin snaps his head from one side to the other, cracking his neck. He sticks his chest out and smirks at Carter with a look that says, *I have saved the day.*

On his way out, Reddick joins Nurse Symon where she is filling out paperwork and kisses her on the cheek, whispering in her ear, "Thanks Babe, I owe you one." She looks up just before he disappears and shouts, "Yes, you do!"

CHAPTER 22

CHRISTOPHER LIES WIDE AWAKE in bed. As his mind races, he can't decide whether or not he'll grow his hair really long like those '80s rock bands, go with more of a Justin Beiber cut—although he thinks that cut may only work on someone younger—or, maybe he'll do a ragged buzz cut and grow some stubble to increase the bad boy image. Then, his mind shifts to David and he smiles. He knew that what they experienced was a pretty special moment. He was so proud of his little brother and knew that he would excel in anything he set his mind to do. Sure, he was a little embarrassed to have to ask his kid brother for help in school, but then, if you can't ask your own family, who can you ask? One thing he knew—if he didn't turn his tour bus around and set it straight, he may not be able to graduate and head to New York. *Wait*, he thought to himself, *do you really have to have a diploma to be a rock star?* Then, the fear set in. What if he couldn't make it as a rock star? *Damn, maybe I'd be locked in Mission Grove Hell! And what about Kym?* They hadn't been hanging out much since last year. After the band competition, some of his pals, and band-mates, said the win went to his head. She even agreed. *What does she know?* He still loved her, but he just wasn't sure that it would be the best thing to try and take her to New York with him. After all, what if he hit it really big, really fast? *She might weigh me down. I'd have to ask her to marry me, I guess,* he thinks. *I'm not ready for that. I'm too young. I have my whole life to do that.*

His mind changes channels; and, he starts thinking about his friends Peter and Jeff. Not really his type of friends, actually, but they certainly took life into their own hands. Just like Uncle Carter. *He was so cool at the diner. Made those cats nearly crap their pants.* He smiles, thinking about it. *I wanted to share that story at dinner, when everyone else was sharing, but noooo...Dad had to go and get all...*

CRASH!

"What?" He loudly whispers, sitting straight up in bed.

He looks around, letting his eyes adjust to the dark, gets out of bed and looks in the backyard, trying to locate the sound. The bright moonlight makes the yard look like a sandy beach. His eyes dart to the garage. *Why's the light—* he stops and thinks.

"Bet it's Jeff and Peter playing a prank to get back at me and Carter," he whispers to himself, his face pushing up against the window. His nervous breathing has caused the glass to fog. He rubs it off and squints to see if he can see anyone. Out of the corner of his eye, he sees a form walking around the side of the house. He starts to leave, then stops to wonder if he should ask Dad for help. *No, I'm man enough to defend our home.* And with that, he slides on a pair of shorts and his Rainbow flip-flops and grabs his aluminum baseball bat on his way out the door.

Christopher tiptoes down the stairs, out the door and around the house, baseball bat raised in the air, ready to strike, when he stops in his tracks.

"Mom! What in the world are you doing?"

Angela is on her knees, planting mums. There are several rows of them. The rows are not very straight, but there are at least a dozen mums planted right in the middle of the backyard. As Christopher thinks about it, he looks around and the mums were planted at exactly the same place where Grace last stood, just before running in the house and...

He stops. The thought makes him lose his breath. He lowers the bat and just stares at Angela.

"Mom. MOM! Hello?"

Angela looks up at Christopher with a smile. The smile changes to confusion. Then, she stands, brushes dirt from her bare knees, and taking her floppy summer hat from her head, squints at Christopher—as though a bright light were in her eyes.

She looks around, in one direction then another, and finally says, "Son, why are you playing baseball in the middle of the night? Don't you know you won't be able to find the balls in the dark?"

෨

Christopher and Angela sit at the kitchen table. Her head is in her hands. His hand is on hers.

"Mom. It's okay. You were just…"

"I don't know what I was," she quietly cries.

"You were just sleepwalking. Everybody does it from time to time."

She looks up and, appreciating the way her boy is looking out for her, reassures him, "No they don't, Son. Not everyone. And not every once in a while." She stares at the table.

"You just couldn't sleep. Needed some exercise, that's all."

"People don't exercise by planting mums," she whispers—her gaze not moving.

"Grandma does."

She finally looks up into his eyes and says, smiling, "Not in the middle of the night."

"At least there was a full moon…so you could see what you were doing," he tries once more.

She laughs, pats his hand and offers, "Did you see the rows I planted? Looks like I was blindfolded."

Finally, they laugh.

After a moment, Christopher yawns, "I think I'm finally ready to sleep."

She looks at the clock on the stove. "Well, by the time you and I get back into bed and shake the chill off from outside, it'll be three. And if my math serves me, I'm on pancake duty in about four hours."

"Aw, Mom. Don't worry about it. Heck, why not sleep in until 8. That way, you can just roll out and drive us to school and Dad can make the pancakes."

"Son, have you tried your father's pancakes lately?"

Standing, he shakes his head. She stands as well and pats his back, adding, "Like I said, see you in about four."

Christopher starts to walk away, but not before she reaches out for a hug. He obliges.

Angela squeezes him tight, smelling his neck. "Hmm…you smell like a little boy who's been outside playing. I love that smell."

He pulls away and she looks him in the eye and adds, "And I love you."

"Love you, too, Mom. 'Night."

Angela turns off the lights as they head upstairs.

He walks into his room and props the bat against the corner wall. She whispers, "Chrissie?"

He smiles big.

"What's funny?"

"Nothing," he hesitates, then, "It's just you haven't called me that since I was David's age."

He kicks off his flip-flops and sits on the bed. She looks out the window. Moonlight blankets the lawn like snow.

Remembering, she smiles. "Can I ask a favor of you?"

"Sure, Mom. Anything."

"For my own reasons, that I'll explain another time, can we keep this…little escape of ours…just between you and me?"

He tilts his head and scrunches his face like he did when he was a young boy. He grins before answering. "Sure thing, Mom. No worries. Our secret."

She blows him a kiss, he blows one back and she closes the door.

CHAPTER 23

CARTER'S HEAD IS POUNDING, not only from the entertainment of last night, but also from the *brutal* entanglement that followed. He rubs his face—his skin is rough, his beard is prickly and his mouth is as dry as if he'd had a glass of sand to drink before bed last night.

He presses his face against the cold bars of the jail cell. *I want to know what time it is. And how much time I have left.* They took his watch along with his smartphone, wallet and pocketknife. He strains to see a clock at the end of the hall. It's almost three.

"Hello? I'm waiting here. Time for my one phone call. It's my right; you know that. Get down here and bring a damn phone!"

☙

Reddick and Durkin are in the squad room. Reddick paces while Durkin fills out paperwork. It's quiet as a morgue. Officer Scott snoozes in the corner; his head leans against the wall. Durkin picks up a phone book and slams it on the counter, startling Scott and waking him up abruptly.

"What? What's th—" Scott looks around, sees nothing different and just scowls at Durkin, mumbling something inaudible under his breath.

"You're not getting paid to nap, Sap!" Durkin barks.

Reddick just stares a hole through him. "You like being a douche, don't you, Durk?" he growls.

"Shut your pie hole, Redneck."

Reddick flares up.

"Hold on. My bad. I mean, *Sergeant* Reddick." He backs down, but only for a moment.

Reddick says, "Look, you know as well as I do that he has one call he can make. And according to the rules, he can make it immediately upon entering the cell."

Durkin looks at him, squints that same *Dirty Harry Wannabe* squint and says, "Show me, Punk. In the big book. Right now."

Reddick is running out of patience. He's about to make his own call about now and he lets Durk know that. "Listen, Feather Duster, in about 15 seconds, I'm going to walk to my desk, pick up that phone," he points directly at it, "and dial our superior officer. And you KNOW you don't want that crap-storm pouring down on your shiny head. Cause if you know anything about one *Captain* Danny Mahler, it's that he likes—and I mean *really* likes, to sleep. And if YOU are the cause of his NOT getting his 7.5 nightly hours…well, there WILL be heck to pay." He is nearly finished, but takes one step back, spins around quickly for added effect, and gets within inches of Durkin's face and adds, "Do. I. Make. Myself. Clear—New Boy?"

Durkin hates the thought of being beat, especially given that he knows he's got a solid case; however, he is the *new boy*, as Reddick so clearly put it, and he decides that, in that instant, there will be another time that he'll put the nail in Carter's proverbial coffin. And with that, he nods and, without saying a word, puts the paperwork in a folder and tosses it on Reddick's desk. He walks down the hall, unlocks the door, motions for Carter to get out, walks him back down the hall and stands him over a chair.

Reddick motions for Durkin to uncuff him. Durkin hesitantly obliges, pushes Carter into the chair and picks up a phone, slamming it down onto the desk with such force, it would be a surprise if it would find a dial-tone if it had to. He then turns to Reddick, smirks at him, then walks down the hall toward the back of the building announcing, "Make your freakin' call, Butt-munch. I gotta take a dump."

The room is completely silent until Carter says, "Charming little man, huh?"

Reddick smiles for the first time this evening then nods toward the phone and says, "Get to it."

Everything seems to move into slow motion, as Carter does an inventory check. He thinks, *Let's see, there are three people I could call. One is standing right in front of me, but that's a conflict of interest. Number two would be Jonathan, but we've had our troubles and I'm not so sure he'd be the best one...*

Carter spins around and waves for Reddick to come closer. There are the ears of Officer Scott at the front desk, a rookie filing paperwork in the opposite corner and a newbie part-timer asleep with his head down on a desk, just outside of earshot.

"What?" Reddick asks.

"Quick. Gimme the numbers of the charges I'm facing."

"Huh?" Reddick asks, processing the request.

"They're going to take me to court. Right?" Reddick nods. "What are the legal case or charge numbers...they're going to use on me."

"Oh. Got it, got it. Let's see, uh...DUI? That'll be a 10-46. RA, resisting arrest, is an 11-73 and, what was the—"

"Attacking an—"

Durkin is coming down the hall.

"Right, uh...12-17."

Carter's mind races.

He repeats: "1046, 1173 and 1217?"

Reddick nods.

"Got it," whispers Carter.

Life speeds back up as Carter picks up the receiver and types a 5-digit code that will make the call untraceable after the fact.

Tap, tap, tap, tap, tap. Then, he punches in an access code, followed by a 10-digit number, from memory. On the second ring, it's picked up.

"Yes?" a voice answers.

Durkin stops to take a sip at the water fountain, midway down the hall. He slurps loudly enough to get attention.

"Alpha, it's Omega. Officer is down. Need immediate assistance. Listen: MGPD. October 46. November 73. December 17. Need affirmative ETA."

He stops and listens.

After a brief moment, an answer comes, "Number: 4. AOK. Over." Click.

Carter hangs up the phone, without acknowledging Durkin, just as he re-enters the room. His back is to Durkin, and he's looking at Reddick. For effect, Carter winks then slowly shakes his head. Reddick plays along and lets his shoulders sag, in apparent disappointment.

"What's up, Gramps? Any luck?" Durkin barks.

Carter says nothing.

"Sounds like you're either calculating the month you'll get out of jail—if ever, or you think your chances of winning the lottery are better than getting laid." He bursts out laughing like it was the funniest thing ever said. The room remains silent.

Finally, Reddick speaks up, "Sorry, Buddy. Doesn't look like there's much I can do." He nods in Durkin's direction. "And as much as I wish this miserable piece of goose-flesh were wrong, I'd say…he's kinda got you over the barrel." Then, for added effect, on the way out the door, he says, "But, just in case, I'll talk to our good buddy, Danny. And see what he thinks. We're having breakfast…" He looks at his watch. "Oh, in about five hours. Sleep tight, pal." He turns and leaves.

"C'mon, Princess," he says, lifting Carter by the arm and putting handcuffs on him. "Might as well get some sleep. Who knows, maybe your *Prince Charming* will come and save your butt."

As they walk down the hall, Durkin finishes, "But I doubt it. We both know fairy tales never come true."

The cell door slams!

CHAPTER 24

THE NEXT MORNING IS business as usual, with a couple of bleary-eyed breakfast participants onboard. Christopher leans against his hand, barely able to keep his eyes open. Angela stands over the pancakes, staring into the bubbles that form on top and thinks to herself, *That looks like it would be such a soft, fluffy pillow.* Jonathan is speed-reading the sports section, then the business section, sipping orange juice between pages. And David, chipper as ever, watches the news on the flat-screen TV on the wall— its volume is just loud enough to hear, but not enough to disturb family conversation, which this particular morning was barely existent.

"More pancakes, anyone?"

"No thanks, Hon. They were great," Jonathan says, smiling at her.

"Hhmm..." Christopher grunts.

"I'll take that as a no, Christopher."

He nods, as he pours another cup of coffee.

"I'll take two, please," David chimes in. "Oh, and is there any way that you could drive me by Dr. Long's place today?"

She stops what she's doing and asks, "Why, Son?"

Jonathan looks up from his paper and raises an eyebrow.

David realizes they must be thinking one thing, when he clearly had other ideas in mind.

"Parents, I just want to pick up some more books. I called his office yesterday and we spoke. He said it was fine."

Angela looks at Jonathan, who returns the look, then shrugs.

"Okay. Sure, Son. Research, is it?" she asks.

He nods, stuffing another fork full of pancakes in his mouth.

"Hhmm…maybe I will make it a short visit with Dr. Long myself. I have a couple of questions I'd like to run by him. Then, perhaps I could join you for lunch," she says to Jonathan. "Sound good?"

"Sounds perfect and I have just the spot," he replies.

In the driveway outside the Matheson home, three vehicles are preparing to leave. Jonathan is just about to step into his Escalade when he looks at Angela, David opening the door to her Volvo and Christopher tossing his bags into the bed of his pickup. Taking in the picture, he says, "Look at us. When's the last time we all three were leaving at the exact same time?" Angela and David look at one another and shrug.

"Uh, don't know, Pops." Christopher says.

"Uh, like never!" He pauses. "Okay, that's my profound moment of the day. Everyone have a great day and know that I love you all!" Jonathan proudly exclaims.

Christopher nods and yawns as he climbs into his truck. Angela blows Jonathan a kiss and he returns it. David gives him a big wink. Jonathan does the same. Within moments, the dust of the driveway settles, and the Matheson family is gone to face another day.

Jonathan has stopped at his favorite neighborhood Starbucks to pick up his daily fix. As he gets out of his SUV, his cell phone slides from his lap and crashes to the pavement, cracking in several places and chipping a corner off.

"That's great," he grumbles under his breath, leaning over to pick it up. Upon further inspection, he sees that it's dead. Tossing it into the passenger side seat, he shakes his head and goes inside, mumbling, "It is what it is."

᠗

Inside Angela's car, David is chattering away about butterflies, or something. Angela's not exactly sure, as her mind has drifted to what happened last night. She looks over at him occasionally to show that she's listening, but with David and his insatiable thirst for knowledge, it can oftentimes get a bit overwhelming. *It's like having my own live-in Wikipedia*, she thinks to herself, again smiling at her son—his eyes sparkle with enthusiasm and she cherishes that about him. Turning her attention back to the road ahead, she returns her thoughts to her clandestine planting of the mums. She shakes her head. *What was I thinking? Oh, I wasn't—that's just it. I don't remember going downstairs and putting on a coat, or walking outside, or going to the garage and pulling out my garden tools, and I certainly don't remember getting those mums from the back of this car and unloading all three dozen...then PLANTING them in rows. What in the world has gotten into me?*

Suddenly, a car in front of her stops without warning and she slams on the brakes, instinctively throwing her right arm across David's chest. They come to a rest. She catches her breath. A few horns blow. Traffic starts back up. And she lets out a big sigh.

David turns to her and says, as only he can do in moments of near tragedy, "Mom, if you weren't enjoying my story, you could have just said 'Sshh...' You didn't have to scare the pancakes outta me to shut me up." He grins.

She grins. "What am I going to do with you?" she asks, vigorously rubbing his neatly combed hair. He swats her hand away and hastily rubs his hair back into place.

᠗

Driving along the highway, Christopher is deep in thought on his way to school. *Seeing Mom planting mums in the middle of the night—that's just wacky...Glad David's gonna help me with my grades. If I don't get them up, I'm gonna be in deep crap...Wonder if Kym is still mad at me for causing a scene at her birthday party. I should call her and set all that straight...Dad sure was chipper today. But then, he usually is—when he and Uncle Carter aren't tossing them back by the grill. Man, Carter sure was cool the way he handled the guys the other day. I'm gonna try that same attitude sometime and see how they like it.*

CHAPTER 25

CARTER'S JAIL CELL REEKS of dried vomit and burnt coffee—not a great combo at 8 A.M. He sits on the edge of the bunk, his eyes going from his boots to Reddick and back. He looks like death warmed over.

"I don't get it. I'm minding my own business—on a weeknight, no less, on a date with the first girl I've gone out with in a year of Sundays...and this CLOWN comes outta nowhere and busts me on not one, but *three* charges?" Carter spits out the words. "Really? How's that happen?"

Reddick leans against the bars of the cell where Carter is currently contained. He shakes his head, "It is strange...on two counts. First, he rarely, if ever, covers that part of town. I mean, he's a newbie. Everyone knows you stick close to home for the first month or so. He's here two weeks and he thinks he's working homicide on *The Streets of San Francisco.*"

"Nice reference." Carter grins. "Are you even old enough to remember that TV show?"

"Yes. Reruns. And thanks."

"And the other reason?"

"Huh?"

"The other reason it's strange that—"

"This is even more interesting," he says, crossing the room. "He wasn't even scheduled to work last night."

Carter frowns. "What?"

Reddick has a clipboard under his arm. He pulls it out and flips over a few pages, looking in the direction of the squad room to see if anyone is nearby, and says, "Yup. You know how it works. Rookies start with *on three-off three*, followed by *on four-off three*, followed by *on five-off two*. This is pretty much SOP for all rookies. And like I said, he's been here just two weeks." He looks back at the paper, "That's *on four-off three*. Last night was an *off* day for him."

"And for me," Carter sardonically adds.

"Yeah, well…" he chuckles.

"Not funny."

"Who's laughing?"

"You are. Feather Duster?" Carter laughs. "Last night, you called Durk a feather duster?" He laughs harder. "Now, THAT is original. I have no idea what it means, but it's damn funny."

Just then, Mahler enters the cell area.

"You girls making funny here?" Mahler cracks in his best *Bad Lieutenant* pose.

"Oohh, scary, Boss," Reddick jokes.

Mahler relaxes and joins the two of them. "Look, I'm on your side, Carter. Well, as much as I can be, considering our history."

Carter just nods.

"However, you were driving while intoxicated." He shakes his head. "Aren't you ever going to learn?"

Carter shakes his head.

"Didn't think so. But then, you served our country. I've always given you loads of slack on that alone. As I was saying, Durk does have you solid on that count. The resisting arrest and excessive force calls are crap. I know you and I know that's not your way unless you're backed in a corner. This guy has a jones for you for some reason."

"Danny, yes, to the DUI, but I swear to you, he tripped me as I was getting out of the truck and he cracked my bean for no reason."

"No. I get it. And I'm sure that's the way it went. However, this is your…" he leans forward to place extra emphasis on the next word, "…*fourth* conviction. The judge ain't gonna like that, and well, frankly, I'm not sure how that's gonna play."

Carter looks him dead in the eye and says, "I've got some help coming."

Reddick looks from Carter to Mahler and back to Carter then asks, "What kind of help?"

After a long moment, Carter quietly says, "The kind of help…that makes things go away."

᠊ᢀ᠊

A gloved hand holds a large gun and takes aim.
BANG! BANG! BANG! BANG! BANG! BANG!
Smoke drifts from the end of the gun.
A motorized sound in the distance gets closer and closer.
Durkin lays his gun down on the counter.
He stands alone inside the shooting range, waiting for the paper target to arrive at his stand.
Pulling the tattered target from the clip, he smiles, staring at the paper man.
All six shots made nearly a perfect circle, within just one inch of the target's heart.
"Nice shot, *Durk*," he growls.
The last one was squarely between the man's eyes.

᠊ᢀ᠊

Carter sits at Reddick's desk, twirling a pencil as Reddick processes the last of the paperwork.
"Man, could I use a shower."
"Ya think?"
"And a cup of coffee. Actually, I'm starved."
Stapling some papers together, Reddick adds, "Wonder why." He looks at Carter's shirt.
Captain Mahler emerges from his office and walks over to Reddick's desk, holding a single paper.
"For the record, I know why I'm helping you," he says looking at Carter, "but for the life of me, tell me why I'd do anything to help *him*?" he adds, nodding at Reddick without looking at him.
"Okay. I give."
Mahler looks around like he's telling a big secret, "Well, this one is trying to horn in on my girl."

"Now, wait just a minute—"

Mahler throws up a hand. "Shut it. I'm the boss. I've got the floor." He leans closer to them. "You remember last summer?" He rolls his eyes. "Of course, anyhow, come to find out our little Nurse Symon had eyes for—"

"You both," Carter interrupts. "I know. We're pals. Who do you think stitched this up?" pointing to his head, "AND helped me keep you both alive?"

They look at one another.

"Look, you both were in a vulnerable place."

"Whatever. Anyhow, she's still, uh, trying to…make up her mind," Mahler sheepishly adds.

Reddick shakes his head and smirks, saying, "No way. She knows which one she wants. She's just in no hurry…before she settles on me." He grins.

"Okay, whatever. Here's the last piece of paper we need to get this deal done." Mahler hands the paper to Reddick. He reads it then looks at Carter with a large look of surprise.

"Yup. Your guy pulled it off," Mahler says. "I don't know HOW, but he did. And FAST." He looks at his watch. "I mean, you're picked up around one, stitched up at two and locked up around three. Here it is, not even 10 yet, and you're out on not one, but *three* charges. Done!"

"How did…uh…the chances of, I mean," Reddick stammers. "It's got to take—"

Carter leans back in his chair, clasps both hands behind his head and smiles, saying, "Good friends. High places."

"Well, I certainly want you on my team," Mahler says. "Always."

"Me too," Reddick adds.

Carter looks at both guys, bites the inside of his mouth, and absently looks out the window—letting the silence hang in the air for effect, and then responds.

"You guys have my back? I'll always have yours. You know that."

"And what I know is that Durkin is due here any minute. And if he sees you walking—let's just say it'll get complicated," Mahler grunts.

"Yeah, but you're the boss and you can shut him up," Reddick finishes.

"True. But all that...*noise* he makes." Mahler shakes his head. "Just annoying." He walks away, adding, "Okay, see you around, Carter," then shouts from inside his office, "Try and stay outta trouble, huh?"

"C'mon, I'll buy you breakfast. It's the least I can do," Reddick suggests.

"Thanks. And you're right," Carter laughs. "I'm so hungry, I'm not even going to shower."

"Oh joy."

"But I could use a clean shirt," Carter says.

"I've got a spare in the car."

Carter heads out the door, a free man. Stepping outside, he takes a long, deep breath and thinks to himself, *Fresh air. What a concept.* Reddick tosses Carter's paperwork in a nearby file cabinet, grabs his cap and keys from his desk, and says, "Derby, here we come."

CHAPTER 26

ANGELA AND DAVID SIT in the waiting room of Dr. Long's office. Angela flips mindlessly through a magazine, while David stares into an aquarium stocked full of exotically colored fish.

Eloise, the receptionist, quietly says, "They're beautiful, aren't they?"

"They sure are," David eagerly replies.

"Doctor Long had some new ones delivered yesterday. Another angel, a half dozen nemos and an eel," she smiles. "Do you like fish?"

"Yes, Ma'am. I like most any living thing."

"That's the truth," Angela adds. "And give him one afternoon and he'll tell you the name of every one of them and where each one comes from."

"Yup," he chirps.

Dr. Long exits his office, escorting Stephan DeAngelo, quietly saying, "Good to meet you and I look forward to our chatting again."

Angela looks up and is caught off-guard by the very handsome man.

"Thank you, Dr. Long," Stephan says with a thick Italian accent. "Ciao."

Stephan starts to leave but turns and catches Angela's eye. Their gaze locks for an instant before he nods, saying politely, "Hello."

"Hello," she says, trying not to stare. *I mean, hello Handsome Man Candy!* she thinks.

Dr. Long interjects, walking over to them, "My apologies. Stephan, please meet Angela Matheson and her son, David."

Angela stands and they shake hands.

"Nice to meet you." A look of surprise registers. "Oh, Pastor Matheson's wife?"

"Yes. And this is David."

"Nice to meet you," David says, shaking Stephan's hand.

"And you as well, David."

David smiles. "I like your accent. Italian, right?"

"Bueno. Yes, David. Very good."

David smiles, then turns to ask Long, "May I get those books now, Dr. Long?"

Long says, "Yes, David," turns to Angela and continues, "Angela, give me just one minute. And Stephan, we'll see you again."

"Yes. Excellent. Thank you."

Long disappears into his office; and, Stephan stands there for a moment before saying, "Your husband is a fine man. I'm happy to be working with him."

Angela looks into his bright green eyes—a sharp contrast to his dark skin and jet black hair, and says, "Yes he is and me too. I mean, I'm happy to…rather, that you're working with him. Except, that I didn't actually know that until now."

She blushes. *Nice, Angela, just keep that witty repartee up and you'll impress everyone.*

"Yes, I moved here recently from Europe and was given this account several weeks ago. It wasn't until just last week that I met Jonathan and then met with his board yesterday. Lovely people."

Angela feels a bit flushed and likes it. *Talking about lovely. Hello, Mr. Italian Man. Whew!* She quietly says, "They are dear, dear people. We love you and them all as our family, really."

He tries to hide a chuckle.

She realizes what she said, "I mean, we love them all…as our own family." *Oh my. I'm not really losing my mind, am I?*

He nods. "I understand. They all seem quite wonderful."

Uh, no, you're the wonderful one, she thinks.

David returns to the waiting room with a short stack of books. "Look what I have, Mom. Dr. Long is going to let me use these for my research."

Angela puts her hand on his shoulder, saying, "That's terrific. I can't wait to hear all about it. Did you thank our friend, Dr. Long?"

"Yes." He turns to Long. "Thanks again."

"My pleasure, David."

"Well, I must run," Stephan excuses himself. "Nice to meet you, Mrs. Matheson."

"Angela."

"Fine, Angela, it is. And quite similar to my last name, DeAngelo."

More like an angel! Okay, stop. Right now. She smiles.

He smiles, turning to David. "David, enjoy your studies."

David responds with, "Ciao!" and sits down in a comfortable chair and begins to read. Stephan looks at Angela with surprise, responds with, "Ciao," and is on his way.

Angela and Long enter the office, but just before the door closes, she turns to catch one last glimpse and mumbles, "Hubba."

ॐ

Angela and Long sit facing one another. Long smiles, waiting for her to gather her thoughts.

"Wow," Angela says quietly but with emphasis.

Long nods. "Nice man."

"And handsome. Whew!"

"Okay." Long smiles.

"Don't get me wrong. I'm happily married and love my Jonathan, but c'mon…I'm not blind," she defends.

"No, I get it. Completely."

Angela stares off into space. He brings her back. "Have you given any more thought to what we spoke about recently?"

Snapping back, she answers, "You mean the prescriptions, or the adoption?"

"Both," Long calmly says.

"Yes, I have."

&

Christopher pulls into the school parking lot, takes his bag from the truck bed and heads toward the building. From the corner of his eye, he sees Jeff and his sidekick, Peter Vaughan. As they approach, he looks around. Given that he's running late, there are very few, if any, students left lounging on the grounds. His stomach tightens.

"What's up, Pretty Boy?" Peter says as he approaches.

"Not much," Christopher says coolly.

"That old man you were with the other day—he your body-guard?" Jeff asks with no emotion.

"That's my uncle. Carter," he says, still walking.

"Uh huh. So you need an old man to do a young man's work?" Peter poses.

Christopher stops walking. "I have no idea what you're talking about, Vaughan, but if you've got something to say, why don't you just say it? Or do you need someone else," nodding toward Jeff, "to tell you what to do?"

This gets Peter agitated.

He circles around, so now Christopher has one bully on either side of him.

"You think you're a tough guy, don't you? A real tough guy," Jeff snarls.

"Not really. But I don't think you guys have the balls to take care of whatever it is you're all wound up about...by yourselves. I mean, if you wanna play fair, this should be one conversation at a time."

He drops his bag to the ground.

Peter takes this as a sign, so he swings.

Christopher ducks at just the right time and lands a punch to Peter's gut. It takes the air out of him.

Bent over, he turns to Jeff and yells, between breaths, "Well, don't just stand there..."

Jeff does just stand there. Waiting.

Christopher stands still. Also waiting.

Peter, still trying to catch his breath, slowly stands up.

As he does, it distracts Christopher.

SMACK!

Jeff's right fist connects squarely with Christopher's jaw at the exact moment he went to turn back.

Christopher loses his balance and, in that moment, Jeff gives him a taste of fury with a kick to his rib cage. Christopher screams in pain and thinks he heard something crack. He gains his ground and at the second Jeff looks at Peter for congratulations, Christopher tackles him to the ground and gets in two good hits to the face before a voice from behind pulls him off.

⤳

Sitting in the waiting area of the principal's office, the three young men are quite the sight. Peter's only visible damage was a red ear from where a teacher had grabbed and pulled him across half a parking lot; his insides were another story.

Jeff had one black eye and a swollen nose. Blood was still seeping from his nose; but, the compress he held to it was doing a pretty good job at keeping it at bay.

Christopher has a cut across his cheek where Jeff's class ring left an impression, but he tries not to show any signs of pain. The much larger problem is that his ribs feel as though someone performed a few rounds of jumping jacks on them.

Principal Vernon Schultz is a tall, thin and well-built man, with a flat-top haircut straight out of the '50s and glasses to match. Schultz opens his door and waves Christopher in. He closes the door, quietly conferring with two teachers outside the room.

ॐ

Dr. Long patiently waits while Angela sits staring at her hands in her lap. She finally says, "Well, I now better understand the dangers of mixing medications, that's for sure. I mean, you should've seen me. And Christopher's face. Not sure which was…more surprising."

A small smile grows upon Long's face, as he quietly says, "That's what I meant by adverse reaction. The medication I prescribed for your depression—"

She instantly looks up. "It's not exactly—"

"Yes it is, Angela. You can pretend and call it whatever you like, but we've discussed this. You suffered the single biggest tragedy a mother—a parent, can ever face. And those close to you know all too well how you have tried to give it more than a fair shot—being *Super Mother* and *Super Wife*. But sometimes—oftentimes, keeping up a front lasts only so long. Something has to eventually give. And if you correct soon enough, you can help repair the damage. That's partly what we're doing here."

"You're right," she whispers.

"And I'm proud of you."

Her mood lightens.

"However, you can NOT mix a sleep aid, such as Ambien, with an anti-depressant—and never with alcohol. No way, no how."

She nods, starts to say something then waves it away.

He continues, "Can you imagine if your family weren't around, or if you were to get in your car and drive somewhere?"

"Oh, I'd never do that," she interrupts.

"Angela! People do it all the time. And some are seriously injured. Or worse."

She looks at him with horror. "Really?"

"Yes, Ma'am. Read about it. There is a drug—rather, a chemical reaction in that particular drug that can effectively erase short-term memory—much like drugs they administer in surgery."

They look at one another. The patient and the doctor. And the friend with the friend. His words weigh heavy on her. She can't decide whether to hug him or scream at the top of her lungs. She finally smiles, takes a deep breath and says, "Thank you."

"My pleasure."

She looks at her watch and says, "Okay, we agreed; I was only a work-in. Half session. So, I have got to run."

"Before you run, remember we never discussed your thoughts on adoption."

"Yes. True. But Rome wasn't built in a day, I seem to recall someone saying to me." She stands and starts toward the door. He follows.

"Fair enough. But next time, let's spend an entire session speaking about just that, okay?" He takes her hands and squeezes them.

"Absolutely. In fact, the more I think about it, the more I think you may be on to something. On many fronts." She kisses his cheek then adds, "Until next time. Ciao!"

Christopher sits alone in the principal's office. He stares at the plaques on the walls. Looking around he sees, by the awards, that his principal is much smarter than he knew. An old, beat-up perforated paddle hung on a peg behind his desk. Inscribed on it were the words, *Spare the Paddle—Spoil the Brattle.* He looks at it and thinks, *Not sure I get it, but then, I don't want to either.* The door opens and Principal Schultz comes in, tossing a file folder on his desk. He lets out an enormous sigh, shakes his head back and forth repeatedly then clucks his tongue and finally sits behind his desk. He allows a long enough stretch of silence to take place to make Christopher as uncomfortable as possible. Christopher fidgets nervously. Schultz stares steadily. *Okay, I'm scared to death. Let's just get this over with and I'll be on my way.*

"Christopher, I like you. I've always liked you. You're a good kid. From a good family. One that I respect. And you *were* a pretty good student, until recently. And trust me, I'm 101% sympathetic to your loss of last year—a tragedy, indeed."

Christopher fidgets and rolls his eyes.

"I'm sorry. I know. You're likely tired of hearing it brought up all the time. Nonetheless, we—you and I, have a real situation on our hands. According to the rules of our school, I am well within my rights to expel you. Permanently.

This gets Christopher's attention.

"However, I am willing to give you ONE more try."

He relaxes just a bit.

"Wait. I'll repeat myself," he says, placing additional emphasis, "That's ONE. More. Try. After today, you get called into my office for anything, and I mean ANY thing and you are done! Do I make myself perfectly clear?"

"Yes, Sir. You do, Sir. And thank you, Sir," Christopher answers.

"Don't thank me. Just work with me. Make me proud. And make your parents proud."

"Yes, Sir."

"Speaking of which," he continues, looking at some notes in the same folder, "I called your mother's cell—the direct contact we were given. It went straight to voicemail. I called your house and got the answering machine. Then, I called your father's cell—straight to voicemail. And then his office and they said he had just stepped out of the building. I left a message. Those are all the contact numbers I have, well, except your cell; but then, you're sitting right here." He smiles then, clearing his throat, says, "So, since you're a senior and we have no contacts responding, perhaps against my better judgment, I'm going to send you home for the rest of the day."

Christopher starts to stand.

"Sit. Not done yet. Your partners in crime are staying here. Both of Jeff's parents work and can't get him until the end of the day. He's recently had his license revoked for some reason I don't care about. And his shadow, Peter? Well, his mother is the school nurse, so that will…take care of itself," he practically mumbles by the end of the sentence.

"But here's the thing, as you're home, I want you to seriously, very seriously, consider these two things. First, what are you going to do with the next five to six months, as you finish your final year? Are you going to apply yourself and get the grades you need to graduate?" He looks in the folder again. "Which, according to this, I'm concerned you may have some serious catching up to do. But I believe you can do it. Now, go home and think about that."

Christopher frowns.

"What?" Schultz asks.

"You said there were two things you wanted me to consider."

"Yes. Good. Thank you. The second thing I want you to consider is where are you going to college? With your musical prowess, I'm sure you're thinking about New York School of the Arts? UCLA has a prestigious music program. If you really hustled, I'm sure you could get into Temple. Philly's a lovely city and their school is top notch. Or, maybe you want to stay close to home and attend Davidson?"

Christopher watches Principal Schultz as he sits back in his chair, propping his elbows on the chair rests and touching his fingertips together by forming a *church*, something that Christopher had seen his father do time and again when he was sitting in contemplation. Christopher can't decide if he wants to say what's on his mind—for fear of the principal telling his parents, but he figures, *What the heck.*

"Actually, I'm not sure I'm going to attend college."

"What?"

"I'm thinking about hitting the road when I graduate—maybe New York, or LA."

"And do what?"

Christopher hesitates just a moment before answering. "And become a rock star!"

Schultz stares at him like he has two heads, slowly shakes his head, rolls his eyes and, pointing to the door, says, "Dismissed!"

CHAPTER 27

OFFICER REDDICK AND CARTER sit in his favorite booth—the one in the far corner but on the front of the building, overlooking the parking lot. This way, Carter can see anyone coming and going, thus eliminating the element of surprise. *I've had enough surprises in my day—enough to last a lifetime*, he thinks to himself. He browses the menu, wondering if he'll venture out and try something new. Nah.

Reddick looks around and says, "I've always liked this place. It's about the only local hangout, besides The Handle, that I frequent."

"Yup. Good, simple food," Carter says, tapping the menu. "It's all in there."

Reddick flips the menu over, then back over. Just then, he looks up to catch Carter make eye contact with someone. From the expression on Carter's face, Reddick has to see what's got his interest, so he turns, looking over his shoulder. Teresa has just finished serving food to one table. As she looks up, she catches Carter's eye.

"Oh yeah. I see what...you see." He turns back around and adds, "Nicely done, Sir."

Carter grins. "Go figure. She's hot. I'm not. She's young. I'm old." He leans closer. "But I'll tell you what..." he shakes his head, "She and I just click." He looks up. "Here she comes."

"Hello, gentlemen. Um, I can only actually attest for one." She winks at Carter. "How about the other?" she says, extending her hand.

Reddick shakes, introducing himself, "Reddick. Sergeant Dennis Reddick, at your service."

"Well, I've had run-ins with the law, as well as," she leans in, "slept with the law. And as I see it, I'd rather hang out with the *good* bad boys," nodding at Carter, "than with the *bad* good boys." She pours them both a cup of coffee, dropping Half & Half containers from her pocket in front of Reddick, but scooting Carter's black coffee in front of him.

Reddick notices, grins and says, "Now, how did you know that?"

She smiles and says, "Just instinct, I guess," then looks toward the serving window and back. "Either that, or been doing this entirely too long. I'll be right back to take your orders, okay?"

"Pleasure to meet you."

Over her shoulder, she shouts, "You too, Dennis!"

"You've got a live one, Batman!"

Watching her walk away, Carter sips his coffee, smiles and grunts, "Uh huh."

ॐ

After getting the boot from school, Christopher drives home. But along the way, he thinks he needs some advice from the one man who will give it to him straight. He gets off the main highway and turns down the bumpy road that leads to Carter's house. Hitting a rough pothole, he flinches as the seatbelt squeezes his rib cage.

"That friggin' hurts," he mumbles, squinting in pain.

Cresting the ridge that hides Carter's property from much of the neighboring land, he is immediately distracted as he spots, several hundred yards from Carter's house, something you don't see every day.

"What is that doing..." he trails off as he sees a sleek, bright red Bell helicopter parked in the middle of Carter's property. Cautious, he stops, spotting a vehicle he doesn't recognize. Black car. Dark windows. *Looks like those cars big city executives use.* He's not sure what to do, but seeing Carter's pickup, he puts it back in gear and approaches, creeping toward the house. *This is about the time I wish Carter had taught me to use a gun—except I hate guns.*

Approaching the house, the man on the front porch looks vaguely familiar, but he doesn't know why. Just then, another man gets out of the black car, looks at the stranger on the front porch, who waves him away. He nods and just stands there. Christopher pulls up and gets out, approaching the man on the front porch.

"You must be Christopher," the man says.

"Yup. And you must be…" he replies.

The man chuckles then starts coughing. After much coughing, he stands and walks toward Christopher with an outstretched hand.

"Randall…Matheson. Your grandfather," he says, reaching for Christopher's hand.

"Damn!" Christopher replies, his jaw hanging wide open.

The man coughs out a crinkly, gooey laugh, like someone choking on fried chicken.

෨

Both Carter and Reddick have finished their meals and are flirting with Teresa.

"Okay, before the real rush comes in, I'm going to have to turn my very interested attentions elsewhere, okay?" coos Teresa, in Carter's direction.

"And I have an idea. Why don't you come to my place tonight for dinner? Let me show you that I can do more than sling the hash…I can actually make the hash, or pork chops, as the case will probably be."

Carter nods, smiling.

Reddick looks at Carter, rolls his eyes and says, "Teresa, look what you've done to my boy."

She laughs. "Oh, he's just wrapped up in my *new car smell*. Reality will settle in soon enough."

Smiling, he says, "Nah, I like the broken-in models. More character."

"Nice, I think," she smirks.

"What time?" Carter asks.

"Around seven?"

"Sounds good."

"And see you another time," she says to Reddick and leaves.

After she's nearly to the kitchen, Reddick turns back around, takes a sip of coffee then quietly says, "Yup. That's a handful."

"I'm up for it."

"No doubt. Hey, before we go, I've been wondering about something."

"What's that?"

"How'd you make that happen so fast?"

"Her?"

"No. Getting out."

Carter clicks into business mode, picks up the check, drops a ten on the table and says, "I'll tell you on the way."

☙

Making their way to his school, Angela and David drive in silence. He looks at her from time to time, but she appears to be lost in her own little world—even mumbling random things that he can't quite make out. Each time he asks her what she said, she doesn't answer, so he assumes she didn't want to be bothered. He finishes reading over his homework, sees that they're getting close to school and finally breaks the silence.

"Mom, you sure have been quiet."

"Huh? Oh, just a lot on my mind. That's all."

"Yeah, me too."

She looks at the books stacked on the seat between them. He picks up an oversized book on butterflies and starts turning the colorful pages.

"I can see that. Is it my imagination, or have you developed an unusual curiosity of late for butterflies."

"Uh huh," he distractedly reads.

"What's that?"

"Yes, Ma'am. An unusual curiosity for butterflies. They're awesome, Mom. Did you know there are literally hundreds upon hundreds of varieties? AND while they differ all around the world, they're basically the same creatures?"

"Well, no...and yes."

He jerks his head toward her, "Huh?"

"No, I didn't know, and yes, I assume they're all the same. Just like us, Son."

"How's that?"

"Well, there are hundreds of millions of people all around the world. But all in all, we're pretty much the same."

He stares out the window, as life rushes by. "Hhmm...guess you're right."

"Speaking of butterflies, why do I get the sneaking suspicion you're up to something?"

"No, I'm not," he interrupts.

"In your bedroom, is what I was going to finish saying."

"Oh, yeah. I am. Top secret. Don't peek. Seriously. You'll ruin the surprise, if you do. You're gonna like it."

"I bet I will."

"My best work yet." He pauses a moment and adds, "And part of the surprise is the best part yet."

Angela pulls into the school parking lot and glances at her watch.

"I know," he says, rolling his eyes. "But this won't take a minute."

"What son? I'm listening."

"I know you are, but I know you also have a lot on your mind. You're not feeling your chipper self and you're having lunch with Dad, so you'll likely have to..."

"Son, what is it? You have my undivided attention. Always. Now, spit it out."

"Not so sure about that," he mumbles. "But here's what I want to share before I run in." He starts putting his books into his book bag. "I know that everything is going to be okay." He snaps and buckles the bag and sets it on his lap.

"Well, uh, okay. Good to know." She looks at him and squints. Then, he squints, playing with her. "Is there more?"

"Gracie told me it's all going to work out just fine."

Angela is caught off-guard. Emotions rush through her. She suddenly feels faint, but tries to keep a quiet face so as to not alarm David.

"W-what's that? Grace...told you...it's all going to be—"

"Just fine," he adds. "Well, she didn't actually say this, but she appeared to me and let me know. It was a real..." he taps his chin, "peaceful feeling I got right after I prayed for Christopher and you and Dad."

She smiles patiently and says softly, "David, I'm trying to follow you. And while this sounds very sweet, what...where did you get these ideas?"

"Mom, it's been known for generations that quite often the souls of those who have gone before, return, even for a short while, to let those they left behind, know that everything will be fine."

Angela isn't sure whether to laugh, or applaud. She is confused.

"And you call this a—"

"Sign. From God." He smiles. "Or, the universe, if you prefer."

"Son, that's nonsense!"

The wind has been sucked from his kite. He slowly begins to descend. A small wrinkle forms in his perfectly smooth forehead and he says, "Wait..."

"Son, what you're saying is not founded in reality. Or, the Bible."

"But I've done extensive research, Mom, and given it a lot of thought and it just makes sense to me."

"Well, I still say it's not founded in reality."

"But Mom, neither is church."

"WHAT?" Angela exclaims.

"Let's face it, the Bible is a group of stories passed from one group to another over hundreds of years. It's—"

She cuts him off, "David Randolph Matheson, that's blasphemy and I won't stand for it!" She's more shocked than angry—perhaps *confused* is the best word.

"Mom, you and Dad always taught us kids to think for ourselves and figure the best way to approach anything in life, right?"

She hesitates just a moment; she knows that what he said is true.

"And you both have worked hard to be able to provide me with a great education at a private school…"

"But you're only 12 years old!

"Mom, I'm 14. And all the better to grasp this…early on." He smiles.

"Yes. I meant to say that. 14." Slowly, her smile turns into a chuckle and they both are laughing.

"Son, you truly are a Matheson. And your father's son. You certainly had me going. And, you're going to do so well in debate—when you get to high school."

"Which, at the rate I'm going, will be much sooner than you think."

She reaches over and places her hand on his cheek and looks lovingly into his eyes and says, "Don't rush, Son. It'll come soon enough. For both of our sakes, please don't rush it."

David reaches for the door handle but she reaches to stop him.

"Hold on one more second, David. While you're doing all this reading and studying and researching that you're doing…" She hesitates, looking for the right words.

"Yes?"

She takes a long, deep breath, lets it out slowly and turns to face him straight on. "Son, while you're researching life, butterflies and such…why don't you help your dear old mother out and help me research our adopting a little girl."

She stops and waits to see what his reaction will be. His eyes open wide. His brow raises high. And his jaw literally drops.

"Really?"

She nods.

"A…sister?"

"Yup. I've been thinking about it a lot and while I may be too old to have another baby—which is likely the case, there are so many families that can't keep their little girls. Besides, we have the perfect home, don't we?"

The look on David's face is precious. His bright blue eyes are processing any number of things and the smile that starts as a tiny dimple, spreads into an ear-to-ear smile that warms her heart and confirms that she may be making the right choice after all.

"That could be so awesome."

"Just one more thing, Son. For now, let's just keep this between you and me. Can we do that?"

"Sure, Mom."

She puts out her hand, closes all fingers except the pinkie—curls it up, and says, "Pinky Promise?"

He does the same, interlocking with her pinky finger and says, "Pinky Promise. Just you and me."

She leans over and kisses David on the check and whispers, "I love you," in his ear.

"Love you too, Mom. That's great news."

He opens the door, jumps out with schoolbag in hand, and is on his way.

She looks in the rearview mirror to watch him run toward the school. Suddenly, he stops, spins around and runs back to her side of the car. She is lowering the window, as he runs up.

Slightly out of breath, he looks her straight in the eye and says, "Gracie thinks it's good news, too!"

He winks at her the way he winks at his father, turns and is gone.

≈

Angela sits in the quiet of the car and absorbs what has just transpired. She smiles, thinking of how quickly life passes by and how she wants desperately to be present for each and every moment. She still can sense the dark clouds of sorrow hanging overhead, but perhaps for the first time in over a year, a tiny ray of sunshine is starting to break through. She starts the car, puts it into gear and backs out of the space. Just as she is about to pull from the lot, something catches her eye. She stops.

Fluttering in front of her windshield, she sees the largest, most colorful butterfly she has ever seen in her life. It flies in several lopsided circles before flying high overhead. She leans forward to follow its flight then slides the sunroof back and watches the happy, bright blue butterfly take flight into the sky and eventually out of sight. The single large tear that runs down her cheek isn't nearly as large as the smile that stretches across her face.

CHAPTER 28

AS REDDICK'S SQUAD CAR merges into oncoming traffic, Carter starts his explanation and has Reddick's full attention.

"Okay. First of all, yes—I was wrong to be drinking and driving. I do need to be more careful, but I guess I was wrapped up in the moment. "

Reddick nods.

"Some habits die hard, so sue me," he continues. "The other two charges, as I said before, were...ARE total bullshit. I don't know what that screwball was up to, but he had it in for me out of the gate."

Reddick nods. "I get that."

"I mean, if I had wanted to be a real jerk, I would have mouthed off and he had a right to push me around. But crack my friggin' skull nearly open? Not acceptable."

Reddick nods. "No argument here."

"Now, I have had the good fortune to have served my country. And I did so proudly. But I have likewise had what some would call the not-so-good fortune to have learned a few...uh...shortcuts to the system."

Reddick listens, slowly nodding.

"Those shortcuts allow people like myself to slip through some cracks. It also helps that I have assistance of the highest order—not necessarily the assistance I would have initially dreamed for, but...it is what it is."

"I get it. I think."

"Here's the bottom line. You're likely—no, you ARE my best friend. I don't have many, so...welcome to my small club. Consider yourself...President."

Reddick smirks and mumbles, "Thanks."

"It's a good thing. Comes with some headaches, perhaps even ones as painful as I'm experiencing now, thanks to that pansy, Durkin," he adds, rubbing the back of his head.

"About those numbers—"

"Code," Carter responds.

"Figured that. And if I stewed on it long enough, I'd likely figure out some of it, but—"

"Okay, watch this. Ever since I was in the marines, from day one, every piece of technical jargon was boiled down to its essence. As I said, a code. There were times we shortened terms, conditions, or instructions, so that *wandering eyes and ears* wouldn't be able to translate quickly."

Reddick drives in silence, nodding.

"Moreover, ALL the branches of the service have a code—a moral code that basically says, in one form or another, *Never leave a man behind.*"

"Absolutely."

"Right. You understand. Now, Pickle Dick, Durkin. Wait—Durkin pickles…"

They laugh.

"Sorry. Just got him up in my hornet's nest and…," he hesitates, "Well, another time."

"I get it."

"Okay, so, we all have *one* person, *one* call we can make that, no matter what it is, or where we are, or whatever thing is going on…personal, business, friends, family—doesn't matter, we know we can make that call and get help. And get it NOW!"

"Who's the he…for you? And how do those numbers—"

"I'll get to the *he* in a minute, but those numbers are easy. Remember I asked you the charge numbers?"

"Yeah, violation abbreviations."

"That's it. Couldn't think of the—"

"Anyhow…"

"Those four digits worked like this: DUI Violation, 1046 becomes *October 46.* Resisting Arrest, 1173 becomes *November 73*—"

"I get it. First two digits become a month—"

"Exactly. Just a way to confuse, or even distract an eavesdropper. So, we begin with—and by the way, the protocol is exactly the same. Always. So that at any moment—especially those when time is short, the message gets delivered quickly. Therefore, we begin with my source's name, which is Alpha—a name we chose a couple of dozen years ago. My name, in relation to his, is Omega."

"Beginning and end. Got it. Like…father and son."

Carter looks at him, doesn't say a word then continues, "Right. Then you've got another universal command, *Officer Down*. And we all know that one."

Reddick nods.

"Follow that with what's needed immediately. In this case, the need was *Immediate Assistance*, followed by another command, which is *LISTEN*. This is where the subversion comes into play. We all know that any altercation has some nearly universal label. I don't care what it is. As I said, if you've been in any branch of the military, everything—right down to taking a leak, comes with a code-word, or code-number."

"Where 1046, 1173 and 1217 came into play."

"Exactly. And then we simply end it with a definitive call to action, or *Need Affirmative ETA*, or when the hell can you be here to save my ass!"

"Got it. A little different than playing *Country Cops* in Mission Grove," he chuckles.

"Yeah, but you, my friend, are of an elite quality. It's just that you probably didn't have the best training, or the ideal opportunities, or…maybe you're just a slacker."

"Then you just waited."

Carter nods.

"And the answer and/or ETA is delivered in the same sort of code. The other end will always say, *Number* which means, stand by for the number of hours it will take for me to get to you. In this case, he said, *Number 4*. He then closes with *AOK* which means it is a *GO MISSION*; nothing will stop him. And of course, close with—"

"*Over*."

"Yup."

Carter casually points to the left, reminding Reddick where to turn.

Reddick gives a signal.

"I think I just went to school."

"Good."

They turn down the familiar bumpy, dusty road and approach the ridge on Carter's property.

"And you're about to meet one of the headmasters."

Reddick whips his head toward Carter.

Carter nods straight ahead.

As they crest the ridge, the blades and bright red body of the Bell helicopter come into full sight.

"Holy Moly," Reddick nearly gasps.

Carter simply says, "Yup."

CHAPTER 29

AS CARTER AND REDDICK pull up, Carter scans the property, the black-windowed car and attending suit and the tree line, just in case. It's then that he spots Christopher's truck. He frowns.

Reddick instinctively checks his weapon. Carter notices.

"You won't need that. Good to have it, but you won't need it."

"Roger."

"I would suggest keeping your eyes on *Mr. Black Suit*. Just in case."

"Cool," Reddick grunts, cracking his neck first to one side then the other.

They park and approach the house. Carter is surprised to see Christopher sitting on the porch talking to Randall.

"Hey, Uncle Carter. Look who's here." He and Randall both stand.

Carter nods to Randall. Randall returns the nod. Carter sees the scratch on Christopher's cheek.

"What happened, Christopher?"

"Oh, some loser named Jeff and—"

"Peter?" Carter interrupts.

"Oh yeah, the guys from the diner. We kinda got into it today."

Carter nods then looks at his watch, "School's not out yet, is it?"

"Nah. I kinda got let go…for the day." Christopher looks at his shoes.

"Expelled?"

"No, not yet. But," he scratches his head, "soon, if I don't get my shi—"

Christopher looks at Randall who shrugs, "Won't offend me, Son."

Carter walks over to Randall and reaches to shake his hand. Randall takes it.

"Thank you, Sir."

The pride in Randall's eyes is evident. He quietly replies, "All in a day's work."

"And it's been a helluva past 24."

"Been there," Randall says.

"Done that," they say in unison.

Carter releases his father's grip—still strong after all these years. He nods toward the helicopter. "Nothin' like subtle."

"Traded the old black one in for a newer model. All they had was red."

"Riiiiiight," Carter mocks. "Always been your favorite color."

"At least they see you coming," Randall coughs. "And going," he adds.

Carter smiles in agreement then nods toward Reddick.

"Sergeant Dennis Reddick, meet Lieutenant Colonel Randall Matheson."

Reddick steps forward and shakes Randall's hand.

"You can call me Randall," he says, squinting into the sun.

"You could call me Dennis, but most people call me Reddick."

"Fair enough. And that," he nods toward the driver, "is Mr. Black. He's my pilot, bodyguard and longtime friend."

Mr. Black salutes the two of them. They salute in return.

"Mr. Black? What is this, *Reservoir Dogs*?" Carter asks.

Christopher chimes in, "Love that movie."

"Me too, Son," Randall smiles. "And that's actually his name."

≈

Jeff sits in detention, staring out the window, bored. His knee bounces up and down quickly—no doubt following a sadistic tune that no one can hear but him. He violently scribbles random dark images on the paper in front of him. A pimple-faced kid across the room picks a booger, rolls it up and tosses it against the blackboard. Jeff squints in disgust and returns to his graphic images. He balls it up and throws it toward the trashcan that sits next to the student picker who jumps. Startled by the paper, the kid whips around to face Jeff.

"You got a problem, Pizza Face?" Jeff barks.

The kid turns red and just stares at him. Jeff can't decide if the kid is angry, blushing, or trying to crap his pants.

"Mind your own business, Fag," the kid says.

Jeff squints, stands and slowly walks across the room. The kid swallows hard, sits up straighter, looks around and when Jeff is a few feet away, jumps up and runs out of the room.

"That's what I thought."

Jeff peeks out into the nearly empty hall. He sees only a student teacher, who is leaning against the wall, talking on the phone. He makes his way down the hall to the boy's gym locker room and steps inside. Grabbing a stack of towels by the door, he walks in confidently, as though he's making a delivery. Several boys are in the shower, yelling and cutting up. Being completely ignored, he walks to a locker, opens it and digging through a pair of jeans, removes a set of car keys and stuffs them in his pocket. Nobody has seen him, so he takes a few dollars that are in the pocket as well, then picks up the same stack of towels and makes his way from the locker room. Nearing the exit, he looks both ways, tosses the stack of towels into an oversized trashcan and shoots out the door, down the sidewalk and across the student parking lot to a car on the far side of the lot—out of view from any of the authorities.

CHAPTER 30

ANGELA ENTERS THE DERBY just as Jonathan pulls in the parking lot. They catch one another's eyes. He smiles. She waves. She goes in and puts her name on the list. Lunchtime is always the busiest time. People come from all around for their authentic southern barbeque, hickory smoked—the real deal. Buster greets Angela at the door.

"Hello, Lovely Lady. Two?" Buster asks, just as Jonathan enters.

"Hey Buster, handsome and chipper as always," Angela compliments.

"You are too kind. And just made my day. Because of that, dessert's on the house. I insist!"

"Oh, you're too much," Angela says, squeezing his arm.

"What she said," Jonathan adds.

Buster takes them to one of the quieter spots in the restaurant and says, "Our newest star employee, Teresa, will be right with you." He smiles and disappears.

"You are the prettiest woman in this place," Jonathan says as they slide into the booth.

Smiling, Angela says, "And you are the best liar—"

"Hold it. Are you insulting my personal taste," he jokingly mocks.

"You're not so bad yourself," she leans closer, "My Love."

He reaches across the table and squeezes her hand.

Teresa approaches the table. "Hello you two. Nice to see you. Our specials today..." She stops, cocks her head to one side and says, "You look awfully familiar."

Angela has a jealous look on her face and thinks, *Now, wait just a minute there Missy—this man is MINE!*

Jonathan is often and regularly noticed because of his place in the community and televised church services on Sunday mornings, so he innocently says, "Well, it could be any number of places. How long have you worked here?"

"Not that long. Maybe four, five months, but I've mostly worked nights. But with my son, it was just too hard. Just recently graduated to days."

Angela takes note. "You have a son? How old is he?"

"17. Goes to Mission Grove High."

"Oh, so does our son."

Teresa stares at Jonathan again and says, "You look so much like a guy I'm dating. Well, not actually dating— we've only been out once, but I think we may go out some more." Self-conscious, she starts to walk away. "I'll just get your—"

Before she can get away, Jonathan asks, "What's his name? I may know him."

She lights up as she says, "Carter. Matheson?"

Jonathan chuckles. Angela joins in. Teresa smiles, but feels like she's on the outside. "What? Is he an ax-murderer? Child molester?"

Jonathan and Angela look at one another and he says, "That's my brother."

The look on her face is priceless. And embarrassed.

"Oh my," she blushes. "Ax-murderer," she mumbles.

"Sorry. It's just funny. He hasn't..." Jonathan looks around to see if Carter's around, "...had a date in so long— he'd probably say he couldn't recall what president was in office the last time he was on a *date*." He laughs. "No, he's a great guy. Big heart. A little too serious for most."

"That's too funny. Okay, I have to get moving here, but *serious*? Not the Carter I just met. Anyhow..." she fans herself, "Nice to meet you, Pastor Matheson. He did tell me that," she shakes his hand, turns to Angela and offers her hand. "And Mrs. Pastor Jonathan...uh..." She shakes her head in total embarrassment.

Laughing, Angela graciously pats her hand and says, "Just call me Angela."

Teresa nods and starts to walk away when Jonathan says, "Just to make it quick and easy, we'll take two Chef Salads with Ranch and two sweet iced teas with extra lemons. And take your time—looks like you have some catching up to do."

The two of them chuckle as Angela leans over and whispers, "Pretty girl. Funny too. But…Carter, an ax-murderer?" They laugh again.

෴

Carter's ax comes slamming down toward the woodpile, splitting the log in half.

"Nice swing, Carter," Randall says to his son.

"Just something I do to keep in shape."

Carter tosses the wood atop the pile, brushes his hands and hands the ax to Christopher.

"So, you came over here to ask me about how to become better at self-defense, huh, Chris?"

"Yes, Sir," he says, running his hand along the edge of the blade, feeling the heft of the ax in his hand. "After what they did to me today—and we were interrupted by the principal, I started thinking of what could happen if nobody was around to help. And while I can usually talk myself out of a situation with one guy…two guys are just a bit much."

"Understood. Hey, it can be a bit much for any man," he turns to Randall and Reddick for confirmation.

"That's right, Son," Randall says. "Your uncle and I have served in the armed forces, but just remember, there are nearly always teammates nearby, watching your back and…helping each other get out of tight spots."

Randall looks at Carter and winks.

Reddick chimes in, "And Christopher, look at us. We almost always travel in pairs. Two cops at a time in a bad situation trumps one anytime."

Christopher is visibly inspired with this encouragement. "Cool. Makes sense," he nods, while taking a position to swing the ax. He picks it up, swings it overhead and it comes down in a THUNK, jarring his teeth and causing the pain in his side to sear like a hot poker. It nearly takes his breath away, but he tries not to show it.

"Damn, that sucked," he says, trying to fit in, but wanting to be home lying down—the pain making it hard to breathe. "I'm not very good, Carter."

"Nah, you just have to take your time, Christopher. First time is always tough. But like anything, practice makes perfect. You'll catch on. And there's plenty here to practice on," he says, pointing to the hundred or so acres of hardwoods that line the back of his property.

"See that stack next to the house? It took time to learn that."

Christopher looks and, sure enough, every log is nearly identical in length.

"Wow. No kidding."

"But it wasn't that neat the first stack—neither will yours be. Give it time. Like playing a drum, or singing a song. The beats and the tunes get better with time."

"Now, when it's time to learn artillery," Randall says, pulling a P226 Sig Sauer Elite Stainless 9MM from the small of his back, "then come see *me*."

"I see your 9 and raise you a 40," Reddick says, drawing his Glock 22 .40 caliber.

"Whoa!" Carter shouts. "Let's put away the heat and just talk…strategy."

"It's okay, Uncle Carter," Christopher says. "I should get home. I've got to do homework and figure out what to tell Dad when he gets home. Not gonna be happy."

"I'll see what I can do," Carter says. "Your dad wasn't always the *angel* he pretends to be today."

Randall interjects, "No kidding. I've got stories on him—hell, on both my boys. No saints in this family."

Christopher walks to Randall and extends his hand, "Nice to meet you, Sir."

Randall shakes his hand and cocks his head to the side like he's waiting for something.

"Grandpa?" Christopher returns.

Still holding his hand, Randall pulls Christopher closer, hugs him and says, "You can call me that. Been waiting 17 years to hear it."

Carter watches the two *strangers* meet for the very first time.

As Christopher pulls away, he says, "Does have a nice ring to it, huh? Will I see you again before you leave?"

"Uh, well…" Randall stammers, looking to Carter for backup. "Let's see how things shake out. I'd love to, Son. Truly, I would. Guess it's going to depend upon—"

"Timing," Carter interrupts. "Got to see if the timing of his visit here, the appointment he has to return to in Florida and…well, if your father will be open to…uh, our getting together."

"Been a very long time since I've seen your father, too, Christopher," Randall quietly says, adding, "He may not be as receptive to it as, say, you are. But let me see, okay?"

Christopher replies, "Fair enough."

"Either way, it was such an honor to get to spend time with you and hear about your music and your dreams of becoming a professional performer, and your girlfriend and all that."

"Wow, you guys really covered a lot of ground in a short time," Carter smirks.

Randall smiles and winks at Christopher and softly says, "Well, we had a lot of catching up to do, right?"

"Yes, Sir. Okay, I'm outta here. Check you all later."

They all wave as he gets in his truck and drives away.

"Good kid," Randall says solemnly.

"And troubled," Carter adds.

"Just like all of us," Reddick finishes.

Carter slaps his hands together and says, "Okay, you gents take a seat on the front porch there and ask *Mr. Black* to stop acting like a statue and join us. I'll slip inside and invite my other friends, Bud and Heineken, to join us too. Then let's debrief so I can learn more about this *mission* I'm about to undertake."

CHAPTER 31

THE DINER HAS SLOWED down considerably and the crowd thinned. Angela and Jonathan are finishing their desert and coffee. Jonathan mindlessly spins his broken cell phone on the table, while Angela people watches.

"So you're sure you don't mind running this by the store and replacing it?"

"Of course not," she looks at her watch, "I don't have to be anywhere until four to pick up David at school." She reaches in her purse. "Here, you want to take mine?" she asks.

"That's okay. I'm going right back to the office—back into meetings."

"Oh, no," she hesitates, looking at the screen, "It's not working either." She pushes a button then sighs, "Duh. It was turned off."

Chuckling, Jonathan says, "I do that sometimes. Freaks me out."

Angela says, "I'll take care of yours," scooping the last bite of apple cobbler, adding, "Hon, did you know there are thousands of various butterflies all around the world?"

"Actually, yes. And let me guess—you've been chatting with our resident professor?" Jonathan grins.

"Yes. He's told you about—"

"At length. That boy of ours is a walking *Wikipedia*."

"But you have to love what that mind..." Angela says as her phone chirps. She picks it up and reads the screen. "Three messages? At this time of day?" A look of panic spreads across her face.

"I'm sure it's Mom. Probably got a second book deal already."

She listens to a message from the principal about Christopher. It sounds like he's in trouble. But she realizes that perhaps she needs to let Christopher handle some of this on his own, as a way to grow up some, especially in the eyes of his father.

She watches Jonathan's eyes take in the world around him and enjoys seeing the similarities in his face and her two boys'. As much as she hurts for Christopher right now, she also hurts herself. Furthermore, she knows that he will be fine. And she will be fine. So, in the spirit of letting little boys grow up, leaving them in the hands of her Heavenly Father, she takes a deep breath and tries to be in the present. She wants to learn to allow herself to watch and appreciate and cherish all that life has to offer. Now, she just has to divert Jonathan's attention, as she's sure the look of shock will garner a litany of questions. *Oh good, Dr. Long just entered the building. Saved by the bell.*

Angela says, "It's nothing. Just school. And you're right—Daphne. But it wasn't a book deal. More like a hair appointment. Wants to know if I can join her tomorrow."

Jonathan nods and looks at his watch and starts to wave for the check.

As Dr. Long and Sammy enter and look for a seat, Angela waves them over.

"Here come Jefferson and Sammy," Angela says.

"I can't stay long," he says quietly. "Gotta get back to finish interviewing new employees. I'd certainly love to stay…" he turns as they approach.

"HELLO!" Jonathan says, not missing a beat.

"Hey, Angela," Sammy says. "You're looking beautiful. Haven't seen you in the library in a long time."

Jonathan and Jefferson shake hands and Jonathan slides over, waving Jefferson to join him.

"We don't want to interrupt," Long says. "We're just slipping in for a late lunch."

"No, it's good. We were just finishing, but let's visit for a moment."

"On second thought, Jefferson," Jonathan says, scooting out of the booth, "Why don't you sit here. That way, when I go to leave, it'll be easier."

Jefferson slides in and says, "Fine," patting Angela's hand. "Long time no see, Girlfriend."

She smiles and squeezes his hand, mouthing, *Thank you*. He nods.

They're all settled as Teresa steps up to the booth. "I see your party's growing!"

 ঌ

By the time Christopher has reached home, between the sucker punch from Jeff and the ax swinging at Uncle Carter's, he is in so much pain that he can barely breathe. *Man, who knew that a couple of punches to the ribs could hurt so bad. How do boxers do it?* Going inside, he looks through the kitchen cabinets for some Tylenol. Nothing. He goes upstairs to his parents' room and looks around. The pain seems to grow with each twist or turn he makes. He rifles through their medicine cabinet, finds some Aspirin and takes a couple, scooping water in his hand from the bathroom sink. *Mom seems to be resting better with the stuff she's been taking—well, besides her 'Midnight in the Garden of Mum & Evil.'* He chuckles at the mash-up.

Walking to her side of the bed, he pulls open the top drawer to find a container of expensive hand cream, a box of Kleenex. *Standard operating procedure for a mom*, he thinks. What's with the tube of some type of lubrication? He pushes that aside. There's a copy of the *New Testament*. *Big surprise*. Some trashy romance novel. *Again, big surprise*. He's about to close the drawer when his hand lands on a small prescription bottle. *Bingo*! He takes it out, looks at the label, *Do not drive...blah, blah...Take with a meal...blah, blah...Can cause drowsiness...blah, blah*. He removes one. *This should work, right? The pain seems to have increased—Okay, maybe two.*

Back downstairs, he pours a glass of milk, downs the two pills and heads to the garage to practice an hour before facing the other music he worries to himself about.

Within twenty minutes, Christopher has passed out and lies on the old sofa—his guitar, still in his lap.

ॐ

Food has arrived for Sammy and Jefferson, and Angela sets down her cup of hot tea. The look of surprise can't hide her excitement.

"What?" Angela exclaims.

"Sure," Long offers. "Why not? It'll be fun. Besides, who wants to do the same thing for Thanksgiving year after year, right?"

"It does sound pretty wonderful, Hon," Angela says to Jonathan, beaming. "I mean, besides the fact we've never spent Thanksgiving any other way...as long as I can remember. Sailing to Florida on a boat does sound divine."

"Actually, it does. And you're sure...?" Jonathan starts to ask.

"Absolutely," Sammy says. "And my *Lady Giselle*, a very comfortable 40 foot yacht—for those keeping score at home, sleeps 6 comfortably and we'd love the company. Something completely different for Thanksgiving!"

Angela's excitement stops the moment she thinks, then looks at Jonathan and asks, "What about Mom and Dad?"

Sammy looks at Jefferson.

"There is an alternative. Weather permitting—and it is supposed to be unseasonably warm this holiday, the boys could sleep under the stars. On nice nights, we often roll out a mat and sleep in sleeping bags. It's quite nice," Jefferson suggests.

"Well, let's think about it. Check our schedules. Talk to the boys. We have several days to decide...right, Jefferson?" Jonathan asks.

"Of course. Take your time. We're going anyway, but having your family be a part of ours," Jefferson says, smiling to Sammy, "would be a bonus."

"Oh, this is an exciting idea! I could use—I think we all could use, something different," Angela beams.

Jonathan slides from the booth, picks up the tab, drops a tip on the table and says, "Well, I really must run. I'm late and have no communication with work..." He looks to Angela.

Reaching for her purse, she replies, "I'll run this to the store then drop by your office on the way to get David."

Jonathan leans over and kisses Angela on the cheek, "Thank you." Turning to Sammy and Jefferson, he adds, "And thank *you* two for the gracious offer. It sounds exciting. Gotta run."

As Jonathan leaves, Angela takes Jefferson's hand and quietly says, "You have no idea what your generous offer could mean to our family. Thank you."

Smiling, he responds, "We all need a little extra help from time to time—who better to receive it from than good friends?"

CHAPTER 32

JEFF PULLS TO the edge of the Matheson property and sits, looking around for any signs of Christopher. *That PK is such a loser*, he thinks. *Time to show him how to respect the big man on campus.* He spots Christopher's truck and slowly drives up the long driveway. He pulls the borrowed car around and faces the street, ready for a quick escape. Quietly closing the door, he goes to the house and looks in the window of the kitchen door. Nothing. He looks around back. The garage. *Probably in there practicing his choir music.* Looking in the small front window to the garage, he can only see Christopher's feet. He pushes the side door in and surprises a groggy Christopher.

"Get up on your feet, Pretty Boy," Jeff growls. "We have some unfinished business to take care of."

Even groggy, Christopher remains coy, "Profound, Wackjob."

"I'll show you wackjob, Pansy-ass," he barks, challenging Christopher to his feet.

Christopher tries to stand, but the painkillers apparently have slowed his motor skills. He hesitates, stands and sways.

"Been drinking, huh? Nice. Then maybe you won't feel this." He swings and connects to Christopher's jaw.

SMACK!

Christopher falls back on the couch, stunned by the hit. He sees stars for a second then tries to stand up. Using the weight of his body, he ducks his head and aims right for Jeff's stomach, pile-driving his body into his opponent's. This takes both boys crashing into some boxes and garden tools and to the floor. Christopher stays down longer than Jeff, who quickly stands and reaches for a garden rake. As Christopher stands, Jeff swings the rake, but Christopher ducks at just the right time, spinning around and punching Jeff in the same spot Jeff hit Christopher earlier in the day.

He hits him again, this time feeling a familiar snap. Jeff drops the rake and screams in agony.

"Doesn't feel too good, does it?"

Jeff tries to catch his breath, wrenching in pain, knowing that if he can hit Christopher in the same spot again, he'll surely break some ribs. He stands and poses to box.

"Really? You're a boxer? Funny, I took you for a badminton player," he returns, spotting a tennis racket on the shelf next to them.

As Jeff's attention is diverted, Christopher instead reaches in the opposite direction and picks up a shovel. At the same time, Jeff has grabbed the tennis racket.

Facing off, they see who has the advantage.

"You had better knock me out, Bitch. 'Cause if you don't, I'll put your head through this racket and then beat you with that shovel!" he barks.

Christopher shifts his weight toward him to make him think he's going to swing. Jeff falls for it and swings with all his might. He misses. Before he can straighten back up, Christopher pulls back and swings—aiming for his body, not his head. *I don't wanna kill the guy, just teach him a lesson*, he thinks in that instant. Jeff, trying to dodge the oncoming shovel, raises his arm in the air at the peak of Christopher's swing. The shovel blade and Jeff's arm collide.

CRACK!

Jeff wails in pain, as his forearm snaps, causing part of the broken bone to penetrate the skin. He falls on the floor, grabbing his arm and writhing in pain.

While Christopher enjoys an instant of victory, he sees the damage he has caused and rushes to help Jeff. He grabs a nearby shop towel, whips it into a tight snake and applies it to Jeff's arm.

"Get the hell away from me," he cries, tears pouring from his eyes, as blood streams down his arm.

"Dude, I'm trying to help you. Just let me. Or you'll be sorry."

Still writhing in pain, he holds his arm—not sure what to do. After a moment, he says, "Okay. But if you're playing—"

"Shut up, Jeff. I may be mad, but I'm not cruel," Christopher quietly says, adding, "unlike you."

Christopher wraps the towel around, creating a tourniquet. He grabs another towel to help with any blood.

"Shit, that hurts. If you hadn't gotten that hit, I'd probably have bashed your head in."

Christopher sees the anger in his eyes start to leave. Jeff's pride wasn't hurting nearly as much as his arm, so he thought he'd give him the space to get out now.

Christopher thinks he sees a hint of a smile, but the grimace of pain hides any hopes of one. He reaches to help Jeff to his feet, who reluctantly obliges.

"I gotta get outta here. I don't feel so good."

"Not a surprise—you've lost a fair bit of blood. You better get to a doctor."

"Yeah, right," he mutters. "First, I get nearly expelled, then before the day's out, I get my arm broken. Mom's gonna love this."

Christopher snorts, "Yeah, well *you* cracked my ribs, Jerky, and the principal says I'm one step away from being tossed. Guess we're both in shit soup."

Christopher picks up the shovel, looks around at the mess they've made and says, "Now, get the heck outta here before I decide to finish you off," lunging at Jeff for effect.

Jeff instinctively jerks, but sees Christopher is kidding and heads for the car.

Outside, Christopher asks, "Truce?"

Jeff keeps walking until he gets to the car, stops, then looks back at Christopher. He waits a long second and says, "For now, anyway."

As he tries to open the door, Christopher shouts, "Let me—"

"I GOT IT!" Jeff winces in pain as he opens the door with his opposite hand. He drives away.

Christopher watches until the car disappears. Still holding the shovel, he looks at the crooked rows of mums planted just the other night.

"Looks like we both had some gardening to do," he mumbles.

CHAPTER 33

CARTER TURNS TO RANDALL and slowly says, while trying to keep the melodrama to a minimum, "Randall, you didn't tell me...my sister...was *black*."

The three men sit on his front porch, staring at a photograph Randall holds. Carter's look of shock is rare. Reddick enjoys this, and looking over their shoulders, he breaks the uncomfortable silence by joking, "Hey, Carter, what's the big deal? It'll be cool knowing you have a *sistuh*!"

Carter cuts him a look, "Very funny."

"African American. Partly," Randall retorts.

"And when did Randall, the racist, get so evolved?" Carter snidely returns.

"Age has a way of changing things, Son."

"But this is a fairly significant detail...you failed to include."

"We didn't have that much time," he responds. "And another reason I thought it better to deliver the news...in person."

"Uh huh."

Reddick's radio squawks, "Sergeant Reddick, this is MGPD. What's your 20? Over."

"Sorry guys—have to take this."

He removes the radio from his belt and walks toward his car. "This is Reddick, HQ, I'm across town..." He trails off.

Randall puts the picture back in the file folder on his lap and, nodding toward Reddick, says, "I know he's a friend, but I wasn't sure how much info to share in front of him."

"He's my friend." He hesitates. "You can...*we* can trust him."

"Enough said." Randall looks at his watch. "I'm heading back shortly. The bird's on a timer," he adds, referring to the helicopter. "Not to mention, him," he nods towards Mr. Black who has remained quiet the entire time.

Black simply nods and says, "Your time is my time, LC."

Carter looks at both men.

"Lieutenant Colonel," Mr. Black says, showing zero emotion.

"Uh huh," Carter responds, then says to Randall, "So, ya wanna tell me how you got me out—and so quickly, now or after you finish…" he nods toward the file.

"Either," Randall says, coughing several times before adding, "Your call."

"Tell me about the mission."

Randall opens the file. Mr. Black picks up a small side table and places it in front of Randall and Carter.

"Thanks," both men say, simultaneously.

Mr. Black returns to his *post* and removes a smartphone and studies it.

Without diverting his attention, Randall answers the question racing through Carter's mind, "He's Black Ops, no pun intended, First Grade and top of his class. Second, he's checking weather patterns for the flight home. And third, he's likely texting his boyfriend."

Carter looks surprised.

"Kidding. Wife. Two boys. Lives just down the street from me. Everything else is true."

Mr. Black smirks, without lifting his eyes from the tiny screen in his hands.

"So, Hope, or rather, Shasta—" Randall starts.

"As in…?"

Randall nods. "The soft drink. She didn't like sharing the name of your mother, so she's referred to herself as Shasta as long as she's lived with us. And that's been," he stops to calculate, "12 years. She's 18. Her mother died from a drug overdose the eve of her sixth birthday. She's been under my roof ever since. Carries some of her late mother's darkness with her—depression, not skin," he half jokes, "but she's a good girl. Just…misdirected."

"And hangs in the wrong places, I see. I mean…a bar? C'mon."

Randall looks at Carter and squints. He says nothing, allowing Carter to fill in the blank.

"Your daughter…" Carter throws up his hands. "Your house. Your rules."

"You remember."

Randall pulls out three more photos.

"These are at least three of the guys we think," he nods to Mr. Black, "WE think…are part of the problem. There may be more. No ideas yet."

Carter picks up the photos and examines them closely, immediately picking up tiny details.

"One light black guy. Two white. One of the white kids likely walks with a limp. Of the two—the built one is left-handed and tattooed. The other—can't see his face as good," he mumbles, pulling the picture closer. "But that mass of hair shouldn't be hard to locate. Picture must have been taken in Florida…Georgia, maybe. Winter, or at least fall. The image of Shasta could be any girl, with that hoodie on. But I'm sure you'll share with me any specifics."

Randall sits back, looks at Mr. Black and smiles, saying, "See?"

"Got the gift," is all Mr. Black says and returns to his screen.

Carter looks from one to the other and says, "C'mon guys. Not tough. The white guy on the left has a shoe that's got a thicker sole than the other. Likely childhood illness. Without it? He's a hop-a-long. The others? The one wearing an oversized watch on his right hand? You see his left hand is on his fork, next to his plate. No utensils on the other side. Plus, he's likely done some jail time, judging from the way he guards his goods. And the tail of a tattoo on his hand—it's just a guess, but from that silly outfit, I'll bet dollars to doughnuts he has at least four—two of which will be about his *girlfriend de jour*, one will be from jail—likely, *Juvee*. And the fourth? Who knows? Maybe a headshot of his pit-bull. And the last part is the easiest. Look at the foliage in the background. Palm trees—maybe palmetto. Thinning. And the shadows are low. Probably lunchtime. It's likely cooler, what with those oversized coats, except that doesn't really mean much. I see kids wear that *costume* in the middle of July."

"Good," is all Randall says, putting the photos in the folder and returning them to his briefcase.

"Why the thought of kidnapping and not runaway, or laying low with friends, or hanging with hoodlums—as the case may be?"

Randall stands and nods toward the open field. "Let's take a walk. My legs need the stretch." Carter nods and they step off the porch and start walking.

"No, don't get up," Carter says sarcastically to Mr. Black. He doesn't.

෨

Randall and Carter walk for a couple of minutes before Randall speaks.

"Black knows everything. Well, that is, except the amount I'm going to pay you for finding Hope—I mean, Shasta."

"Okay, and why…"

Randall interrupts. "Several reasons. Let's start with…you're my son. I may or may not pay this much to a contractor—it happens to be a bonus that it's someone I can trust. Next, I'm going to pay you what they'll be asking for in ransom. The way I see it is, I'll just pay it to you. There's also the fact that…well, while she's my daughter, this could—at the end of the day, be a scam. And if it's *not* a scam, in all likelihood it could become…dangerous."

Carter starts to speak. Randall raises his hand.

"Calculated and cold? Maybe. But c'mon, you don't get where I've been and where I am by being a patsy.

I'm just saying." Randall starts to cough. There are many and they pick up speed, but then die down. Wiping his mouth with a handkerchief, he takes a deep breath then whispers, "Damn ragweed doesn't help matters."

Carter pats him gently on the back and walks along in silence a few moments before saying, "You do know...I'm not doing this for the money."

Randall nods then says with a rasp, "That's part of the reason I'm more than willing to pay you. As I said, and as much as I don't like to think about it, there's the chance you could be in danger."

Carter nods.

"Besides," Randall adds, "you're family." He chuckles, which causes him to cough and finishes, "Sorry to sound like *The Godfather*. I'm not trying to."

They enjoy the humor.

Jeff pulls into the driveway of his mom's apartment and looks around before getting out of the car. Coast is clear. He hops out and walks briskly around back, where he proceeds to unwrap his arm and toss a bloody rag into the trashcan, being sure to push it to the very bottom. When he stands, he sways momentarily—no doubt from the rush of blood to his head from bending over, either that, or the loss of blood. He lets himself in the back door, goes to the bathroom and pulls off the other rag.

"Oh, shit," he says, staring at a black and blue arm—which wasn't so bad. The nastiest part was the splinter of bone from his forearm poking through his skin. It makes him want to faint. He sits on the edge of the bathtub, trying to figure out what to do. *Should I call Dad at work and get him to come help? Mom would be furious.* He hates the thought of living under the roof with a furious mother. *I could try and push the bone back into place. Screw that. The last option? I could just puke.* He sits still, feeling worse by the moment, like he's going to pass out. *I know. I'll call Dad now, tell Mom later, and forget the part about pushing the bone into place. But first...I think I'll puke.*

And he does.

ﾑ

Carter stands in the field surrounding his house, staring at his father. He tries to imagine this moment ever happening. But it is.

"500?"

Randall nods.

"Thousand."

Randall nods again, then adds, "BUT you'll also be recovering something else that she, or *they*, stole from me in the process. It's an oversized leather passport wallet." He snorts, "Mr. Black calls it my *Man Wallet.* Anyhow, it has, or had, about fifty grand in it. In hundreds. It's an emergency fund. I call it my *Plan B*. I don't care about the money. What I care about is a little black book that's sewn into the lining. It'd be impossible for anyone but me—to know it was there. But it's *very* important."

"What are the chances of it still being around?"

"The money? Who knows? But the black book? That's another reason you're here. You're the one to find it. Along with Shasta, of course." He coughs several times— hard enough to make his eyes water. Catching his breath, he continues. "Like I said, the fifty large is nothing."

"But the book..." Carter adds.

"Is worth *five* times what I'll be paying you. Maybe more."

Carter's head whips back, looking Randall dead in the eye.

Randall just nods, "More on that later."

"Slim possibility—still being around."

"Not sure if that's a statement or a question. If they're punks like I expect, the money's gone. If they're dumb—like I'm guessing, the wallet's been tossed."

"If they're smart?" Carter asks, referring to the hidden contents.

"Well, your guess is as good as mine. Something tells me that if Shasta *is* a part of it, she will have kept it around. It also has a security card to my Key West condo, keys to a small boat I keep and... well, there's an extra couple of passports in there."

"Plan B."

He nods, looking into the distance and squints—the same way Carter does when he's chewing on a thought. Carter follows Randall's glance.

"But the price you paid to get me out of jail... "

Randall holds up a single finger, "No. Not jail. *Prison.* With your record? You were going away. For quite some time."

Silence. The air stands still, as though Mother Nature wanted to be sure an exclamation point had been made.

Carter breaks the silence with, "Back to my fee— what you paid to get me off the hook is payment enough."

Randall starts to speak, but Carter interrupts, "Wait. Am I out on bail, or—"

"Son? The pay-*off*, not pay-*ment*...took care of it ALL."

"Okay, how in the hell did you pull that off?"

Randall grins, then starts to walk again. A slight breeze picks up where it left off.

"The judge owed me a favor."

"Musta been a big one."

He nods.

"Why?"

"We were in the same battalion. Way back. When he was moving up the ladder, I was there to help pull."

"How?"

"We were good friends."

"So?"

"And he was gay."

"Oh."

"I was the right person. At the right time. Who happened to have the right hand…on the right strings."

They reach the edge of Carter's property and stop. Carter looks out over his land and then to his dad's world-weary face. He asks, "When do I start?"

Deep-set lines crinkle around Randall's eyes, as a small smile emerges. "Now."

৵

A few minutes later, the Bell helicopter is idling and ready for takeoff. Randall and Carter stand face to face just a few dozen feet from the humming behemoth. Randall looks at his son with pride and says, "I'm proud of you, Son."

Carter won't let himself show the emotion he feels. Instead he responds, "Thanks for bailing me out. And for giving me this opportunity to help."

"Don't let me down."

"I won't—trust me."

"I do," Randall says.

Randall starts towards the helicopter, then stops and adds, "Someone will be by for the car later."

Carter nods.

"And Son?"

"Yes?"

"I plan on seeing the others. Next time."

"Sounds good."

"I will. I promise you that." Randall breaks into a long series of coughs, covering his nose and mouth with a handkerchief.

Mr. Black increases the speed of the blades and the sound of the engines nearly drowns out their conversation. Sand and grass blow into Carter's eyes. He squints to avoid it.

"Safe travels! I'll be in touch!" Carter shouts.

"Roger that!" Randall replies and heads to the helicopter.

Carter looks to the emotionless Mr. Black who gives a *thumbs up* to Carter. Carter nods.

Randall boards, buckles in and gives Carter a relaxed salute. Carter returns the same. And the large red and yellow bird lifts into the air and is gone in an instant. As the trees and the field of grass return to their previous state, Carter takes a deep breath and quietly says, "Godspeed, Dad."

CHAPTER 34

ON THE DRIVE BACK from the school, Angela is excitedly chattering away about the possibility of the family doing something different for Thanksgiving and David is smiling from ear to ear, already imagining sailing the open seas and sleeping under the stars then stepping aboard some deserted island and discovering buried treasures or perhaps a new species of butterfly. His mind races.

"So, can you imagine out in the fresh air, in completely unchartered territory—well, to us, anyway, then spending several glorious days in a warm tropical paradise...not a care in the world? "Angela muses, already basking in the imaginary heat.

"That will be so flippin' cool. I can hardly wait!" David shouts with excitement.

"Yes. And here's what I'm starting to think about already—that is if God wants it to happen and wants for us to soon have a new...addition..." she pulls out the words, as she looks at David's reaction, "...to our family...in the form of...a new sister for you!"

Without missing a beat, he grabs his book bag from the floor and starts to rummage through it, looking for paperwork.

"Aha! Here it is. Mom, I've already started my inquiries into a number of different agencies..."

Angela's cell phone rings.

"... and the one I like the best—"

"Excuse me, Son. Hold that thought." She snaps her phone open. "Hello, it's Angela."

"Hello, Mrs. Matheson. This is Claire, how are you?"

"Just dandy, Claire. Thank you for asking. What can I do for you?"

"I have Jonathan waiting on the line. Can you hold just a quick second, please?"

"Sure."

Angela turns to David and whispers, "I'm holding for Daddy. Remember—our little secret…" She holds up her curled pinky finger. He curls his, interlocking it with hers and they shake.

"Hey, Babe," Jonathan's voice comes on the line.

"Hi, Sweetheart, what's up?"

"Sorry to bother you, but have you had a chance to replace—"

"Been to the store, picked it up and am about 5 minutes from your office."

He sighs, "Thanks, Love. There are some numbers I need and sadly, they're new and not recently backed up on my computer…"

"Well, the guy at the store told me that while the case of the phone was worthless, the inside…date, data card, or whatever it's called…"

"SIM Card," David whispers loudly.

She mouths *Thank you* and says, "L'il P says SIM Card."

"That's it. Perfect. Okay, see you in five. Love you!" Click.

"Love you…" She looks at the phone. "Ooookay. Now, where were we?"

"Let's see. Would that be before or after we were both decadently day-dreaming about our upcoming expedition?" David asks.

"Nicely done. Let's spend a few more moments there, shall we, Co-captain?"

David cups his left hand over his left eye, saluting with his right and saying, "Aye, aye, Matey!"

They share a laugh as they head down the highway.

≈

Nurse Symon puts the finishing touches on the setting of Jeff's cast. He gently touches the bandage that covers four stitches in his brow.

"I don't know which hurt worse—the broken arm, or the gash above my eye."

"Bet they both smart pretty good," Nurse Symon gently encourages.

"Tell you the truth, I didn't feel the cut above my eye. Didn't even see it until I got home and looked in the mirror. Think that probably helped me puke."

"Well, that's good. We all need a little help in that department from time to time," she smiles.

She is cleaning up the bandage papers and cast wrappings when he looks at her and says, "You smell pretty."

Caught off-guard, she blushes then shyly says, "Well, thank you. Uh…that's nice."

Feeling more cocky than usual, Jeff takes it up a notch by asking, "Hey, Nurse Symon, you wanna go out sometime?"

She practically drops the tray of supplies before managing the short answer of, "No."

"Why?" he asks, completely serious.

She holds up two fingers. "One? You're much too young. What are you—15? 16?"

"17," he replies.

Raising an eyebrow, she retorts, "Oh, 17? That's different." She adds, "Uh, NO. I'm 30. Much too old for you."

"But, I'm mature for my age," he says, raising one eyebrow. He winces then raises the other eyebrow that isn't stitched.

"And number two? I have a boyfriend." She stops to add, "Actually two." She smiles and leaves the room and he sighs.

He hears her rubber soles squeak, as she stops abruptly and comes back around the corner, stopping at the side of his bed. "But thanks for the compliment," she smiles. "You're cute—especially with all the hardware."

ॐ

Angela and David walk down the hallway to the church office. As soon as Jonathan opens his office door, David shouts, "Hey, Dad!"

Jonathan waves at David and smiles at Angela as a striking blonde with long, beautiful legs emerges from Jonathan's office. Angela thinks to herself, *Hey, Legs-up-to-here, stay away from the married man.* She looks for Jonathan to exit the office. He doesn't.

The woman is slender, well-shaped and has a perfect complexion. She must be 32, maybe 33. *The perfect age for making babies*, Angela thinks, feeling the *little green monster* raise its head. Heat rushes through her face and out of her control, as she thinks, *Stop it, Angela. She's probably divorced, twice, chain smokes and has an eating disorder.*

Jonathan comes out from his office and greets Angela with a kiss on the cheek. *On the cheek? Hey, we're married here*, she shouts in her head then whispers, "Hello, Love."

"Hey, Babe," Jonathan returns, turning to introduce Angela.

"I'd like you to meet Donna Willamette, our new music director. Donna just moved here recently from Charleston."

The room shifts into slow motion as the unusually striking, ridiculously tall and impeccably-dressed, blue-eyed goddess extends her meticulously manicured hand and says, "Hello. It's a pleasure to meet you, Mrs. Matheson. I've heard such lovely things about you."

Angela nods, thinking, *Who gives a crap where you're from, you mess with my husband and I'll claw your eyes out!* She sweetly replies, "Please, call me Angela, and how nice of my loving husband to say such nice things. I'm sure they're all true." *Did I hit husband a bit too hard?*

"Nice to meet you, Darlene."

"Donna," she corrects gently.

"Silly me. My mind's all aflutter with some recent good news. I apologize. Donna, of course."

Jonathan is oblivious to the electricity in the air and says, "Donna is replacing Geoffrey, who you'll recall is going to the mission field in Nairobi, Kenya."

Angela nods, *How about Beauty Pageant here buy a one-way ticket to Stay The Heck Away From My Husband, Kenya...* "Nice. Welcome aboard," she says.

Angela notices Donna place her hand on Jonathan's arm and coo, "Thanks for all the time today, Pastor Matheson. I'm anxious to be onboard. There's plenty to do to get me started. Gotta run. Nice to meet you, Angela."

Angela tunes out again and thinks she heard, *"Thanks for our playtime today, Pastor Make-Me-A-Son. I'm anxious to climb aboard and let's get the party started. Gotta run around nice little Angela."*

Angela stares blankly as Donna looks from Angela to Jonathan, smiles, then leaves. Jonathan watches her walk away, then turns and asks, "Angela?"

"Huh? Oh, sorry," Angela snaps back. "These...I mean...my head, uh...sorry, Babe, what was it you were saying?"

"Come on, you two. I want to show you something," he says as he starts down the hall. "It's the model of the new Family Center. I'll pull it out of the conference room. It's nice, you'll see."

Absently reaching for David's hand, she thinks she heard Jonathan shout, *C'mon you two. I wanna show you I'm the family sinner. I'll pull it out for you to see!*

She stares at Jonathan like he's wearing no pants.

David tugs on her hand. She looks at David, who has the strangest look on his face. "You okay, Mom?" he asks.

"Yes, Love-bug. Why?"

David looks around like he doesn't want anyone to hear, then says, "You have an awfully funny look on your face."

"Really? Like what?"

"Kinda like when Uncle Carter's had too many adult drinks."

I could use a drink about now—if I drank! Angela's head screams. "I'm okay, Son." She clears her throat. "Now, let's go look at your dad's thingie. I mean, the Family Center model."

CHAPTER 35

TERESA HAS RUSHED AROUND the apartment like a mini tornado and is now tinkling in the last few minutes before Carter arrives. She runs a quick checklist through her head. Pork chops marinating in the fridge. Check. Grill ready to rock. Check. Cold beers on ice. Check. Big salad. Boring, but nice. Check. Twice-baked potatoes with tomatoes, bacon and mushrooms—as a way to appease his *old habits die hard* sensibility. Check.

There's a knock on the door. She checks the clock on the wall and mutters to herself, smiling, "Right on time. Big surprise."

She wipes. Flushes. Washes. Primps. Fluffs. Blots. Breathes. Leaves.

æ

Peeking through the lacy front door curtain, she watches her date survey the building and small front yard. Carter stands at the door—a simple bouquet of flowers in hand. He looks off into the distance. She glances at the clock on the mantle: 7:02. She'd kept him waiting two minutes while she took care of nature. Why was she so nervous? No idea. *Just go with it,* she encourages herself. *Life is short. So you screwed up once before—just don't do it twice.*

She watches him for a second, knowing that these first few dates set the tone for what the rest of the time will be. She likes his mysterious eyes. They are always scanning. For what? She has no idea. They're always staring. At her? She likes that a lot. And the way they laugh together, about anything at all. That is the very best thing. She likes him. And she doesn't want anything to get in the way of that.

She opens the door, as though she had just run up and opened it.

"Hey, there, Sexy Man. Right on time, as you said."

He looks at her. He completely looks at her—not from head to toe, that would be so expected. But he looks into her eyes—into HER. And she feels a jittery buzz roll through her like a wave coming off the ocean and crashing on the beach.

"You look...great!"

And that...is enough.

"Come on in to the humble hacienda."

She looks at the flowers he holds like a high school sweetheart at his very first prom. Her heart melts, but she certainly won't let him see that. It may ruin everything.

"Nice flowers, Carter. Thank you." She gently takes them, allowing her hand to linger on his for a moment or two.

What he hears is, *Thank you for caring enough to stop what you were doing, take a few seconds to go into your backyard and pull together some of nature's finest.*

"You're welcome." He smiles.

"Okay, enough of the hokey-pokey, romantic stuff. Come in and pour us a tiny little..." her hands simulate a very large glass, "...drink and let's have it on the back deck."

"Sounds good."

He follows her through the apartment as she plays tour guide.

"This is my living room," then into the kitchen, "and this is the kitchen."

He's pleasantly surprised. For all the wise-cracking, smart-mouthed, hard-as-nails exterior, Teresa has created a very soothing, peaceful and more than expected feminine oasis for them to enjoy. There are candles everywhere and Christmas tree lights woven through some less-than-hearty indoor trees. She leads them out onto a back deck and spreads her arms like *Vanna White,* displaying a large, handsome grill, smoking hot and ready to go.

"This is the mother ship."

"Impressive."

"Oh yeah." She sticks her chest out proudly. "That, Mr. Carter, is a 5,000 BTU man-sized, Made In The USA, Weber Grill."

He stands there, speechless for a moment then adds, "Barbeque Mecca."

She smiles. "Yep, I only had one thought when buying a grill, *Go Big, Or Go Home.*"

Carter drops to one knee, takes her hand, looks into her eyes, clears his throat and says playfully, "Will you be… my grill master?"

She bursts out laughing, nearly knocking over the bucket of ice that's chilling the beers and responds, "Abso-freakin'-lutely!"

She smells the air, as though something is burning—because it is.

"Dangit! I was trying my hand at some homemade biscuits and I think they're burning!" She darts from the deck and into the kitchen, shouting as she goes, "Make yourself at home!"

He reaches into the cooler, grabs a beer, then finds his way to an oversized beanbag chair in her living room— a remnant, no doubt from the '70s, and takes a long pull on a cold beer.

ॐ

Jonathan and David look at one another with pained looks as they fight the noodles with their chopsticks, while Angela adeptly maneuvers even a simple grain of rice with ease.

"Um, I love Chinese food. It's a nice change, isn't it?" she asks the two.

"Uh huh," Jonathan says, dropping a pile of noodles he had finally managed to pick up.

"Yes, Ma'am," David unenthusiastically responds, having only slightly more success dishing the noodles than his dad.

Jonathan finally goes to a drawer, pulls out two forks and places one next to David and one next to his own plate. He smiles at David and they both proceed to devour the food.

Christopher comes in from the backyard looking like he'd been asleep for days. The three stare at him with surprised looks on their faces.

"What?" Christopher asks through sleepy, glazed-over eyes.

"Nice jammies, Dude," David snickers between bites.

"Christopher, what are you doing outside in…those?" Angela asks.

"Don't you think they're a little…small, Son?" Jonathan asks, trying not to bust out laughing.

Angela looks at him, cocks her head to the side and says, "They are cute. Well, were cute…when you were David's age."

Oblivious to what they're saying, he looks down to see that he is wearing half of his old Spiderman pajamas and a t-shirt that is entirely too small.

"Practicing my guitar," Christopher replies, in half-speed. "What the—" he looks at them, back to the outfit and back to them, scratching his head. He walks to the counter, stops and asks, "Where's the coffee?"

"Son, it's dinner time. Are you okay?" Jonathan asks.

Angela gets up and reaches for a plate. "Here son. You must have fallen asleep. Wait…you never nap during the day. Are you all right?" she asks, reaching to feel his forehead.

"I feel…really…weird. And my side hurts like a—" He stops. "Well, it really hurts," he continues, lifting up his shirt.

Angela gasps. "Oh my heavens," she shouts, bending over to look at his side.

Jonathan jumps from the table, "Christopher! What happened?"

David sits staring, "Wow…"

Christopher stands there, completely bewildered as to why he's wearing his childhood jammies, wanting breakfast but smelling dinner and wondering why he feels like he's inside a huge vat of Jell-O. He hears everything, but it's muffled. His body tingles like it's been shocked. His mouth is dry, and his side feels like it's on fire.

Jonathan helps him to a chair and slowly sits him down, saying, "Son, I've seen this before. It looks like you have some broken ribs."

"I think," Christopher says slowly, "my ribs are broken. And I don't feel so good."

"He may be in shock," David adds.

Jonathan nods and replies, "You may be right, Son." He examines all around the side of Christopher and adds, "From this amount of bruising, I'd say several are, at the very least cracked. We've got to get you to the doctor."

Wasting no time, Angela dials the phone.

"Hello, this is Angela Matheson, Christopher and David's mother. I'm sure Dr. Vaden is gone for the day, but is it possible for us to bring one of our boys in for an X-ray? Yes, it's an emergency. Understood. We'll be there right away. Thank you."

Hanging up, she kicks into *Mom Mode* and heads for her purse and car keys.

Jonathan takes her by the arm and asks, "Honey, need some help?"

"Oh, sorry. Of course. Just called Vaden's office. Closed. The answering service suggested the ER. I think we should get X-rays right away."

"Agreed," he says, turning to David and saying, "Son, please put the food away while I help Christopher get changed. Then, all four of us will head to the ER, okay?"

"Sure thing, Dad."

David begins clearing the table, Jonathan helps Christopher up the stairs and Angela makes another call.

"I'm going to call Mother and let her know what's up," Angela calls out to Jonathan.

From upstairs, he shouts, "Good idea!"

"Hey Chris, why not wear your Batman jammies, instead?" David shouts to his brother, waiting for a reply. He counts three beats then hears Christopher shout in return, "Very funny, Little Man!"

෨

Hotel California plays softly on the stereo in the other room, as Teresa pours Carter another cup of coffee.

"Different having me serve you coffee…in my home."

He smiles, "Much nicer, I'll admit."

"Also, much better wearing this," she looks at her blouse, "than that polyester death trap called a uniform." She laughs.

"And so much more…revealing," he bounces an eyebrow.

"You like?"

"You think?"

She smiles, removing the dishes from the dining room table where they have been talking. He starts to get up to help.

"No, no. Just sit there and relax. I'm just going to get them out of your face. Old habits die hard. Besides, I'm not going to wash them, just move them."

Carter couldn't help but notice the phrase she just used—the one about habits. And now, for whatever reason, he wasn't sure if he said it first, or if she did. It seemed like just another example of their *fit* coming together so nicely.

"Dinner was really good. Your pork chops are as good as I've ever eaten."

"Thanks!" she shouts from the other room. "Learned that from my mom. Her secret was the frying pan." She returns to the dining room. "Mine, as you can see, is the grill."

"Love the grill. You could cook the bottom of my boot on that grill and it'd taste good."

She looks at his boot and says, "Somehow I doubt that." She starts to reach for the boot, and adds, "but I could certainly give it a shot, if you like." She laughs.

He takes her hand and pulls her toward him. She twirls and lands in his lap.

They kiss for a long few moments.

Just then, the front door closes.

She whispers, "My son."

He nods.

She takes his face in her hands and kisses him again.

Someone clears their throat from across the room.

They both look up.

Carter has a look of shock.

Embarrassed, Teresa says, "Son, that's rude. Now, come and meet—"

"Carter?" Jeff nearly shouts.

"Jeff?" Carter replies.

ॐ

Christopher stares at the fluorescent lights overhead; their buzz is nearly trance-like. Angela and Jonathan stand across the room looking at X-rays of Christopher's rib cage. Dr. Peters points to the ribs, explaining, "You see here, here and here?"

They both nod.

He continues, "These darker sections represent cracks. As you'll see, the three ribs along the back side of his rib cage are fractured." He moves to another X-ray, continuing, "And here and here, these two along the front are severely bruised."

They look at one another. "And?" Jonathan asks. "What should we…he…do?"

"You should just take him home, immobilize him for at least a few days. After that, he'll likely heal pretty quickly. He's young, in good shape, and all his vitals tell me he's A-OK. Well, except…"

Angela interrupts, "So, there's no internal damage besides the ribs themselves?"

"Correct. But as I was about to say, he does show traces of a drug in his system. We ran blood tests—just as a precaution, and there seems to be something, rather strong, in his system."

They look at one another in shock.

"That would explain his odd behavior," Jonathan says quietly and Angela nods.

Jonathan asks, "You mean…*drug* drugs? Or—"

"No, not…" shaking his head, then clarifies, "Prescription drugs."

Angela starts to get angry, "How in the world?" She stops, deep in thought.

"What?" Jonathan asks.

"Doctor, can we step outside a moment?" she asks.

Teresa stands across the room, her arms crossed. The mood of the evening has completely changed in just the past few minutes. Carter is still sitting in his chair. Jeff sits across the table.

"You threatened my SON?" she asks, on the brink of a shout.

"Not at all. I simply gave him and his pal a strong suggestion that they take their attitudes out the door."

"Carter, you're more than…three times his age."

"Teresa? Again, I simply spoke authoritatively and did not hurt him in any way, shape or form." He turns and looks directly at Jeff.

"Is this correct, Son?"

He looks at Carter, trying to decide if he will bury him. He thinks better of it, given the fact that he's in his own mess, with no idea how it will turn out. Simpler is better, he decides.

"Yes," he mumbles.

"Then, how in the world did you get your arm broken?"

"Christopher," Jeff says quietly.

"Who?" Teresa asks.

Jeff nods at Carter and says, "His nephew, Christopher."

She slaps her forehead with both hands and says, "Matheson? The pastor's son?"

Carter looks at her and says, "Yeah, my—"

"Oh—"

"Brother," they simultaneously say.

࿚

The Matheson house is dark and quiet. Christopher and David are in bed. All the lights in the house are off except Jonathan's bedside lamp. Angela and Jonathan lie in bed.

"Baby?" Jonathan asks.

"Yes?" Angela softly responds.

"Asleep yet?

"Not yet."

"You do know that I understand your pain, right?" he asks, sweetly.

"Yes, I do."

"And you know that I appreciate everything you do?"

"Yes."

"And while I agree that we all need...a little help...from time to time, we—you and I, have to be careful."

"Agreed."

"Certain things...like prescription drugs...in the wrong hands—"

"I know."

After a long silence, Angela says, "I'm so very sorry."

"I know."

"I've tried to be so strong…for so long."

"And you've done a terrific job."

"But I wanted…her. For so…very long," she softly weeps.

"Me too."

He takes her hand in his and gently squeezes it.

Wiping away tears, she quietly says, "I'm working on getting better."

"And you're doing a great job. But you have to be careful."

"I know. Thank you for understanding."

"It takes time. I get it. Just…be smart."

"I will. I am. Thank you."

Several moments pass then Jonathan raises his arm and says, "Come over here."

She slides over, laying her head on his chest and wrapping an arm around his waist.

He pulls her close, squeezing her tightly.

"That better?" he asks.

"Much."

He kisses her soft cheek and whispers, "I love you."

"I love you, Sweetheart."

He reaches over and turns off the light.

⁊

Teresa and Carter sit on the living room couch, a cushion apart. They stare straight ahead.

"Life's just *full* of surprises, isn't it?" Teresa asks.

"Uh huh."

There's a long silence before he adds, "Not big on surprises. Except Christmas and…"

"Birthdays," they say, simultaneously.

They look at one another. Her stern look slowly morphs into a smirk. "We gotta stop."

"What?" he asks.

"Doing that."

"Doing what?"

"That."

"Why?"

"Not sure. Actually."

Several moments pass before Carter shifts in his seat and finally asks, "Teresa?"

"Yeah, Carter."

"Wanna make out some more?"

"Thought you'd never ask."

CHAPTER 36

THE NEXT MORNING, CARTER is up earlier than
normal. He stands on the front porch watching the sun
come up. He loves the early morning. The start of each new
day is like a clean slate. Fall was arriving quite a bit later
than usual. Nonetheless, this morning, there was a cool nip
in the air. As he stares across his land, he sees the first
colors of fall starting to creep into the very tips of the trees.
Samson happily chews on a stick at Carter's feet.

He's glad that he didn't spend the night with
Teresa. *Too soon*, he thinks to himself. *If it's right, there
will be plenty of time.* He is certainly taken with her, and
she with him. That's more than obvious.

His smartphone rings. He's still trying to get used
to having one. *Did okay without it for so long,* he thinks,
walking inside and pulling it from his coat pocket.

"Hello."

"Morning, Carter. Reddick. But then you probably
saw that on your screen."

"Huh?" Carter looks. "Oh yeah, there you are."

"Sorry to bother you so early, but I know you start
sooner than most and besides, I got some news you'll likely
want to hear."

"I'm all ears."

"Well, I was more than a little surprised when our
good pal, Bobby Durkin, didn't cause much of a stir after
you got let out."

"Uh huh."

"What with the fact that he had you on a trifecta."

"Go on."

"So, I've been keeping an eye on him, just like you
asked. And wondering, as I did before, why he had it so
bad for you."

"And?"

"Two things. First, that clown has practically worn the chief out with questions of how you got released so quickly—how you avoided all *three* violations, all of which carried stiff fines and sentences by themselves. But then my favorite…" He starts to laugh.

Smiling, Carter asks, "What?"

"I heard him actually say to Mahler, 'But Carter got out without even leaving a trail!'"

They both bust out laughing.

"That's got to burn him up."

"You have no idea," Reddick says. "He's just steaming…and taking it out on everyone. What a horse's ass."

"What was the second thing?"

Reddick isn't laughing now.

"Well, that's the part you are *not* going to believe."

෨

Stephan DeAngelo sits very straight in his chair. He appears in complete control. His thick dark hair and bright green eyes alongside his tanned, chiseled good looks and attractive tone of voice shine bright for all to see. They also are a very real distraction for any woman who comes within a hundred feet of him.

Must be nice. But underneath, Long thinks to himself, *there lies so much pain, so much hurt and likely a fair amount of deception. So much work to do.*

"Thank you for agreeing to see me so early. This new job requires so much of my time. If I don't start my day very early, then by the end of it, I have so little time."

"Of course. That's what I'm here for," Long says gently.

"And if I have little time, then I can share so little of it with my daughter. And that is of utmost importance," Stephan continues, looking at his perfectly polished and expensive Italian loafers.

"I understand," Long says.

"My Janabelle is my world. Just everything to me."

Long smiles.

"Do you have children?"

Long hears that so often—a way to bond with their doctor. He shakes his head, knowing his patients will move to the next statement or question without a moment's hesitation.

"That is so sad. I cannot imagine a man of your compassion and love of other people…would not want to share in this beautiful gift of children. They are such a wonder to watch."

Long smiles.

"Dr. Long, why wouldn't you have married? And before you answer, I realize this is my session and it's all about me, but I'm trying to understand the man in front of me. I want to know if I can trust this man. I want to know if I can share my innermost self with a man that should have these things in his life."

Long is touched, but impatient. *But you don't really care. I mean you do, but this is my job. You're nice. We need to move on,* Long thinks to himself.

"Perhaps I have pushed too far," Stephan says, looking down at his hands. "Please accept my apologies."

Long reaches across his desk and slowly turns the framed picture around to face Stephan.

"These were my loves, daughter and wife. They were killed in an automobile crash several years ago."

Stephan is genuinely moved. A tear comes to his eye.

"It was an accident, of sorts. Drunk driver."

Stephan just stares at the photograph. The sadness hangs on his face like a shroud—a completely different look than just moments ago when he spoke of his daughter.

Then, slowly, a smile begins to spread across his face and the wrinkle between his thick eyebrows flattens.

His face is light again. And happy.

"Now, I see," he says, shaking his head. "The happiness was there. So the thing we both know…is that you experienced this sort of happiness, the gift of unconditional love…before."

Long slowly smiles, having just received a lovely gift from a stranger. And new friend.

"Thank you," Dr. Long softly says.

Stephan nods then slowly turns the picture frame around to face Long. He wipes a tear from the corner of his eye and smiles.

Stephan pats the top of the frame ever so gently and whispers, "They still love you."

❧

Carter walks back outside. From the sound of Reddick's voice, he has a strange feeling he's going to need some air.

"Okay, when I heard this, I almost freaked," Reddick says with the most intensity Carter's heard from him in a long time.

"Wait. This is going to be better than hearing how our over-hyped, steroid-riddled ass-wipe can't figure out how his *Number One, Prime Suspect, Good Old Boy* got out of some trumped up charges?"

"Better."

"Oh boy," Carter grunts.

"The only thing that bothers me about this is how it affects my friend."

"Who?"

"You."

"Okay, now you're officially killing me. Let's have it!"

"Your new girlfriend?" Reddick baits for effect.

"Not yet, actually, but go ahead."

"The one who, according to what you told me, was married and then divorced soon thereafter?"

"Uh huh."

Carter waits for the quarter to drop. His sharp, attentive eyes dart back and forth, as his mind races, trying to figure out where this is going.

Then it clicks.

"No! Way!" Carter exclaims.

"Yup."

"NO!"

"YES!"

"Please, for the love of God and everything holy, tell me you're kidding."

"Sorry. But true," Reddick says quietly.

"You are...I am so..." Carter takes a deep breath, starts to lay down his phone, but not before saying, "Hold on. Be right back."

He lays the phone down, steps off the porch and walks around to his woodpile. Picking up a piece of old, hard hickory, he places it on the chopping stump.

He proceeds to chop it into big slabs, firing away at the innocent wood in a controlled rage. They become smaller chunks. He continues to batter them into smaller pieces. He does this until he can practically make a box of toothpicks from the remaining splinters.

Then, after taking a big, long breather, he slams the axe back into its resting place, brushes his shirt of wood fragments, wipes his sweaty palms on his jeans and returns to the conversation.

After taking a deep breath, he picks up the phone and calmly asks, "Wanna grab a cup of coffee?"

Reddick says, "See ya at the diner in 20."

Carter hangs up, tosses the cold coffee from his mug, whistles for Samson to go into the house, slips his phone into his jacket, picks up his keys and drives down the dusty drive.

"What a way to start the day," Carter says to himself.

CHAPTER 37

ANGELA STICKS HER HEAD in the door of Christopher's bedroom. He lies propped up on several pillows, reading a music magazine. Her mind flashes back to when he was just a boy. He had a single snare drum and one cymbal, because that was all they could really afford. But to him, you'd think it was an entire kit. He beat on that drum and smacked that cymbal with all the fury of a professional. Here he was a decade later, with genuine talent. And she was so proud.

"You feeling okay, Sweetheart?" Angela asks.

"I've felt better," Christopher softly says.

"Anything I can get you?"

"Are you going out?"

"Yes. Run some errands and such, but I won't be gone long."

Christopher tries to sit up. That won't work. He grunts in pain. Angela comes in the room and tries to assist.

"What do you need, Baby?"

"Just need to adjust these pillows. Lift this, would you, Mom?"

She lifts the pillow and places it so he's more comfortable. "There."

"Anything else?"

He pats the bed for her to sit. "Just want to chat for one minute."

"Sure." She sits. "What's on your mind?"

He lays the magazine atop a stack on the nightstand next to his bed.

"Just wanted to see how you were doing." He hesitates. "You know, since your late night *outing*. The one with the mums." He chuckles.

Smiling, she says, "Well, they haven't gotten any straighter," she laughs, "and they're not really growing any faster."

"You know what I mean," he says.

She smiles, looking down at her hands, ponders for a moment and then says, "I did something pretty silly, Christopher. I...mixed some prescription drugs that I shouldn't have. Thus, my after-hours gardening."

"Were they something that made you feel really sleepy, like you were as heavy as lead?"

"Actually, yes," she nods.

"And they made you do silly things that you were later told you did but you don't have any recollection of having done?"

She looks puzzled and says, "What?"

"Kinda like when I showed up to dinner in my...Spiderman PJs?"

She laughs. "Yes, that was quite funny. Do you remember the last time you wore those—before yesterday?"

"I'm thinking about David's age, maybe a bit younger."

"Exactly."

He gets more serious and says, "Mom. I have *no* recollection of having done that—"

"But you just said—"

"No. David told me about it this morning. He came in here laughing and told me what I did."

Angela frowns, starts to say something then asks, "Well, what do you remember from last night?"

"That's just it, Mom. I remember going to school yesterday. Getting in a fight with Peter and Jeff. Talking to the principal. Coming home...and that's about it."

"But, your ribs are broken."

He nods slowly. "Yup. I know that."

She tries to piece it together and asks, "But you're pretty sure, and I know this sounds silly, but your ribs were hurt—"

"During the fight, yes."

"I'm still confused. Wait, tell me something, Son. Why did you come into the kitchen, from the backyard, in your PJs?"

"I don't remember doing that, Mom. David told me that's what I did." He rubs his head then says, "I'm confused."

Just then, it hits her.

She straightens up, looks him in the eyes and asks, "Christopher, answer me this—it's no big deal either way, did you go into my medicine cabinet and borrow any prescriptions I have?"

He just sits there staring at the foot of the bed, cocks his head to one side and then the other.

"Wait. I do remember seeing some tube of something that wasn't your ordinary hand-cream and some paperback like you see in truck stops."

She is shocked and embarrassed.

"Oooookay. I got it. You were in my nightstand?"

He looks scared, like he's being attacked.

"Sorry. You're right. No worries about that, but that is what you did, right?"

He nods.

"THOSE are the SAME drugs—prescriptions, I was taking and they just make your short term memory....poof!" Angela says, adding hand gestures for added effect.

"Aaahhh...that explains a lot."

"They can be dangerous, and/or put you in dangerous situations, okay? You don't want to take any more of those, Son. Trust me."

Nodding, he says, "Except they do make everything move in slow motion."

"Yes, they do. But we really need to experience life in normal motion, Son. Dr. Long reminds me of that all the time. And your father would say it's good to be in the moment and see the goodness God can do."

She looks at her watch. "Which reminds me…I have to go. I'm due at Dr. Long's in a very little bit and your father is running David to school for me."

She stands to leave, leans over and kisses him on the top of his head and says, "If there is anything you need, you just call my cell. Okay, Lovebug?"

"Yup. Sounds good. Thank you."

She is just about to close the door when Christopher says, "Mom?"

"Yes, Son."

"PLEASE tell me that nobody took any pictures of me in the Superman jams. I'd really hate for it to end up on Facebook."

She keeps a straight face as she replies, "David did. He thought you wouldn't mind."

"What?"

She laughs. "No, he didn't and it's all okay. Our little secret."

≈

Outside by their cars, Jonathan and Angela share a moment before starting the day. She smiles at David who is buckling himself in the passenger seat of Jonathan's Escalade.

"Smart boy, Son. Daddy will run you to school in just a minute," she says loud enough for him to hear through the glass.

"Okay, Mom," David responds, with a quizzical look on his face.

She adjusts Jonathan's tie and says, "Hon, you were right."

"About what?" he asks, wiping a tiny smudge of lipstick from her face.

"Thanks. About the reason Chris was acting so strange—the pajamas and not really feeling as much pain as he should have been feeling with that much damage."

Nodding, he says, "Your nightstand, right?"

Somewhat embarrassed, she replies, "Yes. But we just had a little talk and I think we're on the same page. Thank you for suggesting that I handle it. You were right."

He smiles and kisses her, "Not saying it to be right. Just saying it because I care. And I think if he sees that you don't think it's a good idea—"

"Absolutely."

He picks up his briefcase and starts to leave.

"By the way, Love?" she says.

"Yes, Babe?" he says turning around and smiling.

"Thanks for taking the professor to kindergarten today. I'm meeting with Dr. Long, running some errands and then I'll be back to tend after *His Majesty*."

"Of course," he chuckles, not even trying to hide a look of complete confusion. "But somehow, I think David's moved passed that stage. Shoot, he'll be in *college* soon enough."

Lost in her own world, she misses the reference, shrugs it off and blows a kiss to David. He catches it and blows it back. She mouths, *I love you*, and waves them off.

Jonathan and David are two miles down the road before Jonathan lets go of what Angela said about David and kindergarten. *Stress. That's all it is. She knew that, right?* he thinks, smiling at his son who stares out the window, watching the world whiz past.

&

Carter arrives at the diner ahead of Reddick, grabs his favorite booth and distracts himself by reading the local paper. He didn't buy newspapers, and he didn't buy this one—he just snagged a copy left behind from the table next to him. His thinking was, *If I need to know something, I'll know it. Most local news is all the same: taxes up, crime down, politicians in, bad guys out. A fender-bender here, a break-in there. Cat in a tree, fugitive on the lam, 20% less at this store, 20% more on that bill—and so it goes.*

Reddick arrives. Carter tosses the paper aside. He sips OJ while nodding at a waitress across the room, gesturing *two coffees*. A nod and a smile and they're on their way.

"Hey, Bro," Reddick says as he sits, removing his cap.

"Hello, Officer," he says in a deadpan tone. "Top of the morning to you."

"Yeah, sorry about starting your day that way."

"No. Like I said—rather hear it from you…" Carter trails off.

The waitress arrives. It's not Teresa. Shorter and less funny. She sets down the two coffees and two menus, adding, "I'll be back in a jiff, Gents."

"Where's Teresa?" Reddick asks.

"At home. Took the day off to stay with *monster*. Guess she thinks either he'll get into more trouble if left alone—most likely, or maybe she can keep him from breaking something else. Me? Don't get it. Let the kid sit on the couch and stuff his face with Twinkies and play video games until he goes blind. Doesn't seem like much of a winner in my book, anyhow."

Reddick looks at him and nods.

"I'm just saying."

Reddick looks around, expecting his creamer—like Teresa delivers, by hand. No such luck from *Ms. Personality Plus*, so he turns around, spots a bowl in the next booth and confiscates it. He rips open two Half & Half packets, two sugars and stirs confidently.

"Y'all set there, Killer?" Carter asks, smirking at Reddick's precise preparation.

"Huh? Yeah. All good," he says, spinning around the menu. He asks, "You eaten yet?"

Carter shakes his head, sipping his coffee. "I'm good."

The waitress reappears and asks for the order.

Reddick says, "Two eggs over easy—runny, but not too runny. 6 slices of bacon—extra crisp. Rye toast—

lightly toasted, no butter. And a side of grits—extra hot, no cheese."

She is still scribbling when Carter saves her the trouble and says, "I'm good." He then turns his attention to his booth-mate.

Reddick looks at him like, *What?*

"Well, *Meg Ryan*, now that you've got that under control—"

"Oh, save it. You're just pissed 'cause your new gal pal happens to be the former Mrs. Bobby Durkin."

Carter sits there for a very long moment, staring at Reddick without a single expression.

Reddick sips his coffee. Then, Carter lets the next cat out of the bag.

"Want to take it…one better?"

Reddick stops sipping and slowly sets his cup down, adding, "No. You can't top that one."

Carter nods.

Reddick shakes his head.

Carter nods. "Wanna know how?"

Reddick squints before nodding.

"My *gal pal*, as you so aptly put it, not only was married to the biggest phlegm ball—but their offspring? Just happens to be…" He looks at Reddick, waiting patiently then continues, "the PUNK that's been hassling Christopher. The one I nearly punched out the other day—sitting in this very booth. The snail slime that just broke my nephews RIBS in four placcs."

Reddick is not happy. He slowly shakes his head from side to side, getting redder in the face by the minute. His nostrils flair and his eyes become beads.

Before Carter will let him explode, he leans over and quietly says, "That, my friend, is exactly how I felt 30 minutes ago."

"Not acceptable," Reddick murmurs.

"So, before I head out on my mission, wanna join me in a little game of payback?"

Reddick snorts, "I'm all in."

CHAPTER 38

BEING FLAT ON HIS back for two days has given Christopher a chance to think about some things—things like, *How am I going to finish school with the kind of grades I need in order to graduate and get out of this town, move to New York or LA and really give this music career a good chance at happening...will Kym and I ever get back together—maybe after she gets off her high horse, like everyone else at school and just realize that the main focus of a group is the lead voice...will Mom ever get over losing her only daughter and will she keep taking those prescriptions—if she does, she may do something sillier, or more dangerous, than planting mums...what will David do in this big house when I leave after graduation—especially with no more siblings to hang out with and teach stuff to...do you think Dad really believes everything he preaches about—I mean, some of it is so far-fetched...what would have happened if that teacher didn't show up in the parking lot—would Jeff and Peter have killed me...they're not that mad with me, are they...what happened to the rest of the afternoon—like why do I remember just little bits and pieces of a second fight with Jeff, and the pajamas— how crazy random was that?*

The phone rings and he jumps. The sudden move causes a shooting pain through his side.

Ring.

He catches his breath and gingerly reaches over and grabs his cell phone.

Ring.

He grimaces from the pain, "Hello?" he squeaks out.

"Hey, Dude, it's me. How ya feeling?" James asks.

"Oh, hey, Choppers. Not too bad."

Christopher and his pals have called James *Choppers* for as long as he can remember. James had been blessed with a perfect smile. That, and his teeth appeared nearly disproportionate to his head. Chicks thought it was handsome. Guys found him goofy. Enemies called him *Chicklets,* because his teeth looked like gum pieces.

"Heard about the fight. Wicked, Dude."

"Yeah, wicked painful, not wicked cool."

"Heard that. Anything broken?" James asks.

"Yeah, like four or five ribs. Some are cracked, but maybe only one or two are actually broken. Not as bad as you might think. But the bruising? It's freakish."

"I bet," James replies.

Christopher and James had been best friends since high school, so the fact that they had fallen out of touch made Christopher sad.

James continued, "You gotta know that guy's trouble, Dude."

"Guy? There were two of them."

"Oh, my bad. I thought it was that kid Jeff."

"Uh, it was Jeff. AND Peter Vaughan."

"Peter? He's just a lot of noise, isn't he?"

"Mostly. But I'll tell you something—his foot to my rib cage made a lot of painful noise."

James chuckles then says, "Yeah, but that Jeff cat? Bad news. New kid in school and a bad home life, I hear. His dad's a cop and not a very nice one."

"Wow, looks like you've done your homework," Christopher cracks.

"Nah. Just listen is all. And just trying…to look out for you."

Christopher would like to believe that, but it rings untrue to him, especially given it'd been months since James called the house.

"Dude? You still there?" James asks.

"Yeah, Chops. Still here. Just in pain."

"Well, I don't want to keep you—"

"No, that's cool," Christopher interrupts. "I got plenty of time. Gonna be pretty much laying right here until we leave for Thanksgiving."

"Huh? You're not gonna be around for Turkey Day? That'll be like the first...ever!"

The two of them played tag football with the neighborhood kids every Thanksgiving, just like clockwork. This year will be different.

"True. But we got invited with my mom's do—, I mean my mom and dad's friends to go on their boat to Florida. Sweet, huh?"

"Very cool, Bro. Should be nice. We're pretty much doing what we always do."

"Eat too much food. Watch too much football. Take long naps."

"You got it!" Choppers laughs. "Well, I gotta run. Heading to class. Thought I'd just check in on you."

"No, I get it. Thanks for calling. Nice to hear from you. And we should get together sometime. Been too long."

"Yeah, since...like last fall, or sometime..." he trails off.

"That's right. Not long after the band competition. We should've stayed in better touch. We're too good of friends to let something silly like that get in the way."

After an uncomfortable pause, James finishes, "Yeah, let's do that. Okay, feel better. And see you around."

"Yeah, Chops. Thanks. Be cool in school, Fool."

He laughs. "Let it ride."

Click.

Christopher lays there for a few minutes, pondering what that was all about. *Why did he call? Just to get caught up? Did he really care? If he did, he would have called before now. Course, I could have called before now, too. What are those cats up to anyhow? Wonder if THEY will ever become something...like I will. Maybe we should play some more together. Wonder how Kym's doing. Betchya she's seeing somebody. Don't want to think about that. I'm hungry.*

ॐ

Angela pulls in the parking lot of Dr. Long's office complex, finds a place to park near the back and sits there several moments. She takes a pill container from her purse and washes one down with water from a bottle. Taking a deep breath, she gets out of the car and heads across the parking lot.

Just then, Stephan DeAngelo walks out.

She reacts. *What is that about, Little Missy? Just settle down,* she thinks to herself. *He's just a man—an extremely handsome, sexy, well-dressed man, but so is your husband. He just doesn't have that accent! What are the chances of them continuing to bump into one another? Oh, I'd like to bump...*

Their eyes meet.

He simply waves. She nearly faints.

He's getting closer. She's getting hotter.

That smile—Wow. My heart—Pow. Okay, Angela, just stop. Not cool. Sooo hot. STOP!

"Hello, Mrs. Matheson," he calmly says—his hand outstretched to shake hers.

"Hello, Mr. DeAngelo," she nervously replies—shaking his hand.

Wow, such soft but manly hands, she thinks.

"You look lovely today. I hope you're well," his full lips speak, as his green eyes sparkle.

And those lips—if I weren't an old married lady, I'd take them for a ride, she ponders before snapping back to reality. "Why I am, thank you. And trust you are," her spinning head blurts, while her knees wobble.

He chuckles.

She hits rewind in her head, catches the slip and, trying to be nonchalant, laughs as though she meant to say that.

"Oops!" she laughs.

"Oops!" he laughs.

Let go of my hand before I toss you on the sidewalk and yell, Oops there I is, she thinks before calmly asking, "In to see our good friend, Dr. Long?"

"Yes, he is such a dear man. Wonderful heart. Has helped me so much, already," he says with such creative phrasing.

How can you not love the Italian accent? "Well, I get off...uh, must be off. To meet him. Dr. Long. So much work to do," she mutters, seemingly unable to stop the silly voices in her head. "Gotta chase the bats from the attic!" she meanders.

He laughs again. This time his head tilts back as the wind blows his dark hair. She can't help but stare.

"Mrs. Matheson?" he asks.

"Oh. Sorry. My son is at home with broken ribs and I guess my mind is wandering. Uh, I mean, wondering if he's okay.

"I understand," he gently says.

She mumbles, "I was trying to recall if I had...well, enough of that," she saves herself, adding, "Thank you for your kind words. You have a handsome day...I mean, lovely day, Stephan."

He does a half-bow, smiles and says, "Ciao!"

She walks toward the building, replaying that little interlude. *Chase the bats from the attic? Really smooth, Angela.*

Carter drives down the highway, his mind changing channels from one topic to another. *I've got 'Mission: Shasta' to prepare for...I want to talk to Christopher about self-defense...May be a good idea to give Durk a little taste of the anguish he pours on others...And need to get Reddick into the next level of rehab so that his hip remains strong and limber...Oh, and don't forget to speak with Teresa—let her know how important she is to me...*

His smartphone rings. He answers before the second ring.

"Carter," he barks.

"And a cheery, good morning to you, Brother," Jonathan says sarcastically.

"Sorry, Jonathan. Was just in my zone. Doing inventory, I guess. How goes it?"

"Good, thanks. I just dropped David at school, picked up a cup of my addiction and you crossed my mind, so I thought I'd call."

Carter smiles. They didn't speak all that often, but always knew they could pick up where they left off at any minute and not miss much.

"Nice to hear from you. What's this I hear through the grapevine that you won't be around for Thanksgiving?"

"Hey, how'd you hear that? It was just decided yesterday. Only a couple of us knew," Jonathan says with surprise.

"Bro. It's me. I know all," he laughs. "I mean, you know I always have a way of staying one step ahead. Try to, anyhow."

"That's true. Uncanny, at times, but certainly true. Anyhow, I basically called to tell you that piece of *top secret information*," he chuckles. "If there were space in the boat…"

"Jonathan that's nice, but—"

Jonathan interrupts, "I know. You probably have a load of wood to chop anyway…or a new secret fort to build on your property, or a new girl to date…"

This catches Carter off-guard.

"You're not the only one that keeps informed, Sir!" Jonathan says slyly.

They laugh again.

"Nice, Johnny. But what I was going to say is that I'm heading out on a…mission, of sorts."

Jonathan gets more serious, "Really? What kind?"

"Private contractor job."

"Where's it taking you?"

"Florida. And surrounding parts."

Silence.

"Hello?" Carter asks.

"Nothing. Just wondering what was so clandestine that—"

"Johnny, it's just business. Someone wants me to help them find someone. That's all."

"Well, that's a relief, I suppose. Wasn't sure if you were..." Jonathan trails off.

"No. I'm not taking...this is different...just a *locate* gig..."

"I guess what came to my mind was—is, *Vengeance is mine, says the Lord.*"

Carter rolls his eyes, takes a breath to keep him from saying anything and quietly responds, "Thank you, Jonathan. I appreciate...your input. It's just business. Nobody's going to get hurt. I hope," he chuckles to lighten the mood.

Jonathan catches on and replies, "Listen, I'll miss having you with us for Thanksgiving. Actually, it would have been fun for you and your new girlfriend to join us."

"Yeah, sounds like it."

"Maybe...like the old days."

Carter gets a sense his kid brother is reaching out to him—for what, he has no idea. But he holds on to the moment.

"Hey, Johnny?"

"Yeah?"

"Thanks for thinking of me."

"Sure thing. Just miss you. And would like to spend some down time together. And I mean, real downtime."

"Soon, okay?"

"Sure thing."

"No, I'm serious. Let's just put something on the books. Let's say before Christmas, for sure. New Year's, at the latest!"

"Done."

"I mean it, Johnny. Don't blow me off and pout like a little girl."

Jonathan chuckles.

"Because I'll turn this truck around, roll right over to that big fancy church office of yours, and—right in front of everyone, pick you up and put you over my knee…like I did when you were just a punk kid!"

Jonathan is laughing loudly now. "Stop!" he coughs. "Come on, stop!" he laughs. "I just about spit my Americano all over the dash!"

"Is that a euphemism for something, Pastor?"

Jonathan burst out again. "Okay, I give," he laughs, takes a deep breath and says, "That was good. Hardest I've laughed in a…long time. Thank you."

"That's what I'm here for. Okay, thanks again for thinking of me. I'll plan on seeing you when I get back, or you all get back—whichever comes first. Then, you and I will kick back and chill."

"Sounds great, Brother. Have fun. Be safe," Jonathan says, adding, "Love you."

"You too. See ya."

Click.

Three miles down the road, Carter is still smiling and enjoying that little slice of family. Man, it felt good to do something right. To do something that made your family feel good, he reflects.

His smile slowly disappears as he ponders, *Now, to take care of some of that family business.*

Angela stands by the window, staring up into the perfectly blue sky, wondering what it would be like to be a cloud—floating, wherever the wind took you.

"Angela?" Dr. Long quietly prods.

She still stares, swaying ever so much.

Dr. Long walks over to where she is. Not to startle her, he steps into her field of vision—just to the side of her.

"Oh, Dr. Long," she pops back to reality. "Sorry. Got caught up in a daydream for a second. I apologize, just processing—" She stops.

"No need to apologize, Angela. Just wanted to be sure you wished to continue."

"Why wouldn't I?"

He smiles, takes her by the hand, leading her back to her chair.

"Well, you've been standing there for the last 20 minutes. We only have a few minutes left in our session and I thought—"

"What?" She is shocked then embarrassed, looking at her watch. "I'm sorry. I was so deep in thought, so much on my mind. Let's just pick back up…"

She stops to recall where that was.

She looks to Dr. Long for some assistance by raising her eyebrows.

"Yes, of course, you had mentioned how incredibly hot Mr. DeAngelo is, and how you have notions about him that are not particularly appropriate…"

She blushes.

"But then I reminded you that fantasy is a part of life—as long as one does not ACT upon said fantasies…"

"Of course."

"Then, good to hear that Christopher is recovering. Glad he'll be okay for our upcoming trip." He smiles.

"Yes. We're all so excited about that."

"And we had just gotten to the point where you had reached out to David to ask him…" Long says, leaning forward.

"Yes. Continue."

"No, Love, that's where you had stopped."

"Yes."

"And where you were going to finish…that thought. You were reaching out to David…perhaps…about school?"

She shakes her head.

"About the trip?"

Frowning, she shakes her head again.

"Perhaps about his new fascination with butterflies?"

She claps her hands.

"Yes. That's it. He loves butterflies. I mean, so much so that he's dedicated his bedroom *light show* to them. Well, we haven't seen it yet, but he's been working so hard on it. Can't wait to see it. He's so talented."

"And Angela, about those butter—"

"Yes. I reached out to him…to help me learn more about adoption!" she is so pleased with herself that it's all coming back.

He patiently smiles.

"May I have some water, please?" she asks, licking her dry lips.

He walks to the cooler in the corner and fills a cup for her.

She watches him walk back and quickly devours the water.

"I am so thirsty. Perhaps—"

He is already walking for another cup.

When she is finished that cup, she's calmer—more focused.

"I think David has found quite a bit of research that will help in my current, and future, considerations of this idea. I feel you're completely right and think that now—while we are still so young, it may be the best time to consider this."

"I'm happy to hear that. What does Jonathan think?"

She stares at her hands.

"Oh. I haven't discussed this with him. Yet."

"Why not? I'm surprised, given that you too are so close." He tries not to let too much emotion show on his face.

"Well, I want to be sure…the timing is right. The kids will be…okay. I will feel…fit enough to…" She trails off.

"I understand. Angela?"

He waits for her to look at him.

Their eyes meet and she smiles, asking, "Yes?"

"You are going to be fine. Depression does not have to be a lifelong situation. The medication you're on?" She nods. "You will eventually be weaned from it," he continues.

"Good."

"And Angela, my dear friend. There is no better mother in the world, than you."

This brightens not only her face but her whole being. She takes in a deep, healing breath, slowly lets it out and seems more peaceful.

He stands, reaches for her hand and says, "Let's stop there today and pick up tomorrow, or the next day. It's completely up to you."

"Sounds terrific. Thank you."

"Of course, I'm sure I or Sammy will be chatting with you about the details of the trip, as to what to pack and such. But there is no pressure and plenty of time. Okay?"

Smiling, she nods, kisses him on the cheek and walks quietly from his office, through the waiting room and back out into the wide-open world.

ॐ

Christopher and Carter sit in the living room of the Matheson home. The large flat screen TV on the wall is on, but muted. Christopher relaxes in Jonathan's recliner, sipping from a Styrofoam cup.

"Thanks for the milkshake, Uncle Carter."

"No worries," he says, staring at the screen with no sound.

"I remember when you and Dad would treat me and David...and Gracie...to these after playing in the yard all day."

Carter smiles at Christopher and nods. "Those were some good days, Son."

Christopher nods.

"How're your sides feeling?"

"Better today, but not great," Christopher says, adding, "as long as I don't move much, or breathe too deeply."

They both grin.

"About that, Christopher. I feel like I should have done more for you the other day when you came over to chat about self-defense and stuff."

"Not your problem, Uncle Carter."

"It sort of is."

"How's that?" Christopher asks, finally looking up from inside his cup.

"Two reasons, I guess. You're family. And you come first—above and beyond everything else in this world. You know that, right?"

Christopher nods.

"I know we've had some...tough spots in the road over the past year, but I think I've shown...I think you see that you and David and your mom and dad mean the world to me. I'd give everything in my life to have you all safe, happy and out of harm's way."

"I know that," Christopher quietly says. "I know."

"So, I should have dropped what I was doing—"

"But Grandpa was there and..." He stops, frowning.

"What is it? You in pain?"

Christopher smiles, "No, I was just thinking. That may be the first time I've ever referred to him as Grandpa. Heck, I didn't even know I *had* one until this week. Weird," he says, staring at the bottom of an empty cup.

Life stops for a moment, as both men consider this.

"I know. And...your dad and I should have—"

"Carter, it's no biggie. You don't have to baby me. I mean, I know life is complicated. I get it. It's just..." He hesitates for several minutes before saying, "It's just that I wish Dad would have put aside whatever feelings he may have had and lived the kind of example he preaches about. *That* is what chaps my ass about Dad sometimes."

"I get it," Carter replies.

"It would have been nice," he snorts, "to have enjoyed that kind of family figure...in my—in *our* lives. All those years are gone."

Carter is sensing a side of Christopher he has never seen before, a young boy who stands on the precipice of manhood. He feels proud and thankful to be here.

"Christopher, I want you to know that I'll do everything in my power to bring our family closer. No matter what that means. I think your grandfather—Dad, is coming around...in a way that I never dreamed possible. Now, don't get me wrong, he was an asshole when we were growing up, but...well, as he says, *Age has a way of changing people*. And I get that more now than ever before. Not to sound corny, Chris, but we're all doing the best we can."

He nods, saying, "I know."

Carter sits on the edge of the couch. "I'm gonna leave in a minute, but the second thing I wanted to say—"

"Oh yeah, I lost count," Christopher says.

Carter is serious. "Family is first. Secondly, self-defense is a precarious thing. You have to understand it, study it, respect it and not be afraid of it. It's what this country is founded upon. It's the reason I, and your granddad, went to war—to protect our freedoms. And whether it's someone on the other side of the world, the other side of the country, or if it's someone on the other side of town...we have to defend ourselves from harm's way. And to be smart about it. Understand?"

"Yes, Sir."

"Good. Now, I gotta roll. I won't be joining you for Thanksgiving—"

"What?"

The look of disappointment nearly crushes Carter.

"No, I have a job to do that's going to take me out of town. But when I get back, I'm going to show you a few things; some will be *tricks of the trade* and others will be good old-fashioned ass-kicking techniques that will protect you from others—whether or not you have a weapon."

Christopher's eyes are wide and he's grinning with anticipation.

Carter stands. Christopher tries and eventually has to ask for help, "Can you give me a hand?"

Helping him up, they walk to the kitchen. Christopher tosses his cup in the trash and leads Carter out the back door.

Looking up into the Carolina blue skies, Christopher takes a deep breath and says, "Been cooped up in this house too long. Feels good to get some fresh air."

Carter puts a hand on his shoulder and says, "I'm proud of you, Chris."

He looks Carter in the eye and asks, "What for?"

"For standing up for yourself. For trying to do the right thing. And most importantly, for always looking out for your family."

"Thanks."

Carter nods and starts walking away.

"Uncle Carter?"

He's at his truck when he stops and looks at Christopher.

"Yeah, Chris?"

"And thanks for coming back home." Christopher tries to suppress any tears, for fear of looking weak to his uncle.

Carter smiles. "You bet."

PART TWO: Elaborate Discoveries

CHAPTER 39

CARTER IS ON THE outskirts of the bedroom community of Mission Grove and heading southbound on I-77, toward his final destination of Miami. He was up early—dressed, packed and on the road before the sun had a chance to peek above the horizon. The local weather may take a turn and it looks as though Thanksgiving weekend, just a few days away, will be more winter-like than expected as a cold front moves down from Canada. *Good thing I'll be in Miami by the time the holiday comes around,* Carter thinks to himself. *Of course, it's all up to the weathermen. And their success record? What, 60, maybe 70%?*

Even at this early morning hour, he can see the low clouds and the threat of a heavy rain, just as local weatherman, Larry Sprinkle, had predicted. Larry Sprinkle. *The original Rain Man,* Carter thinks. *Can't be his original name, can it?*

He checks his watch: 6:55. Wanting to make good time, he pushes the speedometer from 55 to 65 and instinctively checks his rearview. *Another 10 mph isn't going to get noticed. Besides, I've got good people in high places, if the need arises.*

His mind drifts to the two people that are most important to him—besides his family, which are Reddick and Teresa. He's so glad that Reddick and he have become such good pals. They really do have an easy friendship. They're both fiercely independent, happy, driven loners.

Speaking of marriage—had enough of that. Two wives were enough to make you rethink relationships.

Carter flashes back to his marriages. The first was right out of college and just as he entered the marines. She never appreciated his constant deployments and clandestine trips that could take weeks at a time—never knowing if he'd come home able-bodied or disembodied—in a body bag. Besides, she wanted kids and he never thought he'd be much of a father. After all, his role model wasn't all that. So, she distracted herself with a neighbor and was remarried inside a year. Number two was a mistake. Met her at a bar with some friends. She was beautiful, hilarious and rich. She always said money never meant anything to her because she'd always had it and they'd never have to worry for lack of having it. Little did he know that she had a real problem with shoving said money up her perfectly remanufactured nose. He couldn't recall who tired of whom fastest—or first. That one lasted about three years. And as predicted, the drugs dulled both her senses and her sense of humor. She grew boring, bored and busted—ran off with a musician, leaving a note stuck to the fridge that read—he'll never forget it, *Had a blast. Now it's past. Sorry didn't last.* Okay, so maybe she kept some of that humor.

But Teresa? That could be another story. Why mess things up if they're working just fine under separate roofs? *Besides*, he continues to think to himself, *I can't imagine for one minute having Jeff as a stepson, and even worse, having any consistent contact with that deadbeat dad, Durkin.*

Teresa. What did I do to deserve her? Man, have I lucked out? Looks, smarts, sense of humor and legs, to boot. If everything else is as good, I'll have won the lottery.

Carter tries to imagine what it would be like to have a real relationship again. Especially if that relationship is as fun and carefree as this one started. It could happen. We're big kids and don't really want to spend time with someone who doesn't *get it.*

The phone rings.

Finally getting accustomed to his new toy, Carter checks the caller ID.

"You must be reading my mind," he says with a smile.

"I am," Teresa replies, "hoping it reads: *Sexy single dude searching for sassy single lass*, or something like that."

He chuckles. "I doubt I've ever used the word lass in my life, but if you'll answer that ad, I'm game."

"Carter, I was born game."

He grins. "Nice answer."

There's a moment of silence and he speaks before he thinks.

"You miss me already?"

"Duh!"

He passes a convoy of 18-wheelers and they exchange flashing lights.

"Last night, while full of surprises, was actually...perfect," she says quietly.

"Uh huh."

"Nearly perfect. Maybe that'll come another time," she says, whispering, "Right?"

He likes this romantic side of both of them.

"You better believe it."

Trying to stifle a yawn she says, "Well, I know you practically just left, but I wanted to hear your voice. Silly, huh?"

He would blush if he were the blushing type. He was taken with her cute ways—especially with that tough exterior.

"Hello?" she asks.

"I'm here. It's not silly. I was just imagining what you look like right now, all tucked in, warm and cozy, on this dark, cloudy morning."

The light is on next to her bed, so she lifts up the covers to inspect—nothing but a pair of boxer shorts and oversized athletic socks. She chuckles and, lowering her voice, adds, "I'll just leave that to your imagination."

"Nice."

"Thought you'd like that."

His phone beeps.

He looks from the road ahead to the small screen. It's a text from Randall.

"Babe, can you hold just a minute? Don't move."

"Sure."

He clicks a button to read: "May have new development. Call when you can. RM."

He hesitates, but decides to keep it all about her.

"I'm back. It's just business."

"At this hour?" She catches herself and quickly says, "Sorry. Scratch that." Lowering her voice, she adds, "It's none of my business."

He chuckles, quickly putting her at ease, "No worries, just my contact checking in."

"I just want you to know—I'm not that person."

He rolls his eyes.

"I get it. When it becomes something to worry about, I'll tell you. Fair enough?"

"Perfectly," she quietly replies.

She yawns and stretches.

"Well, I'm going to roll back over and try to catch another hour before my boy gets up and I start nurse duties…before I head to the diner for a lunch shift."

"You're a good mother."

"Well, I don't know about all that, but I certainly try. And you're a good kisser."

That catches him off-guard.

"Well, I don't know about all that, but I'll certainly try…to do it again as soon as possible."

"Won't come soon enough."

He laughs.

"How about this?" he asks. "I'll check in later today—maybe, halfway?"

"Sounds good. Or when you get there. No pressure."

"Man, you are easy."

"What!"

"Easy to get along with."

"I know," she giggles. "Just busting your chops."

"Mission accomplished. Okay, I'm ringing off, Miss Boxer Shorts."

"Wait! How did you...?" she asks.

"Part of my mystery. Talk to you later."

"Bye."

With that, she hangs up, throws the covers back, kicks her legs in the air, giggling like a schoolgirl, pulls the covers back to her neck and with a huge smile, lets out a long sigh.

Carter flashes back to last night—the awkward moment when *Jeff plus Teresa equals a hard road. I'll handle it. She's worth it. Besides, we're both big kids,* he thinks, knowing that they'd both seen enough road to know where the potholes were. They talked about it, between make-out sessions, and came to realize that boys will be boys. They also hoped that it would all blow over. And for the most part, Carter agreed. The only part he couldn't let slide was that dork, Durk. But for now, *nothing—and I mean nothing, is going to stand in my way with her.*

Carter gets back to imagining her in those boxers and starts smiling again—all the way down the highway.

CHAPTER 40

THE MATHESON HOME IS still quiet at 6:30 A.M.—
something unusual on pretty much any day of the week.
But now, just days before Thanksgiving, it seems a bit
more unusual, given the fact that they were supposed to be
on the road to Charleston in just under two hours. And they
still had to pack. David must have sensed this, as he shot
upright in bed upon hearing a noise outside the house. He
sat completely still for a moment, trying his best to figure
out its source.

There it was again—a scratching sound. He climbs
out of bed, quietly walks out of his room and down the hall
to the top of the stairs. The sound was coming from the
opposite side of the house. He looks at his parents'
bedroom door; it was closed and no lights were on. Turning
to Christopher's room, he saw that it was also closed. There
it was again. *Probably Jackson scratching to get outside*,
he thought. However, descending the stairs, he peers into
the living room where the family Lab slept every night on
his appointed bed, and upon seeing David, he jumps up—
his tail wagging. And now, he is ready to go, for real.
Walking toward the kitchen to let Jackson out, David hears
the sound again. It was coming from the guest room. He
quietly walks down the hall and to the last room on the
right.

There was Angela, on her hands and knees,
scrubbing the hardwood floors with Murphy's Oil Soap.
The odor was unmistakable.

After a moment, it hits him. She was scrubbing the
spot where Grace had died.

"Mom?" The word catches in his throat.

She continues to scrub, harder and harder. Sweat
forms on her brow and a wisp of hair hangs down in her
face. Her eyes are filled with tears, yet look vacant.

"Mom?" he says louder.

Suddenly, she looks up and says, "Grace?"

The vacant look is slowly replaced with recognition, as she begins to wake. Looking around, she realizes where she is. Embarrassment crosses her face. She stops, drops the brush into the bucket and gets up to sit in a nearby chair. David walks over and takes her hand.

"Mom, are you okay? Why are you…?"

Angela takes a long deep breath, as tears begin to pool in her eyes.

"I was missing Gracie. She should be here with us." A long pause is followed by a deep sigh, as she adds, "It was just too soon."

Her shoulders begin to shake as grief bubbles from deep within. David puts his arms around her and holds her. Leaning her head against his chest, she sobs. The floor creaks behind them, and David turns his head to see Jonathan standing there in his pajamas. Tears are pooled in his eyes, but he manages a strained smile for David. The moment seems to hang for an eternity.

࿇

Within an hour, Daphne and Angela are in the kitchen wrapping and bagging sandwiches and assorted items and packing them in a large cooler. The boys finish breakfast—David fork-loading French toast while reading the paper, and Christopher, slurping cold cereal, while checking emails on his iPhone.

Outside, Stuart and Jonathan pack the SUV.

"Aren't you glad you and Daphne reconsidered, Stuart? It's going to be a neat change of pace—completely different from any other Thanksgiving."

"Yes, Son. Actually, I couldn't believe Daphne nearly passed on the opportunity. We just don't stray very far and haven't really been anywhere since…" He stops to wipe his brow with a handkerchief. Staring into the distance, he continues, "I guess it was our 35th anniversary, when we spent two weeks in San Francisco. She always wanted to see the redwoods. And you know how I love bridges. The Golden Gate is one of our country's true marvels. So, anyway, we both won."

Jonathan closes the tailgate and starts cleaning the windows, saying, "Love that city. Angela still marvels at that drive down the coast to Carmel. Doesn't get much prettier than that."

"No kidding. So, yes, I'm thrilled. Besides, the warm weather will be a really nice change," Stuart adds.

"Nothing like turquoise water and blue skies in the winter to clear the mind," Jonathan says, looking at the dark clouds rolling in off the mountains.

Stuart follows Jonathan's gaze and says, "Yep. We best grab the girls and boys and get on the road."

Jonathan and Stuart look to see Christopher come out dragging behind him a huge duffle bag.

"No, Sir. Not going to happen," Jonathan exclaims, raising his arm to stop Christopher in his tracks.

"But I've got shorts if it's hot, warm stuff if it gets cold, some sports equipment and…"

"Nope. We have to travel light. There are eight of us…on a 6-person boat. Besides, if you can't carry it yourself, it can't go…"

Christopher interrupts. "Yeah, but I've been injured and…"

"Nice try. Besides, it won't be cold beyond today. And only between here and *maybe* Charleston. The only sports equipment you need for the beach is a Frisbee."

Christopher rolls his eyes and heads back in, bumping into David who is carrying both a backpack crammed full of books and a laptop, as he comes out the door.

Jonathan just looks at him. "Really?"

"But, my studies," David says, adding extra sympathetic charm for emphasis.

"How about just the laptop?" Jonathan returns.

"*One* book?" David asks.

Jonathan looks to Stuart who stands aside watching the troops. He shrugs his shoulders.

"Okay. Laptop and *one* book. But, the laptop stays in the car in Charleston and the book can go with you…"

"What?" David interrupts.

"Unless you don't mind running the risk of the laptop accidentally going overboard."

David looks shocked.

"That would never happen."

Jonathan smiles at Stuart and holds the door open, motioning for him to go inside. They leave David standing there contemplating the potential tragedy.

"Would it?" David says quietly, deep in thought.

Leaning out the door, Jonathan says, "And please take Jackson next door. The Fishers have promised to take care of him while we're gone."

"Uh huh," David answers, mindlessly.

Jonathan sees that David can't decide between the laptop and the book. "It'd be a lot easier to replace a book…than a computer," he says gently.

David says, "Good point, Pops." He turns and heads back into the house with the men.

Inside, Angela rinses the last dish and hands it to Daphne, who dries and places it in the cupboard.

"Okay, that's that," Angela says to no one in particular, then adds, "Jonathan, would you take that…" pointing to a basket, "and put it in the car? We're done."

Jonathan looks to Stuart then says, "You sure that's all? I mean, we could take a few dozen of Daphne's biscuits, oh, and maybe a bigger turkey and…"

Angela takes the towel from Daphne, rolls it into a snake and snaps at Jonathan.

"Whoa! Okay, *Uncle!*"

He leans over to kiss her. She rolls her eyes, playing as though she isn't interested. When he hesitates, she grabs his neck and pulls him close for a real kiss.

Stuart says to Daphne, "Hon, you have everything you need?"

Daphne looks to Angela with a look that says *Watch this.* She says, "What? Oh, I haven't started packing yet. Let me just run up to the house and…"

Stuart, almost snookered, starts to say something then shakes his head, "C'mon, woman. Let's hit the road."

The family gathers the last of their things and heads out, climbing into the SUV. All six seatbelts click, and they're rolling down the driveway to the adventure that awaits.

CHAPTER 41

OFFICER DURKIN BARGES INTO the station like a bull in a corral. All the other officers look up from what they're doing and either frown, shake their head or roll their eyes. Reddick does all three then returns to his paperwork. It was still early and, in a town as small as Mission Grove, there wasn't much happening—certainly not before noon, and it was only about 8:30. Durkin, being new, worked the later shift, which he hated, but he had been requested to come in for his three-month evaluation. He wasn't altogether glad about it, not because of the hour—he liked the early morning, but because he was pretty sure he was going to be put through some insignificant paces that would lead nowhere. *I deserve to replace all these slack-ass toy cops and run this place*, he thinks to himself as he takes a seat at Reddick's desk.

Reddick looks up from his papers and stares at Durkin. Thought he'd let the new boy make the first move and see what he had under his cap.

"What are you looking at?" Durkin barks.

"Excuse me?" Reddick replies.

Durkin picks up the morning paper from the corner of Reddick's desk, like it was his desk, and starts reading, but not before expelling noticeable gas. Reddick looks up but is sure to keep his voice low as he delivers the next message.

"Hey Douche-bag, put my newspaper right back where you got it. Then, go find your own spot to sit and pollute. Got it?"

"Screw you, Toy Cop. This isn't your station. What do all you guys in this hick town think—that it's *NYPD Blue*? I came from a *real* station. In a *real* city. And have seen *real* action."

With that, he gets up and walks to the coffee machine and pours himself a cup of coffee, but not before stopping at the front desk and announcing himself.

"Hey, Dough-boy," Durkin says to slightly overweight and very helpful Officer Scott. "Tell Sheriff Mahler I'm here for my nine o'clock. And be sure to let him know I'm early."

Durkin's back is to the front door so he doesn't see that Mahler is coming in at that exact moment. Officer Scott, the gatekeeper, delivers a deadpan message, half of which is only heard by Durkin, while the other half is heard by the rest of the staff.

"Tell him yourself, *Donkey-boy*...Of course, Officer Durkin, I'll let Sheriff Mahler know you're here for your meeting. Oh, here he is now."

Durkin spins around and salutes. Mahler stops in his tracks, looks him up and down then continues past him.

"Take a seat, Durkin. Haven't had my coffee yet."

Durkin obeys like a puppy. Reddick eyeballs Scott, and they share a sneer. Mahler catches Reddick's eye, grins and keeps walking. Durkin does as he's told, but at a different, vacant desk.

Danny Mahler, newly appointed captain, runs the precinct now, having been promoted recently from sergeant. Many in town wondered if he would get the much-envied position, especially given the fact he was caught in a precarious predicament last summer, after he faced foul-play charges. He and Officer Reddick were both caught in compromising positions about the time Carter disappeared. However, now—everything was just dandy.

Mahler walks out of his office and into the main room.

"C'mon, Durkin. Let's have a little chat," Mahler says, nodding for him to follow.

At the exact moment Durkin passes Reddick's desk, Reddick is sure to time his extended foot to reach the nearby chair so that it intersects Durkin's path. Durkin trips just as he nears Mahler's office, but catches himself.

"Reddick!" he shouts before containing his boiling anger—evident by the rush of blood to his face, and forcing a vein in the middle of his forehead to nearly burst.

"My bad," he continues, adding, "Guess I didn't see the chair."

Mahler saw what happened, but shrugs it off and has already turned and gone into his office. Seeing this, Durkin spins back around and growls in a low, husky voice, "Your ass is mine, Redneck. Count on it."

"Ooooh...so menacing," Reddick responds.
Mahler lets Durkin pass then closes the door, but not before rolling his eyes to Reddick. A hearty chuckle rolls through the office, after the door closes

CHAPTER 42

CARTER IS LESS THAN an hour outside Savannah when he decides to take a break, grab some fresh coffee and make two phone calls—one to Randall to see what the latest information is on his mission. He had gotten the text hours ago, but decided to allow for some breathing room, especially given that he'd be there in less than half a day and he doubted that anything urgent would happen in that span of time.

The other phone call would be to his pal, Mack, an old war buddy from The Force—their nickname for the Special Forces. They both took death in stride, defending their country, willing to die, if needed.

Steve "Mack" McKenzie, was a tough son of a bitch, with several tours of duty under his belt. He married his high school sweetheart who lost interest in him, yet gained that of another, while he was away on his first tour of duty. He never remarried, figured it would be better to be lonely than suffer another heartbreak, which inadvertently made him weary of women. Perhaps that similarity wasn't lost on Carter, and their respective proclivities.

Gassed and caffeinated, Carter pulls back onto I-26, but quickly merges onto I-95 and continues making swift work of dissolving the next thirty or so minutes. He dials Mack on a secure line—the second of two cell phones he recently purchased. This one, he uses only when discussing sensitive material.

Mack picks up before the second ring completes.

"Mack's Speed Shop," he answers.

Carter grins at the reference. Mack's is a favorite hangout in the South End section of Charlotte. They serve the best smoked barbecue and the widest varieties of cold beer in town. These two had been known to bury half a pig, half a case and half a mind, on more than several occasions.

"Some things never change," Carter says.

"Nor should they," Mack replies.

"You good?"

"Couldn't be better. You?"

"Aces."

"Swell."

Carter feels lighter, more hopeful. Something about Mack and his upbeat vibe made life, and work, just easier to swallow.

"Care to spare a day or two of undercover work…if the need arises?" Carter asks.

"Any shit-storm of yours is mine."

"Poetic."

"That's what April calls me. A dang poet."

Mack's girlfriend, April, has lived with him on the beach at Tybee Island for 10 years. Although she's 18 years younger, Mack brags that it just works. On more than one occasion, he's told Carter, he never once questioned how the magic worked in their favor. After all, he's faced death overseas and returned home. And she died in the sea but returned.

She got caught in a riptide a few summers back. EMT got there in time to pronounce her *officially* dead. Mack stood over her, mortified, and wouldn't stand for it. So, he pushed the techs aside and went to work on her, relentlessly conducting CPR until she came back. They've never left one another's side since.

Mack couldn't decide whether to sue or kill the EMT who gave up. So, one day while hanging out at a local fish taco stand, he decided to bet the kid—younger by a decade, that he could outswim him. The kid, feeling sorry for the old man and for nearly allowing his girl to remain permanently dead, put up his prized and tricked-out Harley Sportster. Mack put up his vintage dune buggy. Both guys had been eyeing one another's toys for weeks. Thing was,

Mack really wanted that Harley and knew he could win. And he did.

"You're a poet and she's a saint—for putting up with you," Carter says.

"Got that right."

"But then, you got your saint side, too. Saved my bacon more than once."

"Line of duty," Mack chuckles. "But saint? Don't think saints get to Heaven creating all the mayhem I have."

"Into many lives some mayhem must appear."

Mack laughs so loudly that Carter moves the phone away from his ear. Just then, Carter spots a state trooper up ahead. The mostly hidden car sits behind a hedge at the top of an upcoming onramp. He double-checks his speed and taps the cruise button to drop it five, just in case. Passing under the overpass seconds later, he double-checks his rearview and sees the dark sedan still tucked just out of sight. Safe.

"You some kinda *Buddha Warrior* or something, now?" Mack asks.

"Nah, more like…"

"Wait, a woman, that's it!" he interrupts. "See? They keep us young."

"Ya got me. Listen, let's continue this existential chit-chat over some of your chicory coffee." He checks his watch. "I'll be there in less than 20."

"See you in 20. And park down at…

"The Breakfast Club on Main. Got it," Carter confirms and disconnects then dials the second number. The phone rang a number of times before he heard the familiar voice.

"Morning," Randall said before launching a short series of dry coughs.

"You okay?" Carter asks.

"SOP—first thing every morning," he replies, taking a deep breath and adding, "There haven't been any new developments, so I thought it could wait 'til morning."

"Okay."

"My worst fear is that it's a kidnapping," Randall nearly whispers. "But then, you know kids these days...have all kind of crazy notions about what entertainment is."

"Yes, a lot different than the old days."

Both men are quiet.

"Don't worry. She's fine and I'll handle it."

"I'm counting on that, Son." He coughs.

"What's the protocol?"

"Well, I'm moving forward. You remember me telling you a friend of mine had noticed some odd coming and going of late, right?" Randall asks.

"Yes, the security guard. At your entrance."

"Roger. Well, I had him follow that car. You know, to see if there were any patterns."

"And?"

"Sure enough, he has a post office box he frequents."

"Not too odd—" Carter interrupts.

"Except that he does the exact same thing every time. Drives into my subdivision, every couple of days— and he doesn't live here, and then drives straight to one of those personal post office places where people have generic addresses."

"Got it. That is a bit unusual. Unless, like you," Carter chuckles, "he's a creature of habit."

Randall is quiet for several moments before answering, "True."

"But I'm assuming your security friend found something more than that."

Randall breaks into a long series of short, dry coughs, culminating with a long breath. Carter can hear a deep raspy wheeze on the other end of the line.

"You okay, Sir?"

"Yes," he responds after taking a long breath, "just took my breath away."

"What, my astute levels of observation?" Carter jokes.

This got a laugh. Not a big laugh. Not a forced laugh. Carter thought that any laugh was a major accomplishment, as he couldn't recall his father laughing more than a few dozen times in his entire life.

"The reason that's so clever is that you're both correct *and* a smart-ass."

"I'll take anything I can get. If it makes you find the humor in something."

Carter was enjoying the emotional break in the ice between father and son. It had been one too many years before they had any civilized communication.

Randall grunts, "Yeah, I know. A real stick in the mud. Anyway, getting back to business, I had Frank—the security guard, see if he could find anything more. So, he started to dig around. He came up with some story about trying to find his little girl who had run away from home. He had a photo on him and some phony credentials and—"

Carter interrupts, "Wait, what do you mean phony credentials? Security guards don't turn over information for anybody unless—"

"Unless they're FBI," Randall interrupts.

"Oh. Nice. At least that's legal," Carter chuckles.

"Desperate times require—"

"Desperate measures," Carter retorts. "I know. And listen, I'm a big proponent of subterfuge, so you have no complaints here. I'm just surprised it was that easy."

"You don't know Frank. He can be extremely persuasive. In several ways."

Carter lets that percolate a moment before responding. "Okay, so he gets in, spills his story, following a guy he thinks may have something to do with it, spins a tale, persuades this guy and—"

"Girl."

"Huh?"

"The clerk. Attendant. She was a girl."

Carter snorts, "So, it may have been just a bit easier than with a guy."

"What do you think?" Randall whispers. "Like I said, he can be very persuasive—with both sexes. It's a combination of nearly threatening size, balanced out with a genuine demeanor. I've heard women say it's his kind eyes."

"Okay, before we go to commercial break on this episode of *Oprah*, can we just cut to the chase?" Carter jokes.

"You asked." Randall chuckles, dryly. "So, what's your ETA?"

Carter checks his watch. "Well, ordinarily the trip is this side of 10 hours. But I've been giving this some thought, and I'm stopping in Savannah first."

"Oh?"

"Yes. I have an old pal I want to see. And I'm building my backup plan. Just in case."

"Of course you are."

"So, I'm nearly here, and about six or seven to there, depending upon how much time I take. Bottom line, let's say nightfall. Latest."

"Roger that. See you then."

Carter tosses the cell phone on the seat and starts chewing the inside of his mouth, lost in thought. He was already planning one step ahead—old habits die hard. Always watch your back. Mix it up. Stay inconsistent. You never know when someone's watching. To that end, he checks his rearview, decides all is well and takes the next exit, Savannah—Highway 16. Another few minutes and he'll be inhaling sea air and telling tales in the shadow of The Lighthouse, with his partner in crime for what could turn out to be a dangerous expedition.

CHAPTER 43

CHARLESTON IN NOVEMBER IS especially colorful and pleasant. The fall foliage turns a few weeks behind their northern neighbors, and the temperatures have become more comfortable, nearly a dozen degrees warmer than Mission Grove. While the breezes can make for pleasant days, those same breezes can also develop into more furious foes like hurricanes.

Jefferson and Sammy have been watching the meteorological landscape over the past several weeks, tracking any out-of-the-ordinary weather patterns that develop. So far, so good. The violent weather patterns had come earlier this year, and turned east out to sea before reaching land, above Jacksonville, Florida. This gave them confidence of two things. One, the worse had already happened—it had come and gone. Secondly, what remained was merely a small cluster of ordinary thunderstorms—not unusual for this time of year. All in all, it appeared to the weather specialists that it was going to be a temperate and relatively dry late fall and early winter season. Jefferson, being equal parts Boy Scout and optimist, as well as psychotherapist of the highest order, anticipated a vacation of mostly clear skies and smooth sailing. The biggest bonus of all? Meteorologists were expecting the warmest Thanksgiving holiday in memory—perfect for making a southern voyage.

Two days earlier, Jefferson and Sammy had arrived at their second vacation home, two blocks off the marina in downtown Charleston. They wanted to get a head start on the Matheson family and be certain the boat was properly prepped and ready for departure. It was actually the home Sammy grew up in and still occasionally shares with her grandmother. She and Jefferson use it whenever they need a launching point for their sea voyages.

Sammy grew up in Charleston, but moved to Davidson, just outside Mission Grove, nearly two years ago. This was the same time her mother left, moving to Central Florida to follow her *heart-throb-of-the-year*—a man seven years her junior who took a promotion at NASA. Sammy never knew her father, as he left their small family when she was just a baby. Additionally, she was an only child, raised by her mother and grandmother—another reason she tended to cling to those close to her, choosing intimate rather than casual bonds.

Together, she and Jefferson had formed a quick bond about a year ago when he was spending long hours at the Charlotte Library Extension in Davidson.

Jefferson was poring over weather graphs and charts, just for backup, and was busy running a checklist of provisions they would need for just over a week. Sammy was putting the finishing touches on sealing the food in airtight bags and placing the perishables in insulated containers. Sealing certain foods would help extend their freshness, as well as keep them dry in case of water seepage.

"Baby, do you agree we should keep breakfast and lunches, light and fresh? Maybe dried fruits and nuts?" Sammy asks.

Jefferson was lost in thought, sifting through his worn copies of nautical maps.

"Babe?" Sammy prods.

"Huh? Yeah, sounds good," Jefferson answers.

Sammy's not buying it.

"And I was thinking perhaps peanut butter covered sardines for breakfast and maybe fried goat tongue for dinner."

"Perfect. Who doesn't like that?" Jefferson absently responds.

She whistles—the kind you hear from one end of a football field to the other and Jefferson nearly jumps out of his shoes.

"What?!"

She just stares—her hands on her hips.

"Sorry," he softly replies, getting up from his desk and joining her at the kitchen counter. "Pre-occupied double-checking everything."

She puts her cheek out for him to kiss, and he obliges.

"That's better," she says. "I just want it to be perfect. And need your help."

"It's already perfect, Lovey. And I want to say again, what a great suggestion you had inviting our friends to share this holiday with us."

"Thank you. I'm excited. It'll be nice for all of us. Just wish Nana was up to it," Sammy says, stacking all the prepped food and their containers on the counter that divided the kitchen from the open living room.

"I know. Me too. But she'll be fine spending time with her sister and their family in Mount Pleasant. It'll do her good. She can spend time with us back home at Christmas. And up through the first of the year, if she likes," Jefferson says, rolling maps, placing them in waterproof tubes, then exchanging fresh batteries in all the flashlights.

"What can I do next?"

Jefferson looks around at all the provisions and rubs his hands, saying, "I say, we drive down to the marina and give *Lady Giselle* a big hug and stuff her belly with all these goodies."

"Sounds like a plan," Sammy says, saluting him with a hearty, "Aye, aye, Captain!"

An hour outside Charleston, each Matheson is pre-occupied with a variety of diversions. David is creating pencil sketches of butterflies. Christopher flips through a tattered copy of *Rolling Stone*—his head nodding, as he listens through iPod earbuds. Stuart reads a James Patterson paperback—one of the *Alex Cross* stories, while

Daphne works a Sudoku puzzle, twirling a pencil between entries. Angela is asleep, her head resting on a pillow against the window, and Jonathan softly whistles a happy tune for the SUV amphitheater—the same tune he performs nearly every time the family takes a long drive. They all enjoy it.

Daphne taps Jonathan on the shoulder.

"Son-in-law, mind if we make a quick stop? Nana needs to tinkle."

"Sure, no problem," he smiles, looking up ahead for a sign. "I'll grab the next exit."

"Thanks."

David looks up from what he's sketching and says, "Gramma, glad you suggested that. I was just thinking the same thing."

Daphne turns around to face the third seat and smiles, saying, "Great minds think alike, huh?"

About that time, Christopher removes his earbuds, and Stuart folds the corner of his paperback, marking his place, and arches his back, adding, "Good idea, Son. We could all use a break about now."

Giving a turn signal, Jonathan takes the next exit and pulls into one of the mammoth fueling marts scattered all along the North-South interstate corridor. Approaching a fueling bay, Jonathan looks at Angela and gently shakes her arm. She doesn't budge. Everyone unloads and heads into the mart, so he gets out and starts the pump.

He stands there staring into the growing morning light, thinking how this trip would be all the more perfect if Grace were with them, when a large brilliantly colored butterfly enters his peripheral vision. He watches it arc back and forth then circle their SUV, before disappearing above the overhang. Looking first for traffic, Jonathan steps around their vehicle and searches for the butterfly. It's gone. He stands there with a quizzical look on his face, when he notices David standing in the middle of the parking lot, watching him. David smiles and raises his eyebrow as if to say, *See?* Jonathan grins and shakes his head then returns the hose to the pump. As they head inside to pay, Jonathan puts his arm around his smart young man and says, "I hear ya."

CHAPTER 44

SHOOTERS EXPRESS, A LOCAL gun range just off I-85 outside Charlotte, has only four people in the stalls. An enormous black man, dressed in all black, is loading a .45. He seems lost in his own secluded world. On the opposite side of the room two people stand together: a woman, who appears to be a young soccer mom, and an instructor, who is a gray-bearded, pot-bellied older man who looks like he would be more comfortable at a buffet bar than a gun bar. He stands immediately behind her showing the best way to position her arms, nearly whispering things like *Focus* and *Keep your eye on the target* and *Don't let it scare it you*...and other common sense wisdom. She tightly grips a generic-issue .38 revolver, trying to hold it steady.

And there's Officer Durkin, who stares at paper targets an extra 20 yards further away than the other two shooters. His hands seem to rest on an imaginary shelf, hovering four inches above a small array of guns. His hands don't shake an inch. On the actual shelf below lies a .38 revolver—like the housewife's four stalls down, except that it has a longer barrel and a finish of nickel, rather than gunmetal blue. He also has a chrome-plated 9MM. Rounding out the arsenal is a .45 Glock *hand-cannon*. Durkin stands there, simply staring.

Gunshots are infrequent in the stalls to either side. The housewife pulls off a shot, let's out a tiny scream then lays the gun down like it is a red-hot poker. The large dark figure on his opposite side, also four stalls away, sporadically pulls the trigger on one shot after another and another, methodically—as though he's *counting to five* between shots.

Just then, Durkin, hands hovering above the three firearms, suddenly picks up the .38 and squeezes the trigger in five rapid pulls, barely moving the paper target. Not a bullet goes astray. Upon the firing of the last shot, he picks up the 9MM with his left hand and starts firing, at the same time laying the other gun to rest. He fires it ten times—evenly paced, with just enough time to aim the gun between shots. This time, the heavy paper target shows greater damage.

Finally, he picks up the .45 with his right hand, while simultaneously laying down the *9*, then using his left hand as a brace, cups his right hand under the *cannon*. The sound is deafening. He pulls the trigger, unloading ten, eleven, twelve and a *lucky* thirteen rounds—each one hitting the second target further behind the first target. The last several rounds nearly shred the second, beefier composite target. He quietly disassembles the guns, performing this less-than-easy task in less than a fifteen-count.

He stops, takes a deep breath, addresses and then salutes the targets. The black gentleman from down the aisle notices this and displays an unusual expression on his face—something along the lines of *Wacko*.

Durkin touches a button on the wall next to him, and both targets come swooping toward him like war-torn ghosts. Pulling them from their hooks, he looks from one to the other. The first target has not one, but two circles that represent two guns and two different hands. The other target shows two perfectly formed lines—one vertical, the other horizontal. He admires his handiwork and a smile slowly appears on his shadowed face. He whispers, "I'm coming for you, Carter."

Jonathan and David are excitedly chatting as they exit the gas market and make their way back to the car. Stuart and Daphne walk hand-in-hand, squinting into the sun and enjoying the unusual weather. It's then that Jonathan sees the front door of the SUV open, with Angela missing from the front seat. Trying not to cause any panic, he picks up his pace.

"C'mon, Son," he says to David. "Let's see if Mom's still snoozing."

Suddenly, David spots Angela walking aimlessly toward the highway and into oncoming traffic.

"Dad! What's Mom doing?"

David drops his soda and sprints toward his mother. Christopher looks up from his candy bar wrapper at the same moment and, likewise, sprints after David.

"Mom!" David shouts. "Mom, STOP!"

"Mom!" Christopher adds equally as loud. "Over here!"

Taking off like a rocket, Jonathan sprints past both boys and reaches Angela, grabbing her arm just as an 18-wheeler whisks by, laying on his horn and snapping everyone, including himself, back to reality.

Jonathan and Angela whip around as though a cyclone's wind had spun them into a Whirling Dervish routine.

Startled, Angela quickly snaps, "What in the...hello there!" Embarrassed, she says, "Was I sleepwalking again?" Trying to play it off, but knowing that she and her family had just been thrust into serious danger, she manages an awkward laugh and adds, "I was having the most vivid dream and, well, next thing I know...I'm nearly dancing with a Mack truck!"

All three Matheson boys simultaneously exhale. Jonathan offers up a short, quiet prayer of gratitude for the near miss.

"Thank God you're okay," he says, putting his arm around her and nodding for the boys to head back to the car. Stuart and Daphne, just feet away, stand with eyes wide open and mouths agape. They finally exhale, then join the family in heading back to the car. Everyone but Angela is quiet.

"Well, so much for a leg stretch," Angela says, attempting to lighten the mood.

Jonathan takes a second deep, long breath and adds, "Hon, we have so much time for stretching out. What do you say we hop back in and try to give the four-wheel drive a run for her money?"

"Yeah," Christopher and David say, simultaneously.

"Good idea," Stuart adds.

Moments later, the Mathesons are on their way toward Charleston, no worse for the wear for a momentary potty break. Jonathan looks in the rearview mirror, catching Stuart's eye, and raises his eyebrows as if to say, *Close call*. Stuart nods.

Christopher has already climbed back into his musical retreat, while David, not missing a beat of the two men's brief interaction, looks down at his book of colorful butterflies and whispers a tiny prayer that only he can hear. "Thanks, Gracie. I owe you one."

The family is miles down the road when Jonathan, lost in thought, flashes back to the tragedy that nearly happened just moments ago. His heart feels as though it will break at the thought of losing his second favorite girl. Tears pool in his eyes at the thought, as he tries to force a positive thought to replace the pain. He looks over at Angela. She is asleep again—a tiny smile on her lips. She seems to be sleeping a lot lately. *Well, it is vacation. Time for us all to relax. Maybe this trip will do her some good. Do us all some good*, he thinks.

He looks up just in time to see that he had gotten too close to a moving van. Jonathan ignores the instinct to hit the breaks or jerk the wheel as the van, rather fortunately, exits onto an off-ramp at that very moment. His eyes dart from Angela to the rearview, and to the back seat. All is well. Realizing he'd been holding his breath, he relaxes, takes a sip of coffee, pats Angela's hand and turns the cruise control back on. He spots a road sign: Charleston 70 miles. Good, just one more hour and we'll be hitting the high seas. Leaning forward, he scans the horizon and the sky. Clear blue. No clouds. Perfect.

CHAPTER 45

CARTER CRUISES ALONG MAIN Street on downtown Tybee Island, passing Fort Screven that defines the northern part of the island. He passes the legendary DeSoto Hotel—a classy place to unwind and rejuvenate. He drives along what the locals call *Mid-island*, and eventually reaches the southern-most part of the island, where the local grease haunt, The Breakfast Club, lives. It's an eatery that he and his pal had frequented many a time. Their omelets are record-breaking in size, the huevos-rancheros were the perfect remedy for an evening of over-indulgence and the bottomless cup of coffee was worth the two-beans it cost.

He parks along the side of the building, just as Mack had instructed, and deposits a handful of quarters— part of the systematic diversion from which they both operated, especially when engaged in a mission whereby any number of eyes may be following. Today, that wasn't likely the case, but as they say, it never hurts to be cautious.

He passes three houses, crosses a second block and spots Mack's house just across the street, tucked in among a patch of dunes. Forgoing formality, he walks around the side of the house and up onto Mack's deck. There, the master of the house sits, coffee in hand, watching a school of dolphins skim the morning waves on their way to the north end—the place where the river meets the ocean. Carter knows better than to sneak up on him. If you ever caught Mack unawares, you had really gone some; most who had tried would find something on their person broken.

"Lucky Strikes!" Carter shouts, giving a fair warning of the incoming hug that was about to attack his buddy of three decades. Mack could barely turn around before he was *attacked*.

"Mack Attack!" Mack returns, lifting Carter off the ground and threatening to toss him over the deck's banister. They laugh like old times.

"Careful, Old Man, you don't want to throw your back out."

"Not with a little girl like you," Mack laughs, sitting him down. "Coffee?"

"Uh huh."

Lucky was Carter's nickname, given to him a lifetime ago by Mack because he was the luckiest man Mack and their comrades had ever known. Carter was blessed with classic luck, a dose of smooth talk and cool eyes that had gotten him out of more sticky jams than Mack had ever seen.

"Man, you're a sight for sore eyes," Mack jokes.

"And you're a sore sight for eyes," Carter returns.

They fist-bump, shake their heads and turn to face the ocean, like they'd been standing there for hours. As if on cue, April exits the house with two fat, café style mugs, full of steaming hot coffee. She was beautiful, dressed in shorts and a brightly colored tank top. Her long naturally blonde hair was pulled into a ponytail, and her tan was perfect, as always.

"You so scored, Bro," Carter says just loud enough for April to hear. Mack nods.

"Hey, Carter," she coos. "SO good to see your handsome face."

Mack tosses his old coffee over the deck's edge, as she hands out the fresh coffees.

"How can a girl your age be losing her eyesight so soon?"

After a long hug, she pulls away then, in faux shock, asks, "Okay, it's not Christmas. Or, a funeral. So, why are ya here?"

They laugh. Mack gives him a tiny nod and he replies, "Nothin' but a little business. May have to steal your boyfriend for a couple of days. Can you spare him?"

She plays like she's heartbroken then says, "Well, as long as he's with you, I know he'll be safe. I want to hear all about it, but first, why don't we head down to The Breakfast Club and grab some hash!"

"A girl after my own heart," Carter says.

"Hey, I was here first," Mack adds, bumping Carter aside as they head out.

Carter liked her. Thought she was the best thing to ever happen to Mack. And he'd go to his grave defending Mack and the love of his life. He knew Mack would do the same.

And both of them just might find out, soon enough.

≈

Two hours, three omelets and four stacks of pancakes later, the trio is walking back to the beach house. Carter lags behind, handing a couple of singles to a homeless guy sitting on a bench across the parking lot from The Breakfast Club; his head hangs low underneath the large brim of a weathered straw hat.

"Thanks, Mister," the deeply wrinkled man quietly says.

"No worries. Just make it a healthy meal," Carter says, eyeballing an empty bottle tucked under the man's worn sleeping bag, adding, "And not more of that."

The man follows his gaze, sees the bottle then smiles, saying, "Nah, that's from a recent bender. I'm hungry and heading in there...thanks to you."

Carter nods and keeps walking, glancing over his shoulder nearly a block away, to see the lonely man entering the side door of the restaurant.

"C'mon, Lucky. Let's get you on the road. You got some miles to make!" Mack shouts from up ahead.

"Coming!" Carter yells in response, watching the two lovebirds walking hand-in-hand. This made him think of Teresa, and the excitement in his gut knew that something was right about this one; he'd call her as soon as he was on the road.

Moments later, April kisses Carter on the cheek and looks at him with smiling eyes.

"Sure was nice to see you again, Carter. Been too long," she says, elbowing Mack in the ribs. "You'd think thieves as thick as the two of you would've seen each other sooner."

"Aw, it's not his fault. It's been a long—" Mack starts, but is cut off as Carter interjects.

"Right, it's *his* fault…keeping something as lovely as you to himself. I mean, I remember the first time I heard the name April in a phone call a few years back. I figured it was the older, slightly moustached type that he usually went for." Carter smiles at her and winks at Mack.

"Whatever," Mack mumbles, pushing him down the driveway. "Look at the time."

Carter hugs April who then turns and heads back to the house, giving the boys a moment of peace.

"She's a good girl," Mack beams.

"I see that. And a beauty to boot," Carter replies, adding, "Well, I'm off. Like I said, I'll be in touch if I need your help. I should know something inside the next 24."

"I'm in. Just let me know."

"Thanks."

Mack bear hugs Carter. They smack one another's backs—just a bit too hard.

"You been working out, Old Man?" Mack sarcastically asks.

"You know it. And I'm only eleven months older than you, Gran'pa. Talk soon."

As Carter walks down the driveway, Mack shouts, "Carter?"

He turns, "Yeah?"

"Be careful of what you're stepping into. Could be a coupl'a clowns. Could be a coupl'a criminals."

Carter knew what Mack was saying was entirely true. And he had no idea which way this familial pendulum was going to swing. But he knew that if a storm came on strong, he'd have all the backup he needed in his longtime pal.

"Uh huh," Carter replies, tosses a casual salute, turns the corner and is gone.

CHAPTER 46

CARTER CROSSES FROM GEORGIA over the Florida state line, making brisk work of his travel. His mind races from one topic to another: *When am I going to learn more about Shasta's whereabouts? ...Is Dad really dying? ...Does Jonathan believe this trip is legitimate business? What am I going to do with that long, tall drink of water; she has me terribly distracted, but in a good way.*

As he circles Jacksonville and hops on I-295, about to merge back onto I-95, he whistles a random song—one that he recalls from his overseas tour of duty. It's then that his mind flashes back to more troubled times.

Carter reflects. It was the hottest first week of October on record in Afghanistan, 2001, and it was just one of many tours of duty that he would *enjoy* in his illustrious career. He had been called on by his superiors to join the armed forces of the U.S., U.K., France, Australia and the Afghan United Front, known as, *The Northern Alliance.* They had launched *Operation Enduring Freedom.* What had begun as a response to the nightmare of *9-11* would attempt to put an end to a group of terrorists referred to as *Al-Qaeda.*

Carter bites the inside of his cheek, fixating on one thought: *Here we are more than a decade into this ridiculous war, and it's gone from trying to remove the Taliban regime from power, to attempting to battle widespread insurgency—all the while, expanding into neighboring Pakistan, and continuing to be the longest-running war in our history.*

Carter shakes his head, thanking God for the freedom he's been able to enjoy from that cluster-bomb. *Thing is, I'd jump back into duty without a moment's hesitation, if the need arose.*

Out of habit, he scans the overpasses and the low-lying trenches of what was known as *The Speed-trap*

Corridor. He taps his brakes for good measure and decides that all is clear.

No incoming missiles, no rocket launchers, no weapons of mass destruction and no IED's. In fact, not as much as a speed trap—just nice, quiet, easy-going cruise-controlled miles of concrete and asphalt highways, maintained by the state's finest.

His wandering mind finally settles on his favorite pastime, Teresa. Grinning, he snaps back to the present and dials Teresa from memory. Imagine that, already memorized her number and it's only been…

"Hello?" her sexy voice asks.

"Hello," he answers, waiting for that moment when she lights up the other end of the line with that million-dollar smile.

"Oh, hey there! Took me a minute to recall the number. Silly me. Long day. How are you?" she asks, cutting right to it.

"Good, thanks. Just driving. Thinking of you."

"Good answer. Me, too," she responds, in coy fashion.

He loves the way she doesn't miss a trick—dropping into place like a well-oiled machine, or in this case, a sexy woman with oodles of confidence. The long beat gets her attention.

"Are you daydreaming about me while driving? Don't you know that could be dangerous? Both hands on the wheel and eyes on the road, Mister!"

She laughs. He does too.

"Guilty, Your Honor." Beat. "Daydreaming? Yes. Dangerous? Of course, but then my life is spent on the ragged edge of trouble. Don't you know that by now?"

"I certainly do, but it's always nice to hear it, don't-cha-know-see?"

She's a keeper, he thinks—*No doubt*.

"By the way, I almost forgot to thank you for watching the dog."

Silence.

"Hello?"

"That's it? Thanks for watching my dog?" she replies, trying so hard to muffle a laugh.

This catches him off-guard, as he can't tell if she's serious or not. He decides she isn't.

"You're a hot mess," he says. "You know that?"

"Hot for you," she volleys, adding, "You know *that*?"

They laugh like school kids while he cruises down the interstate and Teresa is enjoying getting to know Carter in all the small ways. She smiles, thinking how lucky she is to have met such a good man, someone so very different than her ex-husband. The smile disappears with the thought of Durkin, so she pushes his image aside and continues to listen to Carter talk about his recent stopover in Savannah, and regains the smile on her face.

"Yeah, it was so good to see Mack. I've known him since before our Gulf War experience, but haven't seen him…well, in nearly forever."

"That's nice," she says with a smile in her voice. "He sounds like one of the good guys. Like you."

Carter realizes she's not just being nice, but being real, one of the things he appreciates about her.

"Thanks."

"Is he part of your mission?"

"He could be." He hesitates. "Not trying to be secretive, just keeping things close to my chest for now. I'll share more as it gets revealed. Fair enough?"

"Of course. I get it. You're an international man of mystery and I'm…an international woman of…uh…dog-sitting."

Carter is trying to decide if he should say more but chooses to keep things like they are. Reading his mind, she adds, "And frankly, the less I know, the safer I am." She chuckles. "Isn't that how it works?"

"Actually, yes, to be honest. But also, you're way more than just a dog-sitter. You're a smart, adventuresome, thoughtful, beautiful woman…who also happens to be pretty damn funny!"

She smiles on both the outside and inside, knowing that Carter isn't one for fluff.

"Why, thank you," she says in a deep southern accent, adding, "Golly, you're making me blush!"

"I doubt that!"

Both enjoy the carefree spirit of their newfound relationship.

"Hey, I know you didn't ask, and I'm sure you have, or will have, your hands full with business and all, but *if* you were to happen to want some company…" she hints.

"Already a step ahead of you," he interjects.

"Good. Nice to know we're on the same page… for once."

"Yeah, right," he quips.

"Guess I was just thinking that if you were to get done early and were already down there…in paradise…then perhaps we could enjoy some of that paradise together."

She realizes she's being a little pushy, but she also knows, even in this short time, that Carter won't do anything that he doesn't want to do.

"No, exactly. I was going to mention that. I guess I was just gonna see how things went first."

"But…"

"But," he interrupts. "I realize that women need time to plan things. Guys don't."

She laughs, adding, "You are *so* funny, Carter. I've known you, what—a week? Two weeks?"

"Three. Come Monday."

"See? Even that. Geez, you're *so* much more sensitive than you want to let on."

"Hey, just a minute."

"No, it's a good thing. I just…"

"No, it's not. Well, not all the time. A guy's gotta…"

"Carter. Darling…" she interrupts again, knowing that he's being part funny and part vulnerable, and takes a moment to breathe to be sure she doesn't scare him away. "Man of Mystery…Love of My Life. Okay, well, *Like* of My Life…for now, anyway," she giggles. "I was actually complimenting you. It's a good thing. And trust me, I KNOW you're not the *sensitive* type. Heaven forbid. But it's so stinkin' refreshing to meet a man who isn't afraid to be warm and caring while also being rough and tough and, well, manly!"

He shakes his head and smiles and thinks he may have finally met his match. She got him. And he wasn't afraid to show her. For the first time in his life, Carter felt okay to be himself and not afraid of being hurt, or left alone.

"Thank you, T. I appreciate you saying that."

She sighs, knowing that it's okay—that he *gets* her. And she doesn't have to worry about him stomping on her emotions, while his ego gets in the way. She was serious; it *was* refreshing. Suddenly, she gets that warm tingle all over her body that lets her know she's in a good place. And she enjoys the moment.

"Okay," she whispers.

"Okay," he mirrors.

"Now, about that trip," she says, in her best redneck accent. "You gonna ask this girl out proper like, or you gonna wait around, playing it loosey-goosey, flying by the seat of your pants."

They enjoy yet another hearty laugh, and before hanging up, he reminds her where the spare key is, to make herself at home and to please park around back, even though he rented a car so that he could keep his truck out front—something about his wanting it to look like he was there. She understood, agreed, faux saluted and signed off, begging him for a *second round of beer & barbeque* and some more of that *late-night smooching.*

He agrees to all the above then rings off, feeling lighter than he has in a long time.

CHAPTER 47

THE MATHESONS REACH CHARLESTON just shy of lunchtime. Jonathan exits I-26 and merges onto Meeting Street and eventually makes his way along King Street. Maneuvering through the old cobblestone streets makes for slow going, as tourists flow through the streets like a carnival. The hundred-plus-year-old buildings are decorated for Christmas already, and parking spots are at a premium.

"Tell you what," Jonathan says, breaking the silence. "Before we meet Jefferson and Sammy for lunch at Fleet Landing, I'll swing down toward the French Quarter and South of Broad."

"Hey, that's a book by Pat Conroy," David says from the back seat.

"I've read it, have you?" Daphne asks, leaning over to straighten David's hair.

Christopher is waking up in the back seat and mumbles, "If it's a book published in the last century, he's read it."

David turns around to make a face at Christopher who returns the gesture and musses his recently fixed hair.

"Hey, watch it," David kids. "Gotta look good for the tourists." Turning to Daphne, he answers, "And yes, I read it. Wasn't as good as *Prince of Tides*, but nothing could beat that style."

"But didn't you find *Tides*...depressing?"

"It was dark in tone. But then, depression was so much of the subject matter, right? Much of the angst came from the patriarch in the story. Henry Wingo? Not a good man. And the main character...what was his name?

"Tom," Daphne replies.

"Yeah, Tom. He was mighty bitter. All in all, I think it captured the city of Charleston and the flavor of the

South, while the interaction of the main characters made you want to go to Disneyland after reading it. You know, just to lighten the mood." He laughs at himself.

"My, my, Little Professor, that's quite a recommendation."

"Thanks. Conroy really is the master of the saga."

"And you're the master of the nerds," Christopher jokes.

"Boys!" Jonathan says.

"Straighten up, gentlemen," Daphne adds. "We're almost at the marina."

Angela stretches, looking out the window then spins around toward David and says, while giving him a fist-bump, "I don't know about me, but you look hungry." She knows that's one his of favorite sayings.

"Nice, Mom." David smiles then taps Jonathan on the shoulder. "Hey, Dad?"

"Yes, Son."

"Did you know that the marina is home to the Mega Dock? It covers something like 40 acres of water."

"Actually, I did, Son. I learned all about it, thanks to you, several summers ago when we vacationed on Folly Beach. Remember?"

David frowns, scratching his chin as though deep in thought then says, "That's right, I did take you to school, didn't I?" He grins, as Jonathan shoots him a look.

In between glances at a group of young girls, Christopher chimes in, "Now, if we could only teach you about girls."

"There's plenty of time for that, David. Just don't let your brother rush things," Angela jokes. "Plenty of time."

Jonathan pulls into the small Fleet Landing Restaurant & Bar parking lot and, just as someone is leaving, he snags a spot right in front. Angela whispers, "There's that *Car Karma* of yours again," and kisses his cheek.

"Love, *you're* the good luck charm."

"Oh brother," Christopher and David mock from the back.

Daphne brings the riveting conversation to a close with, "Okay, Matheson troop, bail out, straighten up and fly right. We have a lunch mission on our hands."

"What she said," Stuart adds, stepping out of the SUV and helping Daphne out.

CHAPTER 48

CARTER'S GROWLING STOMACH SOUNDS like a pack of angry bear cubs arguing under his seat. He glances at the clock. There's been no word from Randall, but he knows that he'll be there in plenty of time, so he thinks now is a good enough time as any to stop for lunch. And what better place to stop than Daytona Beach? With that, he disengages the cruise control, so as to not light up his break lights. The reason? He realizes he'd let the last long stretch of highway—the one with a 70 MPH sign, stick in his mind, while the current posted speed had dropped to 55 MPH because of highway construction. And there's a state trooper quickly gaining on him—barreling down the highway. It's just a bit too close for comfort.

"Crap," Carter mumbles. *Orange cones for hundreds of yards means Construction Zone. And if Mr. Trooper were to go through my rental car, what he'd find could draw entirely too much attention and create entirely too many questions.*

The trooper blows past him—no siren, just lights flashing. Must be a high-speed chase or an emergency several miles away. Or, perhaps he's just late for his own lunch date and has grown tired of slow drivers. With that momentary burst of adrenaline behind him, he flips the turn signal, taps the brakes, hits the exit, makes the turn, merges into traffic, spots the truck stop two-hundred yards ahead and nods.

Having traveled a lot, frequenting Petro Shopping Centers, Carter had learned of their *StayFit* program that offered a better alternative to fast food. *One of the few places to eat good food on the road*, he thinks.

Carter is out of the Dodge Charger SRT8—an upgrade from the standard rental, and in the door, grabbing a seat and a menu faster than most people could get unbuckled and around their car to start pumping gas. He had made an art of un-wasted motion—something he'd learned a long time ago in the marines. Oddly enough, that was one of three things he and his father shared. The others were an obsession for being efficient in everything and an unhealthy need for being right, even to a fault—neither of them were ever likely to back down from anything. It just wasn't in their DNA. If they had to lose a limb or their life to get the job done, so be it.

Carter takes a seat at the end of the counter. His back is to the wall with a clear line of sight to the parking lot and his *armored tank*. His eyes scan the room, taking in the wall-to-wall NASCAR memorabilia. Wrecked car hoods, twisted fenders, blown tires—all are attached to the walls and ceiling. It's a hodge-podge of crashed car parts, beer and soda advertising and trucker hats and t-shirts.

Classy.

Nodding, he gets the attention of a tall, lanky waitress with too much make-up. She saunters over, cracking her gum as though it were a contest. Looking him up and down like he's modeling a new suit, she flips on a plastic smile with the automation of a light-switch and pours coffee without asking.

"Sure. Black. Thanks."

"What'll it be, Doll Face?" she asks in a deep, thick-as-molasses southern accent.

"Chef salad and a BLT on white—toasted. Double bacon. Extra crisp."

Pulling a pad from her apron, she sets down the pot of coffee and scribbles his order.

"Sounds good, Darling," she says, pocketing the pad and pen.

"Thanks," he smirks.

"Sure that's all, Honey?" she asks, twitching a phony wink.

"That'll do it. Thanks."

Scooping up the menu, she turns off the smile and retreats to the kitchen window where she shouts the order loud enough for the people pumping gas to hear.

"Subtle," Carter mumbles.

☙

Jefferson and Sammy had reserved the best seat in the house overlooking the water, and the whole gang feasts on fresh seafood, while laughing and sharing their excitement of the upcoming voyage south. Lunch at Fleet Landing was the perfect bridge between a long drive and a long sail. And it would be several days before the Matheson crew would stand on solid land and enjoy a hot shower. The lively conversation over lunch covered a variety of topics. Jefferson explained that the trip would take roughly three days to get there and three days to return. Including Thanksgiving Day, they expected to be traveling under blue skies and warmer than normal temperatures—pending any surprises that Mother Nature wished to spring on them. Everyone seemed perfectly content with that news.

Christopher was unusually open, sharing how he was rethinking his relationship with Kym and was reconsidering getting back with her when they got home. He continued to share how it had become strange not having her as a part of his daily life, especially near the holidays. This surprised the family, as Christopher wasn't much for open displays of emotion. Jonathan suggested that perhaps the *close call* with that punk who picked the fight, and the subsequent length of time lying on his back, may have given him reason to ponder life a bit more.

Angela, perhaps a bit too enthusiastically, showered Christopher with praise for being so vulnerable with the family. This seemed to make him uncomfortable, and it wasn't long before he clammed up, nodded and returned to his interior world. When Jonathan confronted him, asking for more insight, Christopher withdrew once again, now with an excuse about how his ribs were still bothering him. Angela smiled, squeezing Jonathan's knee under the table, and all further inquiries were dropped.

Charismatic David, on the other hand, rattled away while sharing all the research he had done recently on marine life, tide and weather patterns for this time of year and how their oceanic journey was similar to the early Thanksgiving settlers, some 400 years earlier. Everyone was particularly surprised when he revealed that the first Thanksgiving wasn't actually with the pilgrims in 1621, but that this story was made common thinking thanks to a Sarah Hale, one of the most influential women in American history. As a side note, he continued, she wrote *Mary Had a Little Lamb*—another surprising bit of knowledge. The truth was that Sarah so loved the Thanksgiving tradition that she campaigned for nearly 20 years to have that day become a national holiday with a set date, rather than the way states had been celebrating it, which was whenever they wished. She was eventually successful and Thanksgiving on the fourth Thursday of November was born.

When Daphne asked Angela what she was looking forward to most on this trip, Angela thought a few moments before explaining how she was glad to be away from the house and the memories, and how she just needed to let her mind relax. Jefferson nodded his approval, as did everyone else—adding that they were thankful for the same.

Before the close of lunch, Daphne shared her excitement in using some of this time to *marinade* on thoughts of her next cookbook. Everyone enjoyed the play on words. Jefferson expressed his excitement in teaching the boys how to sail in the ocean. Jonathan chimed in with mutual anticipation, while also disclosing a long-held secret—he had never been a particularly good swimmer. This shocked everyone but Angela, and each one assured him that he was safe with them. Sammy was excited to spend time with her two favorite *gal pals*. And Stuart chimed in by saying he just wanted to work on his tan. This drew laughs all around, but he continued with a serious tone by suggesting that they use this trip as part of a *new tradition* by doing something completely different each year. Their response was a resounding shout of approval.

CHAPTER 49

THE WINDOWS ARE DOWN and the sunroof open as Carter enjoys the warm breeze and humid air. Checking the elaborate electronic dash, he eyeballs the weather, local traffic and his GPS location—all with one screen. *Sure beats my old Ford F-150. But then, you can't haul wood, motorcycles or dead bodies in this*, he smirks. Tapping the Sirius Radio button, he scans the stations with a fingertip. Not hearing anything that engages or entertains, he taps the *off* button and returns to the quiet. His left hand *air-surfs* out the window, rising up and down, skimming across the warm, moist air.

Suddenly, the phone rings, breaking the silence. He jumps. *Too much coffee*, he thinks, as he picks up his cell from the passenger seat. Glancing at the screen, he sees that it's Reddick.

"Dennis."

"Carter."

"What's up?"

"Oh, just thought you'd like to hear the latest."

Carter's mind rushes to the options. "Let's see, you've got a new girlfriend—for real, this time."

"I wish, but no," Reddick replies.

"Teresa's pregnant...however, we haven't—"

"Uh no, and not that I even care to know. C'mon, think something we wish would all go away."

"Cancer? War? Famine?"

"Worse."

Carter thinks, grins, then chuckles. "Durkin would swallow dirt?"

"Bingo!" Reddick nearly shouts.

"He's dead?"

"Well, not really. But he is sucking dirt. If graveyard shift for six months is any indication."

"You sound downright giddy. What happened?"

"You know how he's been completely bent out of shape ever since you got released?"

"Sure."

"Well, he cannot seem to let it go. So, Mahler pulled him in his office a few days ago and told him to, quote, *Shut up, fly straight and pull your hours*. Well, he did. For about 24. Then he started melting down again—mouthing off, being belligerent *and* insubordinate to all of us, including Mahler."

"Geez, the guy just won't learn, will he? He needs to realize he's still in the pay-your-dues part of the program," Carter chuckles.

"Exactly, but evidently—after sniffing around a bit, this is his standard MO. He's a hothead who bullies people to get his way."

"He should know, the one person you don't bully is Danny Mahler."

"Well, you'd think so. But in his last gig, in Jersey, he was reprimanded so many times for, get this, aggression and insubordination, they asked him to leave. Why they didn't officially fire him, I have no idea. But he left."

"Okay, so we have a pattern. But why Mission Grove?" Carter asks.

"The obvious? It's cheaper to live and better schools. We have some of the best," Reddick adds. "Plus, his *ex*-wife—your current squeeze, and his son, had moved here shortly before."

"Right."

"And as you likely know, given the proximity you've experienced with Teresa, Oddball followed her here in order to be near his son *and* keep an eye on her."

"Uh huh," Carter replies. "Guess the only other question is, why did Mahler take him on in the first place?"

Nearing the stretch where I-95, Okeechobee Road and the turnpike all merge, Carter sees a jack-knifed semi and two cars. Sirens blare as *Rescue* arrives.

"Ambulance?" Reddick asks, hearing the noise over the phone.

"Yeah. Accident up ahead. Looks like a mess."

"To your point—two reasons, the best I can figure out," Reddick replies.

Carter chuckles.

"What?" Reddick asks.

"It's just funny. Since we've become pals, I've come to realize you've picked up one of my habits."

"What's that?"

"Numbering things. You list things in numbers. Just like me. Do it *all* the time."

A moment of silence, as Reddick thinks. "Huh. I guess you're right. Never thought about it until you mentioned it."

"Yeah, no, it's all good. Just noticed it, probably for the first time. Anyhow, go on, I'm all ears, Buddy."

"First of all," he hesitates. "Now, I'm self-conscious. Anyhow, believe it or not, our friend Durk is an ace shooter."

"Okay. But then, so is Mahler. You're pretty good…"

"And you're the best of all us, but…" Reddick says.

"But what?" Carter interrupts.

"No, he's *really* good. Like, off the charts."

This surprises Carter, as he'd seen him as an out of shape, disgruntled mall cop who couldn't keep a job. "What's the other thing?" he asks.

Reddick sneezes on the other line, causing Carter to move the phone from his ear.

"Bless you…for not blowing my eardrum to bits."

"Sorry. Pepper. Guess where I am."

"Derby. Of course."

"Yup, and your girlfriend is waiting on me. Man, she's smokin' hot."

Carter smiles—at both his pal's use of phrasing, and the fact that he realizes he has a *girlfriend*. And he likes that thought. Looking in the mirror to check traffic, he catches his reflection and wonders if he may even look younger now that he's dating a younger woman—by five years, anyway.

Snapping back, he prods, "Okay, Loverboy, tell me the rest of the story."

"Right. Well, you're gonna really love this. Or not."

"You're killing me."

"Okay, so he's been bounced from not one, but *two* stations in the past handful of years. One in Boston, and the other in Jersey—well, the Pennsylvania/Jersey jurisdiction, his latest."

"Not too unusual, really. There's burnout in all major cities. Besides, like you said, cheaper to live and—"

"Yeah, yeah, but he's a shooter, right?" Reddick whispers.

"Uh huh."

"Well, I got pals in a nearby township—my old stomping grounds..."

"Yeah."

"He was bounced because he shot several guys."

"In the line of duty?" Carter inquires.

"Yeah. Well, thugs, anyway. But it was the *way* he shot them."

Carter rubs his hands on his pants, realizing that his palms are sweating. *Must be the humidity.*

The silence is a bit long.

"You still there?" Reddick asks.

Carter was amazed that someone as laid-back as Reddick could still act like a kid at Christmas.

"You gonna finish this story, or what?" Carter mocks.

"So, he's making a bust. And yes, they were all holding drugs and guns. Yes, they all had a record. But he shot *all five* of them, without missing one of them. And he did it execution style—tap, tap-tap."

The quarter drops. Carter slowly nods, thinking, *I grossly underestimated our Durk.*

"Wait. You said tap, tap-tap."

"Yeah."

"Times 5."

Carter lets it hang there a moment to see if Reddick puts it together.

"Yes, 15. Shots. That's…"

"Exactly," Carter interrupts. "A 15-round. Special upfit. And not…"

"*Standard Issue*. So, not only was he acting out of a potential, self-interest—we'll say for the sake of argument, but carrying his own extra backup."

Carter considers the implications—on several fronts, both his safety and that of Teresa's, and her son's, for that matter.

"So, our boy is a marksman *and* a badass," Carter snidely remarks.

"To quote you, uh-huh. And one more thing…"

"For crying out loud, there's more?"

"He was ALONE when he dropped them."

Surprised, Carter stops and rolls this around.

"No backup?"

"Nope. They were on their way, but he acted solo."

He realizes while it's not the standard way to go, he couldn't be sure it was that odd.

"That's…unusual."

Carter is beginning to get that funny feeling in his gut. A feeling—he didn't like.

"Right. And he was let go, even though the press called him a hero. The suits saw him as a loose cannon—a renegade. And they didn't like the fact that he was both that good and that volatile."

Carter looks down at the speedometer and realizes he's up to 85, scans the mirrors and overpasses and taps the brakes, pulling it back down to a couple of ticks over 70.

"But you need guys like that…"

Reddick interrupts. "No, you need *marksmanship* like that, but not that volatility. Not like that. Look at the way he rubbed us ALL the wrong way—from day one…and for no reason at all. And we're the good guys."

"True."

"What I also can't figure out is why no firing? Why let him walk? Why no record?"

Carter rubs the stubble on his chin and squints, deep in thought. "Unless he's covering for something. Or he's got something on somebody."

"I'll continue to dig. See what I find."

Carter can hear Reddick slurping his coffee on the other end—a habit he finds a bit annoying, but lets it ride. "So, now that we have a better idea of what we're dealing with," he continues, "what are you thinking?"

"Simple. Watch your back."

"I'm so scared." Carter jokes.

"Seriously, Bro. Remember, he got you into jail on three charges that didn't *exactly* exist. And he did it with blunt force. Pun intended. Something tells me if he's that uptight and has such a stiffy for you, he may lean a little harder next time."

"Uh huh."

"And you're dating his ex-wife."

"Lucky Strikes," Carter smirks.

"Whatever," Reddick laughs. "Look, she's happy with you, but dropped him. And he hates it. Plus, you've seen how he handles rejection."

Carter flashes back to those events: him driving, getting stopped then tripped, cracked, cuffed, stitched and dumped in jail. *Not pleasant*, he thinks, adding, "I'll watch my back."

"You should. Cause our friend, my good friend, is not a friend. And something tells me that Durk's the kind of dick that'll drop whoever gets in his way."

Carter lets that sink in before commenting.
"But then he's never seen my bad side…especially when I'm thinking straight. And he does not want to see that. Friend."

CHAPTER 50

GATHERED ON THE MASSIVE expanse of the Charleston City Marina, it was easy to see why the dock was named *2005 National Marina of the Year* by *Marina Dock Age* magazine. The family gathered, staring wide-eyed at the gleaming vessel that would shortly become their temporary home.

"HOLY WOW!" David shouts, standing on the dock's edge. Still staring at the yacht, he adds, "I've never seen anything as beautiful as that. Ever!"

"You said it, Bro," Christopher admires.

"No kidding," Jonathan says.

"That's a beauty, all right," Stuart chimes in.

Jefferson stands tall and proud with both hands on his hips, "Yeah, it's my girl." Looking over at Sammy, he quickly adds, "Well, my *other* girl."

Angela, Sammy and Daphne laugh as they watch all four men stare at the handsome vessel, standing shoulder to shoulder like in a parade.

"I've been on boats most of my life. It began with my father and his love of the water. There was never a weekend, growing up, that we weren't out fishing, skiing, or just laying back and watching life cruise by. I guess it started with kayaks and canoes then skiffs and eventually powerboats. But as soon as I discovered sailing, that's when I knew what I really wanted and I started saving for this. Come on," he waves for them. "Climb aboard!"

Jonathan and Stuart help the ladies aboard, while Christopher and David fetch the luggage.

"Where did you get the name *Lady Giselle* from, Dr. Long?" David asks.

The smile on Jefferson's face becomes faint, "Well, David, that's a two part answer." He looks at Sammy. She blows him a tiny kiss. "Giselle was my daughter's name.

Giselle Marie. And my late wife, Yvonne, I called *My Lady*."

David reaches to put his hand on Jefferson's shoulder, saying quietly, "I'm sorry, Dr. Long."

"Thank you, David. That's kind of you to say."

"I bet they were beautiful."

"Yes, they were," Jefferson nearly whispers. "They've been gone nearly four years now—hard to believe. Giselle would be—let's see," pondering the years, he looks over to Angela.

She smiles and says, "She would have been Gracie's age. This Christmas."

All three women sigh.

"Okay, look," Jefferson says, clapping his hands. "We are here to have FUN. That's what my girls would have wanted. So, what do you say? Is everyone ready to sail the open seas?"

"Yes. Aye, aye. Absolutely. Let's go," several reply, while David pulls up the rear with, "Batten down the hatches and time to shove off!"

David's cheer instantly lightens the mood and prepares them for an exciting holiday journey. Shortly, they're all aboard, cargo is stored and Jefferson is steering the craft through Charleston Harbor, past Fort Sumter National Monument and out into the big, blue Atlantic Ocean, heading south toward sunny Florida.

CHAPTER 51

THE SUN SLOWLY DISSOLVES into the horizon as Lady Giselle glides through the water, causing an occasional splash of cool water to spritz the passengers. Thanks to a particularly strong southwesterly wind, the sails make easy work of propelling the nearly forty-one foot craft. The fiberglass body slices through the water like a razor-sharp knife, helping the crew to relax and enjoy the warmer than normal night air. All except one. Jonathan has been hugging the side rail for the past hour or more, trying not to notice the slight bobble—instead, paying more attention to anything that his eyes can settle upon.

"Any better, Dad?" David asks, leaning over the starboard side next to Jonathan.

Jonathan jumps, "Huh, oh yeah. Peachy."

"I see that. Especially with the color of your face," David jokes.

"Like I said earlier, didn't really spend that much time on the water growing up. Dedicated more of my time to books, girls and football—all things grounded," he chuckles. "Okay, maybe books and football, anyway."

Stuart takes his focus from the cell phone app that Christopher was showing him—the one that shows you the placement of the various stars and constellations, and turns to his son-in-law.

"Son, I don't know why you didn't take Daphne up on the Dramamine. It's fail-proof."

"Just hate to take any chemicals that I...uh...don't—" he suddenly leans over the side and vomits. Wiping his mouth, he turns to David and says, "On second thought, Son, please go get something from your mother. I've had enough of this."

"Good call. Get along, David. The girls should be close to having dinner ready," Stuart says.

"Aye, aye, Captain Number Two!" He salutes and deftly disappears below.

Stuart shrugs. "To quote your boys…I'm just saying."

Christopher, somewhat oblivious, has been engrossed with the same app most of the past hour and finally peels his eyes from his iPhone.

"Pops, you don't look so good."

"Yeah." Jonathan manages a smile. "Thanks for overstating the obvious."

"Kinda like me last summer when I went joy-riding with that hidden hooch from the garage."

Jefferson, who has been listening to the conversation all along, engages the autopilot and takes his hands off the steering wheel, turning to the three and joining them on one of the seats.

"I remember that. Learned some lessons that summer, didn't you, Chris?"

"Several, that's for sure," Christopher boasts.

"Learned any *this* year?" Stuart asks. "Perhaps with those cracked ribs?"

"Very funny. That was different. It wasn't my fault. He came after me."

"And you were just minding your business," Jonathan provokes.

Christopher shifts his weight, making sure not to reveal any pain he was still experiencing. "That's right."

They don't buy it.

"Well, okay. Maybe I had something to do with it. But what I'm trying to say is…" Frustrated, he drops it—just as they all break out laughing.

"Son, it's okay. We're just playing," Jonathan kids. "Just like you were doing with me." He pauses before continuing. "Frankly, Christopher, I think you were smart to stand up. And not let that punk show you up," Jonathan says, looking toward the galley, checking to see if Angela is nearby.

Christopher leans forward, "Really? I thought you'd think I should turn the other cheek and try to save his soul."

"Turn yes, but only after you've fired a warning shot across the bow!" Jonathan adds.

Jefferson chimes in, "Nicely put, Captain."

"Here you go, Pops," David says, bounding up the steps and handing Jonathan a tiny tablet and a bottle of water. "Oh, and dinner is served in five."

"Thanks, Son," Jonathan says, slowly swallowing the pill.

Jefferson rechecks the autopilot, stares up into the expanse of stars and says, "Man, we have really lucked out with this weather. There's barely a cloud for miles, we have a great breeze from who knows where, and we're making good time." Looking at his speed, he adds "And, we're doing six and a half knots."

"That's good, right?" Jonathan asks.

"Oh yes. This is a six, sometimes seven, knot boat. In choppy water, it averages five. At this rate, we'll hit Miami sometime tomorrow. But tonight, with this quiet water and strong back wind, we're cooking with gas."

As if on cue, Daphne pops her head out from the galley and says, "Come and get it!"

Stuart takes Jonathan's elbow as he stands and says, "Ever notice how much time we spend eating?"

"Yeah, great isn't it?" Jefferson says, while Jonathan attempts to hide a belch and says, "Yeah, uh…just great."

Stuart, David and Christopher kid as Jonathan smirks in their direction, adding, "We'll see who laughs last—when the lights go out and you really feel the rock of the water."

Christopher stops laughing and asks, "What?"

CHAPTER 52

CARTER HITS THE OUTSKIRTS of Miami just before
the first wave of drive-home traffic hits. The humidity has
increased, so he turns on the AC, but keeps the windows
down. Swiping his hand across the touch-screen of the
GPS, a dozen emblems pop up. He frowns.

"Screw that," he mumbles and reaches into a worn
duffle bag in the back seat, pulling out a tattered envelope.
Flipping it over, with one eye on the road and the other on
the envelope, he scans the scribbled directions to Randall's
home.
"Better."
Glancing at the overhead signs, he spots the needed
exit, gives a signal and speeds up, merging over one lane at
a time.
In a short while, he's pulling through an iron gate,
having been welcomed by an older but large and very fit
security guard who happens to be packing at least a
Glock—judging from the bulge in his waistband. Carter
shows his driver's license. *Neck* nods and Carter passes
through the gate and into a handsomely appointed enclave
of multi-million dollar homes.

Carter pulls into the *mini-estate* and onto the
cobblestone driveway lined with perfectly manicured
shrubbery and a small stone water fountain with a dancing
angel. He looks up at the three and a half story mini-
mansion on less than an acre but near the water, and shakes
his head, wondering how people can manage to float that
kind of mortgage.
He is greeted at the door by his withering father and
surgically robust wife, and after a few man hugs with *The
Bull* and pleasant double-cheek kisses with Randall's third

wife, Suzanne, the three make their way into the middle of the impressive three-story foyer, sharing pleasantries, while their voices echo off the marble floors and glass entryway.

Carter couldn't help but notice the way she pronounces her name. Most people would say sue-Zan—as in *I can*. Yet, she prefers sue-Zahn—as in *Say Aah*. Carter rolls his eyes, but only in his mind, and graciously smiles. After a brief tour of the palatial spread, they settle in the drawing room—something he generally calls a living room. Carter always found it odd, touring other people's homes, wondering *Why show me yours...I don't want you to see mine.* As another part of the icebreaking and tension relaxing, they share a cocktail from the massive bar.

"You like?" Randall asks, admiring the handsome sculpture of expensive dark woods, adorned with etched and beveled glass, plus a variety of single malt scotches that would make any Irishman proud.

"What's not to like? A big bar with enough wood to build a small barn, enough booze to last until next summer and enough fancy glasses to serve the whole neighborhood," Carter jokes.

"We like to entert-a-i-n," Suzanne says, stretching the last part of entertain to a near ridiculous length. "It's a rather choice neighborhood, with—how shall I say, discreet yet impressive residents."

Carter nearly threw up in his mouth. *The pompous attitude of this one,* he thinks, *her toilet probably smells like a rose garden.* Carter would love to have shared that sentiment with his company, but thought better of it, instead choosing to play along.

"Oh, I would imagine the classy community is decidedly discreet with a plethora of innumerable indiscretions. But I won't tell," he leans forward, getting close to her face, adding, "if you don't."

She hesitates a moment, then a tiny smile breaks at the corners of her well-sculpted mouth as she breaks into a petite chuckle. Carter couldn't tell if she were playing him as much as he was playing her, but when he turned to catch

Randall's sardonic stare, he knew that he had pushed his act a bit far. Randall was not amused—at least, not on the outside.

Suzanne politely smiles and excuses herself. When she is clearly out of earshot, Randall asks, "What are you doing? Can't tell if you've gotten cultured, if you two are flirting, or you just want to get down to business."

Carter clears his throat, looks to see she's not near, then leans close to Randall and whispers, "I have. She is. And, I do."

Randall smiles, saying, "Son, you are a piece of work. Why don't you take a look out back and I'll grab us a cocktail."

"Sounds good," Carter replies as Randall walks to the bar fridge for some ice.

Carter's eyes shift from the setting sun to the gently swaying palm trees, finally settling on the attention-getting three-foot waterfall that cascades into the shallow end of the pool which is surrounded by Randall's immaculately manicured backyard. He shakes his head, thinking *I have never seen a pool-Jacuzzi combo like this.*

Randall approaches with two highballs.

"You like?"

Carter looks up and asks, "The whole get-up, or the U.S. Marines shield painted on the bottom of the pool?"

"Either. Or both," Randall chuckles.

"Original," Carter returns, adding, "So, this is how the other half lives."

"The result of spending one's entire life committed to a cause," Randall says. "You'd know about that, right Son?"

Neither the reference, nor the inference was lost on Carter.

"Uh huh."

"That...and good real estate investments," Randall adds, smiling.

Carter sips his drink, makes a face and adds, "I suppose."

"Too strong for you, Sissy?" Randall grins.

"No. Just never been a big fan of girlie drinks," Carter smirks.

"Right."

Carter's shoulders relax for the first time since hitting the road. Sitting nearly twelve hours wasn't as easy as in the old days, which is why he worked so hard to stay in shape.

"How about you start by telling me what you know?" Carter gets to business.

Randall hesitates. "Not to be insensitive, can we have a drink first and chat business after dinner?"

This was the Randall that Carter had known all his life—a man of contradictions. One minute he was heartbroken—correction, *nearly* heartbroken that his daughter had gone missing. While the next minute he wants to get his drink on and talk old times. But that's what made The Bull what he was. Big. Powerful. And determined to get his way—whatever the cost.

Su-zaahhhne slides open the wall of glass and steps out onto the stone patio, her heels clicking like a metronome. Carter watches her glide toward them. He smells her perfume as soon as she exits the house. *Expensive, no doubt, judging from Randall's handsome abode.*

"Gentlemen," she whispers, "dinner is ready when you are."

Carter thinks she sounds like a movie star from the '40s—a Marilyn-wannabe. She doesn't, however, look like one. *Run hard and put away wet*—is what Carter is thinking. He will certainly convince her to think otherwise—that he is her biggest fan. But for the moment, he just didn't trust her. And he didn't know why.

❧

After dinner, Carter looks through photo albums of Shasta, watches a video of her last birthday and can't believe the resemblance she has to Randall. She has his high forehead shielding deep-set eyes and square chin, yet with the more pronounced African-American nose and lips. She's also tall like Randall, with broad shoulders—looking more mature than her nearly 18 years. Randall's third wife minces few words, expressing her disdain of the situation, and while she doesn't appear to be particularly pleased with the arrangement—having her living under their roof, Randall keeps her in her place, reminding her that she's *his daughter*.

Given the fact that Suzanne is much younger, to the tune of nearly 15 years, and that Randall has fallen very sick, makes Carter wonder if she had anything to do with it. This gets discussed when she leaves the room for coffee and after-dinner drinks, but Randall assures him that it isn't the case. Carter doesn't buy it. Randall motions for Carter to follow him to the sunroom—a screened-in porch of the outdoor pool and cabana area. Judging from the rolled-up wall above, apparently you can swim in the winter and summer—heated and covered in the winter, and screened or uncovered in the summer. Nice.

Carter sips his drink and watches Randall, wondering when he was going to get to business. After all, Carter has a mission.

As if on cue, Randall pulls a paper from his sport coat and hands it to Carter. "Just got this. Nothing particularly creative there."

Carter reads aloud, "Shasta is safe and unharmed. But that won't be the case if you don't meat our demands. One: deliver $500,000 inside a yellow backpack to an address to be provided in the next 24 hours. Two: make the bills unmarked. Three: Do NOT involve the police or military. Four: Divert in any way and she will be hurt."

The several moments of silence are broken when Randall asks, "Note how they misspelled *meet*?"

"Could be a bad speller, or just stupid. Most likely stupid, given that they're screwing with you."

"Roger that. On both counts."

"$500? Not a million?"

"Right."

"Unmarked? Makes sense. But *don't involve the police or the military*?"

"I'm with you."

Emptying his scotch, Carter looks for a place to sit the glass down, but Randall takes it and pours another from the bar.

Carter looks up. "I'm good. Wanna stay sharp."

"Fair enough. What else?" he asks, trying to suppress a cough.

"They said hurt. Not killed, maimed, or delivered in parts…"

"Carter," Randall interrupts.

Carter looks up, realizing he was thinking out loud.

"Sorry. Just seems a bit odd, yes?"

"That's why you're on the job."

"And I am."

Randall puts his hand on his son's shoulder.

"And that note?" Randall adds.

"Yes?"

"Notice how it says, *Deliver $500,000 to an address to be provided in the next 24*. Meaning, deliver to the address in the next 24? Or, in the next 24 the address will be provided?"

"I'm sure it's deliver in 24 after we provide it. But I see what you're saying. It's a little confusing," Carter says.

"Dealing with a half million dollars and a life at stake—doesn't seem like a situation where you want to be…unclear."

Carter grunts, "Uh huh."

Randall slowly nods. "Whoever it is will certainly be sorry they messed with you."

Carter looks at Randall, folds the note and puts it in his pocket, adding, "They'll wish they hadn't messed with either one of us."

CHAPTER 53

TERESA LOOKS AT THE clock, punches out and heads back to the kitchen to grab some takeout from William, the cook who is an older gentleman that everybody likes being around. William has never married. He's been friends with the owner for nearly three decades and prefers working the late shift. He says he likes the fact there isn't as much noise, there's less pressure, and Teresa works that shift. She used to anyway, before moving to days. William misses seeing her each night—always so upbeat and perky. Now, it seems that same perkiness is being shared with that local war hero, Carter.

"Hey, William," Teresa playfully coos.

"Hey, Miss Teresa," he returns, blushing at the attention.

"You 'bout ready to wind it down?"

"Yep. Have to—now that you're leaving."

"You are the sweetest. I miss you, now that I'm working days."

"Aw, you're nice. And I miss you, but it's nice to see you tonight. Anytime is a good time to see you."

"You're my favorite too," she says with a wink. "But I have to admit, working mornings certainly is easier on me, especially with my boy."

He nods while carefully putting her order together, adding more than is customary.

"Here you go. Just a little extra. For you and that boy. I saw him in here not long ago with some friends. He's growing up fast."

"Don't you know it. Maybe too fast. Needs some discipline too, if you know what I mean."

"Well, that new boyfriend of yours may be just the remedy, huh?"

"Huh? What boy—"

"Carter's a good man."

She is caught off-guard and blushes.

"Yes, he is."

William notices and doesn't push any further.

"Not like everybody else…"

"Which is why I like him," she interrupts.

"Good for you. You deserve it," he says, passing the bag through the order window. "You have a good night. Get some rest and I hope to see you soon."

"Thanks, William. For this," she lifts the bag, "and for all those nice words. You're so kind. You take care."

She blows him a kiss and is out the door with what locals call The Derby Diner's Ultra Meatloaf: ground beef, lamb and sausage with a spicy kick that'll have you remembering it for days—that, and double-mashed potatoes along with a side salad big enough to feed a family of four, thanks to William. Teresa hauls the takeout to her old, but reliable Corolla and heads down I-77, first to Carter's house then home to soak her weary body and tired feet in a long, hot bubble-bath.

Durkin sits alone in his large and sparse Lake Norman apartment. It was decorated in *early bachelor*, with an over-sized leather sectional sofa, large flat-screen television on the wall and an over-stuffed recliner—one that had seen better days. Not much else decorated the top floor apartment. Lake Norman was one of the largest man-made lakes in North Carolina and nearly dwarfed Lake Mitchell, a nature-made lake on the edge of Mission Grove. Durkin liked being a bit further from the office. It helped keep his personal business private. He also liked being single again; although, he wasn't completely single—he had a girlfriend. He enjoyed Jen, a sales rep with a local real estate firm, but liked even more the fact that he didn't have to share living space with her. Besides, he'd done it once and swore it wasn't for him. *Carter? He can have my former headache, Teresa. He's got no idea what he's in*

for. The kid? He's kind of a punk. Doubt he'll amount to much. A troublemaker, just like his old man. But married? No thanks. Never again.

Staring at the wall, his mind drifts to Carter and he can feel his body start to stiffen.

I still don't get how that clown got out of jail, he thinks to himself. *I made a clean bust. Guy's a repeat offender. Loose cannon. Troublemaker. Drunk. And I'm a good cop. Probably the best this town's ever seen. So, I know what I'm doing—upholding the law. So what if he's a vet? Big deal. Doesn't give him special privileges. He needs to be taught a lesson. And Mahler? Those two are in cahoots—betchya anything. I'll find out. But him and Teresa? That's crazy. She's too smart for him. Won't last. She'll get tired of his slack ass and dump him. Just like she did me. She deserves that kind of trouble.*

He gets up from the couch, walks to the window and stares out at the lake—his mind, spinning like a tumbler. *Maybe I could roll up on Carter and give him a taste of the Durkin medicine. He's not that tough. Hell, I took him down with one swing. Something to be said for wearing a badge. Smartest way for me to get from third to first shift is to wait my turn. Screw that. Second best way? Push aside Reddick. Least he's not a hick like all the rest. Or, I could become a hero. That'd get Mahler's attention. Move me up the ranks faster. Mahler doesn't like looking stupid. Carter made him look stupid. That's what I'll do.*

Durkin looks at himself in the mirror. *Uniform looks damn good on me*, he thinks, then addresses his image, "You looking at me? Well are ya, Punk? C'mon, Carter, make my day."

With the smirk still frozen on his face, he yanks his holster from the back of the dining room chair, picks up his hat and keys, flips off the lights and is out the door.

৵

It's much later than she had anticipated by the time Teresa finally arrives at Carter's home. Lunch ran extra-long—into the second-shift, in fact. The new girl called in sick, so Teresa agreed to share the second and take a bonus day off so that, when Carter finished his business in Florida, they could escape and reconnect.

She pulls around back, as Carter suggested and, thanks to a recent rain that increased the propensity to slide, comes to a sliding stop. Finding his hidden key above the back door jam, she starts to let herself in, but Samson comes running out the doggie door to greet her—his tail, wagging furiously.

"Hey, Boy! How ya doing?"

Samson, the ruler over Carter's kingdom, does a little happy dance, then sits the moment Teresa waves for him to do so.

"Good boy, Samson."

"You smell the meatloaf?" she asks, adding, "Okay, potty first—meatloaf, second."

As she reaches for the doorknob, he runs straight for the woods.

❧

Durkin parks at the end of Carter's property and heads up the long driveway on foot, his eyes adjusting to the dark. He had no idea Carter lived so far out. No neighbors. No street-lights. *No nothing except a cottage and a plot of land.* He sees Carter's truck out front, and decides to leave his flashlight off, just in case Carter comes out. There's enough light from the moon that he can see the outline of the driveway. He crosses the expanse quickly and is just feet away from the house when he mumbles to himself, "Time to pay you a visit, Old Man."

❧

Entering the kitchen, Teresa fumbles for the overhead light switch next to the refrigerator. Finding it, she flips the switch. Nothing.

She flips it again, as though the second time might be the charm. Nothing.

"Well, that's a fantastic end to my day," she says to the dark.

The storm that blew in over dinner must have blown a fuse. I have no idea where the fuse box would be and I don't have a flashlight, she thinks, then says aloud, "Ah, but the Boy Scout will. Never locks his pickup."

She feels her way across the living room and reaches the front door. It's locked. She shakes it until she realizes it has a deadbolt.

‽

Durkin, now just feet from the house, hears the rattling of the door and stops in his tracks. *Shit, he's planning to take me.* He quickly runs to the side of the house as the door opens. Standing perfectly still, he tries to calm his heavy breathing. *Just stay cool. You're in control.* As he peers around the tall stack of wood, it appears Carter is looking for something in the back of the truck.

Probably his gun!

He reaches for his Glock, thinks better of it and pulls his heavy Maglite from his belt. He slowly approaches and, just as Carter is about to turn around, Durkin swings and cracks him on the head, his body falling with a thud. Turning him over, he flicks on the flashlight and shines it in…Teresa's face.

He's so shocked that he literally jumps back and falls to the ground. Samson approaches, barking loudly, then settles into an evil-sounding, deep growl. He lunges at Durkin and manages to take a mouthful of his forearm, twisting it violently—ripping Durkin's shirt and some flesh.

"OW!" Durkin screams while trying to get to his feet, swinging the flashlight at Samson's head.

Whoosh! He misses as the dog retreats at the last second but is poised to strike again. Durkin shines the bright light in its eyes. This stuns Samson, but not enough to keep him from standing his ground.

"C'mon, Durk," he says aloud—his brain racing to find a solution.

If I take her to the hospital, I'll look stupid. I had no reason to be here and could get kicked off the force. If I take her inside and fix her up, well, why was I here and what would that look like? Besides, with her temper, I'll never hear the end of it. Lucky I was driving the company car and not mine. Wait, I could place a call to the station. But I can't report it as a break-in, because she has a key to the jerk's house! I could report it as a burglary, saying I came up on this person, saw they had a gun and hit them. Wait, why would I be driving all the way out here? Not my jurisdiction.

He looks around, but sees only one home with lights on, nearly a half-mile away.

That's it. I'll call Jen and have her report someone outside the house. I'll respond to it, saying I was in the neighborhood, and then drag her body to the front door. Wait, what if they track the call to the girlfriend. Dammit!

The monster in Durkin's mind slowly stands taller, but also twirls in circles—becoming more deranged by the minute.

Maybe, with that blow, she won't remember anything. There's no way out of this. What the hell have I done?

He hasn't taken his eyes off the dog—the light, shining in its eyes. Samson doesn't budge. Durkin looks around again, hoping nobody has seen him. He doesn't see a way out.

She's a tough cookie. She'll be all right, he thinks, scanning the area once more. He slowly backs away from the growling dog, making his way safely back to the cruiser, and speeds away.

CHAPTER 54

IT'S LATE WHEN RANDALL and Suzanne decide to wrap up the evening. She excuses herself, saying how much she has enjoyed getting to know the *son she never knew*. It rang phony, but Carter smiled graciously, adding something about *that made two of them—as he was getting to know a sister he never knew he had*. Light chuckles between the two new friends helped seal their mutually feigned admiration. *Yeah, right,* he thinks. A couple more pleasantries, a mention of an early morning tennis tournament with the girls at the club, and she leaves the men to themselves, heading upstairs to bed. Randall shows Carter to his enormous and well-appointed office to show off a few trophies.

Carter looks at an entire wall of medals and honors—something fit for a small museum. There was more than a bit of pride in Carter's chest right now, knowing that as much of a tyrant his father had been his whole life, he taught him a good many lessons. Randall stares at the wall of glory with a wistful eye, no doubt remembering the strength and vitality of youth.

"Lot of proud memories," he says softly.

"Uh huh," Carter acknowledges.

Randall picks up a tarnished frame from the credenza behind his desk and joins Carter, handing it to him.

"This was a happier time…wasn't it?" Randall asks.

Carter takes the picture and looks at it—his mind racing back to that day. He nods.

It was the day Carter had decided he wanted to follow in his father's footsteps and become a soldier. Randall was standing tall and proud, wearing a chest full of ribbons. His arm was around Delores. She was a demure woman and so very kind. Carter was reminded of how beautiful she was. She had chestnut hair, bright blue-green eyes and a smile that was at all times inviting and happy. Carter was eighteen, tall and fit. With a full head of thick hair and a wide jaw, he had the beginnings of being a real lady's man—and a hell of a soldier. Little did he know that he would end up fighting in more than a dozen conflicts over the years. And there was Jonathan—ten years old, much softer features than the two soldiers. He was handsome like his dad, but more gentle like his mother. A wide-eyed innocence was always present with Jonathan, a quiet resolve that would suit him just fine later in life.

"Yes, Sir. That was a happy time. Long time ago. Hell, it seems like an eternity," Carter replies, nostalgia hanging in the air like a mist. He thinks, *Those days of innocence are long gone and far away.*

"It was," Randall adds quietly. "I miss your mother. There's never been another like her. Never will be."

Carter's mind fires like a bullet to another time— the instant he saw her die. He feels the acid churn in his stomach. The skin around his skull tightens. *Leave it be*, he thinks—knowing it does no good to live in the past. *Let sleeping memories lie.*

Randall must have felt the shift in energy, as he takes the frame from Carter's hand and says, "Well, enough of memory lane. Time to hit the sack. Got a big day ahead of us."

At that moment, Carter felt a familiar drama play on their familial stage. Father controls the actors, actors follow his orders, and everyone moves to the beat of The Bull's drum.

"Good idea. Kinda bushed myself. It was a long drive," Carter absently replies.

Randall pats his son on the back as he leaves the room, adding, "Make yourself at home. Just stay away from the 40-year-old scotch," turning at the last minute to wink at Carter.

Carter is thrust back in time to an era when *The Lieutenant Colonel* was his dad and not his *boss* and a wink like that meant *You're my boy and everything's okay.* It's also an expression that he's seen Jonathan share with his boys time and again. Oddly enough, it's an old gesture—reserved for another era, one Carter missed coming from his father. And while he appreciated it being shared between his brother and his boys, somehow that simple gesture skipped over Carter, leaving him feeling alone and, once again, on the outside looking in.

Randall is about to leave when he turns back and looks at Carter with that steely eye he often used to employ with his soldiers.

"One more thing. I'm anxious to hear more about your plans for your pal Mack, that is, if you're going to need his assistance. More importantly, I may have another job for you. And him, if it pans out."

All nostalgia evaporates in that instant, as business takes precedence.

"Sir?" Carter replies, fighting the urge to snap to attention.

"Another mission. Maybe more of a business proposition. Either way, it's right up your alley. You'll like it."

Carter hears the word business and it feels like a spider crawling across his neck.

"I'm…liking retirement," Carter responds with no emotion, his attention turning to the wall of glory.

Randall shifts his body, addressing Carter with a fraction more authority.

"I still have a good many allies in the *Corp*. They're creating a new Special Ops division and could really use your expertise—not only of finding people, but of…" He hesitates, choosing his words carefully, "Losing them just as effectively."

He lets the phrase hang in the silence, long enough to hit its mark.

Carter can't help but turn to his father. He wanted to gauge his expression.

"It's a government job with high risk. And high reward. Of many sorts."

Carter is intrigued, but tries to push any interest to the back of his mind.

"I'm enjoying the civie life."

Randall knows that Carter is a soldier first and a civilian second.

"There's also a tremendous amount of money to be made, not that that's ever been a high priority with you."

He sees if that keeps Carter's attention. Carter looks to the wall—the medals, shining like stars awarded for work well done.

"But besides all that, it would be something that'd rid the world of scum…"

Carter barely raises an eyebrow.

Randall is about to let it go when he loads another into the chamber.

"Most important? It'll help keep America safe. And let you leave a legacy for your family."

Carter squints, breathes deeply and slightly nods.

"Interesting," Carter says so quietly that Randall nearly asks him to repeat himself. However, Randall knew exactly what he said. Furthermore, he knew he had his son's full attention.

"I do miss the storm," Carter replies, taking a long beat before adding, "You know what I mean?"

Randall knew exactly what he meant: Desert Storm, the Afghan Storm, the Shit Storm, and pretty much any other storm where Carter could get his hands back in the real game, and not in a small town game called Mission Grove. No, this would be more like, *Mission: Carter*.

"Well, we can talk about it more tomorrow. Let's find Shasta first. We can worry about all that other nonsense later," he tosses it away with just enough nonchalance to let Carter relax, but still chew on. He knew his son very well. After all, he trained him.

"Good idea. Sleep well," is all Carter manages.

He listens to his father ascend the stairs and cross the carpeted floor above him, then walks to the small bar and takes down a crystal glass and a bottle. He pours a handsome serving of the old man's *Glennfiddich Private Vintage* 40-year-old scotch. Carter first lifts his glass to the wall of honor, then to the old black and white photo of his family.

"Here's to you, Mom. God bless."

᠘

Carter wakes up in the middle of the night—still in the recliner where he fell asleep two hours ago. Checking his watch, he sees that it's after 2 A.M. The fatigue had gotten the better of him. It's then he realizes that he'd spent so much time traveling down memory lane that he hadn't spoken to Teresa. In fact, he hadn't spoken to her for some time.

Not good, he thinks, so he retrieves the cell phone from his duffle bag in the corner and dials Teresa's home number. It rings twice.

"Hello, you've reached..." He quickly hangs up, concerned that he might wake her, her son, or both. Thinking more clearly, he dials her cell. It goes straight to voicemail, "Hey there. Teresa here. Leave a message!"

"Hey, Babe, it's me. A bit after 2. Sorry I didn't call earlier. Been traveling down memory lane. Bumpy ride," he nervously chuckles, adding, "Just…give me a ring when you get this. G'night." Then, he dials the diner. *I know it's closed.* It rings and rings.

He disconnects and a nagging thought crawls around in the back of his head like a caged animal. He starts to think about the possible scenarios: *She's working late. Goes to my house. Feeds the dog. Goes home and collapses. She's fine.* But, the other inner voice says, *She would have called. Left a message. Something. Maybe she crashed at my place.* He dials that number. Many rings later, he hangs up. He checks his watch. *2:15 A.M. Should I call Reddick? No, it's late. Just as he's about to toss that idea aside,* he thinks, *Screw that, he's up.* He looks his number up, dials, and the other line picks up before the second ring.

"Yo."

"Hey, Buddy. Sorry to ring so late. Did I wake you?"

"Nah. Got two days off and was just getting caught up on movies."

"Let me guess—*Cops*, or racing."

"Actually both: a Steve McQueen double-header. Watched *LeMans* with dinner. Great flick. And was just catching the end of *Bullitt*."

"You and chase scenes."

They enjoy the inside joke, referring to last summer's chase through the woods—the one where both Carter and Reddick ended up in the lake.

"Anyhow, you didn't call to hear my Netflix lineup. What's up? Miss me?"

"Not actually, but I *am* missing my girl."

"So, call her."

"I did. No answer. Which is strange."

"But it's late."

Carter suddenly feels like a self-conscious high school teenager, worrying that the cheerleader doesn't like him after all.

"Yeah, I know. Silly, I guess. Just weird," Carter mumbles.

Reddick senses that it's important, especially for Carter to call this late.

"When's the last time you spoke?"

"Early this afternoon. She was doing a double. Yeah, that's right you…"

"Yeah, she waited on me. Said something about grabbing a quick break in between, before pulling the second."

Carter feels more self-conscious, but won't let the nagging feeling lie. "You're right. I'm nuts. Maybe the colonel is making me that way. Been a long day. Some emotional shit going on too."

"I get it," Reddick confides, adding, "Tell you what, I'll swing by her place first thing tomorrow on the way to breakfast. Just to be sure. Cool?"

Carter is about to agree when he hesitates.

Silence.

Reddick waits.

Shaking his head, he finally blurts, "Dude, do me a large one, okay? Swing by my house—not sure why, but it's the last place she would have been before heading home. IF she went home. She could have crashed at my place."

Reddick suppresses a sigh and responds, "Okay. No worries."

"Sorry. Probably crazy, but you know me…"

"No, I get it. Your gut's uncanny."

He is already off the couch and putting his boots on when Carter finishes.

"Not sure about all that, but you're not that far away and better safe than sorry, right?"

A short burst of thunder crackles in the background, catching Reddick off-guard. He mumbles, "Whoa."

"Was that thunder?"

"Uh, yes, *Radar*."

"You guys having a storm?"

"Nah. Earlier there was a pretty good one, but it blew over quick."

This makes Carter think, *Storm. Power could have*—"Hey, my power is notorious for kicking off in storms. That fuse box'll blow with even the smallest surge."

"Okay, I'm on my way, Mom. I'll check the box. Find the girl. Save the day. And get back to you."

Carter explains where the main power box is, where he keeps the spare fuses and thanks him for being such a pal. Reddick turns off the TV, grabs his keys and holster and is out the door.

∾

Removing the ransom note from his back pocket, Carter tries to distract himself from needlessly worrying about Teresa. So, given that he isn't sleepy, he starts running random thoughts through his head: *Why $500,000 and not more? Whoever this is has to know the man's good for it. Why'd the 'meet-ball' say military? Why would Shasta disappear if she had all of this wealth?* He looks around. Suddenly, he recalls a photo that Randall showed him of Shasta and some friends, when he and Mr. Black flew in. *Three guys. Two white. One black. Or, he could have been Hispanic or Jamaican. Randall said she was working in a bar. Why? She's smart. The best colleges are at her feet. Makes no sense.*

He tiptoes upstairs to the opposite end of the house from where the parents sleep. Flipping on the light, he looks around. Ordinary girl's room. Only bigger and richer. The enormous four-poster king-sized bed with fancy covers was not your standard teenager's bed. *This room's half the size of my whole house.* Movie posters adorn the walls: Eastwood, Spike Lee, Tarantino and Hitchcock. *Good taste.* He scans the room, looking for photos. Just two. One was Shasta, Randall and Suzanne at a Miami Heat game— looks to be a couple of years ago. The other was Shasta and a light black guy. Looks like a thug, could be a nerd. *Maybe he's a therd*, Carter smirks to himself.

"It's late, I'm punchy," he mumbles aloud.

The guy in the photo was wearing one of those long coats, just like in the other photo. *What's up with that?* He continues looking around. No other photos. *That's crazy— thought girls were all about photos.* He sees some cords on her desk where a laptop likely once sat. *Oh yeah, laptop.* No luck there. He tries to think of what he'd do if he were hiding something in this space.

As he's about to leave the room, he stops. *Under the bed?* Getting down on all fours, he pulls the bedspread up and looks underneath. Nothing. Just before he's about to stand up, his eye catches something. Leaning lower and twisting his neck back at an odd angle, he reaches up between the box-spring cover and the edge of the frame. Pulling at a colored envelope, he tugs until it comes free. A manila envelope falls to the floor. He sits on the bed, first looking to the door and the lights underneath it. Then, he opens the envelope.

CHAPTER 55

OFFICER DENNIS REDDICK CRUISES down I-77 faster than the posted speed limit. *So what,* he thinks, *I'm on official duty.* Looking down at his ripped jeans, running shoes and Temple University sweatshirt—a gift from an old girlfriend, he mumbles, "Okay, not official, but important."

He arrives at the edge of Carter's property in less than 20 minutes. The back tires of his Charger spin in the mud from the recent rainfall then catch as soon as he hits the gravel of the driveway. He frowns as he sees Carter's truck parked out front. *He never parks out front*, he thinks. As his headlights whip past the house and toward his truck, he sees something lying beside the pickup. *Is that...a body?* He hits the breaks, sliding to a stop, and flips on the high-beams. *It is!* He throws the car into Park and looks around. Reaching for his 9MM and Maglite, he gets out and slowly walks toward the truck. The only sounds are those of wind in the trees and a dog barking in the distance. Using the ultra high-beam flashlight, he scans the property in all directions. His body is on high alert, and his mind races to assess the situation.

Comfortable that no one else is in the fringe, he makes his way to the body. He stands over it for a moment, while his eyes adjust.

"Oh Shit!"

Leaning down, he sees a small pool of blood behind Teresa's head. He checks her pulse. It's weak. He lifts her eyelids and shines the light in her eyes. No reaction. Not good. Suddenly, Samson appears out of nowhere, barking. He jumps and flashes the light in his direction.

"C'mon here boy, it's okay."

"Sit." He instantly obeys.

He runs the options through his head. *Call for help? Ambulance?*

"Screw that," he mutters, and gently picks up Teresa and carries her to his car. Laying her in the backseat, he grabs a heavy coat from the trunk and covers her up, then attaches a seatbelt around her waist. He runs back to the house and lets Samson in the open front door. Flipping on the switch, he sees Carter was right. No power.

"You'll be all right. I'll be back later. Good boy."

As he starts to run back to his car, he stops and shines his light around the truck. It's then he sees a set of footprints next to where Teresa had been laying. He estimates it to be a man's boot. *Likely size ten or eleven, deep Vibram soles. On the newer side.*

"I'll get back to you," he says to the night, then runs to his car.

Stepping on the gas, he nearly spins in a complete circle before correcting and ripping down the driveway. *Gotta call Carter, but first the ER,* he thinks while flipping on the police-issue emergency lights hidden in the front grill and in the upper deck of his back window. The speedometer climbs from 65 to 75, then rockets to 95. He can't help but feel a bit like Steve McQueen in *Bullitt.* Only thing, he wasn't being chased—he was doing the chasing.

≈

Carter sits staring at a short stack of photos. They are of Shasta as an infant, a woman who appears to be her mother—judging from the skin tone and features, and Randall, holding baby Shasta. Carter notices a wedding band on Randall's finger, but not on the hand of the woman he assumes is Shasta's mother. While he knows he can't judge a book by its cover, the woman doesn't look like much. She's entirely too skinny, has dark circles and a vacant look in her eyes. *Too many drugs, or too much booze. Or both.* He slides that photo behind the stack, revealing another one that more clearly accentuates her thin body—while at the same time showing just how tall she was. She was just a few inches shorter than Randall's six foot two inch height.

Carter couldn't help but wonder what he and Shasta would have to talk about when they finally met. There was an anxious pang in his gut, and he wasn't sure if it was more panic, fear or just old-fashioned nerves. Of course, the lack of sleep, mixed with the anxiety of Teresa's whereabouts didn't help comfort him.

Just then, the cell phone vibrates in his jeans.

"Hello," Carter says softly, just slightly above a whisper.

Reddick has excused himself from the ER bay where Teresa is getting stitches sewn into the back of her head and walks to the nurses' station.

"Hey, Buddy…you still up? Reddick asks, disregarding the sign overhead instructing people not to use cell phones in the area.

"What do you think? What'd you find?"

Looking down, Reddick sees caked mud on his boots, leaving big chunks of it on the clean, polished floors.

"Well, I have good news and bad news. What first?"

Carter's stomach tightens.

"Give me some good news, will ya?"

"I found Teresa. She's here with me," Reddick says with measured beats, "and she's…okay."

Carter lets out a deep sigh, but isn't thrilled with the hesitant and somewhat generic response. "Okay. What's the bad news…and what's the noise in the background?"

Reddick takes a deep breath. "The noise is the ER. Which is where we are. She's getting some stitches."

"What?" Carter shouts.

"A half-dozen stiches, to be exact. Looks like she may have suffered a concussion. She's coming in and out, but she's mostly out."

Getting more uncomfortable by the minute, Carter stands and paces. "What happened? Give it all to me."

"Okay. I went to your place. The lights were off—you were right. I found her lying on the ground next to your truck. She had evidently been hit on the back of the head. There was a good amount of blood, and I rushed her to the hospital."

"WHAT THE HELL!" Carter shouts, then lowers his voice, looking in the direction of the master bedroom, "How can this…"

"I have no idea, Carter," he interrupts. "It's crazy. I mean, who'd want to hurt her?"

Carter's mind starts running. *This had nothing to do with her. She was in the wrong place at the wrong time.* "There's only one person who—wait, back up. What time did you find her? Where was she on the ground? Was Samson there? And did you see any tracks of any—"

"Whoa, hold on. One at a time. I found her…" He looks at his watch, calculating the time. "Must be almost 20, 23 minutes ago. She was lying beside your truck. On her side. Yes, Samson was there. And on full alert. What was the—oh, there were tracks. I'd say boots." He looks down at the chunks of mud he's left on the floor next to the nurses' station. "Wait…" He lifts his boot up, flicking off some mud. "The prints look just like mine, come to think of it."

Carter's mind is racing, his heart is pounding—along with his head, and he picks up the envelope of pictures, turns off the light and makes his way downstairs. "Hold on just a minute," he says, walking past Randall's bedroom. At the bottom of the stairs, he continues, "Okay, look. There's only one person who has a beef with me. Only one person *stupid* enough to come out to my place in the middle of the night. And only *one* person who hits a woman." He stops. "Wait, whoever it was—and I think I know—didn't mean to hit her. He didn't know she was a *her*. He thought it was me."

"Huh?" Reddick asks. Then, the quarter drops. "Durkin!"

"Has to be. Who else? He came looking for me," Carter continues anxiously, "just like you said he would. You said the power was out, right?"

"Yep."

Carter thinks, replaying the potential scene in his mind. "She showed up...the storm had tripped the box...it was the first time she's at my house...so she didn't know where anything was—she certainly wouldn't have been able to...find...a flashlight."

"Right."

"So, she goes outside..." Carter continues, putting the pieces together, "...digs around my truck—that I told her I left out front just in case anyone came looking for me and..."

"Durk's already there...maybe at the edge of the property, or in the bushes—" Reddick interjects.

"Right. She goes out looking for a flashlight. He comes up on her and..."

"POW!" Reddick blurts on the other end.

"Damn."

"Just like he *powed* you, not long ago."

"Exactly!" Carter replies.

"But, wait, what I don't get—" Reddick stops, as he sees the doctor leave the ER bay and walk toward him. Seeing Reddick on the phone, he nods in the direction of the scrub room—motioning that he has to wash up; his smock is covered in blood.

"Hey, Carter?" Reddick continues, "The doc just left Teresa. Let me go catch him. I'll ring you right back."

"Go."

Reddick rings off. Carter stands in the middle of the grand living room, his mind moving in a blur. *How in the world can I have two major calamities on my hands at one time? I should be there with Teresa. She'd just tell me to do what I came to do.* He looks at his watch. It's nearly 3:30. Rubbing his eyes, he knows he has to get some form of sleep or he won't be worth much tomorrow. *Heck, even two hours will be okay. Whoever the clown is that's playing*

*with Shasta is gonna wish he never dreamt up this game. I
promised Dad I'd have this solved before the end of
Thanksgiving. It will happen.*

The phone in his hand rings.

"Talk to me," Carter barks.

"Okay. She's got six stitches in the back of her
head. Got a concussion from the blow. He's going to keep
her here for the night. Says she has a hard head and should
be okay to go home late tomorrow, but more likely the next
day." He sighs, catching his breath.

"Damn! I should be there."

"No, you should be doing what you're there to do.
I've got your back. Don't worry about a thing."

"Thanks," Carter says quietly. The confidence he
feels with his friend means everything.

Reddick sees an orderly wheeling Teresa out of the
bay and down the hall. He starts following them. "Carter.
I'll hang here long enough to see she's settled in. She's out
and will be for a while, so I'll be back in a few hours."

"Man, I hate for you—"

"Dude, I had two days off anyway. No biggie. Just
gonna watch movies and tinker on the '68. That's all."

Reddick was referring to his 1968 Mustang—just
like the one Steve McQueen drove in the movie. He had
been working on it in his garage for the past two years,
trying to get it up to speed, so to speak. It was his perennial
weekend project.

"Okay. I owe you," Carter says, knowing their
friendship wasn't about keeping score, but also knowing
that, the older he got, the fewer people he could depend on.

"Yeah, and I'll be sure to cash that in," he laughs.

Carter let his shoulders relax. Teresa was in good
hands.

"Okay," Carter says, fatigue starting to take its toll.
"I'm out. Got to get a couple hours of sleep."

"Still no word, huh?" Reddick asks, adding, "You'll
know more soon."

"My guess? First thing."

They ring off and Carter walks down the hall to the guest room, bypasses any bedtime preparations and simply falls into bed. Within seconds, he's out like a light.

Durkin lies in the dark, staring at the ceiling and wondering if Teresa is okay. *I didn't mean to hurt her.* As much as he was angry with her for leaving him, he would never wish her harm. *Carter, on the other hand, is the one I want.* The heat in his chest starts. *Gotta lay low for a while. They'll never track it back to me. Will they?* He begins fixating on that thought, knowing that Carter is tenacious. And Reddick is smart, even though he plays it down. *Come dawn, I'll ride out to Carter's place and erase my tracks. Nobody will ever have a clue.*

CHAPTER 56

LADY GISELLE SLIPS THROUGH the water, hardly creating a sound. The sails are retracted and the yacht is making good time, heading south toward Florida. The running lights are the only things that illuminate the vessel; the stars, however, seem to hang so low you could reach up and touch them.

Jonathan, Angela, Stuart, Daphne, Jefferson and Sammy are down below, where they have been sound asleep all night. David is sleeping across from Christopher, having spent several hours of his evening teaching his older brother about navigating by the stars—something he had learned in the last day and a half, thanks to Jefferson's very patient instruction. Christopher admired how his brother never seemed to tire of learning—a trait that Christopher wished he had.

Lying atop the sleeping bag, Christopher didn't know which he feared more—the constant bad dreams, or the dark, unknown waters all around him.

He tries to enjoy the moment. The warm night air is so much nicer than the approaching weather back home. He stares into the boundless sky—its texture inky black and dotted with diamonds for stars. His mind wanders to his former girlfriend Kym. He imagines how much she would enjoy being on the boat right now. Her love of the water was something he always liked about her. She was a good swimmer, great off the high dive and perfect on a jet ski. She taught him how to master waterskiing three summers ago. Both of their families were on Lake Mitchell, enjoying a church barbecue. He had seen her around school before, but had never seen that much of her—until the day he saw her in a turquoise two-piece. She looked amazing. His mind wandered further, and he thought of the way he missed her laugh and the way her eyes twinkled every time she looked at him. It had been well over a year since the band competition was held in downtown Charlotte. It seemed like an eternity. And that was the time and place where he first started acting like a dork. Unfortunately, he had let winning the competition go to his head and, in the process, lost Kym. She told him that she could never be with anyone as self-centered as he had become—thinking that without him, the group would never amount to anything and how arrogance was just not becoming of a real professional. He'll never forget the way she looked at him with such disappointment. *You're acting like someone I don't even know anymore, Christopher*, he can hear her saying. He realized now that he shouldn't have turned his back on her or his friends. After all, he never went anywhere with his music, and now his grades were in the toilet. He wonders if David will actually be able to help him salvage his grades and pull his sinking ship out of the deep. The metaphor wasn't lost on him, considering his current location, and he chuckles.

"Whatchya thinkin' about?" David quietly asks, hearing Christopher's laugh.

"Huh? Oh, nothing. Just digging staring at the stars," he replies, adjusting his pillow and pulling the sleeping bag around him. "It's gotten cooler, huh?"

"Yeah. This is so great, isn't it?"

David flips his sleeping bag open, jumps up and tip-toes over to the steering column.

"Can you believe this thing has an auto-pilot? How crazy is that?" David's face glows from the panel of dials and switches.

"Yeah, pretty cool. Hey, does that tell us how far away we are?"

David looks over his shoulder to the east where the very first sliver of the morning sun should peek over the horizon shortly. He turns to look to the west where he sees a ridge of civilization and then, looking at the monitors, he calculates.

"I'd say we're less than two hours away," he says, checking his watch. "Maybe ninety minutes. Wouldn't be surprised if we started hearing noise down below soon."

"Well, the quiet was nice while it lasted," Christopher mumbles, smiling at David.

"Yeah. Those kids have been the chatty bunch, haven't they?" David chuckles. "I mean I love all you guys, but spending this much time in this little of a space…you know what I'm saying."

"Yeah, I get it," Christopher replies, tossing the sleeping bag aside. He spins around, planting his bare feet on deck, and stretches toward the sky. As he lifts his arms high, David can see Christopher's rib cage just underneath his t-shirt.

"Hey, your ribs feeling better? The bruises are nearly gone."

"Huh?" Christopher yawns. "Oh yeah, you're right," he says, lifting his shirt higher and rubbing his hand along his belly. "Must be. I nearly forgot about it."

"That's good news."

"Why's that?"

Putting on his flip-flops, he says, "I'm figuring that once we hit land—finally, there must be some jet-skis around so we can venture out on our own."

"And you're not tired of the water yet?"

"Dude, when was the last time we got out of town? A year? Two?"

Christopher thinks about it, rubbing his lightly-stubbled chin and says, "You're right. It was over a year ago, before…" He hesitates, as his mind races back to last summer when Grace died. The smile slowly disappears from his face.

David knows where his big brother's mind just went and he feels dumb for bringing that up, so he jumps on the opportunity to distract him.

"Right, so like, nearly two summers ago. It was Folly Beach, right? You and I were building that sandcastle near…"

Christopher snaps back, looks at his brother knowing what he's up to, and smiles.

"Yeah, Bro. You're right. We were building that sandcastle down at the tip of the island. It was Folly Beach County Park, right? Man, that thing was huge…"

The boys continued their conversation, recalling every detail of that sandcastle—including how many buckets it took to build, how high the tallest part reached and how much fun the five of them had building it.

It was obvious that, in that moment, they both relived the pain of losing Grace, but decided it was time better spent remembering the happier moments.

Jefferson leads Jonathan and Angela topside—steaming cups of coffee in hand. Jefferson greets the two boys, "Morning, gentlemen. Sleep well?"

"It was great," Christopher says, looking at David.

"I never would have imagined sleeping on a moving vessel could be so relaxing," David adds, turning to his father, "Right, Pops?"

Looking much better today, Jonathan nods. "Once I got over the motion of the ocean…I was fine."

Jefferson switches off the auto-pilot and picks up an additional knot or two. Sammy joins the crew, wrapping her arm around Jefferson.

"And who knew you could just put it on auto-pilot and sail through the night," David says.

"Well, given technology these days, sonar with warning systems," he points to the speaker above their heads, "that alert us to danger, along with the lights positioned all around—not to mention her size, it'd be hard *not* to see us coming."

David nods, fascinated with technology.

The bright morning sun slowly peeks above the horizon. It won't be long before she begins warming the seafarers. The long, white shores of southern Florida slowly come into view several miles away, while down below, Daphne and Stuart busily prepare breakfast, chatting away and quite happy to spend this Thanksgiving weekend in an entirely new fashion.

CHAPTER 57

CARTER AND RANDALL GRAB a cup of coffee from the kitchen, jump in Randall's Cadillac and head out to spend several hours driving around looking at the real estate Randall has amassed over the years. Carter knew Randall was wealthy, but not *this* wealthy. The house easily cost five million and he had several expensive cars, plus a small, rustic condo in the Keys that he's had for years and rarely visits. All of this was quite the surprise. Randall shares with Carter that every time he got a raise, or a bonus, he would invest in real estate, saying it was the one thing he knew would always appreciate in value. Addressing the fact that the Florida market had fallen on hard times, Randall counters by referencing everything he has learned about the foreclosure and bankruptcy markets. This allowed him to take advantage of people who had fallen on disadvantaged times. Upon further inquiry, Carter learns that Randall is worth several hundred million—more than he had originally imagined. The fact that nearly parts his hair is when he learns that wife number three stands to inherit a third of it, while Shasta stood to get another third, but not until she turns 21. Carter doesn't even try to learn who gets the remaining third—none of his business. And Randall leaves it to wonder.

"Son, you look like hell," Randall says.
"Didn't sleep very well."
"Was it the bed? I wasn't sure—"
"Bed was fine," Carter interrupts. "Just fine. Mind was racing. A lot to process." He doesn't mention Teresa. Decides it best to stay on point with Shasta.

Just then, Randall's cell phone rings. He looks at it, then to Carter. He appears nervous. Carter shrugs, saying, "Showtime?"

Randall answers, "Hello? Oh, hi John." His shoulders relax.

He moves the phone aside from his mouth and whispers, "My doctor."

After several moments of *Uh huh, right* and *I understand*, along with the look on Randall's face and the fact that color just left his cheeks, Carter is guessing it's not good news. Not to mention Randall has been coughing on and off since Carter arrived, as well as over several recent phone conversations. Carter has a pretty good guess what's coming.

Randall hangs up, coughs deeply several times before rattling off a series of short wet coughs. He catches his breath, wipes his mouth with a handkerchief and just stares straight ahead several minutes before speaking.

"It *is* lung cancer," Randall whispers, adding, "Way back, I originally thought it was just really bad bronchitis, but then I started losing weight and getting weak…"

Carter knew one thing about his father: The Bull wasn't much for melancholy, nor was he apt to whine or complain about much. Carter sits quietly, listening.

"Suzanne has been a princess. Watching out for me. Listening to the never ending coughs, the wheezing in the night…" He hesitates, then stops and tries to lighten the moment. "Well, the good news, I probably have six months to a year."

Carter, having not been close to his father for many years, feels his heart sink. He reaches over and pats Randall's knee. "Hang in there, Sir."

Randall lets a tiny smile lift his sinking cheeks and says, "And I have right now. With you. And, I'm trusting, a bit more time with Hope."

"You bet. That phone call will come and, I guarantee you, I'll have her back and safe under your roof before the Thanksgiving holiday comes to a close. Just like I promised."

Randall chuckles, looks at his watch and replies, "Well, the phone should ring any time now and your personal guarantee has a window of…" he trails off, looking into the distance.

"Piece of cake. Seen a lot worse than this," Carter confides.

"God knows…we all know…you've seen worse."

After a few moments of silence, Carter suggests, "Have you thought about a lung transplant? Money, evidently, can't be an issue."

Randall snorts before answering. "No, it's not. Just don't think this old tank can take the added stress. Too many city miles."

Carter smiles at his father who wasn't one for making very many jokes.

Randall continues, "Besides, haven't treated it with the best of intentions."

"No doubt," Carter adds. "But you know it's an option. If you were open to it."

Randall nods. "Matter of fact, John—the doctor I was just talking to, we discussed it several months ago, when I was in for a follow-up. And just as a precaution, he put me on a list. Said the chances were good to find one— given the window and my wherewithal. We'll see."

"I think you should consider it. Hell, you're only, what—"

"72," Randall interrupts. "Maybe I do have a few miles left. Who knows?"

Carter laughs, "Oh, you got more than a few. You stopped smoking—check. You could back off the booze…"

"Might as well tell me to back off breathing, or eating," Randall jokes.

"At least start exercising. Even a little bit."

Randall waves him away. "Jumping on one of those hamster wheels isn't going to help now."

"But eating right…*better* at least, would help. And what about the gym? You used to kill it in there."

"I do miss those days. Still have some of the strength, just not the size."

"That's what keeps me young," Carter replies.

Randall looks over, grabs Carter's arm and squeezes, "Not bad for an old man."

They laugh and enjoy some father and son time—while they have it.

☞

Durkin sits at the end of the driveway of Carter's property where, hours ago, he committed an act he was sure would have repercussions. He chose not to think about those right now, instead choosing to make haste of getting Teresa some help and hopefully, covering his tracks—if there were any left. Scanning the property, he slowly approaches Carter's truck and gets out. The look on his face said it all, but his next two words confirmed his worst fear.

"Oh shit!"

Teresa wasn't there. He walks around back and sees her car is still there. In the front, all that is left where he last saw her is a dark pool of blood. Whipping his head back and forth in disbelief, his mind races. *Where did she go and what in the hell am I going to do now? WHO found her?*

Suddenly, a deep growl comes from behind. The pain in his forearm reminds him of the attack last night. He slowly reaches for the stun gun on his belt, while turning around a millimeter at a time.

Samson is just feet away. A long ridge of hair stands on end along his large back, and his front teeth are exposed. Durkin aims the stun gun at him and barks, "Stay!" Samson doesn't move. Durkin slowly backs up toward the car. Samson just as slowly steps toward him.

"Stay!"

Samson lunges and Durkin pulls the trigger. 100,000 volts surge through the canine's body, causing him to freeze in place.

Durkin had only used a device like this once in his life and that was on a man he was arresting for drunken and disorderly conduct. The junkie was so hopped up he barely reacted; however, after a couple of extra blasts, he passed out and was carted off to jail.

Samson let out a loud whimper. After a second or two, the dog shook his head, but just stood there. Durkin quickly retreated to his car. *I can't get anything done with that stinkin' mutt around*, he thought. Putting his hand on the 9MM on his side, he stops to consider his next move.

No. Carter would most certainly kill me then. A man and his dog. Whatever. With that, he puts his cruiser into gear and backs down the driveway. Samson is clear-headed by now and follows Durkin at the same pace he retreats. *What about the tracks I left last night? Maybe the rain will have washed them away. What about the tracks I'm leaving now? Man, have I screwed this up.*

᷿

Reddick is sound asleep, slumped in an uncomfortable chair in the corner of the hospital room, as a young man, looking barely old enough to drive, opens the hospital room door. He pulls a plate and matching metal lid from the cart in the hallway, turns to quietly enter the room and CRASH!

This wakes Teresa, and she sits upright in bed, looks around and shouts, "Hey, somebody get the screws outta my head!"

Reddick leaps out of his chair, reaches for a gun on his hip that isn't there and shouts, "What?"

He looks first to Teresa then to the embarrassed young man, feels instantly embarrassed himself and tries to regain composure.

"You all right?" he asks Teresa.

She lets out a long sigh, starts looking around the room, and lifts the covers.

"Where are the keys?" she asks.

"What keys?" Reddick answers.

"To the truck."

"What truck?" He's confused.

She slowly lets her serious expression give way to a sly smile and says, "The one parked on the back of my head."

Reddick's look of shock slowly gives way to a smile, as he gets the joke.

ॐ

Teresa's breakfast plate is empty. In fact, a second one is half gone and she lies against the upright bed. Reddick opens the curtains, allowing the early morning sun to light up the room.

"I can't believe that you're not only awake, but have eaten nearly two entire meals. How?"

"Easy. I'm hungry. And a tough little broad," she smiles.

"I see that. But the doc said your concussion will likely have you looking at plenty of bed rest, maybe several days."

Sipping water through a bent straw, Teresa takes a deep breath and relaxes into her pillows.

"Hey, I hadn't eaten all day yesterday—working a double," referring to the empty dishes. "And as for my head, my daddy always said I nearly arrived as a boy."

"Uh, you were never nearly a boy," Reddick adds.

"I just knew, growing up with two older brothers, there was going to be some roughhousing and if I didn't toughen up quickly, I'd get my butt kicked. So, I just learned to punch back. Harder."

"And that's your secret," Reddick states.

"Okay, enough about that," she dismisses. "When am I out of here? I have a job and a teenager—both full-time duties. And where's my *other* boy?" She smiles.

Reddick enjoys seeing her happy. She deserved it, having a dork for an ex and another dork for a son.

"Doc says you could be out tomorrow." He looks at his watch, adding, "And your other answer is—he's in Miami. We talked until early this morning."

She smiles. "Seems like he's been gone for weeks!"

"He nearly turned around and drove right back here, but…"

"Really? For little ol' me?" she interrupts.

"Whatever. I told him I'd look after you. He has plenty on his plate right now."

She gets quiet. Frowning, she stares at the floor—searching for something.

"What?"

Reaching for the back of her head, her hand touches the shaved part of her scalp and the newly added stiches. She winces. "What about this bullshit? And, who hit me?"

"Well…"

"And WHY?" she says more angrily.

He walks over and sits on the edge of the bed. "Who? I don't want to say anything until I learn more. As for why, Carter and I talked about that just hours ago and he thinks he has a pretty good idea."

They stare at one another, saying nothing. She fidgets with the hospital band wrapped around her wrist, nervously picking at it. He reaches over and touches her hand.

"Look. People do stupid things. Everybody does. Sometimes they make sense. Sometimes they don't. This time, it doesn't. Not yet, anyway."

Starting to relax, she pats his hand. "Thank you."

"But trust me, Carter and I are on this. And we will find out who did this…why they did this. And they'll pay for doing this. 'Kay?"

She nods. He leans over, kisses her forehead and quietly says, "That's from Carter. Now, get some rest."

She reaches up and touches the side of his face. "You're sweet."

"No, I'm not," he says, walking toward the door then adds, "And as for work, as much as I'll miss your taking care of me at the diner, it can wait. You just work on getting better."

"Okay. Doctor Reddick."

He turns to leave, but she stops him by asking, "Dennis?"

Smirking, he holds up a hand and says, "Nobody calls me Dennis but my mother."

"Just wanted to get your attention. Can you do just one more little thing for me?"

"Sure. Name it."

"Can you check on my son? I can't imagine how...wacked out he must be," she says before rolling her eyes and adding, "Lord knows his father isn't looking out for him."

"Will do. Where'll he be?"

She starts to think, looks at the floor and, with a confused look on her face, says, "Uh, I'm not sure. School? Home? I think he's still recuperating from..." She reaches for her head, squinting with pain, "My head hurts and I can't seem to recall..."

"No worries, Teresa. I'll check both. I'm sure he's fine. I'll have him call you."

She pushes the button to lower the back of her bed and quietly says, "Thanks. Now, get outta here. I feel a nap coming on."

He smiles and says, "I'll call Carter in the next few minutes, let him know you're out of the woods and have him ring you later, okay?"

She nods her head, moans in approval and closes her eyes.

With that, Reddick is down the hall, out of the hospital and is approaching his car when the anger starts. *I'm going to roll up on that douche-bag, Durk, and show him how impolite it is to hit a girl. Then, I'm going to take that nightstick, or flashlight, or whatever the hell he hit her with and crack both his knees and then both his elbows. That'll teach that maniac...not to bully people. And NOT to hurt my friends.*

❧

He's nearly two miles down the road before Reddick realizes how heavy he's breathing. Checking his watch, he rubs his tired eyes and scraggly two-day growth and flashes back to his childhood.

He grew up the son of a cop—a man who was used to misappropriation of force. His dad used to take the law into his own hands from time to time. As a youngster, Reddick saw those dealings and recalls his dad saying, *You can't be soft with hard people. You have to take different approaches to teach different lessons.*

He never forgot that. And he was going to take that very advice into consideration when dealing with Officer Durkin, if indeed he was the culprit behind this. The way he had it figured, he would have to take a different approach in order to teach Durkin a different lesson or two. And with that he mumbled, "Breakfast first. Business second."

PART THREE: Hopeful Transitions

CHAPTER 58

THE COCONUT BEACH RESORT was a quaint little spot on the Atlantic Ocean side of Key West. It sat at the corner of Alberta Street and Waddell Avenue, between two of the largest parks on the island and was just a short walk from White Street Pier. If your plans included going shoulder-to-shoulder with tourists during the height of tourist season, you could stroll to just about any flavor of restaurant you could imagine within minutes. The main drags of Truman Avenue, White and Eaton Streets offered all the shopping, eating and people-watching you could possibly need. But if noise is not what you wanted, the slightly secluded and charming Coconut Beach Resort was just right. It didn't look like all that much. But between the heavy foliage of the native palm trees and the lush gardens, not to mention the beach that was literally one block away, it was the perfect place to hide away from it all.

There wasn't a good deal of beachfront on most of Key West mainly because of years of hurricanes that beat the beaches raw, causing erosive mayhem. But then, most people came to Key West to escape—escape the winter doldrums, the hustle-bustle of large cities, the law, an ex, or a current. You couldn't go any further south in the U.S. than right here. And besides, the weather was nearly perfect 365 days out of the year, with the exception of the occasional hurricane.

One of the neatest things that happened around the end of every day, something that locals and visitors alike would notice, was the sunset. People all over the island would stop whatever they were doing at sunset and just watch. They would find a beach, a bench, a car hood or restaurant deck, and simply stop to catch the last glowing burnt-orange colors of a setting sun as she dropped into the vast ocean. It was magical—every single day of the year.

≈

Shasta is eager to get outside and enjoy the perfect weather. She is dressed in a lightweight sundress, sandals and a large-brimmed hat. After double-checking her beach bag for all the necessary items—sunscreen, lip balm, an assortment of hair fixtures, a sketch pad, trashy novel and cell phone, she tosses the bag over her shoulder, grabs the keys from the rattan table by the front door and nearly bounces out of the apartment. She is feeling particularly good today, as she has been working at getting back into shape and it shows.

Heading to her favorite small park on a nearby beach, she plans on meeting up with her boyfriend. She has walked halfway down Seminole and is about to make a right on Reynolds when she passes a couple of girls about her age—part of a cleaning crew for Casa Marina, a massive resort Shasta passes every day on her way to the park. She waves to the girls and they wave back—gesturing that they like her outfit. She beams her brilliant smile and continues on her way.

The Casa, as locals refer to it, takes up nearly four city blocks and is easily the most exclusive and luxurious hotel in the area. The elegant palace is well-known for its more than 1,000 feet of private beach—a rarity on this part of the island. It blends the old traditional Key West with contemporary luxury.

Making her way along Atlantic Boulevard, Shasta sees and smells the familiar sights and sounds of *Salute On The Beach*. At night, the restaurant serves Caribbean-influenced Italian. But on Fridays, Saturdays and Sundays, they open to serve brunch, Italian style, which consisted of café lattes, cappuccinos and espressos, along with breads, biscotti and brioches. The one item they were most famous for was homemade frittatas. People came from all over the

Keys just to sample these enormous, fresh and fluffy dishes. And while the authentic food was the culinary attraction, the locals equally enjoyed sunsets with a cocktail while watching other locals challenge sunburned tourists in friendly games of volleyball, right outside the open-air porch.

Her mind flashes back to her father bringing her to this spot as a child. The former business, called Mr. K's, was famous for their corn dogs, hamburgers and most famously, their soft-serve ice-cream. Many a summer's night, amidst the sweltering humidity, she and her new father—the only one she had ever known, would grab an ice-cream cone and sit, shoulder-to-shoulder, beneath the tall palmetto palms watching the locals play volleyball, silhouetted against the setting sun.

The location was perfect for business, as it's right next to White Street Pier. Years later, and with more money flowing into the local economy, this tourist hotspot had changed clientele, but still retained a loyal audience— thanks in part to good food, a tidy spot of beach and an air of comfortable familiarity.

Removing her sandals, she sinks her feet into the white sand, thinking of how she never tires of the feeling of it between her toes. She notices however, how those same toes are in desperate need of a pedicure. *Later*, she muses to herself, *maybe in celebration of the holiday.*

Shasta finds her favorite spot beneath the shade of three large pine trees nestled together. She drops her bag and slides her sundress over her head, revealing a trim physique in a modest two-piece. A small pink and blue butterfly rests halfway between her hipbone and navel, right at the line of her suit bottom—a birthday gift to herself.

Even though Shasta spent a good deal of her life in and around the beach, she was never a big fan of spending countless hours fine-tuning *the perfect tan*. Part of her reasoning was because she had seen what long hours a day and weeks upon months had done to several friends. They were prematurely wrinkled, looking years older than their driver's license indicated. *Silly. All that work to create great tan lines*, she thought to herself. The other reason, as anyone could see, her light mocha-colored skin didn't need any extended exposure; it was the perfect color. And just to be safe, she applies an extra dose of sunscreen.

Higgs Beach was an official dog park and was adjacent to CB Harvey Beach Park, home to a long row of perfectly aligned bocce ball courts. This particular spot was her favorite. It was the perfect place to read, people watch, enjoy an afternoon snooze, or work on her art. She had loved watercolors since she was a child. There was something so simple, yet elegant about mixing water with color to create intricate designs or minimal landscapes. But today was for relaxing and spending time with her boyfriend. He was actually a somewhat new boyfriend. They met about six months ago at a party a girlfriend of hers was throwing at her parents' home in Wellington, a sophisticated and wealthy neighborhood west of where she lived. Not that her neighborhood was a dump—West Palm Beach had some of the most beautiful and costly homes in Florida. Her father had always provided her with nothing but the best in schools, in sports, and in social activities. But he couldn't provide the one thing she was missing. At 18, she had an itch that needed scratching. And her new beau helped in that department.

The only thing that was causing her anxiety right now was that the new boyfriend had talked her into getting away for the holiday weekend without telling her dad. Of course, the huge knock-down drag-out verbal shouting match between she and her father was certainly enough fuel for the fire to push her rebellious spirit over the edge. They both needed space; and, the new boyfriend provided just the distraction she needed to chill out.

His name was William Dubois, but nobody ever called him William. Some referred to him as *Billy D-Bo*, but most just called him *D-Bo*. She called him Billy, as she thought the abbreviated nickname sounded ghetto. Billy was from New Orleans and biracial like her. Shasta, however, had a white father and a black mother, and her skin was slightly browner than his. Billy got his tightly-curled hair, wide nose and full lips from his father, and his light skin from his mother.

He liked the name D-Bo because of the similarity to the football player, but not because he was, as he called him, a *Super Christian*, but because he thought T-Bo was a kick-ass football player who could do it all. The other similarity both guys shared was their build. Billy's build was like that of a body-builder—tiny waist, broad back and large arms. He said it was natural. Some of their mutual friends thought otherwise. Either way, Shasta thought he was hot—with a capital *H*. Another similarity between T-Bo and D-Bo was their killer smile. Billy could get just about anything he wanted by flashing that perfect smile.

His only downside, according to her, was she didn't find him terribly bright, and at 23, she found it somewhat lazy that bartending was to be his life's dream. The upside? His looks made him great tips, his build made her feel safe and his kiss made her knees weak.

She checks her watch. It's a little after noon and she could feel the first pangs of hunger coming, but knew that Billy would be off work soon and they would run out for a bite to eat, or maybe he'd just bring some takeout from his job. He had picked up more hours at Salute, working whenever he could.

Beneath the shade of her floppy hat with her eyes closed, she daydreams of a fluffy frittata and frothy cappuccino.

"Hey, Beautiful!" a voice shouts in the distance.

She looks up to see Billy strutting towards her. She had a giddy nervousness that made her feel alive. And she liked it.

"Hey, Handsome. 'Bout time you showed up. I was about to eat one of those!" She points to a seagull several feet away.

"Naw, Baby, you don't have to do that. I'm takin' you to lunch. And something nice—not like this place," he says, pointing over his shoulder.

"But I like this place." She slumps her shoulders.

He pulls off his work apron and neatly lays it on the ground, sitting next to her. Pushing her hat back, he leans in and kisses her. She suddenly forgets about lunch.
"Hmm…" she moans. "If I can't have that…maybe I could get me some more of this."

CHAPTER 59

THANKSGIVING HAD ALWAYS HELD a special place in the hearts of the Matheson family. It represented a time when all the family, and the families of their neighborhood and of their church, would come together and share a time of thanks. This year, while celebrating in an entirely different environment, the Matheson family would, nonetheless, come together, bow their heads and give thanks to God for their life and health, to each other for their constant love and affection, and to their church family for their continued support.

After docking his yacht at the Stock Island Marina, Jefferson and the group made their way to their overnight accommodations. They relax on the sunny veranda of the Lopez House, part of The Southernmost Hotel enclave that sat—where else, but at the southern-most point of the continental United States. Here, one could get lost in the constant warmth, the turquoise waters and the remarkable sunsets. Jonathan and Angela smile at the family that sits before them: Christopher, David, Daphne and Stuart, and Jefferson and Sammy.

"This is truly a beautiful day and one for which we are all so very thankful," Jonathan says to the small group.

"Amen," they echo.

Jefferson stands at the opposite end of the table, raises a glass and toasts, "And here's to our extended family—one that we have come to love as our own. And although a tragedy brought us together..."

He looks at each of them, as they simultaneously turn to look at the empty chair which has a lit candle in front of it.

"And even though that accident tried to rip at the fabric of family, we pulled together—each one becoming stronger. Although it's in the loss that we grieve, it is likewise in the memory of her spirit, we remain forever thankful."

"We can't thank you enough, Jefferson," Angela says, "for opening your heart and your home away from home to our family. This holiday will go down in our memories as one of the very best."

"Trust me, Angela, this is as much of a pleasure for us as it is for you," Jefferson replies.

"I second that emotion," Sammy chimes in.

David stands and says he'd like to propose his own toast. "Here's to you and here's to me, and if we ever disagree, then phooey on you and cheers to me!" His innocent words brought together a chuckle and clinking glasses.

The rest of the meal was spent talking about the history of the legendary home that was elegantly poised on Duval Street. Jefferson tells of how his grandmother was the maid to the late author, Ernest Hemingway, and, for nearly two generations, their family celebrated either Thanksgiving, Christmas or New Year's at this most elegant of places.

The stately and historical inn was as grand now as it was when the last bricks were laid more than a century ago. It was constructed in 1896 as a home for Dr. Jeptha Harris and wife, Florida. He was a surgeon in the navy during the Civil War and became a prominent leader in Key West shortly after his arrival on the island. The Harrises took great pride in their magnificent oceanfront home, building it with the utmost attention to detail and with the finest materials that could withstand treacherous hurricanes and lightning storms.

Their early lunch complete, the family decides to split up and spend the rest of the day off by themselves on separate adventures. It was agreed that personal space was needed after spending the past three days within the same few hundred square feet. Jonathan shared of his interest in the history of Fort Zachary Taylor Historic State Park, home to the largest collection of Civil War cannons in the United States. Daphne and Stuart chose to embark upon a leisurely bike ride to Mallory Square to enjoy shopping and people watching. South Beach was very close by and a place that Angela longed to relax for half a day, explaining that she wanted to sit on a piece of still, non-rocking ground and bury her head in a good book. Christopher chose to venture out to the Ernest Hemingway estate only five blocks away. They all looked at him with surprise.

In a moment of surprising vulnerability, Christopher shared that while David loved butterflies, Angela enjoyed romance novels and Jonathan was interested in studying history, he thought that if music never worked out for him, maybe writing would. He went on to reveal that he had been keeping a journal since the week after Grace died. He found solace in the page and courage in the written word and decided that perhaps the Hemingway estate might help distract him from reality. This surprised the whole family. Jefferson spoke about how he saw the most significance in Christopher's *growth*, stating how he felt Christopher had come a long way in just one year. Everyone could see how this encouraged him.

When David learned, thanks to a brochure in the lobby, that the Key West Butterfly and Nature Conservatory was within a stone's throw of where they were sitting, he nearly jumped out of his flip-flops, saying something about it being *a sign*.

Before leaving, Jonathan and Daphne discuss with Angela her *black out* at the truck stop. Angela assures them that she's okay, adding that she'll only walk to a nearby park just a few blocks away, and will use her cell phone to check in later. Since her prescriptions had been left back in

Charleston, and she hadn't had any more *episodes*, they were comfortable with her going off on her own. So, with several hours to play, everyone high-fived and went their separate ways.

CHAPTER 60

THE CROWDS WERE SMALL and handsome at the exclusive Grand Bay Club on Key Biscayne where Randall and Carter were enjoying a rather expensive lunch. Randall had his usual, lobster tails swimming in butter, while Carter—always the creature of habit, wrapped his hands around the largest BLT he had ever seen.

"Son, you could have anything you want and you choose a BLT?" Randall asks, looking at Carter like he wasn't wearing pants.

"Look, you kill yourself the way you want…" he nods at the bowl of warm butter, "and I'll off myself my own way," he adds, chomping on extra-crisp bacon that hung out either side of the triple-decker sandwich.

"Fair enough," Randall returns, nodding for a nearby perfectly tanned and coifed waitress.

"Miss, could my guest bother you for another napkin?" Randall asks, nodding toward the mayo smeared on Carter's chin.

Smiling graciously and exposing perfect white teeth, she responds, "Of course. And for you?" she asks, referencing the butter on Randall's chin.

"Guess you can't take us southern boys anywhere, huh?" Carter jokes.

She disappears and returns before either of them can stop chuckling. Carter takes a long deep breath, soaking in the vista.

"So, this is how the other half lives."

Randall shakes his head and says, "Son, you could have this…if you really wanted it. I seem to recall that you chose to stay in…what's that podunk town called?"

"Mission Grove. And it's not all that…podunk. Just small. And small isn't bad. Besides, look—I'm here, right? I can come and go anytime and anywhere I please. Simple works for me."

Randall picks his teeth with a sweetener packet then proceeds to slurp his light beer. Carter cuts him a look that says *Really*?

"What?"

"See you haven't lost your graceful table manners."

"Yeah, well, I enjoy my food. Just like everything else. I grab what I want…"

"Oh, I know all about that," Carter interrupts, then changes the conversation because he was certain Randall would weave his way around to talking about how he's always worked hard for everything he's gotten.

"You've always taken good care of us," Carter adds, knowing that very shortly Randall would start ranting about how nobody did anything for him. And so forth. So, he moves on, biding time as they wait for *the phone call*.

As if on cue, Randall starts to fidget, scanning the crowd—like they had anything to do with anything. He checks his watch.

"Chill out, Old Man. It's going to ring any moment now. I guarantee it," Carter says in a quiet, confident manner, peering over his sunglasses.

"Sure. Easy for you to play it so cool."

"Hey, it's my sister—" Carter stops, suddenly feeling self-conscious because he's only uttered those words twice in his 49 years.

Randall snorts, "Look at you. You just hit your own button." Randall cackles, following that with a long series of dry coughs. He sounded like he was choking on a chicken bone.

The waitress runs over with a look on her face that says *Please don't die on my shift*.

"Are you all right? Can I get you some water? I know the Heimlich Maneuver, if that helps."

Randall waves her off, still fighting the coughs which have now become a gooey texture, sounding like he swallowed a pound of butter.

"Hold on, or you'll hork up a lung," Carter jokes. Turning to the waitress he nods. "Water would be great. And, no need for the Heimlich, but thanks."

She scurries off to the bar, as Randall retrieves the ever-present handkerchief and wipes his lips. Breathing slowly, he starts to catch his breath. Carter sees small drops of blood on the handkerchief, but keeps comments to himself, trying to change the conversation and take their minds off what will likely come next.

"While Waitress Betty, or whatever her name is, retrieves you a glass of Miami's finest, tell me about the only property that you haven't shown me in…" He turns Randall's wrist toward him, revealing a pricey Rolex. It reads 12:30. "…the last 3 hours and change," he finishes.

Randall starts to speak, but the waitress appears before he can answer and sets down a large glass of water wrapped in a napkin. She bends over just enough to share her tanned and handsomely endowed young figure, which Randall can't possibly dismiss. He takes the glass with one hand, touching her hand with the other then replies in a whisper, "Thank you…" checking her nametag, "Annabeth. You're a life-saver."

She smiles, pats his liver-spotted hand—knowing that lunch will likely pay half her apartment rent for the month, and is on her way. Randall's gaze follows her.

Carter cups his hands around his mouth and, making the sound of a loudspeaker, says, "Attention. Paging Mr. Matheson. Your wife is on Line One."

"Very funny," he mumbles. "Never hurts to look."

Carter shakes his head and rummages through a plate of skinny fries, dipping one in some mayo.

"And we see what looking got you. Two strikes."

Randall looks perturbed but decides to change the conversation.

"So, the only property I haven't shown you, that's within driving distance anyway, is a little three-story resort down on the Keys. I bought it with an old buddy from a local named Jon Spotter. He was a well-known senator. In fact, some locals referred to him as *The Mayor*. We bought back in the '80s when you could get in for cheap. Most of the guests are owners, what we call *lifers*. It's got thirty 2-bedroom/2-bath units and two 1-2's. I own two of the best units, a 2-bedroom suite that I rent out year-round which completely pays for my 1-bed/2-bath extended suite, which I use from time to time, or gift to special friends. Besides loving the location and views, it's also close to the best Waldorf-Astoria resort on the island. On the other side, sits a historical little beauty, The Southernmost House. Big tourist attraction. Wish I could've afforded that joint, back in the day.

"Who knew you'd become Donald Trump of Miami?" Carter smirks.

"But with better hair," Randall replies, running his hands through his wavy salt and pepper hair. "He's still big here, but runs much bigger operations: office towers, hotels, shopping malls. I'm just residential—although there is a little café at the southern-most tip, across from the house I just mentioned. I've been trying to buy it from the owner for a decade now. He won't sell."

"You just haven't given him the right number."

"You're probably right," Randall says, sipping his water and appearing to turn something over in his mind.

"What is it?"

"Just thinking. I'd give everything I have. And I mean *everything*…just to have Shasta back home safe and sound."

He shakes his head.

"Yeah?"

"And if this person…this negotiator…this…"

"Idiot stick," Carter interrupts.

Randall smiles. "Yeah, okay. If he asked for everything, and I knew for some crazy reason I had to give it all up…which I would…I wouldn't be able to do all the things that I still hope to do…" He stops. Carter doesn't say a word.

"In the short time I have left."

"That…isn't going to happen," Carter says, looking his father in the eyes.

CHAPTER 61

SHASTA AND BILLY HAVE clearly been spending time getting to know one another better. The bedspread is a tangled mess at the foot of the bed, Billy lies face down with his right arm hanging off the side, and Shasta lies on her back, breathing deeply with a sheet covering most of her.

"Now, that's what I'm talking about, Baby. You are downright fine!" Billy says between deep breaths.

"Really?"

"Really!"

She's enjoying the afterglow, but wants to make a point about his choice of words. She thinks for a moment then says, "Hon, what I mean is…do you have anything else to say?"

He turns his head from the sliding glass door to face her. "Uh, I'm hungry. How 'bout you?"

She sighs, knowing that as much as she yearns for more, he is good to her and she feels he loves her. And for now, she thinks, that is good enough. Leaning over, she kisses him.

After a minute, he says, "Shasta, you know I love you, right?"

She nods.

"And you know I'd do anything for you, right?"

She nods again.

"And I have *big* plans for you and me, right?"

"Yes."

He pulls her close.

"And I hope you also know that I am working real hard to make it so's we don't have to rely on your daddy for anything else…"

"But…"

He puts his finger on her lips. "I'm not finished. What I mean is, as much as he is probably a good man—he is always going to have you under his thumb telling you what to do, where to go and who to do it with. And that includes me."

She frowns. "He will like you."

He shakes his head, slowly at first, then harder.

"No, he won't. He may put up with me, but he won't...*ever* like me. I think he'll think I'm not good enough for you. But I am, Baby..."

"I know you are, Billy, it's just..."

"What I think? He wants you to have a college-educated guy. But what he doesn't know is..."

Billy takes a deep breath, sits up and stares out at the ocean, silent.

"What is it, Babe?"

He looks over at the clock on the nightstand and rubs his hands together.

"Baby, let's get going. I promised you a nice meal and I'm gonna deliver. Let's go have a proper Thanksgiving."

He stands, pulling his briefs on, and looks around the room.

"Billy, come on. What doesn't my father know? Tell me. Please."

He sees his pants across the room and puts them on. Shasta could tell he was working on something. He tended to do this when he was trying to express himself. She wasn't sure if it was that he had a difficult time expressing his thoughts, or whether he wasn't much for emotional chit-chat—like her father. Or, it could be that he was just scared of falling in love and possibly marrying her. At that moment, she tried to imagine her dad embracing Billy as his son-in-law.

"What your daddy doesn't know is that I'm working hard—been working real hard, to make a good living for us. And I know he gives you everything you want. And there's not much you could possibly need, but here's the thing..."

He stops. She waits.

"I have a few ideas of my own…" he continues. "And I think you'll like them. I'll tell you more at lunch, but let's just say, it involves me…and you, well…*me*…buying a bar right here in Key West…and *you* bartending for me."

This catches her off-guard, as she thought this time was their chance at a romantic getaway. It was his idea for her to sneak into her dad's study, find the keys to this place—one that he never used, Billy reminded her. She liked that he suggested a romantic holiday away from all the noise of the city; but she wasn't big on being devious with her father—until, that is, they got into a verbal fight.

"What are you doing?" he asks.

"What do you mean?"

"You've got that far-away look in your eye again. Don't you like my ideas? It's a good business plan. You. Me. Paradise. I have a name for the bar and everything. I'll tell you about…"

"Billy," she interrupts. "I think you have good ideas. And I love this little place. But it's not ours. And you can't possibly have made enough money to buy a bar…in one of the biggest tourist traps in the South!"

She can tell by his expression that he wasn't happy. What she doesn't want to do is make him angry. He looks around the room, patting his pockets and rummaging through a stack of dirty laundry.

"I've gotta run back to the restaurant. I forgot my wallet," he says, forcing a smile. "How about you jump in the shower and I'll be back in a flash?" He's out the door before she can respond.

She sits there naked, both physically and emotionally, and feels confused and even frightened. She wasn't exactly sure why, although she felt a similar way each time he lost his temper—which was on many occasions. In fact, he had hurt some guys they hung out with, just because they said something he didn't like. She wasn't sure if it was the drugs he used to body-build—a fact she couldn't completely confirm, or if he simply had a bad temper like his dad.

What is it about angry fathers? She didn't know that much about his father, but she recalls a few conversations about how he was beaten as a child. She got out of bed, made it quickly and stepped into the shower. Perhaps the hot water would remove the cloud of doubt she was feeling and clear her head enough to be sure they were on the same page.

࿋

Walking down the street, Billy pulls a small container from his pocket, takes a couple of large pills and swallows them, tossing his head back. He mumbles to himself, going over all the details he had so carefully put together.

Okay, think. Get her old man to bring the money.

He continues to walk, faster now—his eyes, scanning the streets.

It's a quick flight from Miami.

Passing The Casa, he nods at the workers who are changing shifts.

Ha! Working stiffs. Not me—I'm about to be rich!

He takes out his phone, flips it open, searching for the number.

Who's the flunkie? Got my birds in a row!

He finds the number. It reads: Shasta's Dad: Cell.

We're in and out and nobody gets hurt—just like they say in the movies.

His thumb hovers over the SEND button.

Before you know it, I'll be stinkin' rich!

He's about to make the call when the phone rings.

CHAPTER 62

RANDALL AND CARTER ARE seated by the pool under the shade of a massive umbrella. Carter sips a cup of coffee, staring off into the distance and lost in thought, while Randall chatters away. Carter is mainly thinking of what he'll do immediately after getting the call. The other half of his attention involves listening to Randall meander down memory lane. *I'm not sure which I hate more—his former, bitter spirit, or this new 'trying to play nice before I die' attitude. I know he means well. For the most part. But trying to make up for lost time with me…is a little too much a little too late. I'll find this scumbag. I'll make him pay. And Shasta will be home safe and sound. Next week this time, it'll all be a bad dream. But Randall? The way he looks, his health, he'll be lucky to make it 6 months. I've gotta convince him to get serious help. He has the money.* Randall continues to chatter away. *All my life he's been an emotionless prick. Now look at him.* Carter watches the way he wrings his hands—hands that were once so strong. *Poor sap. That wife? He won't even be cold by the time she has a new boyfriend and a new house…And what'll happen to Shasta who won't get any money for another…three years? Her life will be hell.* Carter returns to the present, weaving back into the conversation.

"Yup, your brother always was the high-maintenance one of the two of you."

Carter engages. "When's the last time you even spoke to him, anyway? When he and Angie got married?"

Randall blows out a tiny dry whistle and looks into the distance.

"What's that…twenty years?"

Watching the sun bounce off the water, Carter squints, taking his Ray-Ban's from his pocket, mumbling, "Something like that." He wipes his sunglasses on his shirttail and breathes a long, deep sigh. *Like you even give a—*

"What's on your mind, Carter?"

"Tell me something. Why, after all this time we've been hanging out, you haven't told me anything more about her?"

Randall shakes his head and quietly says, "Hadn't really thought about it, Son." He coughs several times then adds, "Life was going along just fine. We had a bit of a spat. She disappeared. I wigged out. Called you. You're here. And…we'll fix it."

Carter frowns. "You what?"

Before Randall can answer, he continues, "Let's go back a few words. You…had a bit of a…*spat*?"

Randall nods.

"Don't you think that's essential information that could help my POA?"

"I…maybe…but it was just an argument. Well, more like a verbal boxing match, but…" Randall trails off.

Carter rolls his eyes, lets out a big blast of air and says, "Randall, c'mon. A verbal boxing match? Had it occurred to you that just maybe…that spat—*she* was a part of her disappearing?"

"What? No! She and I fight…a lot, actually. She is so stinking stubborn, just like her momma was. She's belligerent and I…just…"

"You *just* nothing! For cryin' out loud." *And here we go,* he thinks. "This certainly adds a twist to the situation and it could mean any number of things."

"Look. She's smart, pretty, outspoken…just like you. Well, not the *pretty* part." He looks at his son and punches his shoulder, "C'mon. Lighten up."

Carter takes a deep breath. "Okay, Sunshine, here's what we know," he says. Holding up a finger he says, "One…she disappeared." Adding another finger, he says, "Two…you and she had a knock down, so that disappearing was likely to cool off…"

"Wait, you don't—"

Carter holds up a hand. "Stop. This is *my* mission."

Randall holds up both hands. "Fair enough."

"Three...we get a note from someone who: (a) can't spell, (b) foreshadows, and (c) has waited too long to respond, given the *urgency* of the situation."

"You're right."

Carter looks at him sympathetically, as the thought comes to him.

"I think I'm starting to see things a bit more clearly. And I'm being honest here. Just talking, okay? Something we haven't done much...like in forever."

Randall nods, managing a tiny smile.

"You're sick. And probably trying to...make up for lost time, or something, but..."

Randall starts to cough and it quickly turns into a long series of strained coughs.

"You okay?"

Randall holds up one hand to stop Carter and with the other, reaches in his pocket to take out an inhaler. Pressing a button, he deeply inhales a burst of medication. The coughing stops and he slowly catches his breath.

"Doc says as things get worse," he holds the inhaler up, "this may be the only thing that'll keep me breathing."

Carter can't decide whether to embrace his father, or get up and leave—ignoring the well of painful memories that bubbles up in his soul. *I just want to find this guy, beat the crap out of him and get back home to Teresa.* He shakes his head.

❧

Walking faster now, and just two blocks from the restaurant, Billy's face appears red as the screen of his phone lights up. Looking at his watch, he screams in his head, *I'm late!*

"Hey, Babe—" Shasta says, flirtatiously.

"I told you I'd be right back! You dressed already?" he shouts.

Her mood changes instantly.

"Drying my hair. I'll be ready by the time you get back. What's wrong?"

Trying to suppress a tantrum, he thinks, *Be cool.* He takes a breath and gently says, "Nothing, Baby. It's just our...reservations are for two o'clock. I don't want to be late."

She pokes her head from the bathroom to look at the clock on the nightstand. It's 1:30.

"That's only 30 minutes!"

"That's right," he chuckles nervously. "Guess I lost track of time. Ya know, gettin' busy and all."

She smiles. "Okay, see you in a few."

"Okay. Bye."

Billy disconnects and stops to think. He spins and looks down the street toward Casa Marina. Smiling, he flips open his phone and scrolls through his contacts.

డ

The country club lunch crowd has thinned out. Randall and Carter are waiting for the valet to bring the car around.

"I'm sorry," Randall says quietly.

"For what?"

"Bringing you into this mess. You're right—it smells funny. And I'll bet you dollars to donuts that—"

Randall's phone rings.

They both stare at the phone. Carter checks his watch—1:32. He nods.

"Randall Matheson."

Silence.

"Hello?" he repeats.

He can hear a muffled sound, like rustling paper or someone covering the mouthpiece.

"Yeah, it's me," Billy says, trying to mask his nerves. "You ready to do this?"

Carter looks to Randall, raising his eyebrows. Randall nods. Carter reaches into his windbreaker pocket and retrieves a tiny box. It has an earpiece attached at one end and a small suction cup at the other. He motions for Randall to drag out the conversation.

"Yes, but I think I have a bad connection. Can you ring me back?"

"Are you shittin' me? No! You're in or out. You want her dead…or alive?"

Billy has stopped a block short of the restaurant—standing in an alley. He looks around.

"Of course I want her *alive*. I'm just having a hard time hearing you."

As the valet opens the driver's door, Randall hands him a ten.

Billy looks at his phone. *Not enough bars, dangit!* He waves the phone in circles overhead.

Carter is already in the car and motioning for Randall to lean the phone toward him.

"Can you hear me now?" Billy asks.

Carter is attached to the back of the phone and placing the other end of the sound amplifier in his ear. He gives a thumbs-up.

"Yes, good." Looking at Carter, Randall asks, "What's next?"

Billy takes a long deep breath. He can feel the confidence surging through his body—either that, or the chemicals he uses to keep him steady.

"Here's the deal. Super-easy. And it has to happen today!"

Randall glances at Carter as looks of surprise hit both of their faces.

"What?" Randall shouts, the pressure instantly building in his head. "You send a note telling me you'll be in touch in what…24 hours? Then, somewhere closer to 72, you finally get back to me? Come on, Punk, I don't think you've got the nerves for this racket!"

Billy feels cornered. And he doesn't like it.

Carter can see the old Randall coming back to life and can practically feel the testosterone in the air. *Glad the old boy isn't giving up just yet.* A car horn toots from behind. Randall looks in the rearview to see a line of cars waiting. He waves and quickly pulls out.

"Listen here, Old Man, I'm the one in charge, so shut it and listen. You catch a flight THIS afternoon. Miami to Key West and meet me—"

"What? Key West?" he whips his head toward Carter. He shrugs.

"There are two more no-stops today: 2:25 and 5:05."

"I can't make the 2:25—it's nearly that now," Randall barks. "You have to at least—"

"I don't have to at least nothin'! Just catch the 5:05. You'll be here by 6, easy. But, I'm telling you, you don't show—we're gone! And you'll never see *Hope* again. You got it, Old Man?"

Randall and Carter look at one another.

"How will I know you?"

"There's only one terminal. It's small. You'll be coming in on Gate 101. As soon as you get inside the terminal, look to your left. You'll see a big piña colada stand. Next to it is a short stack of lockers. Find the oversized lockers on the bottom. The biggest one will have an *Out of Order* sign. Take the key, put the backpack in, and walk to Gate 105 on the opposite side of the room."

"How will I know…?"

"You don't need to know me. I know *you*. And just in case you think you're smart, I'll have some help with me."

Randall looks at Carter like *Really?*

"I hear you."

Billy steps out from the bushes in the alley and starts walking toward the restaurant. He sees the lunch traffic is picking up. A co-worker having a smoke behind the restaurant sees him and shouts, but Billy doesn't hear him.

"And remember, *Idiota*, you won't see your girl until you are in line at Gate 105. Just stand there and wait. I'll see you. You'll have less than 15 minutes before the last flight leaves for Miami. Grab your return tickets, and she'll show up when they call for final boarding at 6:20. And remember, No money? No daughter!"

Randall stays quiet an extra moment, prolonging the stress of the situation.

"Did you hear me? I've got five-hundred thousand reasons you better be paying attention, Jarhead!" Billy says loudly, feeling nervous and amped up at the same time.

There's a long silence as Randall tries his best to check his anger. He can handle the money—no biggie. He will handle this punk—no brainer. But what he has neither the patience nor the stomach for is when someone disrespects either his family, or his service to his country. *He called me a Jarhead?*

"Oh, I heard you. Loud and clear. But now it's your turn to listen. You may think you're in charge now…but trust me…you'll wish you NEVER pulled this stunt! Do you hear me?" he shouts.

CLICK.

Billy's bravado shrivels as fast as it had arrived. He stands there looking at his hands—they're shaking. A cold sweat rushes over him. "Damn," he whispers. *I wasn't expecting a withering old man to be so ballsy. You got all this money, one foot in the grave and a daughter who's done with you. Give up!* He shakes his head, staring at the ground.

A young Cuban kid about nineteen comes running in his direction.

"Billy!" he shouts.

Oblivious, Billy's mind is still racing. *I thought of everything. This was going to be so easy.*

"Billy, what's up?"

Startled, Billy looks up to see his co-worker, Manuel.

"Hey, Manny. What up?"

"Bro, I was yelling from across the parking lot." He reaches in his apron. "Here, you left this next to the register at the bar."

"Damn. Thanks, Man. Yeah, I was punching out, packing my tips in and…"

Just then, something picks at the back of his mind.

"Uh, thanks again," he says, looking through the wallet.

"Esse, it's all there," Manuel says as a scowl crawls across his face. "I didn't take nu'in."

"No, no…it's cool. Just wanted to…make sure I, uh…It's cool, Bro. We're good."

Billy can't decide whether to hug or punch the kid. He was sure the punk was trying to do right, but he can't help but wonder if the old man may have heard this guy yelling his name. *Ain't no way he would've heard. Besides, the old man don't even know me.*

He checks his watch. *Shasta is gonna be wired.*

"Okay, Manny. Thanks again. I owe you."

He holds out his hand. Manny grabs it and they chest bump.

"Cool. See ya later." Manny turns and walks away.

Billy does the math. *Back to the crib. Grab Shasta. Hit lunch. Explain the plan. Make it happen. And sail away.*

CHAPTER 63

ANGELA IS WALKING BACK from the beach, her floppy hat bouncing as she saunters along the quaint island streets. She enjoys the peaceful island, looking at a variety of vegetation that lines the avenues. A light sunburn colors her shoulders and sand sticks to the sun-lotion that coats her legs. *Ah, a nice long shower, a yummy meal and a good night's rest before heading home. I can't wait!*

Her mind is completely preoccupied when she sees a striking girl on the wrap-around porch of The Southernmost House, just a few dozen feet away. Angela, always a lover of fashion, couldn't resist admiring the girl's outfit. She was wearing a spaghetti-strap sundress and adorable sandals, complete with bright toenail polish that matched the flowers in her shear dress. Her cocoa skin completed the elegant look.

She looks exotic. But why on earth does she look familiar? I couldn't possibly know her. Their eyes meet for an instant, but the girl quickly turns, looking in the opposite direction to a distraction just out of sight.

Must be a model from some magazine, she thinks, pulling out and unrolling the recent issue of *Shape* magazine from her bag. *Not on the cover.*

She had spent her entire afternoon reading that magazine and *Safe Haven*, a Nicholas Sparks book, while lounging on a tiny sliver of beach at the Southernmost Beach Café, just across the street from the hotel. She was never without something to read. It was her favorite pastime and the one thing that preoccupied her mind and allowed all the noise of the world to disappear. She liked disappearing. Life had become too painfully real. All she wanted to do, besides raising her two teenage boys, was to rebuild her strength—both physically and mentally. To that end, she'd become preoccupied with the thought of having another girl.

Approaching the steps, she notices the young woman has moved to the street, pacing back and forth, looking from her watch to either end of the street. Just as Angela takes a seat on the enormous porch, she sees her waving to someone in the distance.

"Hello, Beautiful," Jonathan says, kissing the back of Angela's neck.

Angela jumps. "Oh. Hi. And please…don't stop," she coos.

"Whatchya looking at?"

"Oh, just some girl's outfit. You know me—always the fashion police."

Jonathan kisses her cheek, squeezes her shoulders, then walks around and sits next to her.

"How was your time?" Angela asks.

Jonathan suppresses a yawn, then replies, "It was good. I went for a walk, but frankly, I was just so tired…" he looks around, "from sleeping on that tiny cabin bed for three days. I cut my historical jaunt short and snuck back to the room for a nice, long nap—stretched out on that king sized cloud."

"Good for you."

"I see now why they call it the *Perfect Sleeper*…cuz, that's exactly what I was."

CHAPTER 64

RANDALL AND CARTER ARE making good time heading northbound on I-95, back to Palm Beach. The Caddie is humming along at 95 MPH. Randall's mind bounces between anger and compassion toward Shasta. *We shouldn't fight. Spent my whole life doing that. Shouldn't have lost my temper. She's just a young girl. So much different from raising boys. Having a girl is so different. It does something to a man. Hell, I'm just scared. Probably don't have that long. She's all I've got. The boys got lives of their own. But her. I give her a good life. Always tried to do the right thing with her. Screwed up so much of the other. I've got to protect her.*

Flipping his turn signal and barely looking over his shoulder, Randall changes lanes abruptly, deciding to go with another plan. Carter looks at him, raising an eyebrow. Randall looks at him out of the corner of his eye.

"I was gonna fly out of PBI, but screw that. It's an hour we could put to use elsewhere."

"Uh huh."

Randall smirks. "Man of little words." He thinks, *I can only imagine what my boy is cooking on that back burner of his.*

"Private's better than public," Carter says quietly.

"You guessed it."

Carter has remained quiet since they left the country club. He had to focus. And while he was more than willing to do anything he had to in order to help his father—and sister, he didn't want to mess with Randall's plan of action. The Bull was notorious for wanting things done his way, no questions asked. So, Carter was patient before speaking.

"The guy's a punk. I'm a hundred percent sure...now."

Randall nods.

"I've been chasing bad people a long time and I know a punk when I hear one."

"Agreed."

Carter mumbles just loud enough to hear, "Who says *no-stops*? It's *non-stops*."

"You're funny...the way things trickle into that brick of yours," Randall jokes.

"And he was late. Way late. Plus, he sounds dumb. Unpolished."

"And you caught the big tell, right?" Randall asks—his eyes not leaving the road.

"I'm guessing when he referred to her as Hope?"

"Everyone calls her Shasta. Since the day she arrived on my doorstep 10 years ago. Even I call her Shasta now, for crap-sake."

"Did you catch the Spanish?" Carter asks, looking out the window.

"Huh?"

"Idiota. He called you, *Idiota*. Basically, *dumbass* in Spanish."

"Yeah."

"Nothing huge. Don't take it personally." Carter cuts a look in Randall's direction. "Just a detail," Carter quietly adds.

&

Randall picks up his phone, holds down a number that initiates *speed dial* and puts the call on speaker.

Ring.

A voice comes booming across the tiny speaker.

"It's Black. Afternoon, LC. What's up, Sir?"

"You're on speakerphone. Carter's with me."

"Hey, Carter. Long time," Mr. Black says.

"Yup. Too long."

Randall pats Carter's knee.

"Gonna cut to the chase. You busy?" Randall asks.

"Never too busy for business. What can I do you for?"

"I've already shared about my daughter—"

"Kidnapped?"

"Disappeared, but yeah. Still confirming intel."

"Yes, Sir. She okay?"

Randall stops his bravado for a moment, takes a deep inhale to suppress a cough, and looks to Carter for back-up. Carter nods.

"She's fine. But I…*we*…need your help."

"Anything," Black reports.

Randall had already passed the I-95/91 Interchange and was nearly in North Miami by the time he changed his mind to save time. So, he exits at NE 203rd Street, just past the Diplomat Presidential Golf Course and hopped back on I-95, heading south.

"Are you in PB?"

"No, actually at LNA. Giving a hop to an exec who lives on Lake Charleston. What's your 20?"

"Just west of North Miami. Right at that course I took you to play last month."

"The Diplomat. Got it."

"Exactly. Look, I could meet you at FLI, or even North Perry, but…" Randall looks to the sophisticated GPS on his dash. Before he can answer, Black responds.

"No. FLI's a cluster. NP's got construction issues. Just spin back and hit Opa-Locka. I'm done with the suit. Was just burning one in the lounge with some pals. I can be there in…"

Carter smirks, admiring Black's brevity.

Black continues, "I'll drop in less than 20. Good?"

"Perfect. And just one more thing," Randall adds.

"Yes, Sir."

"How much time you got?"

"However much you need," Black bounces back.

Randall looks to Carter. He shrugs, calculates, then holds up two fingers followed by four fingers.

"Twenty-four hours. Tops."

A brief hesitation crackles on the line. "No big. I'll adjust. Anything else?"

Randall mindlessly fidgets, spinning a worn brass Zippo cigarette lighter in his hand, biting the inside of his cheek.

"Should be clean and easy, but...bring some heat. Just in case."

Randall rings off, turns left then right, left again, hits the on-ramp and steps on it.

"I know it's cliché to say," Carter mutters, "but it's times like these I just gotta be cliché."

"What's that, Boy?"

"They have no idea who they're dealing with."

"Damn straight, Lucky."

Carter couldn't help but whip his head toward Randall with a look of surprise.

"You haven't called me that since I came home from Grenada."

Randall snorts and smirks simultaneously, shakes his head and looks at Carter.

"And you better be. Got a reputation to live up to." Randall slaps him hard on the leg.

Carter felt alive again—back in the hunt and doing what he does best. And it was good to see life surging through his old man again. The Bull was back and nowhere near being ready to lie down and die.

CHAPTER 65

DAVID AND CHRISTOPHER ARRIVE and dismount their bikes at the end of the street, just a few yards from the hotel. They had both left their respective tours and bumped into one another, heading back to the hotel. Since they had a little extra time, they had decided to stop at a bicycle shop and rent some wheels for an hour—both agreeing they needed the exercise. Stopping to look at the massive, brightly-colored concrete landmark completely surrounded by photograph-hungry tourists, they joked that the massive marker just a block from their hotel, as well as the café right across the street from their hotel, and even the street on which they were staying, all claimed the *southernmost* moniker. David joked, "Even though we were born and raised in the south…it wasn't the *Southern-most South.*"

After returning the rented bikes, the boys spot their parents, wave to them on the porch, and walk to the end of the short pier to watch the sun that's beginning its descent toward the horizon.

The bonus attraction, Christopher notices, is the growing number of attractive young girls quickly accumulating at the Southernmost Beach Café across the street. He stands a little taller and runs his hands through his thick hair that has gotten lighter by all the exposure to the sun. In fact, the entire family, including Jefferson and Sammy, were a great deal more tanned. They all looked like Bain de Soleil models, *almost*. A small group of bikinied girls gathered on the water's edge look his way and smile. He smiles back.

David flips through a handful of brochures he retrieved from the Butterfly and Nature Conservatory, trying to engage Christopher with his enthusiasm.

"Man, I had a blast at the butterfly museum," David starts. "If you thought you knew about butterflies, you don't know diddly. There were—"

Christopher holds up his hand, interrupting. "David, as much as I'm sure your butterflies were bodacious, I wonder if we could learn all about them on the way back home. I mean, we have a really long trip and well…" he turns toward the sun, but peeking at the girls, "I'd kinda like to…catch these last…memorable moments of the beach…" He stares at the girls. "And all the scenery."

David sees now and says, "Oh, brother." He stuffs his brochures in his ever-present backpack and walks back toward the hotel.

"Hey, you don't have to leave. Just…ya know…chill!" Christopher shouts. David waves him off and continues on his way.

Jefferson and Sammy are rounding the corner just as David hits the hotel front steps.

"How was your day, David?" Sammy asks.

"Great! I was at the Butter—" He stops.

"What, David?"

Feeling self-conscious, David replies, "Well, it was interesting to me…but some people may not find it as…enthralling." He casts a glance over his shoulder to where Christopher now stands in the middle of a gaggle of giggling girls. Jefferson and Sammy look at one another and smile. Putting his arm around David's shoulders, Jefferson says, "Man, I love butterflies. Did you, by any chance, see any of the species Antheraea Mylitta? They're known for a particularly odd…almost *eyeball* pattern on their wings."

David's eyes bug wide open.

"Yes!" David excitedly responds. "They're one of my favorites. They live in oak and apple trees and love humidity."

"Which is why they are so happy here, right?" Jefferson winks at Sammy.

Sammy chimes in, "I've always admired the Swallowtail…"

"Classic!" David interrupts. "And one that most people think of. But are you familiar with what they mean in many cultures and beliefs?"

The trio of butterfly enthusiasts, deeply engrossed in conversation, make their way to join the others on the porch as a perfect holiday slowly comes to a close.

Across the room, a duo of lovebirds enjoy some sparks of their own.

CHAPTER 66

CARTER HAD BEEN SO deeply engrossed in what was happening in Florida that he hadn't given as much thought to home as he had originally wanted. It wasn't that Teresa was far from his thoughts. On the contrary, he found himself thinking of her all the time. He was supremely confident that Reddick would be watching her every move for him and that it wouldn't be long at all before he would return home to help her mend in the best way possible. *It's funny, I've been alone for so long I didn't realize that I don't worry about anything outside my little world. Something tells me that's going to change,* he thinks. Carter lived by the thinking that he could worry about something and it wouldn't change much. Or, he could *not* worry about something and it wouldn't change much.

He was getting used to the newer technology of the smartphones, as they had gotten infinitely smarter than when he was in the service, when life or death depended upon instant communication. With that, he sent a text to Teresa to see how she was doing.

"Hey, Beautiful. How ya feeling?"

Within seconds, he received a reply. "Still got a ridiculous headache, but better. Likely back 2 work in a day or 2."

He smiles, liking this ability to check in without getting *too* distracted.

"Good to hear. Things are heating up. Will check in first thing tomorrow. See you soon. Miss you now."

Teresa knew one thing about Carter—he was a man of simple tastes and few words. For him to admit that he was *missing her* was a pretty big deal. And it was one she didn't take for granted. Even though she was in bed, complete with flannel jammies, socks, a sweatshirt, and a stocking cap to keep her sensitive noggin from getting cold, she longed for him and his warm body. She grinned.

"Thanks 4 checking in," she writes. "Don't worry about me. Just get home safe. Can we PLAY when you come back? Think I need some C-love."

He grinned and looked at Randall who was deep in thought. He signed off with, "You better believe it. Liking FLA. Maybe we should RNR here. Even got a place to PLAY." He waited, watching the screen for more.

Looking up, he sees they are pulling into the Opa-Locka Executive Airport. Randall pulls to the rear hangar, acting as though he knew exactly what he was doing. Because he did. Just as they arrive, Carter's phone pings: "Sun+You+Play = Happy T, XO!"

"Hey, Romeo, heads up. We're here, and from the looks of it..." Randall looks to the sky to see *The Beast*— what he affectionately calls his Bell 429 helicopter, "our man's right on time."

The helicopter approaches the helipad and slowly lands within 100 yards of their car.

"Romeo? What makes you say that?"

Randall turns off the car, turns to Carter, points to his face and says, "Cuz of that thing plastered all across your silly face."

"Oh," he grins even wider.

Randall waits a beat then playfully smacks his son's face. "The only thing that makes you grin like that..." he adds, "is a beautiful woman." He gets out of the car and heads toward Mr. Black, who has already shut down the bird and is crossing the tarmac to join them.

Carter goes to the trunk and retrieves his *kit*—a bag of goodies that he's never without while on a mission.

Mr. Black nods to both men, saying first to Randall, "Afternoon, Sir," then turns to Carter and adds, "Carter? Nice to see me."

Carter smirks.

Randall looks at them both with a steely determination and says, "Gentlemen, ready for *Operation Shasta*?"

CHAPTER 67

MR. BLACK HAS BEEN given a southeast bearing to exit Miami airspace from the tower at Opa-Locka. He pilots The Beast over downtown Miami, then passes directly over Key Biscayne, where Randall and Carter lunched earlier.

"Your country club looks pretty small from up here," Carter pipes in on the headset.

"Hell, it looked small from down there," Randall replies, getting a chuckle from all three.

"You'd think for a $22 BLT, you'd've gotten your Caddy detailed too," Carter jokes.

Randall, sitting in the co-pilot's seat, moves his microphone from his face as he begins a long tirade of coughs. Carter and Black eyeball one another. After Randall catches his breath, thanks to some help from his inhaler, he returns his handkerchief to his pocket, pulls his microphone back into place and starts running the plan.

"Okay, Gents. Given that we'll be there about 30 minutes ahead of the flight suggested by our perp, I'll have my old marine pal, Peter McDuggan, join us. Pete's a retired pilot from my division that I alerted to our situation."

"Why's his name familiar?" Carter interrupts from the backseat.

"Good catch," Randall nods. "He bought the resort with me years back—the one I was telling you about earlier. Been retired and living the life. He still consults on an odd mission, but mostly hangs out at Kiwi—uh, the airport, with some mutual friends. Runs some charters back and forth to Miami. He and I used to pop down to Cuba just for fun. And cigars. You'll like him."

"One of us, huh?" Carter nods.

"He not only has his own bird parked at Kiwi, but has lots of friends who run the airport. So, we'll land near his hanger, get transport to 101, hop up the back ladder, exit as per normal."

"Obviously our perp knows what you look like, but probably not me," Carter says. "So, I'll just head out in front of you. He won't be hard to spot—just look for the nervous beady-eyed punk who's sweating bullets and staring at your yellow backpack which, by the way, wasn't the easiest thing to find on short notice."

"Yeah, real imagination, that one. Guess he needed help spotting it," Randall adds.

"Given that we're private en route and have assistance upon landing, it'll be easy to have this little fella on hand," Carter says, revealing a 9MM Glock in his duffle bag.

"And this," Randall adds, pulling a Beretta from his briefcase.

"And this," Mr. Black chimes in, pulling a Glock .40 from a holster inside his jacket.

"Okay, I see we have the heat. Let's just hope we don't have to use it," Randall says, putting the gun away and scrolling through his phone. "I'll ring Pete and make sure we're good to go."

Mr. Black spends time talking to a number of towers along the Keys, Randall dials in details about potential security issues with Pete, and the loud, rhythmic hum of the helicopter lulls Carter into a trance. He stares out into the ocean blue and ponders, *Maybe I'll renew my copter license and add that to my bag of tricks. Been too long. Teresa would love island hopping from Key to Key some long lazy week. Or three.*

He switches gears back to business as something tickles the back of his mind. *Hope. Shasta. Boyfriend? Randall's money. Real Estate. Key West. Why have us go there? Wait!* He remembers Randall saying something about one piece of property he hadn't told him much about. Just then he overhears Randall's phone conversation.

"How's the property?" Randall asks Pete. "You keeping it booked?" Randall suddenly jerks his head around and looks at Carter. "You saw someone in my unit? No, I haven't been there in, what…a month? Maybe two."

That's when the tumbler starts rolling for Carter.

Randall shakes his head and continues talking, turning back around. "Yeah, probably less than 30, 35 minutes…"

Mr. Black pops Randall on the arm and holds up two fingers then one.

"Correction: 21 minutes."

Carter feels the mental gears click. *Shasta's been gone how long? His property is occupied now, without him knowing?*

Carter snaps his fingers. *I can't believe I didn't see it sooner.* He squeezes Randall's shoulder.

"Hold on, Pete," Randall says, turning to face Carter again.

"The quarter just dropped," Carter says.

"We'll land and see you in less than 20. Bye." He motions for Carter to continue. "What is it?"

"I should have…but by the time I reached you…things back home…"

Randall raises his eyebrows, shakes his head and motions his finger in a circle, pushing Carter to get to it.

"Remember the photo you showed me the day you and Mr. Black paid a visit?"

Randall nods.

"There were three young men in the picture with Shasta."

"Right."

"I'm going to assume one of them was a boyfriend. Or, at the least, an interest."

Randall starts to say something, but stops himself, allowing Carter to continue.

"Okay, so on the phone, our clown refers to Hope. Not Shasta."

"Go on."

"So, it's easy to also assume that one of these guys, close to you and Shasta, knows of your wealth. Maybe even that you're dying. They'll expect you to be weak."

Randall squints, putting the pieces together.

"What?" Carter asks.

"Certainly fits," Randall says, looking at Black. "Tony and I think one of the guys could be this character, Billy. The other two…one with the limp and the other…we got nothing."

Carter nods.

"Couple weeks ago," Black interrupts, "I saw that guy at his house." He nods toward Randall.

Carter listens.

"I just happened to be stopping by with a package when I saw that same character—the one wearing the long coat in the photo, talking to Shasta by the pool. He looked different though. Bigger. Didn't think that much about it at the time."

"Yup," Carter says, turning to stare out the window at the endless miles of turquoise.

"So, this Billy could be…" Carter mumbles.

Randall nods. "Could be."

"Needless to say, you don't want Shasta anywhere near this loser?"

Randall nods, showing little emotion.

"And Mr. Black—Tony, nice to meet the first name, may have tabs on the aforementioned Numbnuts?"

"Well, *if* he's our guy, been in and out of Juvee repeatedly," Black adds. "Mostly, petty theft. The others? No idea."

"My greatest fear," Randall interrupts, "is my girl is involved…with him."

Carter looks from Black to Randall then out the window again, rubbing his three-day beard, exhaling heavily.

"No. It's this Billy character," Carter says, confidently. "He knows you're dying. If he's as close to Shasta as you imagine…he sees you as an easy mark. Puts

Shasta up to lifting that passport wallet and cash. The bonus for you? He doesn't know anything about the black—"

"She wouldn't do that!" Randall interrupts with a bark.

"Okay, so she's a saint. But, for the sake of argument, let's say she did. Maybe she, *or he*...figured with so much you wouldn't miss a little."

Randall nods.

"He's up to something else. I mean, besides working you."

"Like what?" Randall asks, looking to Mr. Black.

"Kid like this? With a record?" He stops a second then adds, "Where'd you say he's from?"

"New Orleans."

Carter adds this to the mix. *Something...,* he thinks. *It's something he said.* "No. I'm certain. He's not *with* Shasta. He's *using* Shasta. And about to turn your *Plan B* into *Plan Zero*."

Randall's been shaking his head, but it slowly comes to a stop. He stares out the window for several minutes then looks at Carter with a look that says *How?*

Carter looks him in the eye and confidently adds, "My gut? They may *be* together, but his *final* plans...don't include her."

CHAPTER 68

A WAITER DELIVERS FRESH lobster to Jonathan and Angela, while a waitress delivers an enormous plate of crab legs to Jefferson and Sammy. Christopher and David get a fried combo platter each, as Daphne and Stuart are served plates of broiled flounder. Everyone admires the spread, and they reach for one another's hands, as Jonathan prays.

"Heavenly Father, thank you for this bounty before us, for the hands that prepared it and for the nourishment we now receive. Thank you for this wonderful time of rest and refreshment. May we always remain grateful for everything you provide for us."

Together they say, "Amen."

"This is awesome. I'm thinking…," David says, "like Grandpa said, maybe *breaking tradition* should become a new tradition."

Jonathan and Angela look to one another and smile.

"We certainly have a great deal to be thankful for, thanks to Jefferson and Sammy's kindness," Jonathan says.

They all nod in approval—their mouths busy with the huge feast.

"Our pleasure. And remember, this is something new for us too," Sammy says.

Jefferson is pulling a large piece of meat from a crab's leg as he adds, "What she said." He looks to David who is likewise stuffing his face.

"Hey Dad, are we officially, like retirees, now?" Christopher asks between bites.

"Why's that, Son?"

Christopher wipes his mouth, nudges David under the table and replies, "Because I don't think, as long as I've been alive, we've ever eaten dinner this early. You think, maybe later, we could put on comfortable shoes and do some laps at a local mall?"

The crowd gets a kick out of that and continues to chatter between bites.

ॐ

While at a not-as-happy table, on the other side of the dining room, Billy and Shasta sip a drink while looking at menus. Shasta is perturbed with Billy's constant checking of his watch.

"Babe, seriously? Are you going somewhere? Got a hot date after this one?"

"Huh? Oh, sorry. No, just, uh, wanted to...," he stalls.

"Wanted to what?"

Frustrated and nervous, he tosses the menu on the table and fidgets with his napkin ring.

"I wanted to make it a surprise. But I guess it's best if I go ahead and tell you now."

Shasta can't decide if she's excited or nervous, judging from his body language. His words make it sound fun and exciting; however, his actions and overall squirrely nature, makes her feel otherwise.

"Well? How bad could it be? It's a holiday...we're together in paradise...we've had a beautiful start to the day," she coos.

"Okay. Here's the thing. I know I haven't officially met your dad yet, the way that I would like to do, but I feel like I know him. And since I want you to be happy, I want you and him to make up and get over this arguing y'alls been doing."

Her body stiffens. She's not liking where this conversation appears to be headed, but knowing that Billy is a pretty simple guy, she's willing to hear him out. So, she takes a deep breath and puts on a phony smile.

"Baby? Any conversations between my father and I aren't your problem."

He starts to get riled up, so she puts her hand on his and continues, "But I'm willing to listen and appreciate your caring about my…relationship with my family. I'm just happy being here with you. So, if you have something to say, just say it."

"I wanted it to be a surprise, but doesn't look like that's gonna happen."

"It's okay."

"I have a surprise coming in from Miami tonight."

"What?"

He squeezes her hand. "Hear me out, Baby. You're gonna like it. Me and my buddy Dwayne, you mighta met him at the restaurant, will get you to the airport. Right after lunch."

"What?"

"Hold on. Here's my plan. It gets better."

She lets out a long sigh, "Okaaaaay."

"I called your dad and asked him to come here and spend some time with you. With us."

She shakes her head back and forth.

"C'mon. You two need to settle down…before we do." He stops to let the words sink in.

Her frown slowly becomes a tiny smile.

"Do you mean…?" she starts to ask, her smile growing bigger.

He smiles, glad that she's hanging in there with him. "Yep. You and I are going to start a new life. Together."

She can't believe her ears. Her mind races. *I know this is too soon, but it feels right. Kind of. So what if he's a loose cannon. So is Daddy. And Billy really loves me.*

He takes another sip of beer and pats her hand. "There's a little bit more…but all part of the bigger plan. And you have to play along with me…if it's going to work."

Shasta's radar feels funky, but she attributes it to nerves. And love. She is bouncing in and out of hearing all the details, but really wants to trust him, so tries to stay with him.

"Okay, okay. Tell me what you need. Oh, Baby, this is so exciting. There are so many things…"

"Baby, first things first, or last…or whatever that saying is. Look, your daddy's coming. He and I talked and he's…uh, excited. Not too sure what I'm up to, but he says he'd trust me."

He trusts you? she thinks, as she struggles for the look on her face to remain steady.

"I just thought it would be nice if he came down here and the two of you spent some time together. While I'm working, you both can get things even-keeled."

"Oh Baby, I don't know."

"You two are gonna patch things up, you'll see. I have to pull some extra shifts at the restaurant and I thought…"

"But…"

"I promised them, Baby. And you know me, I like to keep my promises. It's just a few days of back-to-back work—no biggie."

She wasn't sure she was buying it, but then, people change. And she believed that she saw real change happening with Billy. *He called Dad. That's huge.*

"Here's the thing. I'm going to stay with my buddy, Dwayne, you know—just until you two get things smooth. Don't want your dad to think the wrong thing about me. And in the next one or two days, I'll sit down with your dad…and talk man to man….about the *important* stuff."

Damn, he's serious! How awesome! Could this be…? That still small voice inside clamors for attention, but once again, she pushes it aside because of what she wants to hear.

"You still with me?"

"Yeah, Baby. Just…excited is all. Overwhelmed too, but…"

"I know, I know…" He puts on his biggest smile. "It will be worth the wait." He leans over and kisses her passionately.

CHAPTER 69

THE MATHESON PARTY IS pushing away from the table and preparing to leave when Angela sees the young couple nearly hidden in the corner making out. Christopher notices too and thinks, *Get a room. But she is kinda hot. Him? Dork.*

Angela smiles, admiring the young couple—so obviously in love. Holding Jonathan's hand, she squeezes it. Jonathan, watching the boys, turns to her.

"Yes?"

"Remember those days, Honey?" she nods toward the couple. His eyes follow hers and he sees the couple, but doesn't pay that much attention. She places her hand on the side of his face and kisses him.

David walks up and clears his throat.

"Yes?" Jonathan says, turning around to face the child starving for attention.

"Just wondering if Christopher and I can take one last stroll down to the water before we crash?" David asks.

"I don't see why not."

"Just remember, we're pulling out early," Angela says.

"As in…we catch a shuttle to the marina at seven," Jonathan adds.

"What?"

"We've got to get back home," Jonathan says. "You know how long the trip is."

"Okay," David says, already grabbing the tail of his brother's shirt and pulling him toward the stairs.

Christopher, seeing a group of guys and girls congregating under a streetlight at the end of the pier says, "Sure, let's go. But do me a favor?"

"What?"

"Leave your book bag, I mean, backpack with Dad, okay, Professor?"

David gives him a look and replies, "Yes, it's a backpack. And, okay."

"Trust me, it's for your own good. If you're ever going to meet girls, you've got to back off the geek…and turn on the charm."

The rest of the group makes their way toward the veranda, as Angela looks back to the couple once more. The strangest feeling hits her in the pit of the stomach— something is so familiar.

She makes her way to Jonathan who is deeply engrossed in a conversation with Jefferson about quantum physics. As she passes their table, she could swear she overhears the young man mention the name Randall.

Girl, she thinks to herself, *have another glass of wine.*

CHAPTER 70

THE BRIGHT RED BELL 429 floats just feet above the tarmac of Key West International Airport, before settling firmly upon the concrete. The engines stop, the rotors slowly come to rest and the three men jump out of the bird. Waiting for them, sitting in an old Jeep, is Peter. As the men approach, he gets out of the topless antique and salutes Randall. He nods.

"Hello, LC," Peter says, shaking his pal's hand.
"You know Mr. Black." They nod. "Peter McDuggan, meet my son, Carter."
"Hello Carter. Heard good things about you from your proud pop."
Carter extends his hand and jokes, "Not sure about all that, but nice to meet you, Peter."
Randall looks around. The gate is a few hundred yards across the tarmac. He looks at his watch. It's 5:45.
"The plane's not due to arrive for another 15 minutes. Let's step inside my office and discuss the strategy," Randall says, motioning to the helicopter.
They all climb in.
"Given this is pretty much Carter's mission, I'd like him to get us all up to speed. But first, Pete, tell me anything else you have about having seen someone in my unit."
"Yeah, it was day before yesterday. I'd been bouncing back and forth to Miami, running a charter for some brass from NAS." He turns to Carter to explain, "That's the next Key over. Boca Chica—Naval Air Station. Anyhow, I stopped in my place one night. That's when I saw the lights on. At first, I thought it was you...until I saw a couple leave your place and head in the direction of The Casa. I almost approached them to ask what they were doing, knowing you don't rent that unit to anyone. It was

then that I recognized your daughter. She sure has grown since last I saw her."

"And..." Randall starts.

"Don't know where she got her beauty," Peter interrupts, smacking Randall on the shoulder.

"Always the joker." Randall smirks. "Who was with her?"

"Some guy. No idea. Young. Ethnic. A wall of tats. Reason I say that, he was wearing a wife-beater as they were heading out the door, but pulled on what looked like a uniform—like wait staff, bartender, or something. Noticed he was in really good shape. Buff. Maybe *roids*."

Carter notes everything. He caught himself nodding at nearly every description and stops before asking, "Tattoos? You said several. Happen to notice a snake up the side of his neck?"

Randall and Black look at one another.

"I don't remember your mentioning that," Randall says.

"Come to think of it, it could have been a snake, Carter," Peter adds.

Carter nods to Peter and directs his reply to Randall. "Yeah, I noticed it in the photo you showed me out at my place. Had the photo blown up. It's a gang tat. Looks just like one I first saw on a group of guys at Gitmo, maybe a dozen years ago."

"Guantanamo Bay? When were you—" Randall starts to ask.

"Working a project with the navy. At Camp Echo. I was following an Afghan cell with some buddies. Mainly a consult, but also recon."

This gets a look of surprise from both Randall and Black. Randall realizes he shouldn't be surprised, given he and Carter hadn't been in contact for so many years. That, and the fact that Carter had received such high clearance during his number of tours that he was often called upon by many different arms of the military to *consult* on projects.

He promised himself to learn more about what his son was up to...after they finished this job.

"Anyway, we saw that particular tat on a number of gang factions. We thought it was a coincidence. And I never mentioned it because, frankly, I wasn't sure if that's what I saw, or where this was going," he says to the three men. "But then, when you and I..." Carter raises his eyebrows to Randall, "were having lunch in Biscayne and got the call to go to Key West...well, there was a major shift in my head."

"Do you think this perp has something to do with a terrorist cell?" Peter asks.

"Not sure," Carter says, shaking his head. "I mean, it could be, or have been, a true blue kidnapping. But then, these two jokers tell me about this Billy...I'm trying to think why the money, why the mention of military, why Key West and not his backyard." All three men are nodding, putting the pieces together.

Carter checks his watch. It's 5:50. He checks the sky. *Nothing*.

"Look, this punk thinks we're landing and disembarking inside the next 10 minutes. He's going to be looking for..." He holds up one finger. "An old, sick man with a yellow backpack full of cash. Check." He pats the bag on the floor. "Two..." he holds up another finger. "He'll likely be expecting a second guy."

"But..." Randall starts to say.

"But...what he *won't* be expecting is *three* guys. Mr. Black, a simple-enough looking guy, will be heading out well in front of us. He'll be our first set of eyes. He's not expecting anyone like our war hero here, who has the wherewithal to get us into places we shouldn't be..." he adds, smacking Peter on the knee. "Peter, you'll be on the ground well before they open the gate door. And finally, he, or they, won't be expecting a crusty old nerd caregiver walking alongside our oxygen-tanked mark." He turns to Pete and asks, "Can you make the tank happen?"

"Sure," he answers, immediately pulling out his cell to text someone.

"Wait...," Randall addresses Carter. "What do you mean by crusty old nerd?"

Carter reaches in his bag and pulls over his head a silly sweatshirt that reads: *Save the planet. It's the only one that serves BEER*. It has a fake belly sewn into the front of it, giving the illusion that he is thirty pounds heavier.

"And..."

Carter puts on a pair of nerd glasses and a worn baseball cap that reads *Disneyworld*. He pushes it slightly off-center, making him look daft.

"Doubt anyone would think this guy could fight his way out of an air-sickness bag," Carter jokes.

"Eloquent," Peter smirks.

"Now, if this *is* Billy, we're solid," Carter says.

Mr. Quiet, aka Mr. Black, asks, "What if it's not him?"

"Then...we'll...improvise," Carter replies.

"But you're pretty sure..." Peter begins.

"It's him," Carter confidently nods. "All roads lead to the idiot box. The fact that we're this prepared—and I have my doubts that he will be, tells me we won't even likely have to touch..." his Glock comes from behind his back, "these."

The other three nod.

"And not that I have to say this, but let's *spare* the heat...if we can, okay?" Carter instructs, looking at each man.

Again, all nod in agreement.

Just then, a plane approaches the furthest runway. Carter's checks his watch.

"Right on time. Okay, one last thing. One other slip Numbnuts made, consciously or otherwise, is that he *himself* will be present for the exchange of *goods*." He pats the bag at his feet. "Think about it—his nerves will give him away. What's to our advantage is that nobody would ever imagine that a half-million sleeps inside."

"Agreed," Randall says.

"Where he has the advantage is, we don't know how many people he has working with him. And if he is part of a T-cell, we could be in a lot of heat. And lots of people could get hurt.

"I'm going to help there. Already on it," Peter interjects. "Sorry. Continue."

"No, that's good. Team effort. Okay, and we also don't know if he's willing to grab the backpack and drop the man without hesitation," nodding toward Randall. "Which makes me, and a good many others, potentially collateral damage. Finally, I know for certain, Randall does not care as much about a lousy five-hun...as much as he cares about his girl."

"No shit," Randall says sternly.

"What if..." Peter and Mr. Black speak at exactly the same time. Peter motions for Black to continue.

"I was just gonna ask, what if there's no Shasta? I mean, what if all of this is a crazy set-up?"

Carter squints, starts to say something, checks his watch, wrings his hands and takes a deep breath, finally responding, "No. He won't do that. Not smart enough. That's my gut, anyway. And, if...I repeat...*if* Shasta *is* in on this—"

Randall starts to make a noise, but Carter stops him by grabbing his arm.

"Hold on. There's just no way of our knowing. For sure."

Randall holds up his hands, "As bad as it seems, you're right."

"So, *if* she is, she'll be there." Carter lets the moment hang. "And if they're in it together..." He lets out a short, faint whistle. "They're both dumber than I thought. No offense, Boss."

"No, he's right," Randall looks at the two other men. "There's only one more thing we have to get, besides Shasta."

They all watch Randall when Carter quietly says, "The passport wallet with the book."

"That *little black book*—pardon the cliché, is worth *one helluva lotta money*." Randall's face shows unmistakable determination.

Peter's phone pings. He reads the screen.

"Is that about the tank?" Carter asks, looking out the window to see them push the gate to the plane.

"Roger that. It'll be at the bottom of the stairs, right next to the luggage cart. Oh, and I have a number of extra friends who want to help. That is, if you need them, Carter."

"Absolutely. All the help we can get. Rather have it and not need it than…"

"Need it and not have it," Peter adds, punching buttons on his phone. "Done!"

Carter is pondering something. He's about to get up when something comes out of nowhere. He swings his head toward the opposite end of the runway. *Gitmo. Where did that come from? Instinct. Trust it.* He turns to Peter, checks his watch then asks, "Can you do me a favor?"

"Name it."

Carter hesitates. *Probably nothing.* "What if…" *Gitmo*, he thinks. "Nah, it's not even…"

"What, dammit?" Randall asks.

Peter and Black look out at the tarmac. Peter says, "They're opening the door."

"C'mon, we've got to get moving," Carter says, turning to the men. "We all good?"

All three nod.

"Check your mics, your guns and let's rock," Carter barks.

Each of the men runs a quick check of their rounds and backup clips in their belts, adjusts their hidden lapel mics and exits the chopper, one-by-one.

CHAPTER 71

BILLY AND SHASTA ARE driving to the airport in Dwayne's old pickup truck. Dwayne is Billy's buddy from Miami. He never says much, but he also doesn't bother anyone. He's riding in the bed of the truck—his long hair blowing all over. She certainly didn't see herself as a racist, but she felt uncomfortable around him. *He looks Cuban, or Peruvian. Hell, he could be a terrorist, for all I know. Although they don't ordinarily wear long hair like his, do they?*

She was nervous, thinking about her dad flying in to see her, trying to make amends. It didn't seem like something he would do, but Billy was so sweet to call him and seemed so intent on setting things straight. *Guess you can change, when you set your mind to it.* She's not even sure what they had argued about. Oddly, it seemed like a month ago. *Oh yeah, you don't want me seeing boys who aren't my age. That's crap. I'll see anyone I want*, she thinks, but knowing he was just being a dad—wanting her to be safe and think smart. After all, he provides any and everything she could ever wish for. *But he keeps me on a short leash, gives me a curfew, screens my calls and practically interviews whoever comes to the house. Control freak*, she screams in her head.

"Why did you say your friend was coming again?" she asks, nodding her head to the back of the truck.

"Uh, had to put my car in the shop. Bad gasket, I think. He's cool though. Was down here visiting his grandmother who's retired and lives on the other side of the island."

Sounds like it makes sense. Not sure why it doesn't feel like it, she thinks, adding, "Oh, okay. Is he...are we all gonna go back to Daddy's place in this?"

Billy thinks for a second.

"Sure, why not?" *Spoiled brat.* "We can all fit just fine." *Bitch.* "And it runs good."

Okay, so it's not your daddy's Caddy, he looks on the floorboard, which was filthy and littered with old greasy food wrappers and empty cups. *But it gets us where we need to go.*

"I'll get him to run it over to the carwash while we're inside waiting for your dad. Clean it up real nice," he smiles, thinking, *Yeah, right, and maybe we could get a paint job and curtains, too*!

He looks at his watch. *Dammit, I'm late!*

"That's nice," Shasta says absently. "I just want…I mean, if I'm going to try to, you know, work things out…I just want it all to be perfect."

"It will be," he says, looking at her smooth legs and smiling at her. *Just play along like I told you.* She seems to be getting more and more used to the idea. And this makes them both happy.

"Just hang in there, Baby. We're almost there. And before you know it, we'll all be… "

Billy was looking at Shasta and didn't see a bright red Mazda Miata running a red light at the intersection.

"Billy, watch out!" Shasta screams.

He whips his head around to see a blur of red and cuts the wheel in an instant, just missing the car but nearly tossing Dwayne like a ragdoll from the truck. Recovering the steering and slowing the truck, he checks the back.

Dwayne shoots Billy the bird and quickly checks for his pistol, which fell from the small of his back and slid to the back of the truck bed. He quickly moves over and stuffs the gun in his waistband. He looks to the front.

Billy's eyes are bulging. He frowns in the rearview at Dwayne then quickly looks to Shasta, shifting facial gears.

"You okay, Baby? Man, thanks for yelling. I wouldn'ta seen it."

"I'm fine," she says, trying to catch her breath. "That was close."

Billy pats her leg absently, checking his rearview, side mirrors and looking in all directions, trying to see if there are any police around. Just ahead, he sees the airport and pulls to a special side-gated entrance.

"Baby, you can't go in here," Shasta says with a look of confusion on her face.

"Nah, it's all good. A buddy of mine works here. Uh, actually it's a buddy of Dwayne's. His name's Chuck and he loads luggage on the planes. Cool, huh?"

Shasta didn't see anything particularly odd with that, so she nodded. Looking at the gate up ahead, she saw an armed security officer and wondered how they would get on the other side of the fence.

At that same moment, Billy reaches in the glovebox and takes out a special lanyard. She couldn't read it, as Billy's hand covered most of it, but she managed to see one phrase: *Military Police.* She frowned, but figured maybe Chuck was retired, like her dad, and was working in baggage to keep busy, or stay in shape, or whatever other reason men did stuff after working their entire lives only to get bored come retirement.

Pulling through the gate, Shasta sees a tarmac full of planes, both large and small, helicopters and even those tiny one-seaters that hobbyists flew. She often saw them flying just off the beach, usually over shallow water. She couldn't remember what they were called, but—*Wait, there's a helicopter just like Dad's,* she thinks, looking to the opposite side of the field. *Nah, they all look alike. Besides, those look like military police in that old Jeep.*

Just as the Jeep starts to pull away from the helicopter, a huge black Humvee suddenly appears from nowhere, parking next to their truck and blocking her view.

Dwayne looks at Billy in the rearview mirror as he gets out of the cab.

"Hold on, Baby," he says, smiling in at her. "Let D-Bo get the door for you." Closing the door, he eyeballs Dwayne.

"What? Well, okay now," she mumbles to herself, checking her lipstick in the mirror. *When's the last time he ever did that for me? He IS changing. Imagine that.*

As Billy walks around the truck, he whispers to Dwayne, "Do not let her see them and take your positions as fast as possible. We're late."

"Got it," Dwayne responds, motioning for the guys in the Humvee to stay put. The windows are black, so he can't tell if they saw him or not.

Passing Dwayne, Billy ignores the Humvee, adjusts the gun in his belt and opens the door for Shasta.

"Why, thank you, Baby," she coos, kissing his cheek.

"Anything for you, Babe."

Six months of rough-around-the-edges and suddenly Billy comes to life. Wow, she thinks.

Climbing the stairs to the rear entrance, Billy's mind winds down like a slow-motion recording. The ever-present island breeze seems to suddenly die. The sound of airplanes slowly fades—as though someone is turning down the volume. All that's left is a quiet hum, like an electric fence buzzing through his head.

Glancing over his shoulder, he sees the faces of his four dark-skinned accomplices—three of whom are exiting the Humvee, outfitted in military uniforms. The fourth remained in the driver's seat. Dwayne would provide the signal from the top of the stairs. His job was to not allow anyone to enter or exit, once Billy crossed the threshold. As soon as he did, the three would enter the zone—ready for action.

At the last second, Billy aims his steely gaze at the far edge of the tarmac where he visualizes his final exit.

CHAPTER 72

THE SCENE WAS RIGHT out of a Norman Rockwell painting. However, instead of being on a small-town front porch, this one was located on a tropical island paradise. The family sat side-by-side in lounge chairs on the sand, each one staring quietly at the blue water and red sun— both elements slowly merging as one.

It was as though you could hear a pin drop, if it weren't for the sound of lapping waves, or laughing children nearby. A collective sigh seemed to pervade their thoughts—for this very different Thanksgiving holiday was about to come to a peaceful, yet abrupt close.

Soon, each would return to chores and responsibilities, all of which were needed to keep their normalcy in check. That normalcy had been challenged over the past year and, each one, in their own way, knew deep in their hearts that they were now different.

The loss of Grace had affected them in so many ways. Where there was once a sense of joy, now lived a deep but healing sadness. Where there once was innocence, now intrigue grew. The vacancy had been replaced with victory, and each was learning to cope by setting aside raw grief and replacing it with real grace.

This vacation had made them look outside themselves and see exciting possibilities that lie ahead.

"Whatchya thinkin' about, Babe?" Jonathan asks.

Angela slowly returns to the present and, after several moments, quietly says, "All these months, I've been trying to chase Grace—chase her memory, chase the smell of her hair...the sound of her laughter...the twinkle of her eyes...all of which, at one time lifted my spirits. And I've come to realize, I need to just accept the Grace I had...and the grace I now have, thanks to you and the boys—our family and our friends."

He was quiet for a moment, letting that sink in, and quietly replied, "That's beautiful."

Angela had been wondering for months when the perfect time would arrive for her to say what was resting on her lips. *I can't be afraid of what people will or won't think. It doesn't matter. What matters is family. And building that in any way we see fit.*

"And…" She hesitates, knowing that the next few moments could either bring joy or disappointment, because what Jonathan felt and wanted was just as important, if not more important, than what she wanted.

"And…what?" he asks, turning to face her—her light eyes, sparkling with the reflection of the setting sun.

She hesitates to speak, but knows that the one place in the world she feels the safest is, and always has been, with him. So, she releases a quiet sigh, takes a deep breath and speaks the words she's prayed—for months on end.

"How I want…another child," she replies, watching his reaction, fearing the worst, hoping for the best and trying with all her might, to be happy with the results.

୭

She would never, as long as she lived, ever forget the next sixty seconds.

Jonathan's face went from complete, peaceful stillness and slowly—oh, so slowly, evolved into the biggest, widest, most enthusiastic smile she had ever seen on his face. It was as though the light had been turned back on. She felt, right down to her toes, that all was at peace with the world again.

His eyes went from wide to medium to narrow, as the smile grew across his handsome, sun-kissed face. She could see the tiniest tear form in the corner of one eye, and then grow to envelope both eyes, filling them with crystal tears.

It was then that she absolutely knew the difference. These weren't tears of sadness, but of joy—absolute...pure...and loving...joy.

"I like that idea," he said so quietly she had to move closer to hear. "I like that idea a lot."

CHAPTER 73

CARTER, RANDALL AND MR. Black climb aboard the exterior stairs just in time. Black, in signature all-black suit, white shirt and black tie, proceeds first. His only real *disguise* became reading glasses that he attached to his chiseled face. The difference with these readers, is they had special polycarbonate lenses with multi-purpose built-in infrared lenses. They looked completely normal on the outside, but created a *night-vision-like* characteristic on the inside and were used by bodyguards to indicate spots of extreme heat—like a weapon, especially one that had been fired recently. This time, they would perform that duty, but would be used primarily to protect his 20-10 baby-blues from potential flying shrapnel.

He steps in front of an oversized man wearing cowboy boots and matching hat. *Let me guess, Texas,* he thinks to himself, before motioning for the next passenger—a mother of two toddlers, both of whom were squabbling about how he touched me and she touched me, but he touched me first, and so on. She raises her hand— evidently the hand of God, and they instantly shut up. He lets them go first, on principle alone.

After a nearly full aircraft has deplaned, Carter slides in front of Randall, who by now was wearing a forlorn look on his face and a clear tube in his nose. The tube is attached to an empty oxygen tank he would pull behind him—not that he couldn't use it about now, but it could explode with gunfire, so they had emptied it en route.

Carter and Randall step in front of the last passenger, a gay flight attendant whose teeth were whiter than snow, skin as tan as the leather chair in Carter's house and a haircut that looked like Pee-wee Herman—no kidding.

As Carter approaches the door, he pulls his shirttail out, slacks his jaw and slumps an inch, adding to the masquerade.

"Nice touch," mutters Randall, directly behind him.

Carter approaches the gate entrance, Randall hanging helplessly on his arm, and instantly spots Black approaching the piña colada stand. Alternating his focus between Randall and Black, he notices Black drop a napkin and—looking back at Carter, slightly nods toward the exit door where Dwayne is stationed pretending to read a magazine. Problem is, Black notices the magazine is upside down. *Nice move, rookie*, he thinks.

The minute that Carter's feet touch the shiny tile, he scans the rest of the room. His eyes moved so fast, there was no way they would have made him. It also helped that he was wearing glasses with just enough tint that, from a distance, you couldn't make out where his eyes were looking.

He recognizes not only Billy and Shasta but, counting them—one, two and three *perps*, all of whom are wearing military uniforms he doesn't recognize. Two are covering the remaining exit doors at this end of the terminal. The last one stands next to Billy, just one row from the lockers. He stares up, trying to look as though he is waiting for another departure. He has a direct line of view to his partners who are guarding exits. Carter could tell by their posture they were wired for communication too. The soldier at Billy's side continues to look back and forth from Randall to the rest of the room.

Billy stands near the locker, while Shasta talks to him. Shasta nervously plays with a bracelet on her wrist as they chat, while Billy is obviously watching their every move.

Rookies, Carter thinks to himself, while exaggerating a conversation with Randall, but whispering, "You see the suits at the door?"

"Roger that," Randall says.

Just then, Carter sees Shasta turn and notice Randall. Carter sees that her nervous face can't help hide a smile.

"Randall, look away. Do NOT look toward Billy and Shasta," Carter speaks through gritted teeth. "She just made you and we're not ready."

Something's wrong. Billy's too nervous. She definitely isn't in this, Carter thinks—his mind moving at 90 miles an hour.

"Got it," Randall responds, looking back toward the departure screen over the gate entrance, while appearing to carry on some conversation with Carter. Randall is just mouthing words, while Carter whispers orders.

"Everyone hear me?" Carter looks at Randall while adjusting his collar.

"Roger Black," from Mr. Black.

"Roger Peter," from Peter.

"Okay, Black, you take Exit A," he says, bending over to tie Randall's shoe.

"Copy that," Black responds, making his way to the gate. He looks down at his boarding pass and up at the signs, appearing oblivious.

Carter stands back up and calmly says, "Something's wrong."

"What is it?" Randall asks, just inches from his face, but showing no emotion.

"Don't make eye contact with Shasta until I say *go*," Carter says to Randall then, "Peter, you take Exit B, near you."

"Copy that," Peter responds, taking a baggage dolly from behind a ticket counter and heading in that direction.

Carter pulls a handkerchief from his pocket and, pretending to blow his nose, says into his microphone, "Shasta is *not* part of this. I repeat, Shasta is *not* a partner. Ignore her until we hit the locker. Protect her after we do."

He hears single clicks from all their mics then continues. "The minute we drop and walk away," he says, reaching for the duffle bag attached to Randall's tank,

"Black, take the Soldier 1 clown at door. Peter: Soldiers 2 and 3. I've got Billy. Randall has Shasta. Clear?"

Carter hears both Black and Peter click their open mics. Randall winks at Carter.

ಎ

The next two-and-a-half minutes were like a scene from of a Quentin Tarantino movie—one of those Kung-Fu-Pulp-Fiction-Django-Unchained types, except with even more slow motion.

Carter and Randall make the move toward the lockers—Randall hanging on Carter's arm like he was about to pass out. Carter cuts a glance to Black on his far left, who was taking a position directly in front of Soldier 1's line of fire. They did that back-and-forth shuffle like you do passing a stranger in the hall.

He then looked to Peter who had deftly positioned himself behind the upright steel luggage dolly, already drawing his firearm, but keeping it clearly from sight.

Shasta had turned around—following Billy's gaze, and saw Randall approaching.

"Daddy!" Shasta shouted, throwing her arms into the air.

When Billy saw Carter take the backpack and step toward the locker, he instinctively let go of Shasta's arm and was moving like he was headed toward the lockers.

"Randall, GO." Carter said—his eyes not leaving Billy's.

Billy had lost his game face. And if he wasn't careful, his lack of concentration could cost him his life.

The third soldier spun around—seeing that both Billy and Shasta were exposed, pulled a Sig Sauer from his belt and directed his sight at Carter, hoping to take out the target's protection.

With his gun ready, it was easy for Peter to stop him. He shot Soldier 3 in the meat of his shoulder, just before the man took aim.

The gun flew from the soldier's hand, as he grabbed his shattered shoulder, dropping to the floor like a sack of potatoes.

In the next second, Peter pushed the luggage cart toward Soldier 2, distracting him enough for Peter to literally shoot the gun from his hand—taking a finger in the process. The man's finger never reached the trigger and he began screaming in a language Peter didn't recognize. He dropped to his knees, removing a bandana from his pocket to wrap his bloody hand.

Peter ran over, quickly grabbed both of the guns, and spun around to find Soldier 1 on the ground and Black cuffing his hands behind his back. Black had shot him in the knee, instantly immobilizing the man. Black and Peter nodded to one another, then Black ran out the door to chase after Dwayne.

In the meantime, Randall had grabbed Shasta, pulling them both to the ground.

Carter and Billy stood face to face with their respective guns aimed and ready to fire. However, Carter had his sights at the quarter inch of skin between Billy's beady eyes, while Billy had his gun aimed at Shasta.

In the mayhem, Randall had accidently dropped his gun and it slid across the polished floor, landing near Billy's foot. He stepped on it for effect.

"Drop it, before I drop you," Carter barked.

Billy became strangely calm and Carter wasn't sure if it was the calm before the second storm, or if he was just showing his insanity. Perhaps, a little of both.

"So, you must be the infamous Carter," Billy smirked. His expression reminded Carter of the fat, dumb private in *Full Metal Jacket*, but with better teeth.

"And you must be Numbnuts."

Billy didn't like that. The look on his face showed his tough façade was starting to melt. His bloodshot eyes darted in either direction.

Thanks to Peter, Billy now had one gun pointed at the back of his head and another pointed at the front. One could say he had no way out.

It was then that Billy moved his finger from the safe position to the trigger position. Carter didn't like that, as the playing field just changed.

Carter had to live his life with a finger on the trigger. Metaphysically, it was his destiny. Metaphorically, it was the best way to be real and keep sharp. Realistically, you had to know, *Don't point a loaded gun—with trigger engaged, if you're not willing to fire.*

He knew that not everyone could live that way. Neither should they want to.

As for Billy, he knew life was likely always going to be unfair for him, full of screw-ups, never going anywhere. However, he did know he had some control right now and, as bad as it was, it was about to get even more real in the next few seconds.

"There's no way out, Son," Randall said from the floor, acting like he cared, when everyone in the room knew he didn't.

"Shut up, Old Man, and just die already!" Billy shouts. "This was going fine until you had to screw it up!"

"Billy, what are you doing?" Shasta whimpered. "I thought…"

"Hah! Since when did you start that?" Billy spat.

The look on her face said it all—a combination of *I can't believe you told me you loved me and we were going to make a life together…and…You can rot in Hell, you miserable scumbag.*

In that moment, Carter thought, *I think I'm going to like my new sistuh.*

❧

"Okay, here's how it's going to go," Billy starts, looking at Carter first. "You, Mr. Disneyland, can just kick that bag of cash over here to me."

Carter shakes his head very slowly, for effect.

Billy squints, then starts nodding his head very slowly. "Yes, you are. Or I blow her face away. In fact, I can probably get off two shots—one to daughter, one to Daddy. Call it a two-for-one special," he adds with a stupid laugh.

"How about this, *Juicer*. You lay your gun down, so Mr. Peter there…" he nods behind him and off to the side, "doesn't have to drop you like a dirty shirt."

Billy looks out of the corner of his eye for a nanosecond.

"*If* you do, Shasta's daddy—who is *my* daddy too, will probably let you walk away. Alive."

This gets a strange look from deranged Billy. But he wasn't budging.

"*Riiiiight*," Billy mocks.

"Seriously, Billy? It's just money. All I want is for my daughter to be safe. I don't have any beef with you. Hell, I'll let you keep what's in the bag. And I'll go you one more. I know the judge and can *guarantee* your early release for good behavior."

Everyone could see that Billy was weighing his options. *Maybe he's smarter than we think*, Carter muses to himself. *Nah, this brick will screw it up. That's for sure.*

"I have just one question, Billy—that is, before I pump your body full of hydro-shock." Carter asks, "What was this great plan of yours? C'mon, tell me—one professional to another."

Billy bit.

"I was gonna take the money and Dwayne and I were gonna open a nightclub. In Cuba."

Carter was dumbfounded. "And Dwayne?"

"The pilot," he sneers, nodding toward the tarmac. "And I'm Cuban, not Creole, asshole. You can't touch me once I cross the U.S. line."

That could be true, Carter thinks to himself.

By now, Shasta is torn between being wounded and fed up.

Standing, she asks, "Billy, what about us?" Her sudden movement makes Billy nervous.

She's certainly got our cojones, Carter considers, not moving his gun from Billy's face.

"Don't be stupid, Hope. I mean, *Shasta.* You're too young and dumb to hang with a player like me. I am *so* out of your league."

Shasta shakes her head, staring at him with such disdain that his tough exterior hiccups—but only for a second. "I can't believe...you're such a worthless piece of shit."

I'm liking her more all the time, Carter thinks.

"All of this...nonsense for a *nightclub?*" Randall laughs.

Carter snorts. "Hell, if you had asked, he'd have funded it."

This pulls Billy in.

Randall whips his head toward Carter. "No, I wouldn't."

"You wouldn't even miss it, Old Man," Carter plays along.

This confuses Billy.

Randall looks from Carter to Billy.

"Hey, Monkey, do you honestly think you're going to walk out of here alive...with two of the nation's finest aiming squarely at your insane brain?" Randall spits.

Carter was enjoying seeing his old man bounce back to life.

"Just shut the hell up, toss me that backpack and I'll be on my way," Billy barks.

"Hold on a second. Where's my passport wallet? The one you lifted from my office. The one with a fistful of cash in it?" Randall demands.

Billy laughs, looking at Shasta. "Where do you think the money is? Gone, *Idiota.*"

Carter thinks, *There's the other tell. Spanish.*

"Fine. You spent the cash. But the wallet. It has my passport..." Randall begins to say.

"It's at the condo, Dad," Shasta says quietly. "In my suitcase."

"Who gives a shit about a *wallet*, Shasta? Turning to Carter, he shifts personalities. "You gonna be a man or a *muerto,* Carter?"

I don't know much Spanish, Carter thinks, *but I'm guessing muerto isn't flattering.*

As though he were reading Carter's mind, Billy growls, "Dead man."

Carter smirks. "Yeah, right. Like that's gonna happen."

"For the last time, either you toss me the cash, let me and Dwayne take the money and get the hell out of here..." He points to where Black has Billy's accomplice restrained outside—his bloody face mashed against the glass of the exit door. "And y'all can go about your lives. And that includes *Shasta* the bimbo. *Or*, take your chances. Just remember, you'll be losing a father *and* a daughter."

Randall's had enough. "Listen Punk, you say one more thing about my girl and I'll snap you in half."

Billy slowly moves the aim of his gun from Shasta's head to Randall's chest, pulling the hammer back.

The next moment felt like one of those *YouTube flash mobs*, because with the snap of Peter's fingers, the nearly thirty-odd *pedestrians*—who just four minutes ago had fallen to the floor in fear, quickly stood up, pulled their weapons and aimed directly at Billy's head. The synchronistic maneuver was pure magic.

Carter couldn't help but grin at Billy's expression.

Peter and his crew had done an exceptional job of not only removing all of the real pedestrians from the terminal—including the roughly thirty-five people aboard

American Flight 3477, but had planted nearly three-dozen armed personnel, all dressed in pedestrian attire, in the small terminal. What neither Billy, nor any of the others, could see was the variety of weapons they were also packing, compliments of his pals at Key West's CNIC/NAS, the naval air station.

NAS was the home of America's premiere sophisticated Tactical Combat Training Systems, Joint Interagency Task Force, U.S. Coast Guard and U. S. Army Special Forces Underwater Training School that just so happened to be stationed just five clicks away from where they were standing.

Billy and his compatriots hadn't planned on that.

CHAPTER 74

AS THE LOCAL AUTHORITIES wait for the FBI to arrive, Carter, Randall, Shasta, Mr. Black and Peter stand beside the Bell 429, trying to decide whether to grab Shasta's suitcase and fly back to Miami or take a breather and all crash at Randall's condo.

"I don't know about me, but you look like you could use a drink," Carter says, grinning, looking from one member of the team to the next.

"What's so funny?" Randall asks.

"Nothing. Just something your grandson would say. He's a smart one," Carter adds, with the specific intent to start Randall thinking.

"I'd like to meet him," Shasta smiles. "And the older one is Christopher?"

"Yep. He's talented too—troubled, but talented."

"And there was...a little girl, right?" she asks.

Carter looks at Randall and back to her, nodding. "Yes. Grace." He looks off into the distance and pauses a moment before adding, "She was...special."

After a moment, Randall claps his hands and says, "Okay, what do you say, we hit the condo tonight and fly out first thing in the morning?"

"But first, maybe a little something to wet my whistle," Peter says, trying to blow a whistle, but making no noise. That got a needed laugh.

"And I'm buying the first round!" Randall shouts, motioning for Mr. Black to join him.

"And I'm drinking that first round," Mr. Black echoes.

Wow, that's more animated than I've seen him since I've known him, Carter ponders.

Peter tosses Carter a pair of keys and nods toward a second Jeep sitting next to his.

"You really did think of everything," Carter says, motioning for Randall and Shasta to get in the Jeep. Randall obliges, but Shasta stands there.

"You okay?" Carter asks Shasta.

She looks incredibly sad, looking from the sunset, back to him. She finally says, "Yeah. I'm good. Just thought that today…this weekend…was going to end up a lot…differently. Guess I know the *real* Billy, now."

Carter thinks of several things to say, all of which seem too cliché at a time like this. Instead, he puts an arm around her and says, "People will always show you who they are. Just believe them…the first time."

"That's…pretty profound coming from you. Isn't it? I mean, we just met." She grins.

"Oh, I've got a lot of little sayings. Hang around…I'll teach you some of them."

"Maybe I will." She smiles, kisses his cheek and whispers, "Bro."

Carter glances over to see Randall watching him. They exchange smiles.

"Now, let's get outta here," he says, turning to everyone.

They all nod in agreement, climb into their Jeeps and cross the tarmac, heading toward the sunset and kicking up dust along the way.

𝄢

It would be two days later, when Peter reports to Randall that the rookie duo of Billy and Dwayne, along with the other three mangled *soldiers*, were not expected to be released from prison until such time that, quote, *Jimmy Buffet gave up performing 'island music' for opera.*

Billy and his pals had not only planned and executed a kidnapping, falsified records to gain access through security at an international airport, but did so with the express intent to do harm. They were also carrying illegal weapons, while harboring three former criminals with reported connections to terrorist cells. And they did all of this while attempting the murder of one honored and highly decorated veteran and one decorated, yet *semi-retired,* soldier.

It quickly became apparent that Billy and his duplicitous allies were going away for a very, very long time.

CHAPTER 75

THE GUYS ORDERED DRINKS and were escorted to a table right on the water's edge—compliments of Randall's friend, the manager. Just then, Carter hears his name being shouted from across the beach. He looks around and can't believe what he was seeing. Running toward him was Christopher. From the elevation where Carter stands, he can't see anyone else. As Christopher approaches, they fist-bump, then hug.

"What...are you doing here, Uncle Carter? You said you weren't going to be able to join us for Thanksgiving."

"Well, there was...a change of plans." He winks at Christopher then turns to introduce them. "Everyone, this is my nephew, Christopher. Christopher this is..." pointing to each one respectively, "Peter McDuggan, Tony Black, you know Randall—aka Grandpa, and...uh, my sister, and your Aunt...Shasta. Or, Hope."

"Shasta," she says, smiling. "Please."

Their eyes lock. It was an interesting sight to observe—and everyone did. She and Randall step forward. Christopher shakes Randall's hand first, "Good to see you again, Sir."

"Christopher."

"And nice to meet you...*Aunt* Shasta?" Christopher says, blushing.

The crowd laughs, getting a kick out of watching the expressions of two teenagers meet family they didn't know existed.

"If it helps," Carter says, putting his arm around Christopher, "I just met her myself...on this trip. So, we both got a similar surprise!"

From a distance, David shouts Christopher's name. He spins to see David and waves him over. Running to join the group, David is all smiles—recognizing only Carter. He looks at Randall, cocking his head to the side.

"I'm your grandpa…Randall," he says, his voice beginning to crack.

Randall tries with all his might to fight the tears. He didn't approve of public displays of affection, especially if it involved crying. That didn't stop him from becoming instantly moist in the eyes, which he tried to play down. David stood there, staring.

"Must have sand in my eyes," he jokes, reaching to shake David's hand.

"Such a pleasure to meet you, Sir," David says, in near shock.

"And you…Son. I've got to say…you're as handsome as your father."

❧

As only a mother can, Angela senses her boys are missing. Given that it's getting late and they need to head back to the room and prepare to leave early the next morning, she looks around, but doesn't see them.

"Hon, where are the boys?" she asks Jonathan—his face covered by a weathered hat.

"Huh? Couldn't have gone far," he mumbles. "Christopher's probably getting some last minute phone numbers." He sits up, lifting his hat and smiling at Angela. "And David is probably digging for oil, or slate…or discovering a dinosaur, or something."

He lies back down. "Give 'em ten more minutes. Then we'll head in, okay?" Jonathan says.

Angela stands, stretches and looks toward the sinking sun.

Stuart and Daphne look up from their books. Daphne says, "Honey, I'll join you, if you'd like to take a walk."

"Sure, Mom," Angela responds. "I'd like the company. Been lying around all day."

Stuart and Jefferson start to get up, but Daphne motions for them to stay.

"You guys just hang here. We've got this," she smiles.

"Well, I'm joining you girls. I've finished this," Sammy says, tossing the *Alex Cross* book on her lounge chair, "and could also use the stretch."

Jefferson looks up from his December issue of *Yachting Magazine* and says, "Huh? Yeah. You girls have fun. I'm almost done with this article. Hurry back." He returns to reading.

Angela turns to head down the beach, when she hears her name called.

Whipping around, she sees David waving to her. Both he and Christopher are talking to a group of men— not girls, as she expected.

"Is that...who I...think it is? She says loudly enough for all to hear.

Simultaneously, they follow Angela's gaze and, one by one, stand to get a better view.

"Is that...Dad?" Jonathan's voice drops off.

෧

Randall and Carter are looking toward the beach where Angela, Jonathan and several others are standing. A wave of emotion rolls over Randall.

"C'mon, Old Man. Say hello to your other boy. They'll be thrilled to see you," Carter says, punching Randall playfully and grabbing David by the neck, rubbing the top of his head.

"Why do adults love to do that?" David squirms, asking Christopher the rhetorical question.

"Because they can," Christopher replies.

෧

By now, the group from the café and the group from the hotel meet halfway between the two, at the end of the street, but still on the beach.

"Well, well, well…" Jonathan says, masking his emotions, but glad to see his father.

"Yup. What you said," Carter jokes, reaching out to hug his brother.

Randall and Angela stare at one another. The moment is made all the more awkward by seeing this young, lightly-colored African-American girl with all these military-looking renegades. Angela recognizes her from the hotel restaurant and starts to speak. Carter steps up to break the ice.

"Okay, everybody, relax. We're all family here. Let's start with the strangers first," Carter begins. "And trust me, many are strange. This is Peter, Tony and…Shasta." He smiles, hugging his sister.

Jonathan and Angela can't help but notice the resemblance she has to Randall. The look isn't lost on him, so he speaks up.

"Yes. Shasta—Elizabeth Hope, is my daughter…" Randall looks to Jonathan, adding, "your and Carter's…sister."

The silence hangs in the air for what seems an eternity, until Angela—with tears in her eyes, walks over and says, "Come here, Sweetie," hugging Shasta within an inch of her life.

"Okay. Well….Hey, Sis!" Jonathan finally manages.

"Yeah, yeah, so it'll take some getting used to," Carter quips. "But let me tell you, this girl…is the real deal. With nerves of steel, I might add."

"Whatever," Shasta says, blushing. "Hanging with this rowdy gang…you have to have your game on!"

Jefferson and Sammy are especially enjoying this moment, and Jefferson reflects to a time about a year ago when Jonathan and Angela were just starting to recover. *What a difference a year made*, he thinks.

Jonathan catches Jefferson watching the interaction between Angela, Sammy and Shasta and walks over.

"What's going through that analytical mind of yours, Jefferson?" Jonathan asks.

"It's funny," Jefferson chuckles. "Seems like just yesterday, you were in my office, pouring your heart out, yet having the hardest time trying to take advice…from a *brothuh*."

Laughing, Jonathan replies, "Yeah, well, sometimes it takes a while to teach us old dogs new tricks."

Within moments, both groups merge into one big family. The juxtaposition of the tough and guarded men—each designed from early on to fight and protect the family and country they so loved. While on the other side were the gentle, artistic souls—each man designed from birth to encourage and nurture the family and congregation of friends they so loved.

The glorious sunset seemed to slow its descent, if for no other reason than to keep this perfect moment of reunion, laughter and of love—from stopping. Yes, this Thanksgiving, the Matheson's and their friends had so very much to be thankful for.

Adding a metaphorical and somewhat metaphysical exclamation point to the moment, a big, bright, blue Morpho butterfly flew over just as the family was preparing to head out. David looked up, started to get everyone's attention so they could see it too, but instead just smiled. Watching it fly in wide, happy circles, he quietly whispered, "Happy Thanksgiving, Gracie."

EPILOGUE

CARTER IS DRIVING NORTH on I-95. He is just thirty minutes outside Palm Beach, where he left Randall and Shasta in the rearview, promising to see them both again very soon. The windows are down, the sunroof is open and a song is blaring on the stereo of his rented Dodge Charger. Tapping his toe to the beat, Carter digests the lyrics of the song:

> *I know I won't break your heart*
> *Cause you are in my veins*
> *I never thought this tough old dog*
> *Would share the desert rains...*

The timing was perfect to be hearing those words, especially after the world of heat he'd been through in the past 96 hours.

He had seen old friends, made new ones, gambled the odds, cheated death and mended broken bridges. He had lost sleep, gained weight and come to some pretty meaty decisions. Some of those included: spend more time with family, get to know better those I never knew and just maybe consider settling down again.

Wait, let's not rush it.

Thinking about that topic made him miss Teresa all the more. Checking the clock on his dash, he thinks it could be a little too early to call, in case she's still in recuperation mode.

So in the meantime, he makes just one call and will likely leave the rest of the trip to just the sounds of an American engine burning up highway...and the radio.

He picks up the smartphone, pushes a button and speaks a name. It dials. *Man, I like these toys. Been away from them too long.*

"Yo, what's up, Old Man?" Reddick asks with a smile in his voice.

"Yo, yourself. And if you see an old man…kick his ass!" Carter returns.

"You heading back? Or, has the island life made you forget about us?"

Carter thinks about that a moment before answering.

"Nah. I like the beach, but there's more character in the mountains. Like you!"

Reddick laughs, then says, "Speaking of characters…"

"Let me guess."

"Yep. Durkin. Don't know what got into him, what he did, didn't do, or what someone did to him, but he's been on nothing but A+ good behavior."

"Uh huh."

"I know, I know. Musta taken a good behavior pill, but he's been ridiculously cordial—like Eddie Haskell nice."

"Hate to say it—it won't last," Carter smirks.

"No, you're prolly right."

"On to better thoughts," Carter says.

Carter and Reddick covered all the topics they'd missed jawing about for the past week, like: the girlfriend, the diner, the job, the '68 project and a few other random items. By the time they hit *the weather*, Carter said it was time to ring off. So, they did.

Carter isn't far from Jacksonville when he starts seeing the familiar state patrol cars hiding in the hedges of the glorious I-95. So, he slows his speedometer from 90 to 70.

He took the next several hours to simply reflect. As soon as he got back home, he'd surely be caught up in all the noise around him.

His mind drifted back to the time he had spent with his dad. Randall had certainly been an ass most of his life—not a particularly pleasant man to be around. His lack of emotion and gruff exterior did a pretty good job of alienating most. But the creek of time certainly had a way of washing over and smoothing the rough spots on the stone. While his health was failing quickly, Carter couldn't help but notice an inner peace about him—something he hadn't seen his whole life. Persuading him to check in at the best hospital in Miami, with a top lung specialist—not to mention keeping his name on the donor docket, was likely the one piece of advice Carter ever recalled his father taking from him.

And Shasta? Getting to spend time with her, as well as seeing the interaction between her and Randall was something else. She was about to blossom into an incredible woman—full of spunk, vitality and hope. *Imagine that. Her namesake may just be the inspiration she, and those around her, need to get ahead in life.* He grinned at the thought of getting to spend more time with her. *Maybe I'll invite her up for a spell.*

On the outskirts of Savannah, Carter thought about stopping by to see his pal, Mack. At the end of the day, or week, as the case was, he was glad it wasn't necessary to call on his expertise. In fact, it may have stirred things to a *point of no return.* Instead, he saved time and rang him. They chatted. Carter caught him up on what went down, and before he signed off, wishing love to April, he guaranteed his long-time pal that he'd be calling on him very soon, as he had something coming just around the corner. It was a job right up their alley and one that would take some bad people down. But for now, Carter said he had to cut the chatter on an open line. And so they did.

With one warning from a Georgia state trooper, two Pitt Stops in South Carolina and three corn dogs shared with an old pal in Pineville—a former Secret Service colleague who only went by the name *G*, Carter was soon inside the limits of Mission Grove.

ॐ

With only a few miles left on his journey, Carter was enjoying the solitude. He turned the radio down, picked up the phone and pressed the number 1. The phone autodialed while he listened for the only voice he longed to hear.

"Hello?" the sleepy voice answered.

"Hey," Carter answered, with a smile as wide as a box of Little Debbie's Oatmeal Creme Pies. "You still up?"

After a long silence, a quiet answer—wrapped in a similar smile returned, "Yes?"

"Good, I'll be right there."

Walking down a dusty road
An image in my mind
It wasn't what I was looking for
But rather what I'd find

It seems so long since I could breathe
The laughter in the breeze
It takes no getting used to
I'm handing you the keys

I know I won't break your heart
Cause you are in my veins
I never thought this tough old dog
Would share the desert rains

While my life is nothin' much
More fight than it's worth
I'm thinking just maybe now
To plant us...on this earth.

Faith Fisher, *Desert Rains*, © 2013

ABOUT THE AUTHOR

David Temple is a seasoned writer with works spanning multiple mediums and genres. *Stealing Hope* is the stand-alone sequel to his first suspense novel, *Discovering Grace*, published in 2010.

David earned his Master's in Broadcast Management at Regent University in 1984, and was one of the nation's top radio personalities by the early '90s. Radio was the love of his life, but his itch for challenge and adventure led him into acting, voice-overs, television, screenplay writing, filmmaking and eventually book writing.

As an author, David has discovered that, "A book is where the story lives in its truest form." His passion for storytelling is not new; it's just always searching for the perfect venue.

A master of creative styles, expect the unexpected the next time you see his words, hear his voice, or notice his name as the credits roll.

Information on all of his latest and future projects can be found at: www.davetemple.com

www.ingramcontent.com/pod-product-compliance
Lightning Source LLC
Chambersburg PA
CBHW050901250626
47155CB00001B/51